John Buchan (1875–1940), had a long and successful literary and public career. He was educated in Glasgow, where his father was a Free Church minister in the Gorbals, but his childhood holidays were spent in the Scottish border country.

After graduating at Glasgow University, Buchan took a scholarship to Oxford where he wrote his first two historical novels while still an undergraduate. With interests in law and journalism, he worked for the British High Commission in South Africa at the end of the Boer War. Returning to London in 1903, he eventually became a director of Thomas Nelson the publishers. Buchan worked for the Ministry of Information during the First War, and later wrote a substantial history of the conflict. He became a Tory M.P. for the Scottish Universities from 1927 to 1935, in which year he was appointed Governor-General of Canada as Lord Tweedsmuir.

Buchan took pride in the craft of storytelling and he is probably best known for his Richard Hannay thrillers, with six titles ranging from *The Thirty-Nine Steps* in 1915, to *The Island of Sheep* in 1936. His other fiction includes *John Burnet of Barns* (1898); *Prester John* (1910); *Huntingtower* (1922); *John Macnab* (1925); *Witch Wood* (1927); and *Sick Heart River*, published posthumously in 1941.

Buchan's health had never been strong, yet he achieved an enormous literary output in the course of his life, with no fewer than 30 novels and over 60 non-fiction books, including fine biographies of Walter Scott and James Graham, the Marquis of Montrose, whom he greatly admired. His autobiography, *Memory Hold-the-door*, was published in the year of his death from a cerebral stroke.

JOHN BUCHAN

The Watcher by the Threshold

Shorter Scottish Fiction

EDITED BY
ANDREW LOWNIE

CANONGATE
CLASSICS
79

This edition first published as a Canongate Classic
in 1997 by Canongate Books Ltd, 14 High Street,
Edinburgh EHI ITE. Copyright © The Rt. Hon.
Lord Tweedsmuir of Elsfield, CBE. Introduction
© 1997 Andrew Lownie. All rights reserved.

The publishers gratefully acknowledge general
subsidy from the Scottish Arts Council towards
the Canongate Classics series and a specific grant
towards the publication of this volume.

Set in 10 point Plantin by Hewer Text Composition Services, Edinburgh. Printed and bound
by Caledonian Book Manufacturing, Bishop-
briggs, Glasgow.

British Library Cataloguing-in-Publication Data
A catalogue record for this book is available
on request from the British Library.
ISBN 0 86241 682 5

Contents

Introduction

In popular imagination John Buchan is generally remembered as the author of a series of thrillers that centre around English country houses and London Clubs, an old-fashioned, misogynistic, snobbish and anti-Semitic writer primarily concerned with the British Empire and Establishment. The reality, as is gradually being recognised, is quite different. His thrillers are more sophisticated, profound, ambivalent, better-written and with a greater width of literary reference than their reputation might suggest, and in any case constitute only a fraction of his writing output, which included historical novels, film scripts, comic romances, military history, a legal text book, children's books, biographies, poetry, essays, hundreds of articles and – a particular love – short stories.

Writing to his school and university friend Charles Dick in January 1900, he claimed that 'to a person of my habits the short story is the real form'. By December 1912 *The Bookman*, in a profile of the thirty-seven-year-old writer, was arguing he was 'probably the best modern exponent of the short story' and noting he made 'the short story what a cameo might be when it is cut by the hand of a master'. Buchan wrote about sixty short stories and the majority of them were published in four collections – *Grey Weather* (1899), *The Watcher by the Threshold* (1902), *The Moon Endureth* (1912) and *The Runagates Club* (1928). The exceptions were some stories in *Scholar Gipsies* (1896), in various interwar Nelson Annuals, in the *Scottish Mountaineering Club Journal* and some unpublished stories, recently discovered in his private papers. His first published short story, 'On Cademuir Hill', appeared in the *Glasgow University Magazine* in December 1894 when he was still a teenager and soon, having secured the services of a literary agent, he was publishing stories on a regular basis not just in British papers such as *Macmillan's Magazine, Chambers* and *Blackwoods* but also in American journals such as *The Living Age*. This meant that relatively quickly he found he could support himself from his writing and he soon learnt the importance of a transatlantic appeal.

Another myth, that needs to be scotched, is that Buchan, though born in Perth, should not really be classified as a Scottish writer. What is increasingly becoming clear is that Buchan's interests, both in his life and his writing, remained predominantly Scottish and he deserves to be remembered in the same way as Sir Walter Scott and Robert Louis Stevenson – who were themselves great literary influences on him – as a writer who found fame throughout the world but who drew much of his own inspiration from the country of his birth and especially from its literature, religion and topography. Nowhere is this clearer than in his short stories, half of which are set in Scotland, and which, as can be seen in the following selection, reveal him to be as interested in moorland as Clubland heroes. The stories here largely revolve around the lives of Border shepherds, poachers, gamekeepers and drovers and rely heavily on the use of local dialects. Indeed one of Buchan's great literary gifts in his novels, as well as short stories, was to capture the different forms of Scottish idiom. His Scots stories are unsentimental and largely about temptation, death and retribution and the role played in people's lives by religion, drink or the weather. They are a far cry from either the Kailyard or the adventures of Richard Hannay or Sir Edward Leithen.

It is certainly true that after Hutchesons' Grammar School and Glasgow University, Buchan, like many ambitious Scots before him, headed south and never again lived in Scotland, but the case can easily be made that he retained his love of Scotland and that the country deeply influenced his writing. He regularly visited his parents and siblings, who continued to live in Peebles, and his annual holiday was always spent in Scotland, partly with his family in the Borders and partly staying in the Highlands with friends such as Gerard Craig Sellar on his Ardtornish estate opposite Mull. For twenty years Buchan worked for the Scottish publisher Thomas Nelson and spent some of his time before his marriage in 1907 at their Edinburgh offices. At Nelson he set up a weekly newspaper, *The Scottish Review*, which was an attempt to create a Scottish version of the *Spectator*, a return to the tradition of Francis Jeffrey's *Edinburgh Review*. In it he did much to promote both a new wave of Scottish writers, such as Neil Munro, and reassess more established writers; for example he published some hitherto unknown verse written by R.L. Stevenson at Edinburgh University.

When he decided to pursue a political career he chose to stand not for a local English constituency but for Scottish ones, first as the candidate for Peebles just before the First World War and then as the Conservative Member of Parliament for the Scottish Universities from 1927 to 1935. Among his ambitions as an MP was to be Secretary of State for Scotland and he took a keen interest in Scottish debates, often to the point where he took a strong independent line from the Conservative Party. It is sometimes suggested, on the strength of some selective quotation from his speeches, that Buchan favoured Scottish Home Rule. This is not true. Culturally he was a Scottish Nationalist, but politically he was an enlightened Unionist, prepared to cloak his own views in rhetoric that would appeal to all the Scottish electorate. He recognised the need to respond positively to the burgeoning Scottish Nationalist Movement and that if Conservatives were to continue to enjoy support in Scotland they needed to be more sympathetic to Scottish aspirations. He genuinely believed in devolving more power to Scotland, partly from a desire to remedy a long-standing grievance and partly from a belief that some Scottish matters could best be dealt with at a local level. But though he was prepared to devolve some power he believed that Scotland's interests lay within the Union.

One of his major concerns within this political debate was that Scotland was losing her national identity. He argued in one House of Commons debate: 'In language, literature and art we are losing our idiom, and it seems to many that we are in danger very soon of reaching the point where Scotland will have nothing distinctive to show to the world.' Both in his public work and his writing he tried to redress the balance. As President of the Scottish History Society he successfully won increased government funding to index and preserve various Scottish Record collections. He served on the Board of the new National Library of Scotland, the committee to preserve the site of the Battle of Bannockburn, as a Governor of Gordonstoun School and was, in an apparent oxymoron, President of the Scottish branch of the English Association. Throughout his life, even when abroad, he regularly addressed Caledonian Clubs, Burns and Stevenson dinners and in 1923 was President of the Sir Walter Scott Club. His appointment as Governor-General of Canada in 1935 owed much to his successful tenure as Lord High Commissioner of the Church of Scotland in 1933 and 1934. When he chose a peerage he initially considered an entirely Scottish title – Buchan of Tweed, Buchan of Tweeddale, Buchan of Fruid or Lord Manorwater – eventually deciding on a combination of his Oxford and Border links with Lord Tweedsmuir of Elsfield.

Much of his writing centres around Scotland. His non-fiction included well-reviewed biographies of Montrose and Sir Walter Scott, histories of the Fifteenth Scottish Division and the Royal Scots Fusiliers, *The Kirk in Scotland* (1930) and *The Massacre of Glencoe* (1933). He contributed countless chapters or introductions to books on Scottish subjects: *The Scottish Tongue* (1924), *A History of Peeblesshire* (1925), *The Face of Scotland* (1933), *Scots Heraldry* (1934), to name a few. Eleven of his novels are either entirely or partly set in Scotland, including his best-known novel, *The Thirty-Nine Steps* (1915). Even when the action is ostensibly based elsewhere the landscape is unmistakably Scottish in appearance, whether it is the South African terrain of *Prester John* (1910) or the Canadian wilds of *Sick Heart River* (1941). Buchan's Scottish fictional landscape is very much bound by his own upbringing and experiences. His early historical novels – *Sir Quixote of the Moors* (1895), *John Burnet of Barns* (1898) and *A Lady of Lost Years* (1899) – and the more contemporary *The Half-Hearted* (1900) are set in the Borders; *Prester John* (1910) and *The Free Fishers* (1934) draw on his early upbringing on the Fife coast; *Huntingtower* (1922), *Castle Gay* (1930) and *The Thirty-Nine Steps* (1915) are set in a Galloway remembered from student walking holidays, while *John Macnab* (1925) and parts of *The Three Hostages* (1924) and *Mr Standfast* (1918) come from holidays with friends in the Highlands. It is not just places that are Scottish but also the characters. Who can forget the Glasgow grocer Dickson McCunn, the Gorbals Die-Hards, Andrew Amos, Mrs Brisbane-Brown, Lewis Haystoun and Lord Lamanchas as well as the better known Sandy Arbuthnot and Archie Roylance?

Buchan's interest in poetry is rarely mentioned, yet it is one of the most obvious manifestations of his 'Scottishness'. Many of them in his wartime collection, *Poems Scots and English* (1917), are written in the Doric and he was sufficiently highly regarded as a Scottish poet that when Hugh MacDiarmid published *Northern Numbers* in 1920 and 1921 in an attempt, in his words, to bring together 'certain living Scottish poets', Buchan was included along with Neil Munro, Lewis Spence and MacDiarmid himself. In 1924 Buchan edited *The Northern Muse: an Anthology of Scots Vernacular Poetry*, the first anthology to include some of the poetry produced by the Scottish Literary Renaissance. He was an early champion of Neil Munro, Violet Jacob and of Hugh MacDiarmid, contributing the preface to MacDiarmid's *Sangshaw*. MacDiarmid subsequently was to describe Buchan as 'Dean of the Faculty of Contemporary Scottish Letters' and write of *The Northern Muse* that it stood 'in relation to Scots poetry as Palgrave's Golden Treasury to English'. Indeed one of Buchan's strengths as a writer in general, MacDiarmid also noted, was that the 'books abound in loving and delightful studies of Scottish landscape and shrewd analyses and subtle *aperçus* of Scottish character'.

Apart from their own intrinsic literary merits, Buchan's short stories are interesting for a number of reasons. First, they show how he responded to the environment around him. The early stories, which are included in this book, draw from holidays spent with relations around Peebles

and the life of the Upper Tweed Valley. Later his protagonists will be young Oxford scholars finding mystery, first
in the Scottish countryside and then abroad, particularly in
Africa where Buchan spent two years on Lord Milner's
staff. The First World War, during which Buchan served as
a war correspondent on the Western Front and then ran a
government propaganda organisation, would inspire five
stories, while further tales would be drawn from his post-
war sojourn in the Cotswolds. It is interesting, in tracing
themes in Buchan's work, to see just how many of his own
current interests or those of his family are ascribed to
characters or are central to the books. They include
mountaineering, fishing, birds and walking, all of which
figure in the stories, as well as the novels. As the critic
Patrick Cosgrave has put it: 'He did not metamorphose his
personality when he came to write adventure stories; he
merely relaxed, and indulged some of the whims of his
temperament and imagination.' Two of his stories, for
example, have a mountaineering background. 'Space'
combines Buchan's fascination with the metaphysical
teachings of Bergson and Poincaré with the practical
difficulties of climbing the Chamonix Aiguilles to produce
a haunting story about the nature of reality, while 'The
Knees of the Gods', reproduced here, touches on the
hallucinatory effects of climbing.

Secondly, many of the stories are explorations of themes
subsequently developed in the novels, themes which remain constant even if the locations change. 'The Watcher
by the Threshold' and 'The Outgoing of the Tide' are early
prototypes of the novel, *Witch Wood* (1927), 'Fountainblue'
has similarities with *The Half-Hearted* (1900) and looks
forward to *Sick Heart River* (1941), and 'The Frying-pan
and the Fire', which revolves around a sporting bet, has
parallels with *John Macnab* (1925). It is often assumed that
Buchan's preoccupation with the fragility of civilisation
comes after the First World War or dates from *The Power
House* (1916) with Lumley's famous remark, 'You think
that a wall as solid as the earth separates civilisation from
barbarism. I tell you the division is a thread, a sheet of glass.
A touch here, a push there, and you bring back the reign of

Satan.' In fact Maitland, the central figure in 'Fountain-blue', a story written in 1900, expresses his concern about the 'very narrow line between the warm room and the savage out-of-doors', adding, 'you call it miles of rampart, I call the division a line, a thread, a sheet of glass. But then, you see, you only know one side, and I only know the other.'

The theme of the precarious balance between the civilised and the primitive becomes more explicit in the course of Buchan's writing career. Where in the early short stories the contrast has been between England and Scotland, later it is to be found, for example, between Britain and Africa. Many of the characters exhibit dual personalities, desperate to attune themselves to their more primitive sides, especially the more conventionally successful they become. As one character puts it of Maitland in 'Fountainblue', who turns his back on success to die forgotten in Africa, '. . . he saw our indoor civilisation and his own destiny in so sharp a contrast that he could not choose but make the severance.' Many of Buchan's stories are about the undersides of our personalities. Ladlaw in 'The Watcher by the Threshold', 'a good landlord and respectable country gentleman, now appeared as a kind of horrible genius, a brilliant and malignant satyr', once he becomes possessed by the devil. It is this dual personality, later to figure so prominently in Buchan's villains, to which one of the characters in another of Buchan's short stories, 'The Kings of Orion', refers when he says, 'There's our ordinary self, generally rather humdrum; and then there's a bit of something else, good, bad but never indifferent – and it is that something else which may make a man a saint or a great villain.' Characters are often possessed by powerful atavistic urges as a reaction to the civilised lives they enjoy – so, for example, Maitland in 'Fountainblue' realises that 'the sad elemental world of wood and mountain was far more truly his own than this cosy and elegant civilisation'.

There is often a sacred place, *temenos*, in Buchan's writing, most obviously in the novels *Witch Wood* (1927) and *The Dancing Floor* (1926), but it is also to be found in the stories, either in Scotland as in 'The Green Glen', or in

Africa as in 'The Grove of Ashtaroth'. Place is integral to plot and theme in Buchan, often personifying the border between the primitive and the civilised. As a review of 'The Watcher by the Threshold' put it: 'The mountains are no mere piles of rock, they are the abodes of mystery, of romance, of haunting presences and insubstantial forms.' In that story, for example, the dark mysterious Perthshire woods at More are contrasted with the 'green pastoral country with bright streams and valleys' over the hills at Glenaicill.

Reviewing Buchan's novel, *Sick Heart River* (1941), Graham Greene drew attention to Buchan being 'the first to realise the enormous dramatic value of adventure in familiar surroundings happening to unadventurous men'. He was referring to the thrillers, but his comment could equally apply to the short stories, even these early ones set around Peebles, where the menace comes from the familiar and trusted – streams that flood their banks, hosts who are not what they initially appear, sons who make unusual demonstrations of filial love. Greene also noticed the 'completeness of the world' Buchan created in his books. Buchan's fictional world is already taking shape in these stories, long before many of the people or places appear in the novels. The Clanroyden family are introduced in 'A Reputation', 'The Watcher by the Threshold' and 'Fountainblue', the Sempills in 'The Outgoing of the Tide' and Lady Amysfort in 'The Green Glen'. The Radens, who figure so prominently in *John Macnab*, are in 'The Far Islands' while the Manorwaters appear in 'The Far Islands' as well as the novels, *The Half-Hearted* and *The Dancing Floor*. Even characters who do not appear in the novels tend to reappear in different stories, so Lady Afflint is in both 'A Reputation' and 'The Far Islands', Gideon Scott is the eponymous hero of one story and appears as Gidden Scott in 'The Herd of Standlan', while Jock Rorison features in both 'Streams of Water in the South' and 'Comedy in the Full Moon'. The town of Gledsmuir makes an appearance in six stories and there are numerous references to Clachlans, Callowa, Aller, the Gled, the Forest of Rhynns and St Chad's College at Oxford. *Castle*

Gay, the title of a 1933 novel, is mentioned in 'The Rime of True Thomas', a story written in 1897, and then in 'The Green Glen', Glenaicill is in 'The Watcher by the Threshold' and Machray is referred to in 'Fullcircle'.

Another link with the novels is the use of similar techniques or the reliance on coincidence to drive the plot. In *The Three Hostages* Dr Greenslade described the recipe for writing a thriller as 'fixing on one or two facts which have no obvious connection' and then inventing a connection. 'The reader is pleased with the ingenuity of the solution, for he doesn't realise that the author fixed upon the solution first, and then invented a problem to suit it.' 'The Frying-pan and the Fire' begins with an after-dinner game where 'you invented a preposterous situation and the point was to explain naturally how it came about. Drink, lunacy and practical joking were barred as explanations.' So in the story the Duke of Burminster has to explain just how he came to appear on the station at Langshiels in a dishevelled state to be met by an official reception committee and band.

Buchan had a strong mystical sense and a large number of the short stories have a supernatural element. It may be the power exerted by place, especially a house or an island as in 'Skule Skerry'. Or it may be a spell that only affects certain people and can pass through several generations. Throughout his life Buchan was intrigued by the idea that certain qualities or susceptibilities could be passed from one person to another. His novel, *The Path of the King* (1921), is about how kingship can be passed through different quite ordinary people. In 'The Grove of Ashtaroth' the central character worships an ancient goddess because of his Jewish blood, while in 'The Green Wildebeeste' Andrew du Preez, with his 'touch of the tar brush', is caught in an ancient spell. In 'The Far Islands', included in this volume, Colin Raden inherits the vision of 'The Far Island' first bestowed on a distant ancestor.

Many of the stories involve some encounter with the forces of the unknown and the way in which the 'other' world impinges on the 'ordinary' world. Buchan's susceptibility was heightened at Oxford by attending lectures on pre-Christian cults, by living in rooms at Brasenose, where reputedly a former President of the Brasenose Hellfire Club had been literally snatched by the Devil, and by the influence of Andrew Lang, a neighbour in the Borders, whose *Custom and Myth* dealt with the survival of ancient customs in a modern society. Buchan was also much influenced by his wide reading of Celtic myths, fairy tales, Border ballads, the Bible and Shakespeare, as well as the work of more contemporary writers such as Stevenson, Conan Doyle, Ibsen, Maupassant and Poe, whose *Tales of Mystery and Imagination* he edited for Thomas Nelson in 1911. By education and temperament Buchan was a classicist and his grounding in the classics is evident in his stories, marked as they are by a clear and economical prose style and use of classical imagery. He was also a son of the Manse, brought up to accept an omnipotent and benevolent God and a Devil that was half-humorous and half-earthy, and his Scottish Calvinism was to be an important influence on his writing, including the short stories. At the same time part of the creative tension in his work, as in his life, would come from the fact he was also conversant with the teachings of Erasmus, Galileo and Hume.

Buchan's Scottish stories can be enjoyed at different levels – simply as tales about his own people, as delicate expositions of human character which demonstrate that his gift for strong descriptive writing was apparent from his early twenties, or as explorations of themes to be developed more fully later in his novels. For many of the recurrent Buchan themes are present – the power of place, the use of the sacred place *temenos*, the importance of landscape to plot, the strong descriptive writing, the emptiness of success, the call of the wild, the contrast between the city and the countryside and between England and Scotland, the narrow thread between the primitive and civilised.

Buchan's stories cannot be separated from his novels and are integral to our understanding of his fiction, yet they have received very little critical attention and many are not even recorded in the standard bibliographies. The publication of this selection of stories should help to rectify two gaps in Buchan studies – examination of him as a Scottish writer and as a short story writer – as well as introducing devotees of his novels to another facet of his writing. They give an insight into the versatility of his literary styles and the peculiar cast of his imagination and suggest how he could have developed into an archetypical Scottish writer, more interested in social observation than a gripping yarn. Many stories were clearly written to a deadline, others are highly repetitive or imitative, but some have that mark of greatness, the ability to stay in the mind long after the piece has been read. They are a reminder that John Buchan was a far more accomplished and complex writer than his contemporary reputation has allowed.

Andrew Lownie

On Cademuir Hill

Buchan's first published story, this appeared in the *Glasgow University Magazine* in December 1894 and was included in his first collection, *Scholar Gipsies* (1896). A gamekeeper caught in a poacher's trap reflects back on his life and the role in it played by drink and religion.

I

The gamekeeper of Cademuir strode in leisurely fashion over the green side of the hill. The bright chilly morning was past, and the heat had all but begun; but he had lain long a-bed, deeming that life was too short at the best, and there was little need to hurry it over. He was a man of a bold carriage, with the indescribable air of one whose life is connected with sport and rough moors. A steady grey eye and a clean chin were his best features; otherwise, he was of the ordinary make of a man, looking like one born for neither good nor evil in any high degree. The sunlight danced around him, and flickered among the brackens; and though it was an everyday sight with him, he was pleased, and felt cheerful, just like any wild animal on a bright day. If he had had his dog with him, he would have sworn at it to show his pleasure; as it was, he contented himself with whistling 'The Linton Ploughman', and setting his heels deep into the soft green moss.

The day was early and his way was long, for he purposed to go up Manor Water to the shepherd's house about a matter of some foxes. It might be ten miles, it might be more; and the keeper was in no great haste, for there was abundant time to get his dinner and a smoke with the herd, and then come back in the cool of the evening; for it was summer-time, when men of his class have their holiday. Two miles more, and he would strike the highway; he could see it even now coiling beneath the straight sides of the glen. There it was easy walking, and he would get on quickly; but now he might take his time. So he lit his pipe, and looked complacently around him.

At the turn of the hill, where a strip of wood runs up the slope, he stopped, and a dark shadow came over his face. This was the place where, not two weeks ago, he had chased a poacher, and but for the fellow's skill in doubling, would have caught him. He cursed the whole tribe in his heart. They were the bane of his easy life. They came at night, and took him out on the bleak hillside when he should have been in his bed. They might have a trap there even now. He would go and see, for it was not two hundred yards from his path.

So he climbed up the little howe in the hill beside the firwood, where the long thickets of rushes, and the rabbit-warrens made a happy hunting-ground for the enemies of the law. A snipe or two flew up as he approached, and a legion of rabbits scurried into their holes. He had all but given up the quest, when the gleam of something among the long grass caught his attention, and in a trice he had pulled back the herbage, and disclosed a neatly set and well-constructed trap.

It was a very admirable trap. He had never seen one like it; so in a sort of angry exultation, as he thought of how he would spoil this fine game, he knelt down to examine it. It was no mere running noose, but of strong steel, and firmly fixed to the trunk of an old tree. No unhappy pheasant would ever move it, were its feet once caught in its strong teeth. He felt the iron with his hand, feeling down the sides for the spring; when suddenly with a horrid snap the thing closed on him, pinning his hand below the mid-finger, and he was powerless.

The pain was terrible, agonising. His hand burned like white fire, and every nerve of his body tingled. With his left hand he attempted to loosen it, but the spring was so well concealed, that he could not find it. Perhaps, too, he may have lost his wits, for in any great suffering the brain is seldom clear. After a few minutes of feeble searching and tugging, every motion of which gave agony to his imprisoned hand, he gave it up, and, in something very like panic, sought for his knife to try to cut the trap loose from the trunk. And now a fresh terror awaited him, for he found that he had no knife; he had left it in another coat, which was in his room at home. With a sigh of infinite pain, he stopped the search, and stared drearily before him.

He confusedly considered his position. He was fixed with no possibility of escape, some two miles from the track of any chance passer-by. They would not look for him at home until the evening, and the shepherd at Manor did not know of his coming. Some one might be on the hill, but then this howe was on a remote side where few ever came, unless their duty brought them. Below him in the valley was the road with some white cottages beside it. There were women in those houses, living and moving not far from him; they might see him if he were to wave something as a signal. But then, he reflected with a groan, that though he could see their dwellings, they could not see him, for he was hidden by the shoulder of the hill.

Once more he made one frantic effort to escape, but it was unsuccessful. Then he leant back upon the heather, gnawing his lips to help him to endure the agony of the wound. He was a strong man, broad and sinewy, and where a weaker might have swooned, he was left to endure the burden of a painful consciousness. Again he thought of escape. The man who had set the trap must come to see it, but it might not be that day, nor the next. He pictured his friends hunting up and down Manor Water, every pool and wood; passing and repassing not two hundred yards from where he was lying dead, or worse than dead. His mind grew sick at the thought, and he had almost fainted in spite of his strength.

Then he fell into a panic, the terror of rough 'hard-handed men, which never laboured in their mind'. His brain whirled, his eyes were stelled, and a shiver shook him like a reed. He puzzled over his past life, feeling, in a dim way, that it had not been as it should be. He had been drunk often; he had not been over-careful of the name of the Almighty; was not this some sort of retribution? He strove to pray, but he could think of no words. He had been at church last Sunday, and he tried to think of what he had heard; but try as he would, nothing came to his mind, but the chorus of a drinking-song he had often heard sung in the public-house at Peebles:

> When the hoose is rinnin' round about,
>   It's time eneuch to flit;
> For we've lippened aye to Providence,
>   And sae will we yet.

The irony of the words did not strike him; but fervently, feverishly, he repeated them, as if for the price of his soul. The fit passed, and a wild frenzy of rage took him. He cursed like a fiend, and yelled horrible menaces upon the still air. If he had the man who set this trap, he would strangle the life out of him here on this spot. No, that was too merciful. He would force his arm into the trap, and take him to some lonely place where never a human being came from one year's end to the other. Then he would let him die, and come to gloat over his suffering. With every turn of his body he wrenched his hand, and with every wrench, he yelled more madly, till he lay back exhausted, and the green hills were left again in peace.

Then he slept a sleep which was half a swoon, for maybe an hour, though to him it seemed like ages. He seemed to be dead, and in torment; and the place of his torment was this same hillside. On the brae face, a thousand evil spirits were mocking his anguish, and not only his hand, but his whole body was imprisoned in a remorseless trap. He felt the keen steel crush through his bones, like a spade through a frosted turnip. He woke screaming with nameless dread, looking on every side for the infernal faces of his dreams, but seeing nothing but a little chaffinch hopping across the turf.

Then came for him a long period of slow, despairing agony. The hot air glowed, and the fierce sun beat upon his face. A thousand insects hummed about him, bees and butterflies and little hill-moths. The wholesome smell of thyme and bent was all about him, and every now and then a little breeze broke the stillness, and sent a ripple over the grass. The genial warmth seemed stifling; his head ached, and his breath came in sudden gasps. An overpowering thirst came upon him, and his tongue was like a burnt stick in his mouth. Not ten feet off, a little burn danced over a minute cascade. He could see the dust of spray, which wet the cool green rushes. The pleasant tinkle sang in his ears, and mocked his fever. He tried to think of snow and ice and cold water, but his brain refused to do its part, and he could get nothing but an intolerable void.

Far across the valley, the great forehead of Dollar Law raised itself, austere and lofty. To his unquiet sight, it seemed as if it rolled over on Scrape, and the two played pranks among the lower hills beyond. The idea came to him, how singularly unpleasant it would be for the people there – among them a shepherd to whom he owed two pounds. He would be crushed to powder, and there would be no more of the debt at any rate. Then a text from the Scriptures came to haunt him, something, he could scarce tell exactly, about the hills and mountains leaping like rams. Here it was realised before his very eyes. Below him, in the peaceful valley, Manor Water seemed to be wrinkled across it, like a scrawl from the pen of a bad writer. When a bird flew past, or a hare started from its form, he screamed with terror, and all the wholesome sights of a summer day were wrought by his frenzied brain into terrible phantoms. So true is it that Natura Benigna and Natura Maligna may walk hand in hand upon the same hill-side.

Then came the time when the strings of the reason are all but snapped, and a man becomes maudlin. He thought of his young wife, not six weeks married, and grieved over her approaching sorrow. He wept unnatural tears, which, if any one had been there to see him, would have been far more terrible than his frantic ravings. He pictured to himself in gruesome detail, the finding of his body, how his wife would sob, and his friends would shake their heads, and swear that he had been an honest fellow, and that it was a pity that he was away. The place would soon forget him; his wife would marry again; his dogs would get a new master, and he – ay, that was the question, where would he be? and a new dread took him, as he thought of the fate which might await him. The unlettered man, in his times of dire necessity, has nothing to go back upon but a mind full of vivid traditions, which are the most merciless of things.

It might be about three or four o'clock, but by the clock in his brain it was weeks later, that he suffered that last and awful pain, which any one who has met it once, would walk to the end of the earth to avoid. The world shrank away from him; his wits forsook him; and he cried out, till the lonely rocks rang, and the whaups mingled their startled cries with his. With a last effort, he crushed down his head with his unwounded hand upon the tree-trunk, till blessed unconsciousness took him into her merciful embrace.

II

At nine o'clock that evening, a ragged, unshorn man, with the look of one not well at ease with the world, crept up the little plantation. He had a sack on his back for his ill-gotten plunder, and a mighty stick in case of a chance encounter. He visited his traps, hidden away in little nooks, where no man might find them, and it would have seemed as if trade were brisk, for his sack was heavy, and his air was cheerful. He looked out from behind the dyke at his last snare carefully, as behoved one in danger; and then with a start he crouched, for he saw the figure of a man.

There was no doubt about it; it was his bitterest enemy, the keeper of Cademuir. He made as if to crawl away, when by chance he looked again. The man lay very still. A minute later he had rushed forward with a white face, and was working as if for his life.

In half an hour two men might have been seen in that little glen. One, with a grey, sickened face, was gazing vacantly around him, with the look of some one awakened from a long sleep. By dint of much toil, and half a bottle of brandy, he had been brought back from what was like to have been the longest sleep he had ever taken. Beside him on the grass, with wild eyes, sat the poacher, shedding hysterical tears. 'Dae onything ye like wi' me,' he was saying, 'kick me or kill me, an' am ready. I'll gang to jail wi' ye, to Peebles or the Calton, an' no say a word. But oh –! ma God, I thocht ye were bye wi't.'

Afternoon

'Afternoon', a self-consciously literary tale of a young boy who imagines he is a Jacobite, first appeared in *Scholar Gipsies* (1896) and was inspired by two of Buchan's favourite books – *Lorna Doone* and Kenneth Grahame's *The Golden Age*. Rich in references to Scottish history and Classical literature, it also demonstrates Buchan's ability to evoke the sounds, smells and sights of nature from the very beginning of his literary career.

The Jacobite rushed from the house into the garden, swung himself wildly across a paling, and landed on all fours in the road. It was just past the noon; the cloudless summer day had left its zenith behind it; and the first minute degree of decadence had joined with the sun. July was not yet merged in August; the festival of nature was at its height, and the whole earth throbbed with joy. The hum of bees and the tirra of the lark, the cooing of wood-doves, the far-away calls of haymakers, and the plash of the mill-burn filled the air. It was one great world of flowers, green leaves, and the sunlit heaven above, cool waters, solemn hills, and a blue distance.

The Jacobite was of noble appearance and gallant attire, as became his name. His age might have been twelve, but he was somewhat taller than the common. He was clothed in corduroys, formerly green, now many-coloured as Joseph's coat, and worn at the elbows to the likeness of chamois. Black, short-cut hair, thin shanks though stout as steel, a head held straight above the shoulders, a most cavalier carriage, and there you have him. A sprig of heath and a feather from a crow's wing were stuck in his hat, and in his hand was a well-used stick with a bar nailed thwart-wise, which did duty as a sword. In his belt was a knife with a broken blade, and an old news-sheet, for he made pretence that he carried state papers of high import. He stood there in the road, well-pleased with himself and content with the world. The hurried exit had been but the exuberance of his spirits. He was on no fixed journey bound. With much searching he produced from a deep pocket a George III penny, and spun it in the air. It fell face foremost in the dust, whence he picked it. Now was his course decided, and he turned resolutely to the highway.

In a little he came to a shop, a window in a flower-surrounded cottage, which proclaimed the residence of a wayside trafficker. The Jacobite considered his financial position. He possessed, he reflected, moneys to the extent of one penny and one halfpenny; this found on the road, that given by a benevolent grandfather. So he marched through the honeysuckled entrance, and stood delighted, inhaling the quaint, pleasing odours of bread and ancient brandy-balls, bacon and paraffin. He thought how proud the owner of such a place must be, and wondered mildly how such a man condescended to treat with so small a customer, from which it will be seen that he had no contempt for trade. He bought a pen'orth of treacle toffy, and stowed it about him. Fain would he have expended the other coin, but that it would have left him without supplies – a position he held hateful to the spirit of a cavalier.

Once more he stood in the sunshine, with the world before him and a thousand voices calling him hither and thither. He raced tumultuously over a field of close turf, scattering sheep before him like chaff. Then over a fence and into a byway, where he loitered for a second to fling a stone at a casual rat; and then with a whoop and a skirl of delight he was at the river.

Down its banks he strolled in all the glory of undoubted possession. There was no boy in the place who dared lift hand against him. For had he not fought his way to renown, till in a battle the week before, attended by half the village, he had defeated William Laidlaw, the shepherd's son, who was earning his own living, and so no more in the field of fair encounter, and severely battered the said William's face? From this combat he had been dragged by an irate grandparent, and even now he was dreeing his weird in the loss of his dog, his most faithful ally, who in a lonely kennel sadly bemoaned its master For grown-up persons he cared naught, for he knew by long experience that they were a weak-kneed folk and feeble in the race. So amid the nodding grasses he swung along, whisking the heads off the meadow-sweet with his sword, in most unmilitary fashion, telling himself that he was setting out on a journey as great as erst Sir Galahad or Sir John Mandeville, that sweetest and most truthful of knights. He had his store of provisions in his pocket; he was armed with sword and dagger and a stout heart; with another bellow of defiance he drew his blade and stalked on like Goliath of Gath, or Ajax defying the celestial lightning.

A sound in the bushes, a rustle, a movement, and the Jacobite was on his face, breathing hard and peering warily forth. It was only a thrush, so once more he got upon his feet and advanced. Just where the woods began he had a sharp conflict with a rabbit, which escaped amid a volley of stones. Once inside the cover, among the long, ghostlike firs and tremulous beeches, he felt he was on classic ground. There was every probability that an enchanter lurked among the shadows or a wild-boar in the rocks. To be sure, he had never seen such things, but they must be somewhere about. He clasped his sword a little timorously, but still with strong purpose. The river looked black and unfriendly, a fitting haunt for kelpies and mermaidens.

Soon he came to where another stream entered, a bright, prattling, sunshiny burn, such as his soul loved. Thither he felt his course lay. Now was the time to emulate the heroic John Ridd, when he tracked the Bagworthy stream and met the girl Lorna.

Without doubt some Lorna awaited his coming among the meadows by the water-side. He felt the surer when he reflected that this expedition, too, was not without danger. The land was the ground of a manor-house, watched by zealous gardeners and keepers, full of choice flowers and pleasant fruits as the garden of the Hesperides. He had

once essayed the venture before and met with a sad
discomfiture. While he kept the stream he had fared well
enough, but it so fell out that in the meadow he espied a
horse, and there his troubles began; for, approaching it in
the Indian manner, he crawled under its belly in the most
orthodox way, and proceeded delicately to mount it. The
horse clearly was of no Indian breed, for it made off after
sadly barking his shins. To add to it all, he had to flee
homewards, limping across ploughed lands and through
marshy woods, pursued by two irate grooms and a vocif-
erous coachman. No. There was no lack of danger in that
direction. So for form's sake he pulled his belt tighter,
looked to the edge of his dagger and the point of his sword,
and made a pretence of seeking the aid of Heaven in pious,
knightly fashion.

It was a gracious and comely land he entered upon. The
clear water crooned among irises and white ranunculus or
rippled across broad, shining shallows, or fell in a valorous
plunge over a little cauld. There was no lack of fish, and
had the Jacobite not been on high mission intent he would
have thrown off his jacket and groped for trout beneath the
banks. But not for him now were such sports. The yellow
sunlight clothed the fields as in a cloth of gold, and from
the midst great beech trees raised their masses of rich
browns and cool greens. There were sheep there and
horses, but he did not turn aside, for, like Ulysses, he
had learned from misfortune. The place had an enchanting effect upon his spirits. It was like some domain in
faëry, the slumbrous forest which girt the sleeping princess, or the wood beyond the world. John Ridd was
forgotten, and the Jacobite, forgetful of his special calling, had fled to regions beyond history. He was recalled of
a sudden by an unlooked-for barrier to his progress. The
stream issued from below a high weir, and unfriendly-
looking walls barred its sides.

Without an effort he rose to the occasion. Now was the
opportunity for a master-mind, which had never yet met its
match among the boys of his restricted acquaintance. He
set himself tooth and nail to the wall. Projecting stone and
mossy interstices gave him foothold. In a trice he had

gained the top and was looking into a sort of refined Elysium, a paradise within a paradise. A broad pond had been formed by the stream, whereon sailed a swan and some brave-liveried ducks, and near whose margin floated water-lilies, yellow and white. Clean-shaven turf fell away from the edge, barred by the shadows of trees and bright in many places with half-opened heather. Beyond the water were little glades of the greenest grass, through which came a glimpse of stone and turret. The Jacobite's breath went quick and fast. Things were becoming, he felt, altogether too true to nature. He had come straight upon a castle without so much as a mishap. The burden of his good fortune bore heavily on him; and he was strongly tempted to retreat. But in the end romance prevailed; with wavering footsteps he crept along the edge, ready at a glance to flop among the reeds.

But these violent tactics were not needed. Sleep seemed to have fallen upon the race of grooms and gardeners. Nothing stirred save a linnet, which came down to drink, and a moorhen which scuttled across the pool. Grasshoppers were chirping in the silence, and the faraway sound of a bell came clear and thin through the air. In a little he came to where the pond ceased and the stream began once more, not like the stream in the meadows below, but a slow, dark current among trees and steep mossy banks. Once more the adventurer's heart beat irresolutely; once more his courage prevailed. He scrambled below trailing branches, slipped oftentimes into the shallows, and rolled among red earth till the last vestige of green was gone from his corduroys. But harsh is the decree of fate. Again he came to a barrier – this time a waterfall of great sound and volume.

Joy filled the heart of the Jacobite. This was the water-slide in the Bagworthy wood, and at the top must be the Doone's valley. So with boldness and skill he addressed himself to the ascent. I have no inkling what the real cascade in Devon is like, but I will take my oath it was not more perilous than this. The black rocks were slippery with ooze, few helping boughs of trees were at hand, and the pool at the bottom yawned horrific and

deep. But the Jacobite was skilled in such breakneck
ventures. With the ease of a practised climber he swung
himself from one foothold to another till he gripped the
great rock which stood midway in the stream just at the
summit, and, dripping and triumphant, raised himself to
the dry land.

And there before him on a fallen trunk, in the most lovely
dell that nature ever conceived, sat the Lady.

For a moment the Jacobite, notwithstanding his expectations, was staggered. Then his training asserted itself. He
pulled a torn cap from his head, and 'I thought you would
be here,' said he.

'Who are you?' said the Lady, with the curiosity of her
sex, 'and where do you come from?'

The Jacobite reflected. It was only consistent with
tradition, he felt, to give some account of himself. So he
proceeded compendiously to explain his birth, his ante-
cedents, his calling, and his adventures of the day. He was
delighted with the princess now he had found her. She was
tall and lithe, with hair like gold, and the most charming
eyes. She wore a dress of white, like a true princess, and a
great hat, made according to the most correct canons of
romance. She had been reading in a little book, which lay
face downward at her feet. He thought of all his special
heroines, Helen of Troy and Ariadne, Joan of Arc, the
Queen of Scots, Rosalind, and Amy Robsart, and that most
hapless and beautiful of dames, the wife of the Secretary
Murray. He inwardly decided that the Lady was most like
the last, which indeed was only fitting, seeing that tradition
said that this place was once her home.

'O, you delightful boy,' said the Lady. 'I never met any
one like you before. Tell me what you think of me.'

'You're all right,' said the wanderer, 'only where do you
come from? I hope you're not going to disappear.'

'No, indeed,' said she. 'I come from a place to which you
will go some day, a big, stupid town, where the finest and
the worst things in the world are to be found. I'm here to
escape from it for a little.'

The Jacobite was keenly interested in this account of his
prospective dwelling-place.

'What are the fine things?' he asked. 'Ships and palaces and dogs and guns and – oh, you know what I mean?'

'Yes,' she said, 'these things are there. And the people take very little interest in them. What they chiefly like is money.'

The Jacobite pulled out his halfpenny, and regarded it with critical interest.

'Yes,' she went on, 'and lots of people don't go to bed much at night, but they put on fine clothes and go to other people's houses and have dinner and talk, even when they would rather be at home.'

The Jacobite looked philosophically at his clothes. They could not be called fine. He wasn't given to talking to people whom he didn't like, and he told the Lady so.

'And there are others, who rule the country and don't know anything about it, and are only good for making long speeches.'

'But,' said the Jacobite, incredulously, 'don't they know how to fight, or how do they rule if they don't?'

'They don't know how to fight,' said the Lady sadly; 'and more, they say fighting is wrong, and want to settle everything by talking.'

The Jacobite looked mournfully skyward. If this was true, his future was dismal indeed. He had much skill in fighting, but talk he held in deep contempt.

'But there must be heaps of knights and cavaliers left; or are they all gone to heaven?' said he.

The Lady sighed. 'There are some, but very few, I am afraid. And these mostly go away to foreign lands, where there is still fighting, or they hunt lions and tigers, or they stay at home very sad. And people say there is no such place as heaven, but that all that is left for us when we die is a "period of sensationless, objective existence". Do you know what that means?'

'No,' said the Jacobite, stoutly, 'and I don't care. What awful rot!'

'And they say that there never were such things as fairies, and that all the stories about Hector and Ulysses and William Tell and Arthur are nonsense. But we know better.'

'Yes,' said he, 'we know better. They're true to us, and it is only to stupids that they're not true.'

'Good,' said the Lady. 'There was once a man called Horace, who lived long ago, who said the same thing. You will read his book some day.' And she repeated softly to herself,

> Prætulerim scriptor delirus inersque videri,
> Dum mea delectent mala me vel denique fallant,
> Quam sapere et ringi.

But the Jacobite saw the slanting sun over the treetops, and he knew it was time to go home.

'I am afraid I must go,' he said mournfully. 'When I grow up I will stop all that nonsense. I will hang a lot of them and banish others, and then you will like it, won't you? Will you have some treacle toffy? It is very good.'

'Thank you,' said the Lady, 'it *is* good.'

'Good-bye,' said he, 'I will come and see you when I grow up and go to the place you spoke of.'

'Yes, I am sure you will,' said she, and gave him her hand.

He bent low and kissed it in true cavalier fashion.

'There is the road up there,' she said, 'it's your quickest way.' And she looked after him as he disappeared through the trees.

The road ran east and west, and as the sun bent aslant it, it was one great belt of golden light. The Jacobite was wonderfully elated. What an afternoon he had had, just like a bit out of a book! Now there remained for him the three miles of a walk home; then tea with fresh butter and cakes such as his heart rejoiced in; and then the delights of taking the horses to drink, and riding his pony to the smithy. The prospect was soothing and serene. A mellow gaiety diffused through his being.

And yet he could not get rid of the Lady's news. Ah! There was a true princess for you, one who agreed with him in everything; but how sad was the tale she told! Would he ever have to meet such misfortune? He felt that some day he would, and the notion pained him. But he turned back for a moment to look to the westward. The crimson heart of evening was glowing like a furnace; the long shafts of orange light were lengthening, and the apple-green was growing over the blue. Somehow or other the sight gave him heart. The valiant West, that home of El Dorados and golden cities, whither all the romance of life seems to flee, raised his sinking courage. He would, alone, like Douglas among the Saracens, lift the standard and rout all foolish and feeble folks. Some day, when he was great and tall, he would ride into the city where the Lady dwelt, and, after he had scattered her enemies, would marry her and live happy for evermore.

That for the future. For the present home and tea and a summer evening.

An Individualist

Another story from *Scholar Gipsies* (1896). A man and a tramp meet and discover they have much to learn from each other, particularly about 'the place of ambition in the scale of the virtues'.

The afternoon was fast waning to twilight, and the man who for the last few hours had been alternately sleeping in the heather and dabbling in the rocky pools of the burn awoke to the consciousness of time. He rose and looked around him. Hills crowded upon hills, blue, purple, and black; distant spaces of green meadow; barren pines waving desolately on a scarp; many streams falling in a chain of cascades to the glens; and over all a June sky, clear, deep, and tender. The place was goodly, and the idleness which is inseparable from the true enjoyment of afternoon weather dragged heavily upon him to keep him where he was.

He had come out that morn with his mind a chaos of many cares. Projects, fragments of wise and foolish thoughts, a thousand half-conceptions, had crowded upon him thick and fast, for the habit of unceasing mental toil is not shaken off in an hour. But June and the near presence of great hills are wondrous correctives; they are like an inverted spy-glass, which makes large things seem of the smallest; and ere long he found himself aimless and thoughtless. The drift of clouds, the twitter of mountain linnets, seemed all in the world of moment, and he would have gladly bartered his many plans for some share in this wild lore. And so for that day there was one pervert from the gospel of success in life, till lengthening shadows came and he gathered together his wits and laughed at his folly.

With lingering regrets he set off homewards, and the vista before him was one of work awaiting and a whole host of anxieties. Yet for once in a while he had been at peace, and to don the harness again was not so repellent, now that he had found how it could be shaken off at will. So he went along the grassy hill-path whistling an old air, till he had gained the edge of the decline, and lo! before him went another wayfarer.

It was the figure of a man about the middle height, with a forward stoop, and a walk which was neither shuffle nor stride, but the elegant lounge of the idler. His general aspect was one of breeding and ease; it was not till a nearer approach that one perceived the contradiction of the details. For all things about him were in rags, from the torn cap to the fragmentary shoes, and the pristine excellence of the cloth only served to accentuate its present state of defection. He also whistled as he walked, and his roving eyes devoured the manifold landscape. Then some other mood seemed to take him, and he flung himself on the short hill grass, lying back with his head on his hands.

At the sound of the other's footsteps he sat up and greeted him.

'Good-day,' said the tramp, civilly. 'Do you go far?' Then, as if he had forgotten himself, he went back to his Scots. 'I was wonderin' if ye could tell me the time o' day, sir,' he said, hastily.

The other stopped short and looked at the stranger before him. Something in his frank eye and strange appearance attracted him, for he did not go on, but glanced at his watch and sat down beside him. Darkness was not yet, and the air was as soft as mid-day.

For a few minutes there was silence, and the one broke it with a laugh. 'I seem to have come into a new land to-day,' he said. 'All things have seemed enchanted, and I scarcely know whether I am sleeping or waking. I suppose it is the weather and those great hills.' And even as he spoke he found himself wondering at himself for speaking thus in such company.

But the other reassured him. 'Good,' said he, and again he dropped the dialect. 'At last I have found some one like-minded. You are a—?'

'Oh, I am a man of affairs, busy from year's end to year's end. For eleven months I am chained, but for once in a while I am free. And you—?'

'Oh I,' and the tramp laughed. 'Ulysses, you know. A wanderer is man from his birth. I see we have not so much in common.'

'No,' said the other, 'I am afraid we have not. You see I believe really at the bottom of my heart in getting on in life, and doing one's duty, and that sort of thing. I see that you have no such prejudices.'

'Not a bit of it,' and the tramp whistled lackadaisically. 'It's all a question of nature. Some men – well, some, you know, are born to be good citizens. Others lack the domestic virtues. How does the thing go?

> Non illum tectis ullæ, non mœnibus urbes
> Accepere, neque ipse manus feritate dedisset,
> Pastorum et solis exegit montibus ævum.

'Brunck emends the passage, but the words are good as they are. In them you have my character and watchword.'

'It is the character of many,' said the other. 'We can all hear the Piper if we listen, but some of us stop our ears against him. For myself, this hill air makes me daft, and the smell of heather and burning wood, and the sound of water and the wind. I can sympathise with you. And now I am going back to toil, and it will be very hard for days, till the routine lays its spell over me once more.'

'And for what good?' asked the wayfarer. 'I apologise for asking you the foolish question, but it is the inevitable one in my philosophy.'

'Oh,' said the other, 'I can scarcely tell. For the sake of feeling that one is fighting in the ranks of life and not skulking from the battle line; that one is doing the work for which God has given him talents; to know that one is mixing with men, and playing his part well in the human tragi-comedy. These reasons and many others.'

'Hum,' said the tramp. 'Again I must say, "temper of mind". You will excuse me if I say that they do not commend themselves to me. I cannot see the necessity for making the world a battle-field. It is a pilgrimage, if you like, where it is a man's duty and best wisdom to choose the easiest course. All the pleasure in life can be got apart from the turmoil of the market-place – love and kindness, the taste of bread to a hungry man and water to a thirsty, the delight of rest when tired, and the pleasure of motion when fresh and alert, and, above all, the thousand things of nature.'

'You chose the life? You were not born to it?'

'Born to it?' and the wayfarer laughed again. 'No, I was very little born to it. I shall not trouble you with my story, it is too old-fashioned to amuse you. I had good prospects, as people say, but, as I have said, I lacked the civil virtues. I was too restless to stay long anywhere and too rich to have any need, and the upshot of it all is – this!' And he fingered lovingly the multiform rents in his coat.

Below them, as they talked, ran the sandy hill-road, with its white gravel glistening in the westering sunlight. Far down lay a cottage, which was as clear as if it had been not a score of yards away. Thither a man was walking, a shepherd in his Sabbath clothes, who had been to the country town and was returning laden with many parcels. Distant as it was, the whole scene lay plain before the two. A child, a little girl, ran from the cottage at her father's approach, and clung lovingly to his knee. Then with childish strength she clutched a package, and in another second the pair had entered the house. By some simultaneous impulse both men had directed their eyes to the place and had seen the whole of the little comedy.

And lo! to the other's amazement the tramp's eyes glistened as he looked.

'You do not believe in the domestic virtues?' said the one very slowly.

'Not I,' said the tramp. 'I have told you that I don't. The essence of social life, civil and domestic, is bearing one another's burdens and sharing one another's pleasures. I am an individualist with all my heart. I grant you things would come to a pretty pass if all were of my way of thinking; but there – it is a matter of temperament, and such temperaments are scarce.'

'Is it not,' said his interrogator, 'the old question whether man or nature is the more productive study? You cannot maintain that these hills afford the same view-ground of character as the city and the bustle of

life. I speak solely as a spectator. I do not even ask you to
go down and mix with the crowd and taste its life.' And
there seemed no incongruity in talking thus to the man of
the wayside and many tatters.

'No, no,' said the other. 'God forbid that I should talk so
callously of the sorrows and toils of my fellows. I do not
seek to scrutinise the character of others. All my concern is
with myself. It is not a man's duty to seek out his kind and
strive with them and live among them. All that he must do
is to play his part well as he may chance upon them. It is not
richness and fulness of life that I want. I am not ambitious.
Ease, *ataraxia*, you know, is enough for me.'

'But the rewards?' said the one, questioningly.

'Ah, the rewards! You cannot know them.' And the man's
voice took a new tone. His eyes lit up, and, looking over the
darkening valley, he spoke to his comrade many things, and
sang in his ear ever so sweetly the 'Song of the Open Road'.
He told of the changes of the season – the rigours of winter,
the early flush of spring, the mellow joys of summer, and
autumn with her pomp and decay. He told of clear starlit
nights, when the hill breezes blow over the moors and the
birds wake the sleeper; of windy mornings, when the mist
trails from the hills and dun clouds scud across the sky; of
long hot days in the heather among the odours of thyme and
bog-myrtle and the lark's clear song. Then he changed his
tune, and spoke of the old romance of the wayside, that
romance which gipsies and wanderers feel, of motion amid
rest, of ease in the hurry of the seasons, of progress over the
hills and far away, into that land unknown which dawns
upon the sight with each new morrow. And he spoke, too, of
the human element in it all which is so dear to the man versed
in its mysteries, of heroism amid the sordid, the pathetic in
the coarse, the kindly in the most repulsive. And as he spoke
he grew eloquent with it all, and his hearer marvelled at such
words, till he looked away from the rags to the keen, eager
face, and then he marvelled no more.

But by this time the darkness had all but come, and the
speaker cut himself short, laughing at his own rhetoric.

'Losh, it's comin' on for nicht,' he said, speaking broadly,
as if to point a contrast, 'and time slips by when ye get on the

crack. I'll hae to be movin' if I'm to win to Jock Rorison's the nicht. I aye bide wi' Jock, when I'm hereaways, if I dinna sleep ootbye. Will ye be gaun doun the road?'

'Yes, I go by that way too. I'll be glad to accompany you;' and the two went down the winding path together. Overhead the stars, faint with haze, winked and glittered; and below in the valley a light or two shone out from the blue darkness. The soft, fragrant night airs rustled over the heather, and borne on them came the faint twitter of sleepy birds. To one of the pair all seemed so new, so strange, that it was like an excerpt from the caliph's journal. The wondrous natural loveliness around seemed to be a fitting environment for the strange being at his side; and he reflected somewhat ruefully as he walked that what folk call the romance of life springs in the main from people of hot heads and ill-balanced judgments, who seek to put their imperfect, immature little philosophies into action.

They stopped at the first wayside cottage, and the tramp knocked. The door was opened by a grave-faced woman, for in these uplands the sharp air seems to form the human countenance into a passive mould. But at the sight of the man her eyes brightened and she half-offered admittance.

'I'm no comin' in the now,' he explained. 'I juist ca'ed as I passed to tell ye that as I cam' bye the schule at Callowa', the maister gave me a wheen buiks to tak' to your laddie.'

'Thank ye, and it's rale guid o' ye to bring them. He's awfu' keen o' the readin', and gettin' on uncommon weel. It's a wunnerfu' thing eddication; how it mak's a thing different to some folk. But of course you, that never kenned what it was, canna understand it in the same way.'

'No,' said the tramp humbly, 'we canna, but it's a wunnerfu' thing. Na, I'll no come in. Gude nicht,' and again they took the road.

By the time they crossed the water the darkness had fairly come, and a bright horn rose behind the pines. Somewhere in thicket a bird sang – no nightingale – and the two men stopped to listen. Beyond lay the little hamlet of a dozen houses, a rambling, tangled clachan, looking grey and ghostlike in the night.

At one door he knocked and a man came, an old man bent with age and toil, who greeted them kindly.

'I juist cam' frae your son,' the visitor explained. 'I gave him a ca' in as I was passin'. He's verra weel, and he bade me tell ye that he's comin' ower the morn's week to see ye. I was to tell ye, tae, that he's sold his hoggs at twenty-seven, and that he's bocht Crichope yins this 'ear.'

Again he halted, and this time it was at a very little dwelling somewhat beyond the others, standing alone in its garden of gooseberry and marigold. This time the man who waited at the gate saw a pretty, slim lass stand in the doorway, who blushed at the message which was brought her. For her lover lived many a mile over the hills and saw her but every second Sabbath, so their primitive love-letters were sent by word of mouth. And sometimes there came a present from the market town, and there went back something knitted by the girl's own fair fingers; and so the harmless comedy was played, as it is played and will be played all the world over.

Once more the two went on their way, the one silent, the other humming a light country catch. The mind of the one was occupied with many problems, among them that hard one of the adjustment of a man to his neighbours, and the place of ambition in the scale of the virtues. Somehow or other his pride of intellect, of strength, seemed to be deserting him, and in its place there came a better feeling, humble and kindly, a sense that the world is full of more things than any man has ever writ in black and white.

But now it was the cross-road where their paths were severed. They had known each other a bare hour, and now they were the fastest friends. At parting the one shook the other's hand. 'You are a very pretty kind of individualist,' he said.

A Journey of Little Profit

Buchan contributed three stories to *The Yellow Book*, Aubrey Beardsley's magazine of the Aesthetic movement that during its thirteen issues published such writers as George Gissing and W.B. Yeats. John Betjeman in his 'The Arrest of Oscar Wilde at the Cadogan Hotel' sums up the surprise with which this association is often greeted:

> So you've brought me the latest *Yellow Book*
> And Buchan has got in it now;
> Approval of what is approved of
> Is as false as a well-kept vow.

In fact Wilde had been arrested by the time Buchan started writing for the paper. This story was published in April 1896 and was later included in *Grey Weather* (1899). A drover, driving his sheep between Edinburgh and Glasgow, takes refuge at a remote farmhouse where he enters into a Faustian pact with his landlord, who mysteriously has the same name.

———————————

> The Devil he sang, the Devil he played
>   High and fast and free.
> And this was ever the song he made,
>   As it was told to me.
> Oh, I am the king of the air and the ground,
>   And lord of the seasons' roll,
> And I will give you a hundred pound,
>   If you will give me your soul!
>   from *The Ballad of Grey Weather*

The cattle market of Inverforth is, as all men know north of the Tweed, the greatest market of the kind in the land. For days in the late Autumn there is the lowing of oxen and the bleating of sheep among its high wooden pens, and in the rickety sale-rings the loud clamour of auctioneers and the talk of farmers. In the open yard where are the drovers and the butchers, a race always ungodly and law-despising, there is such a Babel of cries and curses as might wake the Seven Sleepers. From twenty different adjacent eating-houses comes the clatter of knives, where the country folk eat their dinner of beef and potatoes, with beer for sauce, and the collies grovel on the ground for stray morsels. Hither come a hundred types of men from the Highland cateran with scarce a word of English, and the shentleman-farmer of Inverness and Ross, to lowland graziers and city tradesmen, not to speak of blackguards of many national-ities and more professions.

It was there I first met Duncan Stewart of Clacham-harstan, in the Moor of Rannoch, and there I heard this story. He was an old man when I knew him, grizzled and wind-beaten; a prosperous man, too, with many herds like Jacob and much pasture. He had come down from the North with kyloes, and as he waited on the English-men with whom he had trysted, he sat with me through the long day and beguiled the time with many stories. He had been a drover in his youth, and had travelled on foot the length and breadth of Scotland; and his memory went back hale and vigorous to times which are now all but historical. This tale I heard among many others as we sat on a pen amid the smell of beasts and the jabber of Gaelic:

'When I was just turned of twenty-five I was a wild young lad as ever was heard of. I had taken to the droving for the love of a wild life, and a wild life I led. My father's heart would be broken long syne with my doings, and well for my mother that she was in her grave since I was six years old. I paid no heed to the ministrations of godly Mr Macdougall of the Isles, who bade me turn from the error of my ways, but went on my own evil course, making siller, for I was a braw lad at the work and a trusted, and knowing the inside of every public from the pier of Cromarty to the streets of York. I was a wild drinker caring in my cups for neither God nor man, a great hand with the cards, and fond of the lasses past all telling. It makes me shameful to this day to think on my evil life when I was twenty-five.

'Well, it chanced that in the back of the month of September I found myself in the city of Edinburgh with a flock of fifty sheep which I had bought as a venture from a drunken bonnet-laird and was thinking of selling somewhere wast the country. They were braw beasts, Leicester every one of them, well-fed and dirt-cheap at the price I gave. So it was with a light heart that I drove them out of the town by the Merchiston Road along by the face of the Pentlands. Two or three friends came with me, all like myself for folly, but maybe a little bit poorer. Indeed, I cared little for them, and they valued me only for the whisky which I gave them to drink my health in at the parting. They left me on the near side of Colinton, and I went on my way alone.

'Now, if you'll be remembering the road, you will mind that at the place called Kirk Newton, just afore the road begins to twine over the Big Muir and almost at the head of the Water o' Leith, there is a verra fine public. Indeed, it would be no lee to call it the best public between Embro' and Glesca. The good wife, Lucky Craik by name, was an old friend of mine, for many a good gill of her prandy have I bought; so what would I be doing but just turning aside for refreshment? She met me at the door, verra pleased-like to see me, and soon I had my legs aneath her table and a basin of toddy on the board before me. And whom did I find in the same place but my old comrade Toshie Maclean from the backside of Glen-Lyon. Toshie and I were acquaintances so old that it did not behoove us to be parting quick. Forbye the day was chill without; and within the fire was grand and the crack of the best.

'Then Toshie and I got on quarrelling about the price of Lachlan Farawa's beasts that he sold at Falkirk; and, the drink having aye a bad effect on my temper, I was for giving him the lie and coming off in a great rage. It was about six o'clock in the evening and an hour to nightfall, so Mistress Craik comes in to try and keep me. "Losh, Duncan," says she, "ye'll never try and win ower the muir the nicht. It's mae than ten mile to Carnwath, and there's nocht atween it and this but whaups and heathery braes." But when I am roused I will be more obstinate than ten mules, so I would be going, though I knew not under Heaven where I was going till. I was too full of good liquor and good meat to be much worth at thinking, so I got my sheep on the road an a big bottle in my pouch and set off into the heather. I knew not what my purpose was, whether I thought to reach the shieling of Carnwath, or whether I expected some house of entertainment to spring up by the wayside. But my fool's mind was set on my purpose of getting some miles further in my journey ere the coming of darkness.

'For some time I jogged happily on, with my sheep running well before me and my dogs trotting at my heels. We left the trees behind and struck out on the proad grassy path which bands the moor like the waist-strap of a sword. It was most dreary and lonesome with never a house in view, only bogs and grey hillsides and ill-looking waters. It was stony, too, and this more than aught else caused my Dutch courage to fail me, for I soon fell wearied, since much whisky is bad travelling fare, and began to curse my folly. Had my pride no kept me back, I would have returned to Lucky Craik's; but I was like the devil, for stiff-neckedness and thought of nothing but to push on.

'I own that I was verra well tired and quite spiritless when I first saw the House. I had scarce been an hour on the way, and the light was not quite gone; but still it was geyan dark, and the place sprang somewhat suddenly on my sight. For, looking a little to the left, I saw over a little strip of grass a big square dwelling with many outhouses, half farm and half pleasure-house. This, I thought, is the verra place I have been seeking and made sure of finding; so whistling a gay tune, I drove my flock toward it.

'When I came to the gate of the court, I saw better of what sort was the building I had arrived at. There was a square yard with monstrous high walls, at the left of which was the main block of the house, and on the right what I took to be the byres and stables. The place looked ancient, and the stone in many places was crumbling away; but the style was of yesterday and in no way differing from that of a hundred steadings in the land. There were some kind of arms above the gateway, and a bit of an iron stanchion; and when I had my sheep inside of it, I saw that the court was all grown up with green grass. And what seemed queer in that dusky half-light was the want of sound. There was no neichering of horses, nor routing of kye, nor clack of hens, but all as still as the top of Ben Cruachan. It was warm and pleasant too, though the night was chill without.

'I had no sooner entered the place than a row of sheep-pens caught my eye, fixed against the wall in front. This I thought mighty convenient, so I made all haste to put my beasts into them; and finding that there was a good supply of hay within, I leff them easy in my mind, and turned about to look for the door of the house.

'To my wonder, when I found it, it was open wide to the wall; so, being confident with much whisky, I never took thought to knock, but walked boldly in. There's some careless folk here, thinks I to myself, and I much misdoubt if the man knows aught about farming. He'll maybe just be a town's body taking the air on the muirs.

'The place I entered upon was a hall, not like a muirland farmhouse, but more fine than I had ever seen. It was laid with a verra fine carpet, all red and blue and gay colours, and in the corner in a fireplace a great fire crackled. There were chairs, too, and a walth of old rusty arms on the walls, and all manner of whigmaleeries that folk think ornamental. But nobody was there, so I made for the staircase which was at the further side, and went up it stoutly. I made scarce any noise so thickly was it carpeted, and I will own it kind of terrified me to be walking in such a place. But when a man has drunk well he is troubled not overmuckle with modesty or fear, so I e'en stepped out and soon came to a landing where was a door.

'Now, thinks I, at last I have won to the habitable parts of the house; so laying my finger on the sneck I lifted it and entered. And there before me was the finest room in all the world; indeed I abate not a jot of the phrase, for I cannot think of anything finer. It was hung with braw pictures and lined with big bookcases of oak well-filled with books in fine bindings. The furnishing seemed carved by a skilled hand, and the cushions and curtains were soft velvet. But the best thing was the table, which was covered with a clean white cloth and set with all kind of good meat and drink. The dishes were of silver and as bright as Loch Awe water in an April sun. Eh, but it was a braw braw sight for a drover! And there at the far end, with a great pottle of wine before him, sat the master.

'He rose as I entered, and I saw him to be dressed in the pink of town fashion, a man of maybe fifty years, but hale and well-looking, with a peaked beard and trimmed moustache and thick eyebrows. His eyes were slanted a thought, which is a thing I hate in any man, but his whole appearance was pleasing.

'"Mr Stewart?" says he courteously, looking at me. "Is it Mr Duncan Stewart that I will be indebted to for the honour of this visit?"

'I stared at him blankly, for how did he ken my name?

'"That is my name," I said, "but who the tevil tell't you about it?"

'"Oh, my name is Stewart myself," says he, "and all Stewarts should be well acquaint."

'"True," said I, "though I don't mind your face before. But now I am here, I think you have a most gallant place, Mr Stewart."

'"Well enough. But how have you come to't? We've few visitors."

'So I told him where I had come from, and where I was going, and why I was forwandered at this time of night among the muirs. He listened keenly, and when I had finished, he says verra friendly-like, "Then you'll bide all night and take supper with me. It would never be doing to let one of the clan go away without breaking bread. Sit ye down, Mr Duncan."

'I sat down gladly enough, though I own that at first I did not half-like the whole business. There was something unchristian about the place, and for certain it was not seemly that the man's name should be the same as my own, and that he should be so well posted in my doings. But he seemed so well-disposed that my misgivings soon vanished.

'So I seated myself at the table opposite my entertainer. There was a place laid ready for me, and beside the knife and fork a long horn-handled spoon. I had never seen a spoon so long and queer, and I asked the man what it meant. "Oh," says he, "the broth in this house is very often hot, so we need a long spoon to sup it. It is a common enough thing, is it not?"

'I could answer nothing to this, though it did not seem to me sense, and I had an inkling of something I had heard about long spoons which I thought was not good; but my wits were not clear, as I have told you already. A serving man brought me a great bowl of soup and set it before me. I had hardly plunged spoon intil it, when Mr Stewart cries out from the other end: "Now, Mr Duncan, I call you to witness that you sit down to supper of your own accord. I've an ill name in these parts for compelling folk to take meat with me when they dinna want it. But you'll bear me witness that you're willing."

' "Yes, by God, I am that," I said, for the savoury smell of the broth was rising to my nostrils. The other smiled at this as if well-pleased.

'I have tasted many soups, but I swear there never was one like that. It was as if all the good things in the world were mixed thegether – whisky and kale and shortbread and cocky-leeky and honey and salmon. The taste of it was enough to make a body's heart loup with fair gratitude. The smell of it was like the spicy winds of Arabia, that you read about in the Bible, and when you had taken a spoonful you felt as happy as if you had sellt a hundred yowes at twice their reasonable worth. Oh, it was grand soup!

' "What Stewarts did you say you comed from?" I asked my entertainer.

' "Oh," he says, "I'm connected with them all, Athole Stewarts, Appin Stewarts, Rannoch Stewarts; and a' I've a heap o' land thereaways."

' "Whereabouts?" says I, wondering. "Is't at the Blair o' Athole, or along by Tummel side, or wast the Loch o'Rannoch, or on the Muir, or in Mamore?"

' "In all the places you name," says he.

' "Got damn," says I, "then what for do you not bide there instead of in these stinking lawlands?"

'At this he laughed softly to himself. "Why, for maybe the same reason as yoursel, Mr Duncan. You know the proverb, 'A' Stewarts are sib to the Deil.'"

'I laughed loudly; "Oh, you've been a wild one, too, have you? Then you're not worse than mysel. I ken the inside of every public in the Cowgate and Canongate, and there's no another drover on the road my match at fechting and drinking and dicing." And I started on a long shameless catalogue of my misdeeds. Mr Stewart meantime listened with a satisfied smirk on his face.

'"Yes, I've heard tell of you, Mr Duncan," he says. "But here's something more, and you'll doubtless be hungry."

'And now there was set on the table a round of beef garnished with pot-herbs, all most delicately fine to the taste. From a great cupboard were brought many bottles of wine, and in a massive silver bowl at the table's head were put whisky and lemons and sugar. I do not know well what I drank, but whatever it might be it was the best ever brewed. It made you scarce feel the earth round about you, and you were so happy you could scarce keep from singing. I wad give much siller to this day for the receipt.

'Now, the wine made me talk, and I began to boast of my own great qualities, the things I had done and the things I was going to do. I was a drover just now, but it was not long that I would be being a drover. I had bought a flock of my own, and would sell it for a hundred pounds, no less; with that I would buy a bigger one till I had made money enough to stock a farm; and then I would leave the road and spend my days in peace, seeing to my land and living in good company. Was not my father, I cried, own cousin, thrice removed, to the Macleans o' Duart, and my mother's uncle's wife a Rory of Balnacroy? And I am a scholar too, said I, for I was a matter of two years at Embro' College, and might have been roaring in the pulpit, if I hadna liked the drink and the lassies too well.

'"See," said I, "I will prove it to you;" and I rose from the table and went to one of the bookcases. There were all manner of books, Latin and Greek, poets and philosophers, but in the main, divinity. For there I saw Richard Baxter's "Call to the Unconverted", and Thomas Boston of Ettrick's "Fourfold State", not to speak of the *Sermons* of half a hundred auld ministers, and the "Hind let Loose", and many books of the covenanting folk.

'"Faith," I says, "you've a fine collection, Mr What's-your-name," for the wine had made me free in my talk. "There is many a minister and professor in the Kirk, I'll warrant, who has a less godly library. I begin to suspect you of piety, sir."

'"Does it not behoove us," he answered in an unctuous voice, "to mind the words of Holy Writ that evil communications corrupt good manners, and have an eye to our company? These are all the company I have, except when some stranger such as you honours me – with a visit."

'I had meantime been opening a book of plays, I think by the famous William Shakespeare, and I here proke into a loud laugh. "Ha, ha, Mr Stewart," I says, "here's a sentence I've lighted on which is hard on you. Listen! 'The Devil can quote Scripture to advantage.'"

'The other laughed long. "He who wrote that was a shrewd man," he said, "but I'll warrant if you'll open another volume, you'll find some quip on yourself."

'I did as I was bidden, and picked up a white-backed book, and opening it at random, read: "There be many who spend their days in evil and wine-bibbing, in lusting and cheating, who think to mend while yet there is time; but the opportunity is to them for ever awanting, and they go down open-mouthed to the great fire."

'"Psa," I cried, "some wretched preaching book, I will have none of them. Good wine will be better than bad theology." So I sat down once more at the table.

'"You're a clever man, Mr Duncan," he says, "and a well-read one. I commend your spirit in breaking away from the bands of the kirk and the college, though your father was so thrawn against you."

'"Enough of that," I said, "though I don't know who telled you;" I was angry to hear my father spoken of, as though the grieving him was a thing to be proud of.

' "Oh, as you please," he says; "I was just going to say that I commended your spirit in sticking the knife into the man in the Pleasaunce, the time you had to hide for a month about the backs o' Leith."

' "How do you ken that," I asked hotly, "you've heard more about me than ought to be repeated, let me tell you."

' "Don't be angry," he said sweetly; "I like you well for these things, and you mind the lassie in Athole that was so fond of you. You treated her well, did you not?"

'I made no answer, being too much surprised at his knowledge of things which I thought none knew but myself.

' "Oh yes, Mr Duncan. I could tell you what you were doing today, how you cheated Jock Gallowa out of six pounds, and sold a horse to the farmer of Haypath that was scarce fit to carry him home. And I know what you are meaning to do the morn at Glesca, and I wish you well of it."

' "I think you must be the Devil," I said blankly.

' "The same, at your service," said he, still smiling.

'I looked at him in terror, and even as I looked I kenned by something in his eyes and the twitch of his lips that he was speaking the truth.

' "And what place is this, you . . ." I stammered.

' "Call me Mr S.," he says gently, "and enjoy your stay while you are here and don't concern yourself about the lawing."

' "The lawing!" I cried in astonishment, "and is this a house of public entertainment?"

' "To be sure, else how is a poor man to live?"

' "Name it," said I, "and I will pay and be gone."

' "Well," said he, "I make it a habit to give a man his choice. In your case it will be your wealth or your chances hereafter, in plain English your flock or your—"

' "My immortal soul," I gasped.

' "Your soul," said Mr S., bowing, "though I think you call it by too flattering an adjective."

' "You damned thief," I roared, "you would entice a man into your accursed house and then strip him bare."

' "Hold hard," said he, "don't let us spoil our good fellowship by incivilities. And, mind you, I took you to witness to begin with that you sat down of your own accord."

' "So you did," said I, and could say no more.

' "Come, come," he says, "don't take it so bad. You may keep all your gear and yet part from here in safety. You've but to sign your name, which is no hard task to a college-bred man, and go on living as you live just now to the end. And let me tell you, Mr Duncan Stewart, that you should take it as a great obligement that I am willing to take your bit soul instead of fifty sheep. There's no many would value it so high."

' "Maybe no, maybe no," I said sadly, "but it's all I have. D'ye no see that if I gave it up, there would be no chance left of mending? And I'm sure I do not want your company to all eternity."

' "Faith, that's uncivil," he says; "I was just about to say that we had had a very pleasant evening."

'I sat back in my chair very down-hearted. I must leave this place as poor as a kirk-mouse, and begin again with little but the clothes on my back. I was strongly tempted to sign the bit paper thing and have done with it all, but somehow I could not bring myself to do it. So at last I says to him: "Well, I've made up my mind. I'll give you my sheep, sorry though I be to lose them, and I hope I may never come near this place again as long as I live."

' "On the contrary," he said, "I hope often to have the pleasure of your company. And seeing that you've paid well for your lodging, I hope you'll make the best of it. Don't be sparing on the drink."

'I looked hard at him for a second. "You've an ill name, and an ill trade, but you're no a bad sort yoursel, and, do you ken, I like you."

' "I'm much obliged to you for the character," says he, "and I'll take your hand on't."

'So I filled up my glass and we set to, and such an evening I never mind of. We never got fou, but just in a fine good temper and very entertaining. The stories we telled and the jokes we cracked are still a kind of memory with me, though I could not come over one of them. And then, when I got sleepy, I was shown to the brawest bedroom, all hung with pictures and looking-glasses, and with bed-clothes of the finest linen and a coverlet of silk. I bade Mr S. good-night, and my head was scarce on the pillow ere I was sound asleep.

'When I awoke the sun was just newly risen, and the frost of a September morning was on my clothes. I was lying among green braes with nothing near me but crying whaups and heathery hills, and my two dogs running round about and howling as they were mad.'

Politics and the May-Fly

When Buchan was ennobled in 1935 he considered as a title Lord Manorwater, the name he gives one of the characters in this story about the clash between a Tory farmer and his Radical ploughman. The story, included in *Grey Weather* (1899), appeared in *Chambers Magazine* in May 1896 and the following month in the Boston magazine, *The Living Age*. In the magazine versions the town at the centre of the events was called Marchthorn but in the book was changed to Gledsmuir, a name Buchan used in a number of subsequent stories.

The farmer of Clachlands was a Tory, stern and unbending. It was the tradition of his family, from his grandfather, who had been land-steward to Lord Manorwater, down to his father, who had once seconded a vote of confidence in the sitting member. Such traditions, he felt, were not to be lightly despised; things might change, empires might wax and wane, but his obligation continued; a sort of perverted *noblesse oblige* was the farmer's watchword in life; and by dint of much energy and bad language, he lived up to it.

As fate would have it, the Clachlands ploughman was a Radical of Radicals. He had imbibed his opinions early in life from a speaker on the green of Gledsmuir, and ever since, by the help of a weekly penny paper and an odd volume of Gladstone's speeches, had continued his education. Such opinions in a conservative countryside carry with them a reputation for either abnormal cleverness or abnormal folly. The fact that he was a keen fisher, a famed singer of songs, and the best judge of horses in the place, caused the verdict of his neighbours to incline to the former, and he passed for something of an oracle among his fellows. The blacksmith, who was the critic of the neighbourhood, summed up his character in a few words. 'Him,' said he, in a tone of mingled dislike and admiration, 'him! He would sweer white was black the morn, and dod! he would prove it tae.'

It so happened in the early summer, when the land was green and the trout plashed in the river, that Her Majesty's Government saw fit to appeal to an intelligent country. Among a people whose politics fight hard with their religion for a monopoly of their interests, feeling ran high and brotherly kindness departed. Houses were divided against themselves. Men formerly of no consideration found themselves suddenly important, and discovered that their intellects and conscience, which they had hitherto valued at little, were things of serious interest to their betters. The lurid light of publicity was shed upon the lives of the rival candidates; men formerly accounted worthy and respectable were proved no better than whited sepulchres; and each man was filled with a morbid concern for his fellow's character and beliefs.

The farmer of Clachlands called a meeting of his labourers in the great dusty barn, which had been the scene of many similar gatherings. His speech on the occasion was rigorous and to the point. 'Ye are a' my men,' he said, 'an' I'll see that ye vote richt. Y're ueddicated folk, and ken naething aboot the matter, sae ye just tak' my word for't, that the Tories are in the richt and vote accordingly. I've been a guid maister to ye, and it's shurely better to pleesure me, than a wheen leein' scoondrels whae tramp the country with leather bags and printit trash.'

Then arose from the back the ploughman, strong in his convictions. 'Listen to me, you men,' says he; 'just vote as ye think best. The maister's a guid maister, as he says, but he's nocht to dae wi' your votin'. It's what they ca' inteemedation to interfere wi' onybody in this matter. So mind that, an' vote for the workin'-man an' his richts.'

Then ensued a war of violent words.

'Is this a meetin' in my barn, or a pennywaddin?'

'Ca't what ye please. I canna let ye mislead the men.'

'Whae talks about misleadin'? Is't misleadin' to lead them richt?'

'The question,' said the ploughman solemnly, 'is what you ca' richt.'

'William Laverhope, if ye werena a guid plooman, ye wad gang post-haste oot o' here the morn.'

'I carena what ye say. I'll stand up for the richts o' thae men.'

'Men!' – this with deep scorn. 'I could mak' better men than thae wi' a stick oot o' the plantin'.'

'Ay, ye say that noo, an' the morn ye'll be ca'in' ilka yin o' them *Mister*, a' for their votes.'

The farmer left in dignified disgust, vanquished but still dangerous; the ploughman in triumph mingled with despair. For he knew that his fellow-labourers cared not a whit for politics, but would follow to the letter their master's bidding.

The next morning rose clear and fine. There had been a great rain for the past few days, and the burns were coming down broad and surly. The Clachlands Water was chafing by bank and bridge and threatening to enter the hay-field, and every little ditch and sheep-drain was carrying its tribute of peaty water to the greater flood. The farmer of Clachlands, as he looked over the landscape from the doorstep of his dwelling, marked the state of the weather and pondered over it.

He was not in a pleasant frame of mind that morning. He had been crossed by a ploughman, his servant. He liked the man, and so the obvious way of dealing with him – by making things uncomfortable or turning him off – was shut against him. But he burned to get the upper hand of him, and discomfit once for all one who had dared to question his wisdom and good sense. If only he could get him to vote on the other side – but that was out of the question. If only he could keep him from voting – that was possible but unlikely. He might forcibly detain him, in which case he would lay himself open to the penalties of the law, and be nothing the gainer. For the victory which he desired was a moral one, not a triumph of force. He would like to circumvent him by cleverness, to score against him fairly and honourably on his own ground. But the thing was hard, and, as it seemed to him at the moment, impossible.

Suddenly, as he looked over the morning landscape, a thought struck him and made him slap his legs and chuckle hugely. He walked quickly up and down the gravelled walk.

'Losh, it's guid. I'll dae't. I'll dae't, if the weather juist hauds.'

His unseemly mirth was checked by the approach of someone who found the farmer engaged in the minute examination of gooseberry leaves. 'I'm concerned aboot thae busses,' he was saying; 'they've been ill lookit to, an' we'll no hae half a crop.' And he went off, still smiling, and spent a restless forenoon in the Gledsmuir market.

In the evening he met the ploughman, as he returned from the turnip-singling, with his hoe on his shoulder. The two men looked at one another with the air of those who know that all is not well between them. Then the farmer spoke with much humility.

'I maybe spoke rayther severe yestreen,' he said. 'I hope I didna hurt your feelings.'

'Na, na! No me!' said the ploughman airily.

'Because I've been thinking ower the matter, an' I admit that a man has a richt to his ain thochts. A'body should hae principles an' stick to them,' said the farmer, with the manner of one making a recondite quotation.

'Ay,' he went on, 'I respect ye, William, for your consistency. Ye're an example to us a'.'

The other shuffled and looked unhappy. He and his master were on the best of terms, but these unnecessary compliments were not usual in their intercourse. He began to suspect, and the farmer, who saw his mistake, hastened to change the subject.

'Graund weather for the fishin',' said he.

'Oh, is it no?' said the other, roused to excited interest by this home topic. 'I tell ye by the morn they'll be takin' as they've never ta'en this 'ear. Doon in the big pool in the Clachlands Water, at the turn o' the turnip-field, there are twae or three pounders, and aiblins yin o' twae pund. I saw them mysel' when the water was low. It's ower big the noo, but when it gangs doon the morn, and gets the colour o' porter, I'se warrant I could whup them oot o' there wi' the flee.'

'D' ye say sae?' said the farmer, sweetly. 'Weel, it's a lang time since I tried the fishin', but I yince was keen on 't. Come in bye, William; I've something ye micht like to see.'

From a corner he produced a rod, and handed it to the other. It was a very fine rod indeed, one which the owner had gained in a fishing competition many years before, and treasured accordingly. The ploughman examined it long and critically. Then he gave his verdict. 'It's the brawest rod I ever saw, wi' a fine hickory butt, an' guid greenhert tap and middle. It wad cast the sma'est flee, and haud the biggest troot.'

'Weel,' said the farmer, genially smiling, 'ye have a half-holiday the morn when ye gang to the poll. There'll be plenty o' time in the evening to try a cast wi' 't. I'll lend it ye for the day.'

The man's face brightened. 'I wad tak' it verra kindly,' he said, 'if ye wad. My ain yin is no muckle worth, and, as ye say, I'll hae time for a cast the morn's nicht.'

'Dinna mention it. Did I ever let ye see my flee-book? Here it is,' and he produced a thick flannel book from a drawer. 'There's a maist miscellaneous collection, for a' waters an' a' weathers. I got a heap o' them frae auld Lord Manorwater, when I was a laddie, and used to cairry his basket.'

But the ploughman heeded him not, being deep in the examination of its mysteries. Very gingerly he handled the tiny spiders and hackles, surveying them with the eye of a connoisseur.

'If there's anything there ye think at a' like the water, I'll be verra pleased if ye'll try 't.'

The other was somewhat put out by this extreme friendliness. At another time he would have refused shamefacedly, but now the love of sport was too strong in him. 'Ye're far ower guid,' he said; 'thae twae paitrick wings are the verra things I want, an' I dinna think I've ony at hame. I'm awfu' gratefu' to ye, an' I'll bring them back the morn's nicht.'

'Guid-e'en,' said the farmer, as he opened the door, 'an' I wish ye may hae a guid catch.' And he turned in again, smiling sardonically.

The next morning was like the last, save that a little wind had risen, which blew freshly from the west. White cloudlets drifted across the blue, and the air was as clear as spring-water. Down in the hollow the roaring torrent had sunk to a full, lipping stream, and the colour had changed from a turbid yellow to a clear, delicate brown. In the town of Gledsmuir, it was a day of wild excitement, and the quiet Clachlands road bustled with horses and men. The labourers in the field scarce stopped to look at the passers, for in the afternoon they too would have their chance, when they might journey to the town in all importance, and record their opinions of the late Government.

The ploughman of Clachlands spent a troubled forenoon. His nightly dreams had been of landing great fish, and now his waking thoughts were of the same. Politics for the time were forgotten. This was the day which he had looked forward to for so long, when he was to have been busied in deciding doubtful voters, and breathing activity into the ranks of his cause. And lo! the day had come and found his thoughts elsewhere. For all such things are, at the best, of fleeting interest, and do not stir men otherwise than sentimentally; but the old kindly love of field-sports, the joy in the smell of the earth and the living air, lie very close to a man's heart. So this apostate, as he cleaned his turnip rows, was filled with the excitement of the sport, and had no thoughts above the memory of past exploits and the anticipation of greater to come.

Mid-day came, and with it his release. He roughly calculated that he could go to the town, vote, and be back in two hours, and so have the evening clear for his fishing. There had never been such a day for the trout in his memory, so cool and breezy and soft, nor had he ever seen so glorious a water. 'If ye dinna get a fou basket the nicht, an' a feed the morn, William Laverhope, your richt hand has forgot its cunning,' said he to himself.

He took the rod carefully out, put it together, and made trial casts on the green. He tied the flies on a cast and put it ready for use in his own primitive fly-book, and then bestowed the whole in the breast-pocket of his coat. He had arrayed himself in his best, with a white rose in his button-hole, for it behoved a man to be well dressed on such an occasion as voting. But yet he did not start. Some fascination in the rod made him linger and try it again and again.

Then he resolutely laid it down and made to go. But something caught his eye – the swirl of the stream as it left the great pool at the hay-field, or the glimpse of still, gleaming water. The impulse was too strong to be resisted. There was time enough and to spare. The pool was on his way to the town, he would try one cast ere he started, just to see if the water was good. So, with rod on his shoulder, he set off.

Somewhere in the background a man, who had been watching his movements, turned away, laughing silently, and filling his pipe.

A great trout rose to the fly in the hay-field pool, and ran the line up-stream till he broke it. The ploughman swore deeply, and stamped on the ground with irritation. His blood was up, and he prepared for battle. Carefully, skilfully he fished, with every nerve on tension and ever-watchful eyes. Meanwhile, miles off in the town the bustle went on, but the eager fisherman by the river heeded it not.

Late in the evening, just at the darkening, a figure arrayed in Sunday clothes, but all wet and mud-stained, came up the road to the farm. Over his shoulder he carried a rod, and in one hand a long string of noble trout. But the expression on his face was not triumphant; a settled melancholy overspread his countenance, and he groaned as he walked.

Mephistopheles stood by the garden-gate, smoking and surveying his fields. A well-satisfied smile hovered about his mouth, and his air was the air of one well at ease with the world.

'Weel, I see ye've had guid sport,' said he to the melancholy Faust. 'By-the-bye, I didna notice ye in the toun. And losh! man, what in the warld have ye dune to your guid claes?'

The other made no answer. Slowly he took the rod to pieces and strapped it up; he took the fly-book from his pocket; he selected two fish from the heap; and laid the whole before the farmer.

'There ye are,' said he, 'and I'm verra much obleeged to ye for your kindness.' But his tone was of desperation and not of gratitude; and his face, as he went onward, was a study in eloquence repressed.

The Herd of Standlan

Arthur Mordaunt, a distinguished politician, almost drowns whilst fishing but is saved by Gidden Scott, who then questions why he saved the man. First published in the magazine *Black and White* in June 1896, it was one of the stories in *Grey Weather* (1899).

When the wind is nigh and the moon is high
  And the mist on the riverside,
Let such as fare have a very good care
  Of the Folk who come to ride.
For they may meet with the riders fleet
  Who fare from the place of dread;
And hard it is for a mortal man
  To sort at ease with the Dead.

from *The Ballad of Grey Weather*

When Standlan Burn leaves the mosses and hags which gave it birth, it tumbles over a succession of falls into a deep, precipitous glen, whence in time it issues into a land of level green meadows, and finally finds its rest in the Gled. Just at the opening of the ravine there is a pool shut in by high, dark cliffs, and black even on the most sunshiny day. The rocks are never dry but always black with damp and shadow. There is scarce any vegetation save stunted birks, juniper bushes, and draggled fern; and the hoot of owls and the croak of hooded crows is seldom absent from the spot. It is the famous Black Linn where in winter sheep stray and are never more heard of, and where more than once an unwary shepherd has gone to his account. It is an Inferno on the brink of a Paradise, for not a stone's throw off is the green, lawn-like turf, the hazel thicket, and the broad, clear pools, by the edge of which on that July day the Herd of Standlan and I sat drowsily smoking and talking of fishing and the hills. There he told me this story, which I here set down as I remember it, and as it bears repetition.

'D'ye mind Airthur Morrant?' said the shepherd, suddenly.

I did remember Arthur Mordaunt. Ten years past he and I had been inseparables, despite some half-dozen summers' difference in age. We had fished and shot together, and together we had tramped every hill within thirty miles. He had come up from the South to try sheep-farming, and as he came of a great family and had no need to earn his bread, he found the profession pleasing. Then irresistible fate had swept me southward to college, and when after two years I came back to the place, his father was dead and he had come into his own. The next I heard of him was that in politics he was regarded as the most promising of the younger men, one of the staunchest and ablest upstays of the Constitution. His name was rapidly rising into prominence, for he seemed to exhibit that rare phenomenon of a man of birth and culture in direct sympathy with the wants of the people.

'You mean Lord Brodakers?' said I.

'Dinna call him by that name,' said the shepherd, darkly. 'I hae nae thocht o' him now. He's a disgrace to his country, servin' the Deil wi' baith hands. But nine year syne he was a bit innocent callant wi' nae Tory deevilry in his heid. Well, as I was sayin', Airthur Morrant has cause to mind that place till his dying day'; and he pointed his finger to the Black Linn.

I looked up the chasm. The treacherous water, so bright and joyful at our feet, was like ink in the great gorge. The swish and plunge of the cataract came like the regular beating of a clock, and though the weather was dry, streams of moisture seamed the perpendicular walls. It was a place eerie even on that bright summer's day.

'I don't think I ever heard the story,' I said casually.

'Maybe no,' said the shepherd. 'It's no yin I like to tell'; and he puffed sternly at his pipe, while I awaited the continuation.

'Ye see it was like this,' he said, after a while. 'It was just the beginning o' the back-end, and that year we had an awfu' spate o' rain. For near a week it poured hale water, and a' doon by

Drumeller and the Mossfennan haughs was yae muckle loch.
Then it stopped, and an awfu' heat came on. It dried the grund
in nae time, but it hardly touched the burns; and it was rale
queer to be pourin' wi' sweat and the grund aneath ye as dry as
a potato-sack, and a' the time the water neither to haud nor
bind. A' the waterside fields were clean stripped o' stooks, and
a guid wheen hay-ricks gaed doon tae Berwick, no to speak o'
sheep and nowt beast. But that's anither thing.

'Weel, ye'll mind that Airthur was terrible keen on fishing.
He wad gang oot in a' weather, and he wasna feared for ony
mortal or naitural thing. Dod, I've seen him in Gled wi' the
water rinnin' ower his shouthers yae cauld March day playin'
a saumon. He kenned weel aboot the fishing, for he had
traivelled in Norroway and siccan outlandish places, where
there's a heap o' big fish. So that day – and it was a Setterday
tae and far ower near the Sabbath – he maun gang awa' up
Standlan Burn wi' his rod and creel to try his luck.

'I was bidin' at that time, as ye mind, in the wee cot-house at
the back o' the faulds. I was alane, for it was three year afore I
mairried Jess, and I wasna begun yet to the coortin'. I had
been at Gledsmuir that day for some o' the new stuff for killing
sheep-mawks, and I wasna very fresh on my legs when I gaed
oot after my tea that night to hae a look at the hill-sheep. I had
had a bad year on the hill. First the lambin'-time was snaw,
snaw ilka day, and I lost mair than I wad like to tell. Syne
the grass a' summer was so short wi' the drought that the
puir beasts could scarcely get a bite and were as thin as
pipe-stapples. And then, to crown a', auld Will Broun,
the man that helpit me, turned ill wi' his back, and had to
bide at hame. So I had twae man's work on yae man's
shouthers, and was nane so weel pleased.

'As I was saying, I gaed oot that nicht, and after lookin'
a' the Dun Rig and the Yellow Mire and the back o'
Cramalt Craig, I cam down the burn by the road frae the
auld faulds. It was geyan dark, being about seven o'clock
o' a September nicht, and I keepit weel back frae that
wanchancy hole o' a burn. Weel, I was comin' kind o'
quick, thinkin' o' supper and a story book that I was
readin' at the time, when just abune that place there, at the
foot o' the Linn, I saw a man fishing. I wondered what ony

body in his senses could be daein' at that time o' nicht in sic a dangerous place, so I gave him a roar and bade him come back. He turned his face round and I saw in a jiffey that it was Mr Airthur.

'"O, sir," I cried, "What for are ye fishing there? The water's awfu' dangerous, and the rocks are far ower slid."

'"Never mind, Scott," he roars back cheery-like. "I'll take care o' mysel'."

'I lookit at him for twa-three meenutes, and then I saw by his rod he had yin on, and a big yin tae. He ran it up and doon the pool, and he had uncommin wark wi' 't, for it was strong and there was little licht. But bye and bye he got it almost tae his feet, and was just about to lift it oot when a maist awfu' thing happened. The tackets o' his boots maun hae slithered on the stane, for the next thing I saw was Mr Airthur in the muckle hungry water.

'I dinna exactly ken what happened after that, till I found myself on the very stone he had slipped off. I maun hae come doon the face o' the rocks, a thing I can scarcely believe when I look at them, and a thing no man ever did afore. At ony rate I ken I fell the last fifteen feet or sae, and lichted on my left airm, for I felt it crack like a rotten branch, and an awfu' sairness ran up it.

'Now, the pool is a whirlpool as ye ken, and if anything fa's in, the water first smashes it against the muckle rock at the foot, then it brings it round below the fall again, and syne at the second time it carries it doon the burn. Weel, that was what happened to Mr Airthur. I heard his heid gang dunt on the stane wi' a sound that made me sick. This must hae dung him clean senseless, and indeed it was a wonder it didna knock his brains oot. At ony rate there was nae mair word o' swimming, and he was swirled round below the fa' just like a corp.

'I kenned fine that nae time was to be lost, for if he once gaed doun the burn he wad be in Gled or ever I could say a word, and nane wad ever see him mair in life. So doon I got on my hunkers on the stane, and waited for the turnin'. Round he came, whirling in the foam, wi' a lang line o' blood across his brow where the stane had cut him. It was a terrible meenute. My heart fair stood still. I put out my airm, and as he passed I grippit him and wi' an awfu' pu' got him out o' the current into the side.

'But now I found that a waur thing still was on me. My left airm was broken, and my richt sae numbed and weak wi' my fall that, try as I micht, I couldna raise him ony further. I thocht I wad burst a bloodvessel i' my face and my muscles fair cracked wi' the strain, but I would make nothing o' 't. There he stuck wi' his heid and shouthers abune the water, pu'd close until the edge of a rock.

'What was I to dae? If I once let him slip he wad be into the stream and lost forever. But I couldna hang on here a' nicht, and as far as I could see there wad be naebody near till the mornin', when Ebie Blackstock passed frae the Head o' the Hope. I roared wi' a' my power; but I got nae answer, naething but the rummle o' the water and the whistling o' some whaups on the hill.

'Then I turned very sick wi' terror and pain and weakness and I kenna what. My broken airm seemed a great lump o' burnin' coal. I maun hae given it some extra wrench when I hauled him out, for it was sae sair now that I thocht I could scarcely thole it. Forbye, pain and a', I could hae gone off to sleep wi' fair weariness. I had heard o' men sleepin' on their feet, but I never felt it till then. Man, if I hadna warstled wi' mysel, I wad hae dropped off as deid's a peery.

'Then there was the awfu' strain o' keepin' Mr Airthur up. He was a great big man, twelve stone I'll warrant, and weighing a terrible lot mair wi' his fishing togs and things. If I had had the use o' my ither airm I micht hae taen off his jacket and creel and lichtened the burden, but I could do naething. I scarcely like to tell ye how I was tempted in that hour. Again and again I says to mysel, "Gidden Scott," say I, "what do ye care for this man? He's no a drap's bluid to you, and forbye ye'll never be able to save him. Ye micht as weel let him gang. Ye've dune a' ye could. Ye're a brave man, Gidden Scott, and ye've nae cause to be ashamed o' givin' up the fecht." But I says to mysel again: "Gidden Scott, ye're a coward. Wad ye let a man die, when there's a breath in your body? Think shame o' yoursel, man." So I aye kept haudin' on, although I was very near bye wi' 't. Whenever I lookit at Mr Airthur's face, as white's death and a' blood, and his een sae stelled-like, I got a kind o' groo and felt awfu' pitiful for the bit laddie. Then I thocht on his faither, the auld Lord, wha was sae built up in him, and I couldna bear to think o' his son droonin' in that awfu' hole. So I set mysel to the wark o' keepin' him up a' nicht, though I had nae hope in the matter. It wasna what ye ca' bravery that made me dae't, for I had nae ither choice. It was just a kind o' dourness that runs in my folk, and a kind o' vexedness for sae young a callant in sic an ill place.

'The nicht was hot and there was scarcely a sound o' wind. I felt the sweat standin' on my face like frost on tatties, and abune me the sky was a' misty and nae mune visible. I thocht very likely that it micht come a thunder-shower and I kind o' lookit forrit tae't. For I was aye feared at lichtning, and if it came that nicht I was bound to get clean dazed and likely tummle in. I was a lonely man wi' nae kin to speak o', so it wouldna maitter muckle.

'But now I come to tell ye about the queer side o' that nicht's wark, whilk I never telled to nane but yoursel, though a' the folk about here ken the rest. I maun hae been geyan weak, for I got into a kind o' doze, no sleepin', ye understand, but awfu' like it. And then a' sort o' daft things began to dance afore my een. Witches and bogles and brownies and things oot o' the Bible, and leviathans and brazen bulls – a' cam fleerin' and flauntin' on the tap o' the water straucht afore me. I didna pay muckle heed to them, for I half kenned it was a' nonsense, and syne they gaed awa'. Then an auld wife wi' a mutch and a hale procession o' auld wives passed, and just about the last I saw yin I thocht I kenned.

' "Is that you, Grannie?" says I.

' "Aye, it's me, Gidden," says she; and as shure as I'm a leevin' man, it was my auld grannie, whae had been deid thae sax year. She had on the same mutch as she aye wore, and the same auld black stickie in her hand, and, Dod, she had the same snuff-box I made for her out o' a sheep's horn when I first took to the herdin'. I thocht she was lookin' rale weel.

' "Losh, Grannie," says I, "Where in the warld hae ye come frae? It's no canny to see ye danderin' about there."

' "Ye've been badly brocht up," she says, "and ye ken nocht about it. Is't no a decent and comely thing that I should get a breath o' air yince in the while?"

' "Deed," said I, "I had forgotten. Ye were sae like yoursel I never had a mind ye were deid. And how d' ye like the Guid Place?"

' "Wheesht, Gidden," says she, very solemn like, "I'm no there."

'Now at this I was fair flabbergasted. Grannie had aye been a guid contentit auld wumman, and to think that they hadna let her intil Heeven made me think ill o' my ain chances.

' "Help us, ye dinna mean to tell me ye're in Hell?" I cries.

' "No exactly," says she, "But I'll trouble ye, Gidden, to speak mair respectful about holy things. That's a name ye uttered the noo whilk we dinna daur to mention."

' "I'm sorry, Grannie," says I, "but ye maun allow it's an astonishin' thing for me to hear. We aye counted ye shure, and ye died wi' the Buik in your hands."

' "Weel," she says, "it was like this. When I gaed up till the gate o' Heeven a man wi' a lang white robe comes and says, 'Wha may ye be?' Says I, 'I'm Elspeth Scott.' He gangs awa' and consults a wee and then he says, 'I think, Elspeth my wumman, ye'll hae to gang doon the brae a bit. Ye're no quite guid eneuch for this place, but ye'll get a very comfortable doonsittin' whaur I tell ye.' So off I gaed and cam' to a place whaur the air was like the inside of the glass-houses at the Lodge. They took me in wi'oot a word and I've been rale comfortable. Ye see they keep the bad part o' the Ill Place for the reg'lar bad folk, but they've a very nice half-way house where the likes o' me stop."

' "And what kind o' company hae ye?"

' "No very select," says she. "There's maist o' the ministers o' the countryside and a pickle fairmers, tho' the maist o' them are further ben. But there's my son Jock, your ain faither, Gidden, and a heap o' folk from the village, and oh, I'm nane sae bad."

' "Is there naething mair ye wad like then, Grannie?"

' "Oh aye," says she, "we've each yae thing which we canna get. It's a' the punishment we hae. Mine's butter. I canna get fresh butter for my bread, for ye see it winna keep, it just melts. So I've to tak jeely to ilka slice, whilk is rale sair on the teeth. Ye'll no hae ony wi' ye?"

' "No," I says, "I've naething but some tobaccy. D' ye want it? Ye were aye fond o' 't."

' "Na, na," says she. "I get plenty o' tobaccy doon bye. The pipe's never out o' the folks' mouth there. But I'm no speakin' about yoursel, Gidden. Ye're in a geyan ticht place."

' "I'm a' that," I said. "Can ye no help me?"

' "I micht try." And she raxes out her hand to grip mine. I put out mine to tak it, never thinkin' that that wasna the richt side, and that if Grannie grippit it she wad pu' the broken airm and haul me into the water. Something touched my fingers like a hot poker; I gave a great yell; and ere ever I kenned I was awake, a' but off the rock, wi' my left airm aching like hell-fire. Mr Airthur I had let slunge ower the heid and my ain legs were in the water.

'I gae an awfu' whammle and edged my way back though it was near bye my strength. And now anither thing happened. For the cauld water roused Mr Airthur frae his dwam. His een opened and he gave a wild look around him. "Where am I?" he cries, "Oh, God!" and he gaed off intil anither faint.

'I can tell ye, sir, I never felt anything in this warld and I hope never to feel anything in anither sae bad as the next meenutes on that rock. I was fair sick wi' pain and weariness and a kind o' fever. The lip-lap o' the water, curling round Mr Airthur, and the great *crush* o' the Black Linn itsel dang me fair silly. Then there was my airm, which was bad eneuch, and abune a' I was gotten into sic a state that I was fleyed at ilka shadow just like a bairn. I felt fine I was gaun daft, and if the thing had lasted another score o' meenutes I wad be in a madhouse this day. But soon I felt the sleepiness comin' back, and I was off again dozin' and dreamin'.

'This time it was nae auld wumman but a muckle black-avised man that was standin' in the water glowrin' at me. I kenned him fine by the bandy-legs o' him and the broken nose (whilk I did mysel), for Dan Kyle the poacher deid thae twae year. He was a man, as I remembered him weel, wi' a great black beard and een that were stuck sae far in his heid that they looked like twae wull-cats keekin' oot o' a hole. He stands and just stares at me, and never speaks a word.

' "What d'ye want?" I yells, for by this time I had lost a' grip o' mysel. "Speak, man, and dinna stand there like a dummy."

' "I want naething," he says in a mournfu' sing-song voice; "I'm just thinkin'."

' "Whaur d' ye come frae?" I asked, "and are ye keepin' weel?"

' "Weel," he says bitterly. "In this warld I was ill to my wife, and twa-three times I near killed a man, and I stole like a pyet, and I was never sober. How d' ye think I should be weel in the next?"

'I was sorry for the man. "D' ye ken I'm vexed for ye, Dan," says I; "I never likit ye when ye were here, but I'm wae to think ye're sae ill off yonder."

' "I'm no alane," he says. "There's Mistress Courhope of the Big House, she's waur. Ye mind she was awfu' fond o' gumflowers. Weel, she canna keep them Yonder, for they a' melt wi' the heat. She's in an ill way about it, puir body." Then he broke off. "Whae's that ye've got there? Is't Airthur Morrant?"

' "Ay, it's Airthur Morrant," I said.

' "His family's weel kent doon bye," says he. "We've maist o' his forbears, and we're expectin' the auld Lord every day. May be we'll sune get the lad himsel."

' "That's a damned lee," says I, for I was angry at the man's presumption.

'Dan lookit at me sorrowfu'-like. "We'll be gettin' you tae, if ye swear that gate," says he, "and then ye'll ken what it's like."

'Of a sudden I fell into a great fear. "Dinna say that, Dan," I cried; "I'm better than ye think. I'm a deacon, and 'll maybe sune be an elder, and I never swear except at my dowg."

' "Tak care, Gidden," said the face afore me. "Where I am, a' things are taken into account."

'"Then they'll hae a gey big account for you," says I. "What-like do they treat you, may be?"

'The man groaned.

'"I'll tell ye what they dae to ye doon there," he said. "They put ye intil a place a' paved wi' stanes and wi' four square walls around. And there's naething in 't, nae grass, nae shadow. And abune you there's a sky like brass. And sune ye get terrible hot and thirsty, and your tongue sticks to your mouth, and your eyes get blind wi' lookin' on the white stane. Then ye gang clean fey, and dad your heid on the ground and the walls to try and kill yoursel. But though ye dae't till a' eternity ye couldna feel pain. A' that ye feel is just the awfu' devourin' thirst, and the heat and the weariness. And if ye lie doon the ground burns ye and ye're fain to get up. And ye canna lean on the walls for the heat, and bye and bye when ye're fair perished wi' the thing, they tak ye out to try some ither ploy."

'"Nae mair," I cried, "nae mair, Dan!"

'But he went on malicious-like, –

'"Na, na, Gidden, I'm no dune yet. Syne they tak you to a fine room but awfu' warm. And there's a big fire in the grate and thick woollen rugs on the floor. And in the corner there's a braw feather bed. And they lay ye down on 't, and then they pile on the tap o' ye mattresses and blankets and sacks and great rolls o' woollen stuff miles wide. And then ye see what they're after, tryin' to suffocate ye as they dae to folk that a mad dowg has bitten. And ye try to kick them off, but they're ower heavy, and ye canna move your feet nor your airms nor gee your heid. Then ye gang clean gyte and skirl to yoursel, but your voice is choked and naebody is near. And the warst o' 't is that ye canna die and get it ower. It's like death a hundred times and yet ye're aye leevin'. Bye and bye when they think ye've got eneuch they tak you out and put ye somewhere else."

'"Oh," I cries, "stop, man, or you'll ding me silly."

'But he says never a word, just glowrin' at me.

'"Aye, Gidden, and waur than that. For they put ye in a great loch wi' big waves just like the sea at the Pier o' Leith. And there's nae chance o' soomin', for as sune as ye put out your airms a billow gulfs ye down. Then ye swallow water and your heid dozes round and ye're chokin'. But ye canna die, ye must just thole. And down ye gang, down, down, in the cruel deep, till your heid's like to burst and your een are fu' o' bluid. And there's a' kind o' fearfu' monsters about, muckle slimy things wi' blind een and white scales, that claw at ye wi' claws just like the paws o' a drooned dog. And ye canna get away though ye fecht and fleech, and bye and bye ye're fair mad wi' horror and choking and the feel o' thae awfu' things. Then—"

'But now I think something snapped in my heid, and I went daft in doonricht earnest. The man before me danced about like a lantern's shine on a windy nicht and then disappeared. And I woke yelling like a pig at a killing, fair wud wi' terror, and my skellochs made the rocks ring. I found mysel in the pool a' but yae airm – the broken yin – which had hankit in a crack o' rock. Nae wonder I had been dreaming o' deep waters among the torments o' the Ill Place, when I was in them mysel. The pain in my airm was sae fearsome and my heid was gaun round sae wi' horror that I just skirled on and on, shrieking and groaning wi'oot a thocht what I was daein'. I was as near death as ever I will be, and as for Mr Airthur he was on the very nick o' 't, for by this time he was a' in the water, though I still kept a grip o' him.

'When I think ower it often I wonder how it was possible that I could be here the day. But the Lord's very gracious, and he works in a queer way. For it so happened that Ebie Blackstock, whae had left Gledsmuir an hour afore me and whom I thocht by this time to be snorin' in his bed at the Head o' the Hope, had gone intil the herd's house at the Waterfit, and had got sae muckle drink there that he was sweered to start for hame till aboot half-past twal i' the night. Weel, he was comin' up the burnside, gey happy and contentit, for he had nae wife at hame to speir about his ongaeings, when, as he's telled me himsel, he heard sic an uproar doon by the Black Linn that made him turn pale and think that the Deil, whom he had long served, had gotten him at last. But he was a brave man, was Ebie, and he thinks to himsel that some fellow-creature micht be perishin'. So he gangs forrit wi' a' his pith, trying to think on the Lord's

Prayer and last Sabbath's sermon. And, lookin' ower the edge, he saw naething for a while, naething but the black water wi' the awfu' yells coming out o' 't. Then he made out something like a heid near the side. So he rins doon by the road, no ower the rocks as I had come, but round by the burnside road, and soon he gets to the pool, where the crying was getting aye fainter and fainter. And then he saw me. And he grips me by the collar, for he was a sensible man, was Ebie, and hauls me oot. If he hadna been geyan strong he couldna hae dune it, for I was a deid wecht, forbye having a heavy man hanging on to me. When he got me up, what was his astonishment to find anither man at the end o' my airm, a man like a corp a' bloody about the heid. So he got us baith out, and we twae baith senseless; and he laid us in a safe bit back frae the water, and syne gaed off for help. So bye and bye we were baith got home, me to my house and Mr Airthur up to the Lodge.'

'And was that the end of it?' I asked.

'Na,' said the shepherd. 'I lay for twae month there ravin' wi' brain fever, and when I cam to my senses I was as weak as a bairn. It was many months ere I was mysel again, and my left airm to this day is stiff and no muckle to lippin to. But Mr Airthur was far waur, for the dad he had gotten on the rock was thocht to have broken his skull, and he lay long atween life and death. And the warst thing was that his faither was sae vexed about him that he never got ower the shock, but dee'd afore Airthur was out o' bed. And so when he cam out again he was My Lord, and a monstrously rich man.'

The shepherd puffed meditatively at his pipe for a few minutes.

'But that's no a' yet. For Mr Airthur wad tak nae refusal but that I maun gang awa' doon wi' him to his braw house in England and be a land o' factor or steward or something like that. And I had a rale fine cottage a' to mysel, wi' a very bonny gairden and guid wages, so I stayed there maybe sax month and then I gaed up till him. "I canna bide nae longer," says I. "I canna stand this place. It's far ower laigh, and I'm fair sick to get hills to rest my een on. I'm awfu' gratefu' to ye for your kindness, but I maun gie up my job."

He was very sorry to lose me, and was for giein' me a present o' money or stockin' a fairm for me, because he said that it was to me he owed his life. But I wad hae nane o' his gifts. "It wad be a terrible thing," I says, "to tak siller for daein' what ony body wad hae dune out o' pity." So I cam awa' back to Standlan, and I maun say I'm rale contentit here. Mr Airthur used whiles to write to me and ca' in and see me when he cam North for the shooting; but since he's gane sae far wrang wi' the Tories, I've had naething mair to dae wi' him.'

I made no answer, being busy pondering in my mind on the depth of the shepherd's political principles, before which the ties of friendship were as nothing.

'Ay,' said he, standing up, 'I did what I thocht my duty at the time and I was rale glad I saved the callant's life. But now, when I think on a' the ill he's daein' to the country and the Guid Cause, I whiles think I wad hae been daein' better if I had just drappit him in.

'But whae kens? It's a queer warld.' And the shepherd knocked the ashes out of his pipe.

Streams of Water in the South

The title of the story comes from Psalm 126 – 'As streams of water in the South/Our bondage, Lord, recall' – and this becomes a refrain throughout the story. Written in 1896, it appeared in slightly different versions (rather unusually) in two of Buchan's collections of short stories – *Grey Weather* (1899) and *The Moon Endureth* (1912). It is yet another exploration of the relationship between the country folk of the Upper Tweed Valley and the forces of nature.

As streams of water in the South,
Our bondage, Lord, recall.
Psalm CXXVI
Scots Metrical Version

I

It was at the ford of the Clachlands Water in a tempestuous August that I, an idle boy, first learned the hardships of the Lammas droving. The shepherd of the Redswirehead, my very good friend, and his three shaggy dogs, were working for their lives in an angry water. The path behind was thronged with scores of sheep bound for the Gledsmuir market, and beyond it was possible to discern through the mist the few dripping dozen which had made the passage. Between raged yards of brown foam coming down from murky hills, and the air echoed with the yelp of dogs and the perplexed cursing of men.

Before I knew I was helping in the task, with water lapping round my waist and my arms filled with a terrified sheep. It was no light task, for though the water was no more than three feet deep it was swift and strong, and a kicking hogg is a sore burden. But this was the only road; the stream might rise higher at any moment; and somehow or other those bleating flocks had to be transferred to their fellows beyond. There were six men at the labour, six men and myself, and all were cross and wearied and heavy with water.

I made my passages side by side with my friend the shepherd, and thereby felt much elated. This was a man who had dwelt all his days in the wilds, and was familiar with torrents as with his own doorstep. Now and then a swimming dog would bark feebly as he was washed against us, and flatter his fool's heart that he was aiding the work. And so we wrought on, till by midday I was dead-beat, and could scarce stagger through the surf, while all the men had the same gasping faces. I saw the shepherd look with longing eye up the long green valley, and mutter disconsolately in his beard.

'Is the water rising?' I asked.

'It's no rising,' said he, 'but I likena the look o' yon big black clud upon Cairncraw. I doubt there's been a shoor up the muirs, and a shoor there means twae mair feet o' water in the Clachlands. God help Sandy Jamieson's lambs, if there is.'

'How many are left?' I asked.

'Three, fower – no abune a score and a half,' said he, running his eye over the lessened flocks. 'I maun try to tak twae at a time.'

So for ten minutes he struggled with a double burden, and panted painfully at each return. Then with a sudden swift look up-stream he broke off and stood up. 'Get ower the water, every yin o' ye, and leave the sheep,' he said, and to my wonder every man of the five obeyed his word.

And then I saw the reason of his command, for with a sudden swift leap forward the Clachlands rose, and flooded up to where I had stood an instant before high and dry.

'It's come,' said the shepherd in a tone of fate, 'and there's fifteen no ower yet, and Lord kens how they'll dae't. They'll hae to gang roond by Gledsmuir Brig, and that's twenty mile o' a differ. 'Deed, it's no like that Sandy Jamieson will get a guid price the morn for sic sair forfochen beasts.'

Then with firmly gripped staff he marched stoutly into the tide till it ran hissing below his armpits. 'I could dae't alane,' he cried, 'but no wi' a burden. For, losh, if ye slippit, ye'd be in the Tod's Pool afore ye could draw breath.'

And so we waited with the great white droves and five angry men beyond, and the path blocked by a surging flood. For half an hour we waited, holding anxious consultation across the stream, when to us thus busied there entered a newcomer, a helper from the ends of the earth.

He was a man of something over middle size, but with a stoop forward that shortened him to something beneath it. His dress was ragged homespun, the cast-off clothes of some sportsman, and in his arms he bore a bundle of sticks and heather-roots which marked his calling. I knew him for a tramp who long had wandered in the place, but I could not account for the whole-voiced shout of greeting which met him as he stalked down the path. He lifted his eyes and looked solemnly and long at the scene. Then something of delight came into his eye, his face relaxed, and flinging down his burden he stripped his coat and came toward us.

'Come on, Yeddie, ye're sair needed,' said the shepherd, and I watched with amazement this grizzled, crooked man seize a sheep by the fleece and drag it to the water. Then he was in the midst, stepping warily, now up, now down the channel, but always nearing the farther bank. At last with a final struggle he landed his charge, and turned to journey back. Fifteen times did he cross that water, and at the end his mean figure had wholly changed. For now he was straighter and stronger, his eye flashed, and his voice, as he cried out to the drovers, had in it a tone of command. I marvelled at the transformation; and when at length he had donned once more his ragged coat and shouldered his bundle, I asked the shepherd his name.

'They ca' him Adam Logan,' said my friend, his face still bright with excitement, 'but maist folk ca' him "Streams o' Water".'

'Ay,' said I, 'and why "Streams of Water"?'

'Juist for the reason ye see,' said he.

Now I knew the shepherd's way, and I held my peace, for it was clear that his mind was revolving other matters, concerned most probably with the high subject of the morrow's prices. But in a little, as we crossed the moor toward his dwelling, his thoughts relaxed and he remembered my question. So he answered me thus, –

'Oh, ay; as ye were sayin', he's a queer man, Yeddie – aye been; guid kens whaur he cam frae first, for he's been

trampin' the countryside since ever I mind, and that's no
yesterday. He maun be sixty year, and yet he's as fresh as
ever. If onything, he's a thocht dafter in his ongaein's and
mair silent-like. But ye'll hae heard tell o' him afore?'

I owned ignorance.

'Tut,' said he, 'ye ken nocht. But Yeddie had aye a queer
crakin' for waters. He never gangs on the road. Wi' him it's
juist up yae glen and doon anither, and aye keepin' by the
burnside. He kens every water i' the warld, every bit sheuch
and burnie frae Gallowa' to Berwick. And he kens the way
o' spates the best I ever seen, and I've heard tell o' him
fordin' waters when nae ither thing could leeve i' them. He
can weyse and wark his road sae cunnin'ly on the stanes
that the roughest flood, if it's no juist fair ower his heid,
canna upset him. Mony a sheep has he saved to me, and it's
mony a guid drove wad never hae won to Gledsmuir
market but for Yeddie.'

I listened with a boy's interest in any romantic narration.
Somehow, the strange figure wrestling in the brown stream
took fast hold on my mind, and I asked the shepherd for
further tales.

'There's little mair to tell,' he said, 'for a gangrel life is
nane o' the liveliest. But d'ye ken the langnebbit hill that
cocks its tap abune the Clachlands heid? Weel, he's got a
wee bit o' grund on the tap frae the Yerl, and there he's
howkit a grave for himsel'. He's sworn me and twae-three
ithers to bury him there, wherever he may dee. It's a queer
fancy in the auld dotterel.'

So the shepherd talked, and as at evening we stood by his
door we saw a figure moving into the gathering shadows. I
knew it at once, and did not need my friend's 'There gangs
"Streams o' Water"' to recognise it. Something wild and
pathetic in the old man's face haunted me like a dream, and as
the dusk swallowed him up, he seemed like some old Druid
recalled of the gods to his ancient habitation of the moors.

II

Two years passed, and April came with her suns and rains,
and again the waters brimmed full in the valleys. Under the

clear, shining sky the lambing went on, and the faint bleat of sheep brooded on the hills. In a land of young heather and green upland meads, of faint odours of moor-burn, and hill-tops falling in clean ridges to the sky-line, the veriest St Anthony would not abide indoors; so I flung all else to the winds and went a-fishing.

At the first pool on the Callowa, where the great flood sweeps nobly round a ragged shoulder of hill, and spreads into broad deeps beneath a tangle of birches, I began my labours. The turf was still wet with dew and the young leaves gleamed in the glow of morning. Far up the stream rose the grim hills which hem the mosses and tarns of the tableland, whence flow the greater waters of the country-side. An ineffable freshness, as of the morning alike of the day and the seasons, filled the clear hill air, and the remote peaks gave the needed touch of intangible romance.

But as I fished, I came on a man sitting in a green dell, busy at the making of brooms. I knew his face and dress, for who could forget such eclectic raggedness? – and I remembered that day two years before when he first hobbled into my ken. Now, as I saw him there, I was captivated by the nameless mystery of his appearance. There was something startling to one, accustomed to the lack-lustre gaze of town-bred folk, in the sight of an eye as keen and wild as a hawk's from sheer solitude and lonely travelling. He was so bent and scarred with weather that he seemed as much a part of that woodland place as the birks themselves, and the noise of his labours did not startle the birds that hopped on the branches.

Little by little I won his acquaintance – by a chance reminiscence, a single tale, the mention of a friend. Then he made me free of his knowledge, and my fishing fared well that day. He dragged me up little streams to seques-tered pools, where I had astonishing success; and then back to some great swirl in the Callowa where he had seen monstrous takes. And all the while he delighted me with his talk, of men and things, of weather and place, pitched high in his thin, old voice, and garnished with many tones of lingering sentiment. He spoke in a broad, slow Scots, with so quaint a lilt in his speech that one seemed to be in an elder time among people of a quieter life and a quainter kindliness.

Then by chance I asked him of a burn of which I had heard, and how it might be reached. I shall never forget the tone of his answer as his face grew eager and he poured forth his knowledge.

'Ye'll gang up the Knowe Burn, which comes doun into the Cauldshaw. It's a wee tricklin' thing, trowin' in and out o' pools i' the rock, and comin' doun out o' the side o' Caerfraun. Yince a merry-maiden bided there, I've heard folks say, and used to win the sheep frae the Cauldshaw herd, and bile them i' the muckle pool below the fa'. They say that there's a road to the Ill Place there, and when the Deil likit he sent up the lowe and garred the water faem and fizzle like an auld kettle. But if ye're gaun to the Colm Burn ye maun haud atower the rig o' the hill frae the Knowe heid, and ye'll come to it wimplin' among green brae faces. It's a bonny bit, lonesome but awfu' bonny, and there's mony braw trout in its siller flow.'

Then I remembered all I had heard of the old man's craze, and I humoured him.

'It's a fine countryside for burns,' I said.

'Ye may say that,' said he gladly, 'a weel-watered land. But a' this braw south country is the same. I've traivelled frae the Yeavering Hill in the Cheviots to the Caldons in Galloway, and it's a' the same. When I was young, I've seen me gang north to the Hielands and doun to the English lawlands, but now that I'm gettin' auld I maun bide i' the yae place. There's no a burn in the South I dinna ken, and I never cam to the water I couldna ford.'

'No?' said I. 'I've seen you at the ford o' Clachlands in the Lammas floods.'

'Often I've been there,' he went on, speaking like one calling up vague memories. 'Yince, when Tam Rorison was drooned, honest man. Yince again, when the brigs were ta'en awa', and the Back House o' Clachlands had nae bread for a week. But oh, Clachlands is a bit easy water. But I've seen the muckle Aller come roarin' sae high that it washed awa' a sheepfauld that stood weel up on the hill. And I've seen this verra burn, this bonny clear Callowa,

lyin' like a loch for miles i' the haugh. But I never heeds a
spate, for if a man just kens the way o't it's a canny,
hairmless thing. I couldna wish to dee better than just
be happit i' the waters o' my ain countryside, when my legs
fail and I'm ower auld for the trampin'.'

Something in that queer figure in the setting of the hills
struck a note of curious pathos. And towards evening as we
returned down the glen the note grew keener. A spring
sunset of gold and crimson flamed in our backs and turned
the pools to fire. Far off down the vale the plains and the sea
gleamed half in shadow. Somehow in the fragrance and
colour and the delectable crooning of the stream, the
fantastic and the dim seemed tangible and present, and
high sentiment revelled for once in my prosaic heart.

And still more in the breast of my companion. He
stopped and sniffed the evening air, as he looked far over
hill and dale and then back to the great hills above us.
'Yon's Crappel, and Caerdon, and the Laigh Law,' he said,
lingering with relish over each name, 'and the Gled comes
doun atween them. I haena been there for a twalmonth,
and I maun hae another glisk o't, for it's a braw place.'
Some bitter thought seemed to seize him, and his mouth
twitched. 'I'm an auld man,' he cried, 'and I canna see ye a'
again. There's burns and mair burns in the high hills that
I'll never win to.' Then he remembered my presence, and
stopped. 'Ye maunna mind me,' he said huskily, 'but the
sicht o' thae lang blue hills makes me daft, now that I've
faun i' the vale o' years. Yince I was young and could get
where I wantit, but now I am auld and maun bide i' the
same bit. And I'm aye thinkin' o' the waters I've been to,
and the green heichs and howes and the linns that I canna
win to again. I maun e'en be content wi' the Callowa, which
is as guid as the best.'

I left him wandering down by the streamside and telling
his crazy meditations to himself.

III

A space of years elapsed ere I met him, for fate had carried
me far from the upland valleys. But once again I was afoot

on the white moor roads; and, as I swung along one
autumn afternoon up the path which leads from the Glen
of Callowa to the Gled, I saw a figure before me which I
knew for my friend. When I overtook him, his appearance
puzzled and troubled me. Age seemed to have come on him
at a bound, and in the tottering figure and the stoop of
weakness I had difficulty in recognising the hardy frame of
the man as I had known him. Something, too, had come
over his face. His brow was clouded, and the tan of weather
stood out hard and cruel on a blanched cheek. His eye
seemed both wilder and sicklier, and for the first time I saw
him with none of the appurtenances of his trade.

He greeted me feebly and dully, and showed little wish to
speak. He walked with slow, uncertain step, and his breath
laboured with a new panting. Every now and then he would
look at me sidewise, and in his feverish glance I could
detect none of the free kindliness of old. The man was ill in
body and mind.

I asked him how he had done since I saw him last.

'It's an ill world now,' he said in a slow, querulous voice.
'There's nae need for honest men, and nae leevin'. Folk
dinna heed me ava now. They dinna buy my besoms, they
winna let me bide a nicht in their byres, and they're no like
the kind canty folk in the auld times. And a' the countryside
is changin'. Doun by Goldieslaw they're makkin' a dam for
takin' water to the toun, and they're thinkin' o' daein' the
like wi' the Callowa. Guid help us, can they no let the works
o' God alane? Is there nae room for them in the dirty
lawlands that they maun file the hills wi' their biggins?'

I conceived dimly that the cause of his wrath was a
scheme for waterworks at the border of the uplands, but
I had less concern for this than his strangely feeble health.

'You are looking ill,' I said. 'What has come over you?'

'Oh, I canna last for aye,' he said mournfully. 'My auld
body's about dune. I've warkit it ower sair when I had it,
and it's gaun to fail on my hands. Sleepin' out o' wat nichts
and gangin' lang wantin' meat are no the best ways for a
long life'; and he smiled the ghost of a smile.

And then he fell to wild telling of the ruin of the place and
the hardness of the people, and I saw that want and bare

living had gone far to loosen his wits. I knew the countryside, and I recognised that change was only in his mind. A
great pity seized me for this lonely figure toiling on in the
bitterness of regret. I tried to comfort him, but my words
were useless, for he took no heed of me; with bent head and
faltering step he mumbled his sorrows to himself.

Then of a sudden we came to the crest of the ridge where
the road dips from the hill-top to the sheltered valley. Sheer
from the heather ran the white streak till it lost itself among
the reddening rowans and the yellow birks of the wood.
The land was rich in autumn colour, and the shining waters
dipped and fell through a pageant of russet and gold. And
all around hills huddled in silent spaces, long brown moors
crowned with cairns, or steep fortresses of rock and shingle
rising to foreheads of steel-like grey. The autumn blue
faded in the far sky-line to white, and lent distance to
the farther peaks. The hush of the wilderness, which is far
different from the hush of death, brooded over the scene,
and like faint music came the sound of a distant scythe-
swing, and the tinkling whisper which is the flow of a
hundred streams.

I am an old connoisseur in the beauties of the uplands,
but I held my breath at the sight. And when I glanced at my
companion, he too had raised his head, and stood with
wide nostrils and gleaming eye revelling in this glimpse of
Arcady. Then he found his voice, and the weakness and
craziness seemed for one moment to leave him.

'It's my ain land,' he cried, 'and I'll never leave it. D'ye
see yon lang broun hill wi' the cairn?' and he gripped my
arm fiercely and directed my gaze. 'Yon's my bit. I howkit it
richt on the verra tap, and ilka year I gang there to mak it
neat and orderly. I've trystit wi' fower men in different
pairishes, that whenever they hear o' my death, they'll
cairry me up yonder and bury me there. And then
I'll never leave it, but lie still and quiet to the warld's
end. I'll aye hae the sound o'water in my ear, for there's five
burns tak' their rise on that hillside, and on a' airts the glens
gang doun to the Gled and the Aller.'

Then his spirit failed him, his voice sank, and he was
almost the feeble gangrel once more. But not yet, for again

his eye swept the ring of hills, and he muttered to himself names which I knew for streams, lingeringly, lovingly as of old affections. 'Aller and Gled and Callowa,' he crooned, 'braw names, and Clachlands and Cauldshaw and the Lanely Water. And I maunna forget the Stark and the Lin and the bonny streams o' the Creran. And what mair? I canna mind a' the burns, the Howe and the Hollies and the Fawn and the links o' the Manor. What says the Psalmist about them?

> "As streams of water in the South,
> Our bondage, Lord, recall."

Ay, but yon's the name for them. "Streams o' water in the South."'

As we went down the slopes to the darkening vale I heard him crooning to himself in a high, quavering voice the single distich; then in a little his weariness took him again, and he plodded on with no thought save for his sorrows.

IV

The conclusion of this tale belongs not to me, but to the shepherd of the Redswirehead, and I heard it from him in his dwelling, as I stayed the night, belated on the darkening moors. He told me it after supper in a flood of misty Doric, and his voice grew rough at times, and he poked viciously at the dying peat.

'In the last back-end I was at Gledfoot wi' sheep, and a weary job I had and sma' credit. Ye ken the place, a lang dreich shore wi' the wind swirlin' and bitin' to the bane, and the broun Gled water choked wi' Solloway sand. There was nae room in ony inn in the town, so I bude to try a bit public on the Harbour Walk, where sailor-folk and fishermen feucht and drank, and nae dacent men frae the hills thocht o' gangin'. I was in a gey ill way, for I had sell't my beasts dooms cheap, and I thocht o' the lang miles hame in the wintry weather. So after a bite o' meat I gangs oot to get the air and clear my heid, which was a' rammled wi' the auction-ring.

'And whae did I find, sittin' on a bench at the door, but the auld man Yeddie? He was waur changed than ever. His lang hair was hingin' ower his broo, and his face was thin and white as a ghaist's. His claes fell loose about him, and he sat wi' his hand on his auld stick and his chin on his hand, hearin' nocht and glowerin' afore him. He never saw nor kenned me till I shook him by the shouthers, and cried him by his name.

' "Whae are ye?" says he, in a thin voice that gaed to my hert.

' "Ye ken me fine, ye auld fule," says I. "I'm Jock Rorison o' the Redswirehead, whaur ye've stoppit often."

' "Redswirehead," he says, like a man in a dream. "Redswirehead! That's at the tap o' the Clachlands Burn as ye gang ower to the Dreichil."

' "And what are ye daein' here? It's no your countryside ava, and ye're no fit noo for lang trampin'."

' "No," says he, in the same weak voice and wi' nae fushion in him, "but they winna hae me up yonder noo. I'm ower auld and useless. Yince a'body was gled to see me, and wad keep me as lang's I wantit, and had aye a guid word at meeting and pairting. Noo it's a' changed, and my wark's dune."

'I saw fine that the man was daft, but what answer could I gie to his havers? Folk in the Callowa glens are as kind as afore, but ill weather and auld age had put queer notions intil his heid. Forbye, he was seeck, seeck unto death, and I saw mair in his ee than I likit to think.

' "Come in-by and get some meat, man," I said. "Ye're famishin' wi' cauld and hunger."

' "I canna eat," he says, and his voice never changed. "It's lang since I had a bite, for I'm no hungry. But I'm awfu' thirsty. I cam here yestreen, and I can get nae water to drink like the water in the hills. I maun be settin' out back the morn, if the Lord spares me."

'I mindit fine that the body wad tak nae drink like an honest man, but maun aye draibble wi' burn water, and noo he had got the thing on the brain. I never spak a word, for the maitter was bye ony mortal's aid.

'For lang he sat quiet. Then he lifts his heid and looks awa ower the grey sea. A licht for a moment cam intil his een.

' "Whatna big water's yon?" he said, wi' his puir mind aye rinnin' on waters.

' "That's the Solloway," says I.

' "The Solloway," says he; "it's a big water, and it wad be an ill job to ford it."

' "Nae man ever fordit it," I said.

' "But I never yet cam to the water I couldna ford," says he. "But what's that queer smell i' the air? Something snell and cauld and unfreendly."

' "That's the salt, for we're at the sea here, the mighty ocean."

'He keepit repeatin' the word ower in his mouth. "The salt, the salt! I've heard tell o' it afore, but I dinna like it. It's terrible cauld."

'By this time an on-ding o' rain was coming up frae the water, and I bade the man come indoors to the fire. He followed me, as biddable as a sheep, draggin' his legs like yin far gone in seeckness. I set him by the fire, and put whisky at his elbow, but he wadna touch it.

' "I've nae need o' it," said he. "I'm fine and warm;" and he sits staring at the fire, aye comin' ower again and again, "The Solloway, the Solloway. It's a guid name and a muckle water." But sune I gaed to my bed, being heavy wi' sleep, for I had traivelled for twae days.

'The next morn I was up at six and oot to see the weather. It was a' changed. The muckle tides lay lang and still as our ain Loch o' the Lee, and far ayont I saw the big blue hills o' England shine bricht and clear. I thankit Providence for the day, for it was better to tak the lang miles back in the sun than in a blast o' rain.

'But as I lookit I saw folk comin' up frae the beach cairryin' something atween them. My hert gied a loup, and "Some puir, drooned sailor body," says I to mysel', "whae has perished in yesterday's storm." But as they cam nearer I got a glisk which made me run like daft, and lang ere I was up on them I saw it was Yeddie.

'He lay drippin' and white, wi' his puir auld hair lyin' back frae his broo and the duds clingin' to his legs. But oot o' the face there had gane a' the seeckness and weariness. His een were stelled as if he had been lookin' forrit to something, and his lips were set like a man on a lang errand.

And mair, his stick was grippit sae firm in his hand that nae man could lowse it, so they e'en let it be.

'Then they tell't me the tale o't, how at the earliest licht they had seen him wanderin' alang the sands, juist as they were putting out their boats to sea. They wondered and watched him, till of a sudden he turned to the water and wadit in, keeping straucht on till he was oot o' sicht. They rowed a' their pith to the place, but they were ower late. Yince they saw his heid appear abune water, still wi' his face to the other side; and then they got his body, for the tide was rinnin' low in the mornin'.

'We brocht him up to the house and laid him there till the folk i' the town had heard o' the business. Syne the procurator-fiscal came and certifeed the death, and the rest was left to me. I got a wooden coffin made and put him in it, juist as he was, wi' his staff in his hand and his auld duds about him. I mindit o' my sworn word, for I was yin o' the four that had promised, and I ettled to dae his bidding. It was saxteen miles to the hills, and yin and twenty to the lanely tap whaur he had howkit his grave. But I never heedit it. I'm a strong man, weel used to the walkin', and my hert was sair for the auld body. Now that he had gotten deliverance from his affliction, it was for me to leave him in the place he wantit. Forbye, he wasna muckle heavier than a bairn.

'It was a long road, a sair road, but I did it, and by seven o'clock I was at the edge o' the muirlands. There was a braw mune, and a' the glens and taps stood out as clear as midday. Bit by bit, for I was gey tired, I warstled ower the rigs and up the cleuchs to the Gled-head; syne up the stany Gled-cleuch to the lang grey hill which they ca' the Hurlybackit. By ten I had come to the cairn, and black i' the mune I saw the grave. So there I buried him, and though I'm no a releegious man, I couldna help sayin' ower him the guid words o' the Psalmist –

> "As streams of water in the South,
> Our bondage, Lord, recall."'

So if you go from the Gled to the Aller, and keep far over the north side of the Muckle Muneraw, you will come in time to a stony ridge which ends in a cairn. There you will see the whole hill country of the south, a hundred lochs, a myriad streams, and a forest of hill-tops. There on the very crest lies the old man, in the heart of his own land, at the fountain-head of his many waters. If you listen you will hear a noise as of a swaying of trees or a ripple on the sea. It is the sound of the rising of burns, which, innumerable and unnumbered, flow thence to the silent glens for evermore.

At the Article of Death

Another story from *Grey Weather* (1899), 'At the Article
of Death' appeared in *The Yellow Book* in January 1897,
alongside tales by Henry James and Kenneth Grahame.
It is one of Buchan's bleakest stories as a dying shepherd
reviews his life and finds no consolation in the religion he
hoped might sustain him.

Nullum
Sacra caput Proserpina fugit.

A noiseless evening fell chill and dank on the moorlands.
The Dreichil was mist to the very rim of its precipitous face,
and the long, dun sides of the Little Muneraw faded into
grey vapour. Underfoot were plashy moss and dripping
heather, and all the air was choked with autumnal heavi-
ness. The herd of the Lanely Bield stumbled wearily
homeward in this, the late afternoon, with the roof-tree
of his cottage to guide him over the waste.

For weeks, months, he had been ill, fighting the battle of
a lonely sickness. Two years agone his wife had died, and as
there had been no child, he was left to fend for himself. He
had no need for any woman, he declared, for his wants were
few and his means of the scantiest, so he had cooked his
own meals and done his own household work since the day
he had stood by the grave in the Gledsmuir kirkyard. And
for a little he did well; and then, inch by inch, trouble crept
upon him. He would come home late in the winter nights,
soaked to the skin, and sit in the peat-reek till his clothes
dried on his body. The countless little ways in which a
woman's hand makes a place healthy and habitable were
unknown to him, and soon he began to pay the price of his

folly. For he was not a strong man, though a careless onlooker might have guessed the opposite from his mighty frame. His folk had all been short-lived, and already his was the age of his father at his death. Such a fact might have warned him to circumspection; but he took little heed till that night in the March before, when, coming up the Little Muneraw and breathing hard, a chill wind on the summit cut him to the bone. He rose the next morn, shaking like a leaf, and then for weeks he lay ill in bed, while a young shepherd from the next sheep-farm did his work on the hill. In the early summer he rose a broken man, without strength or nerve, and always oppressed with an ominous sinking in the chest; but he toiled through his duties, and told no man his sorrow. The summer was parchingly hot, and the hillsides grew brown and dry as ashes. Often as he laboured up the interminable ridges, he found himself sickening at heart with a poignant regret. These were the places where once he had strode so freely with the crisp air cool on his forehead. Now he had no eye for the pastoral loveliness, no ear for the witch-song of the desert. When he reached a summit, it was only to fall panting, and when he came home at nightfall he sank wearily on a seat.

And so through the lingering summer the year waned to an autumn of storm. Now his malady seemed nearing its end. He had seen no man's face for a week, for long miles of moor severed him from a homestead. He could scarce struggle from his bed by mid-day, and his daily round of the hill was gone through with tottering feet. The time would soon come for drawing the ewes and driving them to the Gledsmuir market. If he could but hold on till the word came, he might yet have speech of a fellow man and bequeath his duties to another. But if he died first, the charge would wander uncared for, while he himself would lie in that lonely cot till such time as the lowland farmer sent the messenger. With anxious care he tended his flickering spark of life – he had long ceased to hope – and with something like heroism looked blankly towards his end.

But on this afternoon all things had changed. At the edge of the water-meadow he had found blood dripping from his lips, and half-swooned under an agonizing pain at his heart.

With burning eyes he turned his face to home, and fought his way inch by inch through the desert. He counted the steps crazily, and with pitiful sobs looked upon mist and moorland. A faint bleat of a sheep came to his ear; he heard it clearly, and the hearing wrung his soul. Not for him any more the hills of sheep and a shepherd's free and wholesome life. He was creeping, stricken, to his homestead to die, like a wounded fox crawling to its earth. And the loneliness of it all, the pity, choked him more than the fell grip of his sickness.

Inside the house a great banked fire of peats was smouldering. Unwashed dishes stood on the table, and the bed in the corner was unmade, for such things were of little moment in the extremity of his days. As he dragged his leaden foot over the threshold, the autumn dusk thickened through the white fog, and shadows awaited him, lurking in every corner. He dropped carelessly on the bed's edge, and lay back in deadly weakness. No sound broke the stillness, for the clock had long ago stopped for lack of winding. Only the shaggy collie which had lain down by the fire looked to the bed and whined mournfully.

In a little he raised his eyes and saw that the place was filled with darkness, save where the red eye of the fire glowed hot and silent. His strength was too far gone to light the lamp, but he could make a crackling fire. Some power other than himself made him heap bog-sticks on the peat and poke it feebly, for he shuddered at the ominous long shades which peopled floor and ceiling. If he had but a leaping blaze he might yet die in a less gross mockery of comfort.

Long he lay in the firelight, sunk in the lethargy of illimitable feebleness. Then the strong spirit of the man began to flicker within him and rise to sight ere it sank in death. He had always been a godly liver, one who had no youth of folly to look back upon, but a well-spent life of toil lit by the lamp of a half-understood devotion. He it was who at his wife's death-bed had administered words of comfort and hope; and had passed all his days with the thought of his own end fixed like a bull's eye in the target of his meditations. In his lonely hill-watches, in the weariful lambing days, and on droving journeys to faraway towns, he had whiled the hours with self-communing, and self-examination, by the help of a rigid Word. Nay, there had been far more than the mere punctilios of obedience to the letter; there had been the living fire of love, the heroical attitude of self-denial, to be the halo of his solitary life. And now God had sent him the last fiery trial, and he was left alone to put off the garments of mortality.

He dragged himself to a cupboard where all the appurtenances of the religious life lay to his hands. There were Spurgeon's sermons in torn covers, and a dozen musty 'Christian Treasuries'. Some antiquated theology, which he had got from his father, lay lowest, and on the top was the gaudy Bible, which he had once received from a grateful Sabbath class while he yet sojourned in the lowlands. It was lined and re-lined, and there he had often found consolation. Now in the last faltering of mind he had braced himself to the thought that he must die as became his possession, with the Word of God in his hand, and his thoughts fixed on that better country, which is an heavenly.

The thin leaves mocked his hands, and he could not turn to any well-remembered text. In vain he struggled to reach the gospels; the obstinate leaves blew ever back to a dismal psalm or a prophet's lamentation. A word caught his eye and he read vaguely: 'The shepherds slumber, O King, . . . the people is scattered upon the mountains . . . and no man gathereth them . . . there is no healing of the hurt, for the wound is grievous.' Something in the poignant sorrow of the phrase caught his attention for one second, and then he was back in a fantasy of pain and impotence. He could not fix his mind, and even as he strove he remembered the warning he had so often given to others against death-bed repentance. Then, he had often said, a man has no time to make his peace with his Maker, when he is wrestling with death. Now the adage came back to him; and gleams of comfort shot for one moment through his soul. He at any rate had long since chosen for God, and the good Lord would see and pity His servant's weakness.

A sheep bleated near the window, and then another. The flocks were huddling down, and wind and wet must be coming. Then a long dreary wind sighed round the dwelling, and at the same moment a bright tongue of flame shot up from the fire, and queer crooked shadows flickered over the ceiling. The sight caught his eyes, and he shuddered in nameless terror. He had never been a coward, but like all religious folk he had imagination and emotion. Now his fancy was perturbed, and he shrank from these uncanny shapes. In the failure of all else he had fallen to the repetition of bare phrases, telling of the fragrance and glory of the city of God. 'River of the water of Life,' he said to himself, . . . 'the glory and honour of the nations . . . and the street of the city was pure gold . . . and the saved shall walk in the light of it . . . and God shall wipe away all tears from their eyes.'

Again a sound without, the cry of sheep and the sough of a lone wind. He was sinking fast, but the noise gave him a spasm of strength. The dog rose and sniffed uneasily at the door, a trickle of rain dripped from the roofing, and all the while the silent heart of the fire glowed and hissed at his side. It seemed an uncanny thing that now in the moment of his anguish the sheep should bleat as they had done in the old strong days of herding.

Again the sound, and again the morris-dance of shadows among the rafters. The thing was too much for his failing mind. Some words of hope – 'streams in the desert, and' – died on his lips, and he crawled from the bed to a cupboard. He had not tasted strong drink for a score of years, for to the true saint in the uplands abstinence is a primary virtue; but he kept brandy in the house for illness or wintry weather. Now it would give him strength, and it was no sin to cherish the spark of life.

He found the spirits and gulped down a mouthful – one, two, till the little flask was drained, and the raw fluid spilled over beard and coat. In his days of health it would have made him drunk, but now all the fibres of his being were relaxed, and it merely stung him to a fantasmal vigour. More, it maddened his brain, already tottering under the assaults of death. Before he had thought feebly and greyly, now his mind surged in an ecstasy.

The pain that lay heavy on his chest, that clutched his throat, that tugged at his heart, was as fierce as ever, but for one short second the utter weariness of spirit was gone. The old fair words of Scripture came back to him, and he murmured promises and hopes till his strength failed him for all but thought, and with closed eyes he fell back to dream.

But only for one moment; the next he was staring blankly in a mysterious terror. Again the voices of the wind, again the shapes on floor and wall and the relentless eye of the fire. He was too helpless to move and too crazy to pray; he could only lie and stare, numb with expectancy. The liquor seemed to have driven all memory from him, and left him with a child's heritage of dreams and stories.

Crazily he pattered to himself a child's charm against evil fairies, which the little folk of the moors still speak at their play, –

> Wearie, Ovie, gang awa',
> Dinna show your face at a',
> Ower the muir and down the burn,
> Wearie, Ovie, ne'er return.

The black crook of the chimney was the object of his spells, for the kindly ingle was no less than a malignant twisted devil, with an awful red eye glowering through smoke.

His breath was winnowing through his worn chest like an autumn blast in bare rafters. The horror of the black night without, all filled with the wail of sheep, and the deeper fear of the red light within, stirred his brain, not with the far-reaching fanciful terror of men, but with the crude homely fright of a little child. He would have sought, had his strength suffered him, to cower one moment in the light as a refuge from the other, and the next to hide in the darkest corner to shun the maddening glow. And with it all he was acutely conscious of the last pangs of mortality. He felt the grating of cheekbones on skin, and the sighing, which did duty for breath, rocked him with agony.

Then a great shadow rose out of the gloom and stood shaggy in the firelight. The man's mind was tottering, and once more he was back at his Scripture memories and vague repetitions. Aforetime his fancy had toyed with green fields, now it held to the darker places. 'It was the day when Evil Merodach was king in Babylon,' came the quaint recollection, and some lingering ray of thought made him link the odd name with the amorphous presence before him. The thing moved and came nearer, touched him, and brooded by his side. He made to shriek, but no sound came, only a dry rasp in the throat and a convulsive twitch of the limbs.

For a second he lay in the agony of a terror worse than the extremes of death. It was only his dog, returned from his watch by the door, and seeking his master. He, poor beast, knew of some sorrow vaguely and afar, and nuzzled into his side with dumb affection.

Then from the chaos of faculties a shred of will survived. For an instant his brain cleared, for to most there comes a lull at the very article of death. He saw the bare moorland room, he felt the dissolution of his members, the palpable ebb of life. His religion had been swept from him like a rotten garment. His mind was vacant of memories, for all were driven forth by purging terror. Only some relic of manliness, the heritage of cleanly and honest days, was with him to the uttermost. With blank thoughts, without hope or vision, with naught save an aimless resolution and a causeless bravery, he passed into the short anguish which is death.

At the Rising of the Waters

The story of the events that befell a farmer, Robert Linklater, one night in September 1880, it demonstrates the unsentimentality of country people when faced with the forces of nature. The story was first published in *Chamber's Journal* in March 1897, to which Buchan had become a regular contributor, and subsequently in *Grey Weather* (1899).

In mid-September the moors are changing from red to a dusky brown, as the fire of the heather wanes, and the long grass yellows with advancing autumn. Then, too, the rain falls heavily on the hills, and vexes the shallow upland streams, till every glen is ribbed with its churning torrent. This for the uplands; but below, at the rim of the plains, where the glens expand to vales, and trim fields edge the wastes, there is wreck and lamentation. The cabined waters lip over cornland and meadow, and bear destruction to crop and cattle.

This is the tale of Robert Linklater, farmer in Clachlands, and the events which befell him on the night of September 20th, in the year of grace 1880. I am aware that there are characters in the countryside which stand higher in repute than his, for imagination and love of point and completeness in a story are qualities which little commend themselves to the prosaic. I have heard him called 'Leein' Rob', and answer to the same with cheerfulness; but he was wont in private to brag of minutest truthfulness, and attribute his ill name to the universal dullness of man.

On this evening he came home, by his own account, from market about the hour of six. He had had a week of festivity. On the Monday he had gone to a distant cattle-show, and on Tuesday to a marriage. On the Wednesday he had attended upon a cousin's funeral, and, being flown with whisky, brought everlasting disgrace upon himself by rising to propose the health of the bride and bridegroom. On Thursday he had been at the market of Gledsmuir, and, getting two shillings more for his ewes than he had reckoned, returned in a fine fervour of spirit and ripe hilarity.

The weather had been shower and blast for days. The grey skies dissolved in dreary rain, and on that very morn there had come a downpour so fierce that the highways ran like a hillside torrent. Now, as he sat at supper and looked down at the green vale and red waters leaping by bank and brae, a sudden fear came to his heart. Hitherto he had had no concern – for was not his harvest safely inned? But now he minds of the laigh parks and the nowt beasts there, which he had bought the week before at the sale of Iverforth. They were Kyloe and Galloway mixed, and on them, when fattened through winter and spring, lay great hopes of profit. He gulped his meal down hurriedly, and went forthwith to the garden-foot. There he saw something that did not allay his fears. Gled had split itself in two, at the place where Clachlands water came to swell its flow, and a long, gleaming line of black current stole round by the side of the laigh meadow, where stood the huddled cattle. Let but the waters rise a little, and the valley would be one uniform, turgid sea.

This was pleasing news for an honest man after a hard day's work, and the farmer went grumbling back. He took a mighty plaid and flung it over his shoulders, chose the largest and toughest of his many sticks, and set off to see wherein he could better the peril.

Now, some hundreds of yards above the laigh meadow, a crazy wooden bridge spanned the stream. By this way he might bring his beasts to safety, for no nowt could hope to swim the red flood. So he splashed through the dripping stubble to the river's brink, where, with tawny swirl, it licked the edge of banks which in summer weather stood high and flower-decked. Ruefully he reflected that many good palings would by this time be whirling to a distant sea.

When he came to the wooden bridge he set his teeth manfully and crossed. It creaked and swayed with his weight, and dipped till it all but touched the flow. It could not stand even as the water was, for already its mid prop had lurched forward, like a drunken man, and was groaning at each wave. But if a rise came, it would be torn from its foundations like a reed, and then heigh-ho! for cattle and man.

With painful haste he laboured through the shallows which rimmed the haughlands, and came to the snake-like current which had even now spread itself beyond the laigh meadow. He measured its depth with his eyes and ventured. It did not reach beyond his middle, but its force gave him much ado to keep his feet. At length it was passed, and he stood triumphant on the spongy land, where the cattle huddled in mute discomfort and terror.

Darkness was falling, and he could scarcely see the homestead on the affronting hillside. So with all speed he set about collecting the shivering beasts, and forcing them through the ring of water to the bridge. Up to their flanks they went, and then stood lowing helplessly. He saw that something was wrong, and made to ford the current himself. But now it was beyond him. He looked down at the yellow water running round his middle, and saw that it had risen, and was rising inch by inch with every minute. Then he glanced to where aforetime stood the crazy planking of the bridge. Suddenly hope and complacency fled, and the gravest fear settled in his heart; for he saw no bridge, only a ragged, saw-like end of timber where once he had crossed.

Here was a plight for a solitary man to be in at nightfall. There would be no wooden bridge on all the water, and the nearest one of stone was at distant Gledsmuir, over some score of miles of weary moorland. It was clear that his cattle must bide on this farther bank, and he himself, when once he had seen them in safety, would set off for the nearest farm and pass the night. It seemed the craziest of matters, that he should be thus in peril and discomfort, with the lights of his house blinking not a quarter mile away.

Once more he tried to break the water-ring and once more he failed. The flood was still rising, and the space of green which showed grey and black beneath a fitful moon was quickly lessening. Before, irritation had been his upper feeling, now terror succeeded. He could not swim a stroke, and if the field were covered he would drown like a cat in a bag. He lifted up his voice and roared with all the strength of his mighty lungs, 'Sammle', 'Andra', 'Jock', 'come and help 's', till the place rang with echoes. Meantime, with strained eyes he watched the rise of the cruel water, which crept, black and pitiless, over the shadowy grey.

He drove the beasts to a little knoll, which stood somewhat above the meadow, and there they stood, cattle and man, in the fellowship of misfortune. They had been as wild as peat-reek, and had suffered none to approach them, but now with some instinct of peril they stood quietly by his side, turning great billowy foreheads to the surging waste. Upward and nearer came the torrent, rising with steady gurgling which told of great storms in his hills and roaring torrents in every gorge. Now the sound grew louder and seemed almost at his feet, now it ceased and nought was heard save the dull hum of the main stream pouring its choking floods to the sea. Suddenly his eyes wandered to the lights of his house and the wide slope beyond, and for a second he mused on some alien trifle. Then he was brought to himself with a pull as he looked and saw a line of black water not three feet from the farthest beast. His heart stood still, and with awe he reflected that in half-an-hour by this rate of rising he would be with his Maker.

For five minutes he waited, scarce daring to look around him, but dreading each instant to feel a cold wave lick his boot. Then he glanced timorously, and to his joy it was scarce an inch higher. It was stopping, and he might yet be safe. With renewed energy he cried out for aid, till the very cattle started at the sound and moved uneasily among themselves.

In a little there came an answering voice across the dark. 'Whae's in the laigh meedy?' and it was the voice of the herd of Clachlands, sounding hoarse through the driving of the stream.

'It's me,' went back the mournful response.

'And whae are *ye*?' came the sepulchral voice.

'Your ain maister, William Smail, forewandered among water and nowt beast.'

For some time there was no reply, since the shepherd was engaged in a severe mental struggle; with the readiness of

his class he went straight to the heart of the peril, and
mentally reviewed the ways and waters of the land. Then he
calmly accepted the hopelessness of it all, and cried loudly
through the void, –

'There's nae way for't but juist to bide where ye are. The
water's stoppit, and gin mornin' we'll get ye aff. I'll send a
laddie down to the Dow Pule to bring up a boat in a cairt.
But that's a lang gait, and it'll be a sair job gettin' it up, and
I misdoot it'll be daylicht or he comes. But haud up hour
hert, and we'll get ye oot. Are the beasts a' richt?'

'A' richt, William; but, 'od man! their maister is cauld.
Could ye no fling something ower?'

'No, when there's twae hunner yairds o' deep water
atween.'

'Then, William, ye maun licht a fire, a great muckle
roarin' fire, juist fornenst me. It'll cheer me to see the
licht o' 't.'

The shepherd did as he was bid, and for many minutes
the farmer could hear the noise of men heaping wood, in
the pauses of wind and through the thicker murmur of the
water. Then a glare shot up, and revealed the dusky forms
of the four serving-men straining their eyes across the
channel. The gleam lit up a yard of water by the other
bank, but all mid-way was inky shadow. It was about eight
o'clock, and the moon was just arisen. The air had
coldened and a light chill wind rose from the river.

The farmer of Clachlands, standing among shivering and
dripping oxen, himself wet to the skin and cold as a stone,
with no wrapping save his plaid, and no outlook save a
black moving water and a gleam of fire – in such a position,
the farmer of Clachlands collected his thoughts and mus-
tered his resolution. His first consideration was the safety of
his stock. The effort gave him comfort. His crops were in,
and he could lose nothing there; his sheep were far removed
from scaith, and his cattle would survive the night with
ease, if the water kept its level. With some satisfaction he
reflected that the only care he need have in the matter was
for his own bodily comfort in an autumn night. This was
serious, yet not deadly, for the farmer was a man of many
toils and cared little for the rigours of weather. But he

would gladly have given the price of a beast for a bottle of whisky to comfort himself in his emergency.

He stood on a knuckle of green land some twenty feet long, with a crowd of cattle pressing around him and a little forest of horns showing faintly. There was warmth in these great shaggy hides if they had not been drenched and icy from long standing. His fingers were soon as numb as his feet, and it was in vain that he stamped on the plashy grass or wrapped his hands in a fold of plaid. There was no doubt in the matter. He was keenly uncomfortable, and the growing chill of night would not mend his condition.

Some ray of comfort was to be got from the sight of the crackling fire. There at least was homely warmth, and light, and ease. With gusto he conjured up all the delights of the past week, the roaring evenings in market ale-house, and the fragrance of good drink and piping food. Necessity sharpened his fancy, and he could almost feel the flavour of tobacco. A sudden hope took him. He clapped hand to pocket and pulled forth pipe and shag. Curse it! He had left his matchbox on the chimney-top in his kitchen, and there was an end to his only chance of comfort.

So in all cold and damp he set himself to pass the night in the midst of that ceaseless swirl of black moss water. Even as he looked at the dancing glimmer of fire, the moon broke forth silent and full, and lit the vale with misty glamour. The great hills, whence came the Gled, shone blue and high with fleecy trails of vapour drifting athwart them. He saw clearly the walls of his dwelling, the light shining from the window, the struggling fire on the bank, and the dark forms of men. Its transient flashes on the waves were scarce seen in the broad belt of moonshine which girdled the valley. And around him, before and behind, rolled the unending desert waters with that heavy, resolute flow, which one who knows the floods fears a thousandfold more than the boisterous stir of a torrent.

And so he stood till maybe one o'clock of the morning, cold to the bone, and awed by the eternal silence, which choked him, despite the myriad noises of the night. For there are few things more awful than the calm of nature in her madness – the stillness which follows a snowslip or the monotony of a great flood. By this hour he was falling from his first high confidence. His knees stooped under him, and he was fain to lean upon the beasts at his side. His shoulders ached with the wet, and his eyes grew sore with the sight of yellow glare and remote distance.

From this point I shall tell his tale in his own words, as he has told it me, but stripped of its garnishing and detail. For it were vain to translate Lallan into orthodox speech, when the very salt of the night air clings to the Scots as it did to that queer tale.

'The mune had been lang out,' he said, 'and I had grown weary o' her blinkin'. I was as cauld as death, and as wat as the sea, no to speak o' haein' the rheumatics in my back. The nowt were glowrin' and glunchin', rubbin' heid to heid, and whiles stampin' on my taes wi' their cloven hooves. But I was mortal glad o' the beasts' company, for I think I wad hae gane daft mysel in that muckle dowie water. Whiles I thocht it was risin', and then my hert stood still; an' whiles fa'in', and then it loupit wi' joy. But it keepit geyan near the bit, and aye as I heard it lip-lappin' I prayed the Lord to keep it whaur it was.

'About half-past yin in the mornin', as I saw by my watch, I got sleepy, and but for the nowt steerin', I micht hae drappit aff. Syne I begood to watch the water, and it was rale interestin', for a' sort o' queer things were comin' doun. I could see bits o' brigs and palin's wi'oot end dippin' in the tide, and whiles swirlin' in sae near that I could hae grippit them. Then beasts began to come by, whiles upside doun, whiles soomin' brawly, sheep and stirks frae the farms up the water. I got graund amusement for a wee while watchin' them, and notin' the marks on their necks.

' "That's Clachlands Mains," says I, "and that's Nether Fallo, and the Back o' the Muneraw. Gudesake, sic a spate it maun hae been up the muirs to work siccan a destruction!" I keepit coont o' the stock, and feegured to mysel what the farmer-bodies wad lose. The thocht that I wad keep a' my ain was some kind o' comfort.

'But about the hour o' twae the mune cloudit ower, and I saw nae mair than twenty feet afore me. I got awesome cauld, and a sort o' stound o' fricht took me, as I lookit into that black, unholy water. The nowt shivered sair and drappit their heids, and the fire on the ither side seemed to gang out a' of a sudden, and leave the hale glen thick wi' nicht. I shivered mysel wi' something mair than the snell air, and there and then I wad hae gien the price o' fower stirks for my ain bed at hame.

'It was as quiet as a kirkyaird, for suddenly the roar o' the water stoppit, and the stream lay still as a loch. Then I heard a queer lappin' as o' something floatin' doun, and it sounded miles aff in that dreidfu' silence. I lisrened wi' een stertin', and aye it cam' nearer and nearer, wi' a sound like a dowg soomin' a burn. It was sae black, I could see nocht, but somewhere frae the edge o' a cloud, a thin ray o' licht drappit on the water, and there, soomin' doun by me, I saw something that lookit like a man.

'My hert was burstin' wi' terror, but, thinks I, here's a droonin' body, and I maun try and save it. So I waded in as far as I daured, though my feet were sae cauld that they bowed aneath me.

'Ahint me I heard a splashin' and fechtin', and then I saw the nowt, fair wild wi' fricht, standin' in the water on the ither side o' the green bit, and lookin' wi' muckle feared een at something in the water afore me.

'Doun the thing came, and aye I got caulder as I looked. Then it was by my side, and I claught at it and pu'd it after me on to the land.

'I heard anither splash. The nowt gaed farther into the water, and stood shakin' like young birks in a storm.

'I got the thing upon the green bank and turned it ower. It was a drooned man wi' his hair hingin' back on his broo, and his mouth wide open. But first I saw his een, which glowered like scrapit lead out o' his clay-cauld face, and had in them a' the fear o' death and hell which follows after.

'The next moment I was up to my waist among the nowt, fechtin' in the water aside them, and snowkin' into their wet backs to hide mysel like a feared bairn.

'Maybe half an 'oor I stood, and then my mind returned to me. I misca'ed mysel for a fule and a coward. And my legs were sae numb, and my strength sae far gane, that I kenned fine that I couldna lang thole to stand this way like a heron in the water.

'I lookit round, and then turned again wi' a stert, for there were thae leaden een o' that awfu' deid thing staring at me still.

'For anither quarter-hour I stood and shivered, and then my guid sense returned, and I tried again. I walkit backward, never lookin' round, through the water to the shore, whaur I thocht the corp was lyin'. And a' the time I could hear my hert chokin' in my breist.

'My God, I fell ower it, and for one moment lay aside it, wi' my heid touchin' its deathly skin. Then wi' a skelloch like a daft man, I took the thing in my airms and flung it wi' a' my strength into the water. The swirl took it, and it dipped and swam like a fish till it gaed out o'sicht.

'I saw doun on the grass and grat like a bairn wi' fair horror and weakness. Yin by yin the nowt came back, and shouthered anither around me, and the puir beasts brocht me yince mair to myself. But I keepit my een on the grund, and thocht o' hame and a' thing decent and kindly, for I daurna for my life look out to the black water in dreid o' what it micht bring.

'At the first licht, the herd and twae ither men cam' ower in a boat to tak me aff and bring fodder for the beasts. They fand me still sittin' wi' my heid atween my knees, and my face like a peeled wand. They lifted me intil the boat and rowed me ower, driftin' far down wi' the angry current. At the ither side the shepherd says to me in an awed voice, –

' "There's a fearfu' thing happened. The young laird o' Manorwater's drooned in the spate. He was ridin' back late and tried the ford o' the Cauldshaw foot. Ye ken his wild cantrips, but there's an end o' them noo. The horse cam' hame in the nicht wi' an empty saddle, and the Gled Water rinnin' frae him in streams. The corp'll be far on to the sea by this time, and they'll never see't mair." '

' "I ken," I cried wi' a dry throat, "I ken; I saw him floatin' by." And then I broke yince mair into a silly greetin', while the men watched me as if they thocht I was out o' my mind.'

So much the farmer of Clachlands told me, but to the countryside he repeated merely the bare facts of weariness and discomfort. I have heard that he was accosted a week later by the minister of the place, a well-intentioned, phrasing man, who had strayed from his native city with its familiar air of tea and temperance to those stony uplands.

'And what thoughts had you, Mr Linklater, in that awful position? Had you no serious reflection upon your life?'

'Me,' said the farmer; 'no me. I juist was thinkin' that it was dooms cauld, and that I wad hae gien a guid deal for a pipe o' tobaccy.' This in the racy, careless tone of one to whom such incidents were the merest child's play.

Prester John

Yet another of Buchan's stories which reveal his ability to describe weather and terrain, and to cast an affectionate, if sly, look at Border folk and their preoccupation with religion. It appeared in *Chamber's Journal* in June 1897 and then in *Grey Weather* (1899).

Or he, who in the wilderness, where no man travels and few may live, dwelled in all good reason and kindness.

Chronicle of S. Jean de Remy

The exact tale of my misadventure on that September day I can scarcely now remember. One thing I have clear in my mind – the weather. For it was in that curious time of year when autumn's caprices reach their height either in the loveliest of skies or a resolute storm. Now it was the latter, and for two days the clear tints of the season had been drowned in monotonous grey. The mighty hill-streams came down like fields in breadth, and when the wind ceased for a time, the roar of many waters was heard in the land. Ragged leaves blocked the path, heather and bracken were sodden as the meadow turf, and the mountain backs were now shrouded to their bases in mist, and now looming ominous and near in a pause of the shifting wrack.

In the third day of the weather I was tempted by the Evil One and went a-fishing. The attempt was futile, and I knew it, for the streams were boiling like a caldron, and no man may take fish in such a water. Nevertheless, the blustering air and the infinite distance of shadowy hill-top took hold on me so that I could not choose but face the storm. And, once outside, the north wind slashed and buffeted me till my breath was almost gone; and when I came to the river's edge, I looked down on an acre of churning foam and mountainous wave.

Now, the way of the place is this. The Gled comes down from flat desolate moorlands to the narrower glen, which in turn opens upon the great river of the countryside. On the left it is bounded by gentle slopes of brown heather, which sink after some score of miles into the fields of a plain; but to the right there lies a tract of fierce country, rugged and scarred with torrents; while at the back of all rise the pathless hills which cradle the Callowa and the Aller. It is a land wild on the fairest summer noon, but in the autumn storms it is black as a pit and impregnable as a fortress.

As ill-fortune would have it, I raised a good fish in my first pool, ran it, and lost it in a tangle of driftwood. What with the excitement and the stinging air my blood grew high, I laughed in the face of the heavens, and wrestled in the gale's teeth for four miles up-stream. It was the purest madness, for my casting-line was blown out of the water at almost every gust, and never another fish looked near me. But the keenness abode with me, and so it happened that about midday I stood at the foot of the glen whence the Cauldshaw Burn pours its troubled waters to the Gled.

Something in the quiet strength of the great brown flood attracted me against my better judgment. I persuaded myself that in this narrower vale there must be some measure of shelter, and that in its silent pools there were chances of fish. So, with a fine sense of the adventurous, I turned to the right and struck up by the green meadow-lands and the lipping water. Before me was a bank of mist; but even as I looked it opened, and a line of monstrous blue shoulders, ribbed and serrated with a thousand gullies, frowned on my path. The sight put new energy into my limbs. These were the hills which loomed far to the distant lowlands, which few ever climbed, and at whose back lay a land almost unknown to man. I named them to myself with the names which had always been like music to my ear – Craigcreich, the Yirnie, the two Muneraws, and the awful precipice of the Dreichil. With zest I fell to my fishing, and came in a little to the place where the vale ceased and the gorge began.

Here for the first time my efforts prospered, and I had one, two, and three out of the inky pots, which the spate had ringed and dappled with foam. Then, from some unknown cause, the wind fell, and there succeeded the silence which comes from a soaked and dripping world. I fished on and on, but the stillness oppressed me, and the straight craigs, tipped with heather and black with ooze, struck me with something like awe.

Then, ere I knew, I had come to the edge of the gorge, and was out on the peat-moss which gives the Cauldshaw its birth. Once more there came a clearing in the mist, and hill-faces looked out a little nearer, a little more awful. Just beyond that moss lay their foot, and over that barrier of heath and crag lay a new land which I had not yet seen, and scarcely heard of. Suddenly my whole purpose changed. Storm or no storm, I would climb the ridge and look down on the other side. At the top of the Little Muneraw there rose two streams – one, the Callowa, which flowed to the haughlands and meadows of the low country; the other, the Aller, which fought its way to the very centre of the black deserts, and issued some fifty miles distant on another seaboard. I would reach the top, haply see the sight I had often longed for, and then take my weary way down the Callowa home.

So, putting up my rod and strapping tight my creel, I set my face to the knuckle of these mountains which loomed beyond the bog. How I crossed that treacherous land I can scarcely tell, for the rain had left great lagoons which covered shifting sand and clinging mud. Twice I was bogged to my knees, but by dint of many flying leaps from heather to heather, and many lowly scrambles over loose peat, I came to the hard ground whence the slope began. Here I rested, panting, marvelling greatly at my foolhardiness and folly. When honest men were dwelling in comfort at home, I in my fool's heart chose to be playing cantrips among mosses and scaurs and pathless rocks. I was already soaked and half tired, so in no great bodily ease I set myself to the ascent.

In two hours I had toiled to the front shoulder of the Muneraw, and sat looking down on a pit of mist whence three black lochs gleamed faint and shadowy. The place was hushed save for the croak of ravens and the rare scream of a hawk. Curlews and plovers were left far below; the place was too wild for rushes or bracken; and nothing met the eye but stunted heather, grey lichen-clad boulders, and dark craigs streaked with the fall of streams. I loosened a stone and sent it hurling to the loch below, and in a trice the air was thick with echoes of splash and rush and splinter.

Then once more I set my face to the steep and scrambled upward. And now there came to trouble me that very accident which I most feared; for the wind brought the accursed mist down on me like a plaid, and I struggled through utter blindness. The thickness of mirk is bad enough, but the thickness of white, illimitable ether is worse a thousandfold, for it closes the eye and mazes the wits. I kept as straight as might be for what I knew was the head of the hill, and now upon great banks of rotten granite, now upon almost sheer craigs, I made my track. In maybe an hour the steeps ceased, and I lay and panted on a flat bed of shingle, while the clammy mist drenched me to the bone.

Now for the first time I began to repent of my journey, and took grace to regret my madcap ploy. For the full perils of the place began to dawn upon me. I was here, in this dismal weather, a score of miles from any village, and nigh half as many from the nearest human habitation. A sprain or a broken limb would mean death, and at any moment I might step over a cliff-face into eternity. My one course of safety lay in finding the Callowa springs, and following the trickle to the glens. The way was long, but it was safe, and sooner or later I must come to a dwelling-house.

I knew well that the Callowa rose on the south side of the Muneraw, and the Aller somewhere on the north. But I had lost all sense of direction, I had no compass, and had it not been for the wind, I should have been without guidance. But I remembered that it had blown clear from the north on all my way up the Gled, and now, as I felt its sting on my cheek, I turned with it to what I guessed to be the south. With some satisfaction I began to descend, now sliding for yards, now falling suddenly in a rocky pool, whence a trickle issued among a chaos of stones. Once I came to a high fall, which must have been wonderful indeed had the water been of any size, but was now no more than a silver thread on a great grey face. Sometimes I found myself in ravines where the huge sides seemed to mock the tiny brawling water. A lurking fear began to grow upon me. Hitherto I had found no loch, though I had gone for miles. Now, though I had never been at Callowa head, I had seen it afar off, and knew that the Back Loch o' the Muneraw lay near the source. But now the glen was opening, peat and heather were taking the place of stone, and yet I had seen no gleam of water.

I sat down to consider, and even as I looked the mist drew back again. And this was what I saw. Brown bog lay flat down a valley, with a stream in its midst making leaden pools. Now there are bogs and bogs, and some are harmless enough; but there was that in the look of this which I could not like. Some two miles down the stream turned, and a ridge of dark and craggy hills fronted the eye. Their edges were jagged, and their inky face was seamed and crossed with a thousand little cataracts. And beneath their shadow lay the cruel moss, with flows and lochs scattered over it like a map on a child's slate.

To my wonder, in the very lee of the hill I saw what seemed to be a cottage. There was a stunted tree, a piece of stone wall, and a plain glimpse of a grey gable-end. Then I knew whither I had come. The wind had changed. I had followed north for south, and struck the Aller instead of the Callowa. I could not return over that fierce hill and those interminable moorland miles. There was naught to be done save to make for the stones, which might be a dwelling. If the place was ruined, I would even sleep the night in its shelter, and strive to return in the morning. If it was still dwelled in, there was hope of supper and bed. I had always heard of the Aller as the wildest of all waters, flowing, for most of its course, in a mossland untenanted of man. Something of curiosity took me, in spite of my weariness, to meet with a dweller in this desert. And always as I looked at the black hills I shuddered, for I had heard men tell of the Caldron, where no sheep ever strayed, and in whose sheer-falling waters no fish could live.

I have rarely felt a more awful eeriness than in crossing that monstrous bog. I struck far from the stream, for the Aller, which had begun as a torrent, had sunk into links of unfathomable moss-holes. The darkening was coming on, the grim hills stood out more stark and cruel, and the smell of water clung to my nostrils like the odour of salt to a half-drowned man. Forthwith I fell into the most violent ill-temper with myself and my surroundings. At last there was like to be an end of my aimless wanderings, and unless I got through the moss by nightfall, I should never see the morning. The thought nerved me to frantic endeavour. I was dog-tired and soaked to the marrow, but I plunged and struggled from tussock to tussock and through long black reaches of peat. Anything green or white I shunned, for I had lived too long in wildernesses to be ignorant that in the ugly black and brown lay my safety.

By-and-by the dusk came, and a light was kindled in the cottage, at which sign of habitation I greatly rejoiced. It gave me new heart, and when I came to a more level place I ran as well as my wearied legs would suffer me. Then for my discomfiture I fell into a great bed of peat, and came out exceeding dirty. Still the flare grew nearer, and at last, about seven o'clock, just at the thickening of darkness, I reached a stone wall and a house-end.

At the sound of my feet the door was thrown open, and a string of collies rushed out to devour me. At their tail came the master of the place, a man bent and thin, with a beard ragged and torn with all weathers, and a great scarred face roughly brown with the hill air and the reek of peat.

'Can I stay—' I began, but my words were drowned in his loud tone of welcome.

'How in the warld did ye get here, man? Come in, come in; ye'll be fair perished.'

He caught me by the arm and dragged me into the single room which formed his dwelling. Half-a-dozen hens, escaping from the hutch which was their abode, sat modestly in corners, and from a neighbouring shed came the lowing of a cow. The place was so filled with blue fine smoke that my eyes were dazed, and it was not till I sat in a chair by a glowing fire of peats that I could discern the outlines of the roof. The rafters were black and finely polished as old oak, and the floor was flagged with the grey stones of the moor. A stretch of sacking did duty for a rug, and there the tangle of dogs stretched itself to sleep. The furnishing was of the rudest, for it was brought on horseback over barren hills, and such a portage needs the stoutest of timber. But who can tell of the infinite complexity of the odour which filled the air, the pungency of peat, varied with a whiff of the snell night without and the comfortable fragrance of food?

Meat he set before me, scones and oaten-cakes, and tea brewed as strong as spirits. He had not seen loaf-bread, he told me, since the spring, when a shepherd from the Back o' the Caldron came over about some sheep, and had a loaf-end for his dinner. Then, when I was something recovered, I sat again in the fireside chair, and over pipes of the strongest black we held high converse.

'Wife!' he said, when I asked him if he dwelt alone; 'na, na, nae woman-body for me. I bide mysel', and bake my bakings, and shoo my breeks when they need it. A wife wad be a puir convanience in this pairt o' the warld. I come in at nicht, and I dae as I like, and I gang oot in the mornings, and there's naebody to care for. I can milk the coo mysel', and feed the hens, and there's little else that a man need dae.'

I asked him if he came often to the lowlands.

'Is 't like,' said he, 'when there's twenty mile o' thick heather and shairp rock atween you and a level road? I naether gang there, nor do the folk there fash me here. I havena been at the kirk for ten 'ear, no since my faither dee'd; and though the minister o' Gledsmuir, honest man, tries to win here every spring, it's no' often he gets the length. Twice in the 'ear I gang far awa' wi' sheep, when I spain the lambs in the month o' August, and draw the crocks in the back-end. I'm expectin' every day to get word to tak' off the yowes.'

'And how do you get word?' I asked.

'Weel, the post comes up the road to the foot o' the Gled. Syne some o' the fairmers up the water tak' up a letter and leave it at the foot o' the Cauldshaw Burn. A fisher, like yersel', maybe, brings it up the glen and draps it at the herd's cottage o' the Front Muneraw, whaur it lies till the herd, Simon Murddock, tak's it wi' him on his roonds. Noo, twice every week he passes the tap o' the Aller, and

I've gotten a cairn there, whaur he hides it in an auld tin box among the stanes. Twice a week I gang up that way mysel', and find onything that's lyin'. Oh, I'm no' ill off for letters; I get them in about a week, if there's no' a snawstorm.'

The man leant forward to put a fresh coal to his pipe, and I marked his eyes, begrimed with peat smoke, but keen as a hawk's, and the ragged, ill-patched homespun of his dress. I thought of the good folk in the lowlands and the cities who hugged their fancies of simple Arcadian shepherds, who, in decent cottage, surrounded by a smiling family, read God's Word of a Saturday night. In the rugged man before me I found some hint of the truth.

'And how do you spend your days?' I asked. 'Did you never think of trying a more kindly countryside?'

He looked at me long and quizzically.

'Yince,' he said, 'I served a maister, a bit flesher-body doun at Gledfoot. He was aye biddin' me dae odd jobs about the toun, and I couldna thole it, for I'm a herd, and my wark's wi' sheep. Noo I serve the Yerl o' Callowa, and there's no' a body dare say a word to me; but I manage things according to my ain guid juidgement, wi'oot ony "by your leave". And whiles I've the best o' company, for yince or twice the Yerl has bided here a' nicht, when he was forewandered shooting amang thae muirs.'

But I was scarce listening, so busy was I in trying to picture an existence which meant incessant wanderings all day among the wilds, and firelit evenings, with no company but dogs. I asked him if he ever read.

'I ha'e a Bible,' he said doubtfully, 'and I whiles tak' a spell at it to see if I remember my schulin'. But I'm no keen on books o' ony kind.'

'Then what in the name of goodness do you do?' said I.

Then his tongue was unloosed, and he told me the burden of his days; how he loved all weather, fighting a storm for the fight's sake, and glorying in the conquest; how he would trap blue hares and shoot wild-fowl – for had he not the Earl's leave? – and now and then kill a deer strayed among the snow. He was full of old tales of the place, learned from a thousand old sources, of queer things that happened in these eternal deserts, and queer sights which he and others than himself had seen at dawning and sunset. Some day I will put them all down in a book, but then I will inscribe it to children and label it fantasy, for no one would believe them if told with the circumstance of truth. But, above all, he gloried in the tale of the changes of sky and earth, and the multitudinous lore of the hills. I heard of storms when the thunder echoed in the Caldron like the bleating of great sheep, and the man sat still at home in terror. He told with solemn eyes of the coming of snow, of masterful floods in the Aller, when the dead sheep came down and butted, as he said, with their foreheads against his house-wall. His voice grew high, and his figure, seen in the red glare of the peats, was like some creature of a tale.

But in time the fire sank, the dogs slumbered, our pipes went out, and he showed me my bed. It was in the garret, which you entered by a trap from the shed below. The one window had been shattered by some storm and boarded up with planks, through whose crevices I could see the driving mist and the bog lying dead under cover of night. I slept on rough blankets of homespun, and ere I lay down, in looking round the place, I came upon a book stuck fast between the rafters and the wall. It was the Bible used to brush up the shepherd's learning, and for the sake of his chances hereafter I dragged it forth and blew the dust from it.

In the morning the mist had gone, and a blue sky shone out, over which sudden gusts swept like boats on a loch. The damp earth still reeked of rain; and as I stood at the door and watched the Aller, now one line of billows, strive impetuous through the bog-land, and the hills gleam in the dawning like wet jewels, I no more wondered at the shepherd's choice. He came down from a morning's round, his voice bellowing across the uplands, and hailed me from afar. 'The hills are no vera dry,' he said, 'but they micht be passed; and if I was sure I wadna bide, he wad set me on my way.' So in a little I followed his great strides through the moss and up the hill-shoulder, till in two hours I was breathing hard on the Dreichil summit, and looking down on awful craigs, which dropped sheerly to a tarn. Here he stopped, and, looking far over the chaos of ridges, gave me my directions.

'Ye see yon muckle soo-backit hill – yon's the Yirnie Cleuch, and if ye keep alang the taps ye'll come to it in an 'oor's time. Gang doun the far shouther o't, and ye'll see a burn which flows into a loch; gang on to the loch-foot, and ye'll see a great deep hole in the hillside, what they ca' the Nick o' the Hurlstanes; gang through it, and ye'll strike the Criven Burn, which flows into the Callowa; gang doun that water till it joins the Gled, and syne ye're no' abune ten mile from whaur ye're bidin'. So guid-day to ye.'

And with these lucid words he left me and took his swinging path across the hill.

The Moor Song

This story has appeared in slightly different versions, under varied names and in several books. It was first published as 'Song of the Moor' in *Macmillan's Magazine* in July 1897 and the following month in *The Living Age*, as 'The Moor Song' in *Grey Weather* (1899) and as 'The Rime of True Thomas' in *The Moon Endureth* (1912) and in the 1918 American edition of *The Watcher by the Threshold*. Simon Etterick, a 'great godly man', has a strange encounter with a bird who tells him about the history of his family and the area. As is the case in several of Buchan's stories, the supernatural element is left rather ambivalent and he includes one of his own poems in the text – here 'The Ballad of Grey Weather'.

THE TALE OF THE RESPECTABLE WHAUP
AND THE GREAT GODLY MAN

This is a story that I heard from the King of the Numidians, who with his tattered retinue encamps behind the peat-ricks. If you ask me where and when it happened I fear that I am scarce ready with an answer. But I will vouch my honour for its truth; and if any one seek further proof, let him go east the town and west the town and over the fields of Nomansland to the Long Muir, and if he find not the King there among the peat-ricks, and get not a courteous answer to his question, then times have changed in that part of the country, and he must continue the quest to His Majesty's castle in Spain.

Once upon a time, says the tale, there was a Great Godly Man, a shepherd to trade, who lived in a cottage among heather. If you looked east in the morning, you saw miles of moor running wide to the flames of sunrise, and if you turned your eyes west in the evening, you saw a great confusion of dim peaks with the dying eye of the sun set in a crevice. If you looked north, too, in the afternoon, when the life of the day is near its end and the world grows wise, you might have seen a country of low hills and haughlands with many waters running sweet among meadows. But if you looked south in the dusty forenoon or at hot mid-day, you saw the far-off glimmer of a white road, the roofs of the ugly little clachan of Kilmaclavers, and the rigging of the fine new kirk of Threepdaidle.

It was a Sabbath afternoon in the hot weather, and the man had been to kirk all the morning. He had heard a grand sermon from the minister (or it may have been the priest, for I am not sure of the date and the King told the story quickly) – a fine discourse with fifteen heads and three parentheses. He held all the parentheses and fourteen of the heads in his memory, but he had forgotten the fifteenth; so for the purpose of recollecting it, and also for the sake of a walk, he went forth in the afternoon into the open heather. The air was mild and cheering, and with an even step he strolled over the turf and into the deeps of the moor.

The whaups were crying everywhere, making the air hum like the twanging of a bow. *Poo-eelie, Poo-eelie*, they cried, *Kirlew, Kirlew, Whaup, Wha- -up*. Sometimes they came low, all but brushing him, till they drove settled thoughts from his head. Often had he been on the moors, but never had he seen such a stramash among the feathered clan. The wailing iteration vexed him, and he *shoo'd* the birds away with his arms. But they seemed to mock him and whistle in his very face, and at the flaff of their wings his heart grew sore. He waved his great stick; he picked up bits of loose moor-rock and flung them wildly; but the godless crew paid never a grain of heed. The morning's sermon was still in his head, and the grave words of the minister still rattled in his ear, but he could get no comfort for this intolerable piping. At last his patience failed him and he swore unchristian words. 'Deil rax the birds' thrapples,' he cried.

At this all the noise was hushed and in a twinkling the moor was empty. Only one bird was left, standing on tall

legs before him with its head bowed upon its breast, and its
beak touching the heather.

Then the man repented his words and stared at the thing
in the moss. 'What bird are ye?' he asked thrawnly.

'I am a Respectable Whaup,' said the bird, 'and I kenna
why ye have broken in on our family gathering. Once in a
hundred years we foregather for decent conversation, and
here we are interrupted by a muckle, sweerin' man.'

Now the shepherd was a fellow of great sagacity, yet he
never thought it a queer thing that he should be having talk
in the mid-moss with a bird. Truth, he had no mind on the
matter.

'What for were ye making siccan a din, then?' he asked.
'D' ye no ken ye were disturbing the afternoon of the holy
Sabbath?'

The bird lifted its eyes and regarded him solemnly. 'The
Sabbath is a day of rest and gladness,' it said, 'and is it no
reasonable that we should enjoy the like?'

The shepherd shook his head, for the presumption
staggered him. 'Ye little ken ye what speak of,' he said.
'The Sabbath is for them that have the chance of salvation,
and it has been decreed that Salvation is for Adam's race
and no for the beasts that perish.'

The whaup gave a whistle of scorn. 'I have heard all that
long ago. In my great-grandmother's time, which 'ill be a
thousand years and mair syne, there came a people from
the south with bright brass things on their heads and breasts
and terrible swords at their thighs. And with them were
some lang-gowned men who kenned the stars and would
come out o' nights to talk to the deer and the corbies in
their ain tongue. And one, I mind, foregathered with my
great-grandmother and told her that the souls o' men flitted
in the end to braw meadows where the gods bide or gaed
down to the black pit which they ca' Hell. But the souls o'
birds, he said, die wi' their bodies and that's the end o'
them. Likewise in my mother's time, when there was a
great abbey down yonder by the Threepdaidle Burn which
they called the House of Kilmaclavers, the auld monks
would walk out in the evening to pick herbs for their
distillings, and some were wise and kenned the ways of

bird and beast. They would crack often o'nights with my ain family, and tell them that Christ had saved the souls o' men, but that birds and beasts were perishable as the dew o' heaven. And now ye have a black-gowned man in Threepdaidle who threeps on the same owercome. Ye may a' ken something o' your ain kitchen-midden, but certes! ye ken little o' the warld beyond it.'

Now this angered the man, and he rebuked the bird. 'These are great mysteries,' he said, 'which are no to be mentioned in the ears of an unsanctified creature. What can a thing like you wi' a lang neb and twae legs like stilts ken about the next warld?'

'Weel, weel,' said the whaup, 'we'll let the matter be. Everything to its ain trade, and I will not dispute with ye on metapheesics. But if ye ken something about the next warld, ye ken terrible little about this.'

Now this angered the man still more, for he was a shepherd reputed to have great skill in sheep and esteemed the nicest judge of hogg and wether in all the countryside. 'What ken ye about that?' he asked. 'Ye may gang east to Yetholm and west to Kells, and no find a better herd.'

'If sheep were a',' said the bird, 'ye micht be right; but what o' the wide warld and the folk in it? Ye are Simon Etterick o' the Lowe Moss. Do ye ken aucht o' your forebears?'

'My father was a God-fearing man at the Kennel-head, and my grandfather and great-grandfather afore him. One o' our name, folk say, was shot at a dyke-back by the Black Westeraw.'

'If that's a',' said the bird, 'ye ken little. Have ye never heard o' the little man, the fourth back from yoursel', who killed the Miller o' Bewcastle at the Lammas Fair? That was in my ain time, and from my mother I have heard o' the Covenanter, who got a bullet in his wame hunkering behind the divot-dyke and praying to his Maker. There were others o' your name rode in the Hermitage forays and burned Naworth and Warkworth and Castle Gay. I have heard o' an Etterick, Sim o' the Redcleuch, who cut the throat o' Jock Johnson in his ain house by the Annan side. And my grandmother had tales o' auld Ettericks who rade wi' Douglas and the Bruce and the ancient Kings o'

Scots; and she used to tell o' others in her mother's time, terrible shock-headed men, hunting the deer and rinnin' on the high moors, and bidin' in the broken stane biggings on the hill-taps.'

The shepherd stared, and he, too, saw the picture. He smelled the air of battle and lust and foray, and forgot the Sabbath.

'And you yoursel',' said the bird, 'are sair fallen off from the auld stock. Now ye sit and spell in books, and talk about what ye little understand, when your fathers were roaming the warld. But little cause have I to speak, for I too am a down-come. My bill is two inches shorter than my mother's, and my grandmother was taller on her feet. The warld is getting weaklier things to dwell in it, ever since I mind mysel'.'

'Ye have the gift o' speech, bird,' said the man, 'and I would hear mair.' You will perceive that he had no mind of the Sabbath day or the fifteenth head of the forenoon's discourse.

'What things have I to tell ye when ye dinna ken the very hornbook o' knowledge? Besides, I am no clatter-ven-geance to tell stories in the middle o' the muir, where there are ears open high and low. There's others than me wi' mair experience and a better skill at the telling. Our clan was well acquaint wi' the reivers and lifters o' the muirs, and could crack fine o' wars and the taking of cattle. But the blue hawk that lives in the corrie o' the Dreichil can speak o' kelpies and the dwarfs that bide in the hill. The heron, the lang solemn fellow, kens o' the greenwood fairies and the wood elfins, and the wild geese that squatter on the tap o' the Muneraw will croak to ye of the merrymaidens and the girls o' the pool. The wren – he that hops in the grass below the birks – has the story of the "Lost Ladies of the Land", which is ower auld and sad for any but the wisest to hear; and there is a wee bird bides in the heather – hill-lintie men call him – who sings the "Lay of the West Wind", and the "Glee of the Rowan Berries". But what am I talking of? What are these things to you, if ye have not first heard the Moor-Song, which is the beginning and end o' all things?'

'I have heard no songs,' said the man, 'save the sacred psalms o' God's Kirk.'

'Bonny sangs,' said the bird. 'Once I flew by the hinder end o' the Kirk and I keekit in. A wheen auld wives wi' mutches and a wheen solemn men wi' hoasts! Be sure the Moor-Song is no like yon.'

'Can ye sing it, bird?' said the man, 'for I am keen to hear it.'

'Me sing,' cried the bird, 'me that has a voice like a craw! Na, na, I canna sing it, but maybe I can tak ye where ye may hear it. When I was young an auld bog-blitter did the same to me, and sae began my education. But are ye willing and brawly willing? – for if ye get but a sough of it ye will never mair have an ear for other music.'

'I am willing and brawly willing,' said the man.

'Then meet me at the Gled's Cleuch Head at the sun's setting,' said the bird, and it flew away.

Now it seemed to the man that in a twinkling it was sunset, and he found himself at the Gled's Cleuch Head with the bird flapping in the heather before him. The place was a long rift in the hill, made green with juniper and hazel, where it was said True Thomas came to drink the water.

'Turn ye to the west,' said the whaup, 'and let the sun fall on your face, then turn ye five times round about and say after me the Rune of the Heather and the Dew.' And before he knew, the man did as he was told, and found himself speaking strange words, while his head hummed and danced as if in a fever.

'Now lay ye down and put your ear to the earth,' said the bird, and the man did so. Instantly a cloud came over his brain, and he did not feel the ground on which he lay or the keen hill-air which blew about him. He felt himself falling deep into an abysm of space, then suddenly caught up and set among the stars of heaven. Then slowly from the stillness there welled forth music, drop by drop like the clear falling of rain, and the man shuddered, for he knew that he heard the beginning of the Moor-Song.

High rose the air, and trembled among the tallest pines and the summits of great hills. And in it were the sting of rain and the blatter of hail, the soft crush of snow and the rattle of thunder among crags. Then it quieted to the low sultry croon which told of blazing mid-day when the streams are parched and the bent crackles like dry tinder. Anon it was evening, and the melody dwelled among the high soft notes which mean the coming of dark and the green light of sunset. Then the whole changed to a great pæan which rang like an organ through the earth. There were trumpet notes in it and flute notes and the plaint of pipes. 'Come forth,' it cried; 'the sky is wide and it is a far cry to the world's end. The fire crackles fine o' nights below the firs, the smell of roasting meat and wood smoke is dear to the heart of man. Fine, too, is the sting of salt and the risp of the north-wind in the sheets. Come forth, one and all, to the great lands oversea, and the strange tongues and the fremit peoples. Learn before you die to follow the Piper's Son, and though your old bones bleach among grey rocks, what matter, if you have had your bellyful of life and come to the land of Heart's Desire?' And the tune fell low and witching, bringing tears to the eyes and joy to the heart; and the man knew (though no one told him) that this was the first part of the Moor-Song, the 'Song of the Open Road', the 'Lilt of the Adventurer', which shall be now and ever and to the end of days.

Then the melody changed to a fiercer and sadder note. He saw his forefathers, gaunt men and terrible, run stark among woody hills. He heard the talk of the bronze-clad invader, and the jar and clangour as flint met steel. Then rose the last coronach of his own people, hiding in wild glens, starving in corries, or going hopelessly to the death. He heard the cry of Border foray, the shouts of the poor Scots as they harried Cumberland, and he himself rode in the midst of them. Then the tune fell more mournful and slow, and Flodden lay before him. He saw the flower of Scots gentry around their king, gashed to the brest bone, still fronting the lines of the south, though the paleness of death sat on each forehead. 'The flowers of the Forest are gone,' cried the lilt, and through the long years he heard the cry of the lost, the desperate, fighting for kings over the water and princes in the heather. 'Who cares?' cried the air. 'Man must die, and how can he die better than in the stress of fight with his heart high and alien blood on his sword?

Heigh-ho! One against twenty, a child against a host, this is
the romance of life.' And the man's heart swelled, for he
knew (though no one told him) that this was the 'Song of
Lost Battles', which only the great can sing before they die.

But the tune was changing, and at the change the man
shivered, for the air ran up to the high notes and then down
to the deeps with an eldrich cry, like a hawk's scream at
night, or a witch's song in the gloaming. It told of those who
seek and never find, the quest that knows no fulfilment.
'There is a road,' it cries, 'which leads to the Moon and the
Great Waters. No changehouse cheers it, and it has no end;
but it is a fine road, a braw road – who will follow it?' And
the man knew (though no one told him) that this was the
'Ballad of Grey Weather', which makes him who hears it
sick all the days of his life for something which he cannot
name. It is the song which the birds sing on the moor in the
autumn nights, and the old crow on the tree-top hears and
flaps his wing. It is the lilt which old men and women hear
in the darkening of their days, and sigh for the unforget-
table; and love-sick girls get catches of it and play pranks
with their lovers. It is a song so old that Adam heard it in the
Garden before Eve came to comfort him, so young that
from it still flows the whole joy and sorrow of earth.

Then it ceased, and all of a sudden the man was rubbing
his eyes on the hillside, and watching the falling dusk. 'I
have heard the Moor-Song,' he said to himself, and he
walked home in a daze. The whaups were crying, but none
came near him, though he looked hard for the bird that had
spoken with him. It may be that it was there and he did not
know it, or it may be that the whole thing was only a dream;
but of this I cannot say.

The next morning the man rose and went to the manse.

'I am glad to see you, Simon,' said the minister, 'for it
will soon be the Communion Season, and it is your duty to
go round with the tokens.'

'True,' said the man, 'but it was another thing I came to
talk about,' and he told him the whole tale.

'There are but two ways of it, Simon,' said the minister.
'Either ye are the victim of witchcraft, or ye are a self-deluded

man. If the former (whilk I am loth to believe), then it behoves ye to watch and pray lest ye enter into temptation. If the latter, then ye maun put a strict watch over a vagrom fancy, and ye'll be quit o' siccan whigmaleeries.'

Now Simon was not listening, but staring out of the window. 'There was another thing I had it in my mind to say,' said he. 'I have come to lift my lines, for I am thinking of leaving the place.'

'And where would ye go?' asked the minister, aghast.

'I was thinking of going to Carlisle and trying my luck as a dealer, or maybe pushing on with droves to the South.'

'But that's a cauld country where there are no faithfu' ministrations,' said the minister.

'Maybe so, but I am not caring very muckle about ministrations,' said the man, and the other looked after him in horror.

When he left the manse he went to a Wise Woman, who lived on the left side of the Kirk-yard above Threepdaidle burn-foot. She was very old, and sat by the ingle day and night, waiting upon death. To her he told the same tale.

She listened gravely, nodding with her head. 'Ach,' she said, 'I have heard a like story before. And where will you be going?'

'I am going south to Carlisle to try the dealing and droving,' said the man, 'for I have some skill of sheep.'

'And will ye bide there?' she asked.

'Maybe aye, and maybe no,' he said. 'I had half a mind to push on to the big toun or even to the abroad. A man must try his fortune.'

'That's the way of men,' said the old wife. 'I, too, have heard the Moor-Song, and many women, who now sit decently spinning in Kilmaclavers, have heard it. But a woman may hear it and lay it up in her soul and bide at hame, while a man, if he get but a glisk of it in his fool's heart, must needs up and awa' to the warld's end on some daft-like ploy. But gang your ways and fare ye weel. My cousin Francie heard it, and he went north wi' a white cockade in his bonnet and a sword at his side, singing "Charlie's come hame". And Tam Crichtoun o' the

Bourhopehead got a sough o' it one simmer's morning, and the last we heard o' Tam he was killed among the Frenchmen fechting like a fair deil. Once I heard a tinkler play a sprig of it on the pipes, and a' the lads were wud to follow him. Gang your ways, for I am near the end o' mine.' And the old wife shook with her coughing.

So the man put up his belongings in a pack on his back and went whistling down the Great South Road.

Whether or not this tale have a moral it is not for me to say. The King (who told it me) said that it had, and quoted a scrap of Latin, for he had been at Oxford in his youth before he fell heir to his kingdom. One may hear tunes from the Moor-Song, said he, in the thick of a storm on the scarp of a rough hill, in the low June weather, or in the sunset silence of a winter's night. But let none, he added, pray to have the full music, for it will make him who hears it a footsore traveller in the ways o' the world and a masterless man till death.

A Reputation

'A Reputation', one of the stories in *Grey Weather*
(1899), first appeared in *Macmillan's Magazine* in February 1898 and in *The Living Age* the following April.
The influence of Buchan's circle at Oxford is apparent in
this story about male friendship and Arnold Layden is
probably a composite of three of them – Arnold Ward,
Raymond Asquith and Aubrey Herbert. The story has
certain similarities to his novel, *The Half-Hearted* (1900),
written at the same time, while the emptiness of success
was to be a major theme in all of his writing.

I

It was at a little lonely shooting-box in the Forest of Rhynns
that I first met Layden, sometime in the process of a wet
August. The place belonged to his cousin Urquhart, a
strange man well on in years who divided his time between
recondite sport and mild antiquities. We were a small party
of men held together by a shifty acquaintance of those who
meet somewhere and somehow each autumn. By day we
shot conscientiously over mossy hills or fished in the many
turbid waters; while of an evening there would be much
tobacco and sporting-talk interspersed with the sleepy,
indifferent joking of wearied men. We all knew the life
well from long experience, and for the sake of a certain
freshness and excitement were content to put up with
monotonous fare and the companionship of bleak moorlands. It was a season of brown faces and rude health, when
a man's clothes smelt of peat, and he recked not of letters
accumulating in the nearest post-town.

To such sombre days Layden came like a phœnix among
moorfowl. I had arrived late, and my first sight of him was

at dinner, where the usual listless talk was spurred almost to brilliance by his presence. He kept all the table laughing at his comical stories and quaint notes on men and things, shrewd, witty, and well-timed. But this welcome vivacity was not all, for he cunningly assumed the air of a wise man unbending, and his most random saying had the piquant hint of a great capacity. Nor was his talk without a certain body, for when by any chance one of his hearers touched upon some matter of technical knowledge, he was ready at the word for a well-informed discussion. The meal ended, as it rarely did, in a full flow of conversation, and men rose with the feeling of having returned for the moment to some measure of culture.

The others came out one by one to the lawn above the river, while he went off with his host on some private business. George Winterham sat down beside me and blew solemn wreaths of smoke toward the sky. I asked him who was the man, and it is a sign of the impression made that George gave me his name without a request for further specification.

'That's a deuced clever chap,' he said with emphasis, stroking a wearied leg.

'Who is he?' I asked.

'Don't know, – cousin of Urquhart's. Rising man, they say, and I don't wonder. I bet that fellow is at the top before he dies.'

'Is he keen on shooting?' I asked, for it was the usual question.

Not much, George thought. You could never expect a man like that to be good in the same way as fools like himself; they had better things to think about. After all, what were grouse and salmon but vanities, and the killing of them futility? said Mr Winterham, by way of blaspheming his idols.

'I was writing to my sister, Lady Clanroyden, you know,' he went on, 'and I mentioned that a chap of the name of Layden was coming. And here she writes to me to-day and can speak about nothing but the man. She says that the Cravens have taken him up, and that he is going to marry the rich Miss Clavering, and that the Prime Minister said to somebody that he would be dashed if this chap wasn't the best they had. Where the deuce did I leave Mabel's letter?' And George went indoors upon the quest.

Shortly after Layden came out, and soon we all sat watching the dusk gather over miles of spongy moor and vague tangled birchwoods. It is hard for one who is clearly the sole representative of light amid barbarism to escape from a certain seeming of pedantry and a walk aloof and apart. I watched the man carefully, for he fascinated me, and if I had admired his nimble wits at dinner, the more now did I admire his tact. By some cunning art he drove out all trace of superiority from his air; he was the ordinary good fellow, dull, weary like the rest, vastly relishing tobacco, and staring with vacant eyes to the evening.

The last day of my visit to the Forest I have some occasion to remember. It was marked by a display of weather, which I, who am something of a connoisseur in the thing, have never seen approached in this land or elsewhere. The morning had been hazy and damp, with mist over the hill-tops and the air lifeless. But about mid-day a wind came out of the south-west which sent the vapour flying, and left the tops bald and distant. We had been shooting over the Cauldshaw Head, and about five in the afternoon landed on a spur of the Little Muneraw above the tarn which they call the Loch o' the Threshes. Thence one sees a great prospect of wild country, with birchwoods like smoke and sudden rifts which are the glens of streams. On this afternoon the air was cool and fine, the sky a level grey, the water like ink beneath dull-gleaming crags. But the bare details were but a hundredth part of the scene; for over all hung an air of silence, deep, calm, impenetrable, – the quiet distilled of the endless moors, the grey heavens, the primeval desert. It was the incarnate mystery of Life, for in that utter loneliness lay the tale of ages since the world's birth, the song of being and death as uttered by wild living things since the rocks had form. The sight had the glamour of a witch's chant; it cried aloud for recognition, driving from the heart all other loves and fervours, and touching the savage elemental springs of desire.

We sat in scattered places on the hillside, all gazing our fill of the wild prospect, even the keepers, to whom it was a matter of daily repetition. None spoke, for none had the gift of words; only in each mind was the same dumb and unattainable longing. Then Layden began to talk, and

we listened. In another it would have been mere imperti-
nence, for another would have prated and fallen into easy
rhetoric; but this man had the art of speech, and his words
were few and chosen. In a second he was done, but all had
heard and were satisfied; for he had told the old tale of the
tent by the running water and the twin candle-stars in
heaven, of morning and evening under the sky and the
whole lust of the gipsy life. Every man there had seen a
thousandfold more of the very thing he spoke of, had gone
to the heart of savagery, pioneering in the Himalayas,
shooting in the Rockies, or bearing the heat of tropical
sport. And yet this slim townsman, who could not shoot
straight, to whom Scots hills were a revelation of the
immense, and who was in his proper element on a London
pavement, – this man could read the sentiment so that
every hearer's heart went out to answer.

As we went home I saw by his white face that he was
overtired, and he questioned me irritably about the for-
warding of letters. So there and then I prayed Heaven for
the gift of speech, which makes a careless spectator the
interpreter of voiceless passion.

II

Three years later I found myself in England, a bronzed
barbarian fresh from wild life in north Finland, and glad of a
change to the pleasant domesticity of home. It was early
spring, and I drifted to my cousin's house of Heston, after
the aimless fashion of the wanderer returned. Heston is a
pleasant place to stay in at all times, but pleasantest in spring,
for it stands on the last ridge of a Devon moor, whence rolls a
wide land of wood and meadow to a faint blue line of sea.
The hedgerows were already bursting into leaf, and brim-
ming waters slipped through fresh green grasses. All things
were fragrant of homeland and the peace of centuries.

At Heston I met my excellent friend Wratislaw, a
crabbed, cynical, hard-working, and sore-battered man,
whose excursions in high politics had not soothed his
temper. His whole life was a perpetual effort to make
himself understood, and as he had started with somewhat

difficult theories his recognition had been slow. But it was sure; men respected him sincerely if from afar; in his own line he was pre-eminent, and gradually he was drawing to himself the work in a great office of State where difficulty was equally mated with honour.

'Well, you old madman,' he cried, 'where have you been lost all these months? We heard marvellous stories about you, and there was talk of a search-party. So you chose to kill the fatted calf here of all places. I should have gone elsewhere; it will be too much of a show this week.'

'Who are coming?' I groaned resignedly.

'Lawerdale for one,' he answered. I nodded; Lawerdale was a very great man in whom I had no manner of interest. 'Then there are Rogerson, and Lady Afflint and Charlie Erskine.'

'Is that the lot?'

'Wait a moment. Oh, by Jove, I forgot; there's Layden coming, the great Layden.'

'I once met a Layden; I wonder if it's the same man.'

'Probably, – cousin of Urquhart's.'

'But he wasn't commonly called "great" then.'

'You forget, you barbarian, that you've been in the wilderness for years. Reputations have come and gone in that time. Why, Layden is a name to conjure with among most people, – Layden, the brilliant young thinker, orator, and writer, the teacher of the future!' And Wratislaw laughed in his most sardonic fashion.

'Do you know him?' I asked.

'Oh, well enough in a way. He was a year below me at Oxford, – used to talk in the Union a lot, and beat me hollow for President. He was a harebrained creature then, full of ideals and aboriginal conceit; a sort of shaggy Rousseau, who preached a new heaven and a new earth, and was worshipped by a pack of schoolboys. He did well in his way, got his First and some 'Varsity prizes, but the St Chad's people wouldn't have him at any price for their fellowship. He told me it was but another sign of the gulf between the real and the ideal. I thought then that he was a frothy ass, but he has learned manners since, and tact. I suppose there is no doubt about his uncommon cleverness.'

'Do you like him?'

Wratislaw laughed. 'I don't know. You see, he and I belong to different shops, and we haven't a sentiment in common. He would call me dull; I might be tempted to call him windy. It is all a matter of taste.' And he shrugged his broad shoulders and went in to dress.

At dinner I watched the distinguished visitor with interest. That he was very much of a celebrity was obvious at once. He it was to whom the unaccountable pauses in talk were left, and something in his carefully modulated voice, his neatness, his air of entire impregnability, gave him a fascination felt even by so unemotional a man as I. He differed with Lawerdale on a political question, and his attitude of mingled deference and certainty was as engaging to witness as it must have been irritating to encounter. But the event of the meal was his treatment of Lady Afflint, a lady (it is only too well known) who is the hidden reef on which so many a brilliant talker shipwrecks. Her questions give a fatal chance for an easy and unpleasing smartness; she leads her unhappy companion into a morass of 'shop' from which there is no escape, and, worst of all, she has the shrewdness to ask those questions which can only be met by a long explanation and which leave their nervous and short-winded victim the centre of a confusing silence. I have no hesitation in calling Layden's treatment of this estimable woman a miracle of art. Her own devices were returned upon her, until we had the extraordinary experience of seeing Lady Afflint reduced to an aggrieved peace.

But the man's appearance surprised me. There was nothing of the flush of enthusiasm, the ready delight in his own powers, which are supposed to mark the popular idol. His glance seemed wandering and vacant, his face drawn and lined with worry, and his whole figure had the look of a man prematurely ageing. Rogerson, that eminent lawyer, remarked on the fact in his vigorous style. 'Layden has chosen a damned hard profession. I never cared much for the fellow, but I admit he can work. Why, add my work to that of a first-class journalist, and you have an idea of what the man gets through every day of his life. And then think of the amount he does merely for show: the magazine

articles, the lecturing, the occasional political speaking. All
that has got to be kept up as well as his reputation in society.
It would kill me in a week, and, mark my words, he can't
live long at that pitch.'

I saw him no more that night, but every paper I picked up
was full of him. It was 'Mr Layden interviewed' here, and
'Arnold Layden, an Appreciation' there, together with
paragraphs innumerable, and the inscrutable allusions in
his own particular journal. The thing disgusted me, and yet
the remembrance of that worn-out face held me from
condemning him. I am one whose interest lies very little
in the minute problems of human conduct, finding enough
to attract me in the breathing, living world. But here was
something which demanded recognition, and in my own
incapable way I drew his character.

I saw little of him during that week at Heston, for he was
eternally in the train of some woman or other, when he was
not shut up in the library turning out his tale of bricks. With
amazing industry he contrived to pass a considerable
portion of each day in serious labour, and then turned
with weary eyes to the frivolity in which he was currently
supposed to delight. We were the barest acquaintances, a
brief nod, a chance good-morning, being the limits of our
intimacy; indeed, it was a common saying that Layden had
a vast acquaintance, but scarcely a friend.

But on the Sunday I happened to be sitting with Wratislaw on an abrupt furze-clad knoll which looks over the park
to meadow and sea. We had fallen to serious talking, or the
random moralising which does duty for such among most
of us. Wratislaw in his usual jerky fashion was commenting
on the bundle of perplexities which made up his life, when
to us there entered a third in the person of Layden himself.
He had a languid gait, partly assumed no doubt for
purposes of distinction, but partly the result of an almost
incessant physical weariness. But to-day there seemed to be
something more in his manner. His whole face was listless
and dreary; his eyes seemed blank as a stone wall.

As I said before, I scarcely knew him, but he and
Wratislaw were old acquaintances. At any rate he now
ignored me wholly, and flinging himself on the ground

by my companion's side, leaned forward, burying his face in his hands.

'Oh, Tommy, Tommy, old man, I am a hopeless wreck,' he groaned.

'You are overworking, my dear fellow,' said Wratislaw; 'you should hold back a little.'

Layden turned a vacant face toward the speaker. 'Do you think that is all?' he said. 'Why, work never killed a soul. I could work night and day if I were sure of my standing-ground.'

Wratislaw looked at him long and solemnly. Then he took out a pipe and lit it. 'You'd better smoke,' he said. 'I get these fits of the blues sometimes myself, and they go off as suddenly as they come. But I thought you were beyond that sort of thing.'

'Beyond it!' Layden cried. 'If I had had them years ago it might have saved me. When the Devil has designs on a man, be sure that the first thing he does is to make him contented with himself.'

I saw Wratislaw's eyebrows go up. This was strange talk to hear from one of Layden's life.

'I would give the world to be in your place. You have chosen solid work, and you have left yourself leisure to live. And I – oh, I am a sort of ineffectual busy person running about on my little errands and missing everything.'

Wratislaw winced; he disliked all mention of himself, but he detested praise.

'It's many years since I left Oxford; I don't remember how long, and all this time I have been doing nothing. Who is it talks about being "idly busy"? And people have praised me and fooled me till I believed I was living my life decently. It isn't as if I had been slack. My God, I have worked like a nigger, and my reward is wind and smoke! Did you ever have the feeling, Tommy, as if you were without bearings and had to drift with your eyes aching for solid land?'

The other shook his head slowly, and looked like a man in profound discomfort.

'No, of course you never did, and why should you? You made up your mind at once what was worth having in the world and went straight for it. That was a man's part. But I thought a little dazzle of fame was the heavenly light. I liked to be talked about; I wanted the reputation of brilliance, so I utilised every scrap of talent I had and turned it all into show. Every little trivial thought was stored up and used on paper or in talk. I toiled terribly, if you like, but it was a foolish toil, for it left nothing for myself. And now I am bankrupt of ideas. My mind grows emptier year by year, and what little is left is spoiled by the same cursed need for ostentation. "Every man should be lonely at heart"; whoever said that said something terribly true, and the words have been driving me mad for days. All the little that I have must be dragged out to the shop-window, and God knows the barrenness of that back-parlour I call my soul.'

I saw that Wratislaw was looking very solemn, and that his pipe had gone out and had dropped on the ground.

'And what is the result of it all?' Layden went on. 'Oh, I cannot complain. It is nobody's fault but my own; but Lord, what a pretty mess it is!' and he laughed miserably. 'I cannot bear to be alone and face the naked ribs of my mind. A beautiful sight has no charms for me save to revive jaded conventional memories. I have lost all capacity for the plain, strong, simple things of life, just as I am beginning to realise their transcendent worth. I am growing wretchedly mediocre, and I shall go down month by month till I find my own degraded level. But thank God, I do not go with my eyes shut; I know myself for a fool, and for the fool there is no salvation.'

Then Wratislaw rose and stood above him. I had never seen him look so kindly at any one, and for a moment his rough, cynical face was transfigured into something like tenderness. He put his hand on the other's shoulder. 'You are wrong, old man,' he said; 'you are not a fool. But if you had not come to believe yourself one, I should have had doubts of your wisdom. As it is, you will now go on to try the real thing, and then – we shall see.'

III

The real thing, – Heaven knows it is what we are all striving after with various degrees of incompetence. I looked forward to the transformation of this jaded man with an interest not purely of curiosity. His undoubted cleverness, and the habitual melancholy of his eyes, gave him a certain romantic aloofness from common life. Moreover, Wratislaw had come to believe in him, and I trusted his judgment.

I saw no more of the man for weeks, hearing only that his health was wretched and that he had gone for a long holiday to the south. His private income had always been considerable, and his work could very well wait; but his admirers were appalled by the sudden cessation of what had been a marvellous output. I was honestly glad to think of his leisure. I pictured him once more the master of himself, gathering his wits for more worthy toil, and getting rid of the foolish restlessness which had unnerved him. Then came a chance meeting at a railway-station, where he seemed to my hasty eyes more cheerful and well looking; and then my wanderings began again, and London gossip, reputation, and chatter about letters were left a thousand miles behind.

When I returned I had almost forgotten his name; but the air of one's own land is charged with memories, and the past rises on the mind by degrees till it recovers its former world. I found Wratislaw looking older, grimmer, and more irritable, ready to throw books at me for tantalising him with glimpses of an impossible life. He walked me fiercely through Hyde Park, full of abrupt questions as of old, and every ready with his shrewd, humorous comment. Then in my turn, I fell to asking him of people and things, of the whole complication of civilised life from which I had been shut off for years. Some stray resemblance in a passing face struck me, and I asked about Layden.

Wratislaw grunted savagely. 'In a way I am grateful to the man for showing me that I am a fool.'

'Then he has gone back to his old life?' I asked, not without anxiety.

'Listen to me,' he said gruffly. 'His health broke down, as you know, and he went abroad to recover it. He stopped work, dropped out of publicity, and I thought all was well. But the man cannot live without admiration; he must be hovering in its twopenny light like a moth round a candle.

So he came back, and, well, – there was a repetition of the parable of the seven devils. Only he has changed his line. Belles-lettres, society small-talk, everything of that kind has gone overboard. He is by way of being earnest now; he talks of having found a mission in life, and he preaches a new gospel about getting down to the Truth of Things. His trash has enormous influence; when he speaks the place is crowded, and I suppose he is in hopes of becoming a Force. He has transient fits of penitence, for he is clever enough to feel now and then that he is a fool, but I was wrong to think that he could ever change. Well, well, the band-playing for the ruck, but the end of the battle for the strong! He is a mere creature of phrases, and he has got hold of the particular word which pleases his generation. Do you remember our last talk with him at Heston? Well, read that bill.'

He pointed to a large placard across the street. And there in flaming red and black type I read that on a certain day under the auspices of a certain distinguished body Mr Arnold Layden would lecture on The Real Thing.

Comedy in the Full Moon

This story from *Grey Weather* (1899), originally entitled
'A Midsummer Night's Tale' and published in *Chambers
Journal* in December 1898, looks forward to several of
Buchan's novels, including *The Half-Hearted* (1900), *The
Gap in the Curtain* (1932) and *John Macnab* (1925). It
also displays Buchan's fascination with a sacred place –
temenos – here called the Fairy Knowe. In the story he
gently mocks a superstition which revolves around two
people meeting at midsummer under a full moon.

I

'I dislike that man,' said Miss Phyllis, with energy.

'I have liked others better,' said the Earl.

There was silence for a little as they walked up the
laurelled path, which wound by hazel thicket and fir-wood
to the low ridges of moor.

'I call him Charles Surface,' said Miss Phyllis again, with
a meditative air. 'I am no dabbler in the water-colours of
character, but I think I could describe him.'

'Try,' said the Earl.

'Mr Charles Eden,' began the girl, 'is a man of talent. He has
edged his way to fortune by dint of the proper enthusiasms and
a seductive manner. He is a politician of repute and a lawyer of
some practice, but his enemies say that like necessity he knows
no law, and even his friends shrink from insisting upon his
knowledge of politics. But he believes in all honest enthusiasms,
temperance, land reform, and democracy with a capital D; he
is, however, violently opposed to woman suffrage.'

'Every man has his good points,' murmured the Earl.

'You are interrupting me,' said Miss Phyllis, severely.
'To continue, his wife was the daughter of a baronet of

ancient family and scanty means. Her husband supplied the element which she missed in her father's household, and today she is popular and her parties famous. Their house is commonly known as the Wilderness, because there the mixed multitude which came out of Egypt mingle with the chosen people. In character he is persuasive and good-natured; but then good-nature is really a vice which is called a virtue because it only annoys a man's enemies.'

'I am learning a great deal tonight,' said the man.

'You are,' said Miss Phyllis. 'But there, I have done. What I dislike in him is that one feels that he is the sort of man that has always lived in a house and is out of place anywhere but on a pavement.'

'And you call this a sketch in water-colours?'

'No, indeed. In oils,' said the girl, and they walked through a gate on to the short bent grass and the bouldered face of a hill. Something in the place seemed to strike her, for she dropped her voice and spoke simply.

'You know I am town-bred, but I am not urban in nature. I must chatter daily, but every now and then I grow tired of myself, and I hate people like Charles Eden who remind me of my weakness.'

'Life,' said the Earl, 'may be roughly divided into – But there, it is foolish to be splitting up life by hairs on such a night.'

Now they stood on the ridge's crest in the silver-grey light of a midsummer moon. Far up the long Gled valley they looked to the towering hills whence it springs; then to the left, where the sinuous Callowa wound its way beneath green and birk-clad mountains to the larger stream. In such a flood of brightness the far-distant peaks and shoulders stood out clear as day, but full of that hint of subtle and imperishable mystery with which the moon endows the great uplands in the height of summer. The air was still, save for the falling of streams and the twitter of nesting birds.

The girl stared wide-eyed at the scene, and her breath came softly with utter admiration.

'Oh, such a land!' she cried, 'and I have never seen it before. Do you know I would give anything to explore these solitudes, and feel that I had made them mine. Will you take me with you?'

'But these things are not for you, little woman,' he said. 'You are too clever and smart and learned in the minutiae of human conduct. You would never learn their secret. You are too complex for simple, old-world life.'

'Please don't say that,' said Miss Phyllis, with pleading eyes. 'Don't think so hardly of me. I am not all for show.' Then with fresh wonder she looked over the wide landscape.

'Do you know these places?' she asked.

'I have wandered over them for ten years and more,' said the Earl, 'and I am beginning to love them. In other ten, perhaps, I shall have gone some distance on the road to knowledge. The best things in life take time and labour to reach.'

The girl made no answer. She had found a little knoll in the opposite glen, clothed in a tangle of fern and hazels, and she eagerly asked its name.

'The folk here call it the Fairy Knowe,' he said. 'There is a queer story about it. They say that if any two people at midsummer in the full moon walk from the east and west so as to meet at the top, they will find a third there, who will tell them all the future. The old men speak of it carefully, but none believe it.'

'Oh, let us go and try,' said the girl, in glee. 'It is quite early in the evening, and they will never miss us at home.'

'But the others,' said he.

'Oh, the others,' with a gesture of amusement. 'We left Mr Eden talking ideals to your mother, and the other men preparing for billiards. They won't mind.'

'But it's more than half a mile, and you'll be very tired.'

'No, indeed,' said the girl, 'I could walk to the top of the farthest hills tonight. I feel as light as a feather, and I do so want to know the future. It will be such a score to speak to my aunt with the prophetic accent of the things to be.'

'Then come on,' said the Earl, and the two went off through the heather.

II

If you walk into the inn-kitchen at Callowa on a winter night, you will find it all but deserted, save for a chance traveller who is storm-stayed among the uncertain hills. Then men stay in their homes, for the place is little, and the dwellers in the remoter parts have no errand to town or village. But in the long nights of summer, when the moon is up and the hills dry underfoot, there are many folk down of an evening from the glens, and you may chance on men drinking a friendly glass with half a score of miles of journey before them. It is a cheerful scene – the wide room, with the twilight struggling with the new-lit lamp, the brown faces gathered around the table, and the rise and fall of the soft southern talk.

On this night you might have chanced on a special gathering, for it was the evening of the fair-day in Gled-fost, and many shepherds from the moors were eating their suppers and making ready for the road. It was then that Jock Rorison of the Redswirehead – known to all the world as Lang Jock to distinguish him from his cousin little Jock of the Nick o' the Hurlstanes – met his most ancient friend, the tailor of Callowa. They had been at school together, together they had suffered the pains of learning; and now the one's lot was cast at the back of Creation, and the other's in a little dark room in the straggling street of Callowa. A bottle celebrated their meeting, and there and then in the half-light of the gloaming they fell into talk. They spoke of friends and kin, and the toils of life; of village gossip and market prices. Thence they drifted into vague moralisings and muttered exhortation in the odour of whisky. Soon they were amiable beyond their wont, praising each other's merit, and prophesying of good fortune. And then – alas for human nature! – there came the natural transition to argument and reviling.

'I wadna be you, Jock, for a thousand pounds,' said the tailor. 'Na, I wadna venture up that lang mirk glen o' yours for a' the wealth o' the warld.'

'Useless body,' said the shepherd, 'and what for that?'

'Bide a' nicht here,' said the tailor, 'and step on in the mornin'. Man, ye're an auld freend, and I'm wae to think that aucht ill should befa' ye.'

'Will ye no speak sense for yince, ye doited cratur?' was the ungracious answer, as the tall man rose to unhook his staff from the chimney corner. 'I'm for stertin' if I'm to win hame afore mornin'.'

'Weel,' said the tailor, with the choked voice of the maudlin, 'a' I've to say is that I wis the Lord may protect ye, for there's evil lurks i' the dens o' the way, saith the prophet.'

'Stop, John Rorison, stop,' again the tailor groaned. 'O man, bethink ye o' your end.'

'I wis ye wad bethink o' yin yoursel'.'

The tailor heeded not the rudeness . . . 'for ye ken a' the auld queer owercomes about the Gled Water. Yin Thomas the Rhymer made a word on 't. Quoth he,

"By the Gled side
The guid folk bide." '

'Dodsake, Robin, ye're a man o' learnin' wi' your poetry,' said the shepherd, with scorn. 'Rhymin' about auld wives' havers, sic wark for a grown man!'

A vague recollection of wrath rose to the tailor's mind. But he answered with the laborious dignity of argument, –

'I'm no sayin' that a' things are true that the body said. But I say this – that there's a heap o' queer things in the warld, mair nor you nor me nor onybody kens. Now, it's weel ken't that nane o' the folk about here like to gang to the Fairy Knowe . . .'

'It's weel ken't nae siccan thing,' said the shepherd, rudely. 'I wonder at you, a kirk member and an honest man's son, crakin' siccan blethers.'

'I'm affirmin' naething,' said the other, sententiously. 'What I say is that nae man, woman, or child in this parish, which is weel ken't for an intelligent yin, wad like to gang at the rising o' the mune up the side o' the Fairy Knowe. And it's weel ken't, tae, that when the twae daft lads frae the Rochan tried it in my faither's day and gaed up frae opposite airts, they met at the tap that which telled them a' that they ever did and a' that was ever like to befa' them, and put the fear o' death on them for ever and ever. Mind, I'm affirmin' naething; but what think ye o' that?'

'I think this o' 't – that either the folk were mair fou than the Baltic or they were weak i' the heid afore ever they set out. But I'm tired o' hearin' a sensible man bletherin', so I'm awa' to the Redswirehead.'

But the tailor was swollen with pride and romance, and filled with the audacity which comes from glasses replenished.

'Then I'll gang a bit o' the road wi' ye.'

'And what for sae?' said the shepherd, darkly suspicious. Whisky drove care to his head, and made him the most irritable of friends.

'I want the air, and its graund munelicht. Your road gangs by the Knowe, and we micht as weel mak the experiment. Mind ye, I'm affirmin' naething.'

'Will ye no haud your tongue about what ye're affirmin'?'

'But I hold that it is a wise man's pairt to try all things, and whae kens but there micht be some queer sicht on that Knowe-tap? The auld folk were nane sae ready to be inventin' havers.'

'I think the man's mad,' was the shepherd's loud soliloquy. 'You want me to gang and play daft-like pranks late at nicht among birks and stanes on a muckle knowe. Weel, let it be. It lies on my road hame, but ye'd be weel serv't if some auld Druid cam out and grippit ye.'

'Whae's blethering now,' cried the tailor, triumphantly. 'I dinna gang wi' only supersteetions. I gang to get the fresh air and admire the wonderfu' works o' God. Hech, but they're bonny.' And he waved a patronising finger to the moon.

The shepherd took him by the shoulder and marched him down the road. 'Listen,' said he, 'I maun be hame afore the morn, and if ye're comin' wi' me ye'll hae to look smerter.' So down the white path and over Gled bridge they took their way, two argumentative figures, clamouring in the silent, amber spaces of the night.

III

The farmer of the Lowe Moss was a choleric man at all times, but every now and again his temper failed him utterly. He was florid and full-blooded, and the hot weather drove him wild with discomfort. Then came the torments of a dusty market and completed the task; so it fell out that on that evening in June he drove home at a speed which bade fair to hurry him to a premature grave, and ate his supper with little thankfulness.

Then he reflected upon his manifold labours. The next day was the clipping, and the hill sheep would have to be brought down in the early morning. The shepherds would be at the folds by seven, and it would mean rising in the small hours to have the flocks in the low fields in time. Now his own shepherd was gone on an errand and would not be back till the morrow's breakfast. This meant that he, the wearied, the sorely tried, must be up with the lark and tramping the high pastures. The thought was too much for him. He could not face it. There would be no night's rest for his wearied legs, though the Lord knew how he needed it.

But as he looked through the window a thought grew upon his mind. He was tired and sore, but he might yet manage an hour or two of toil, if a sure prospect of rest lay at the end. The moon was up and bright, and he might gather the sheep to the low meadows as easily as in the morning. This would suffer him to sleep in peace to the hour of seven, which was indulgence indeed to one who habitually rose at five. He was a man of imagination and hope, who valued a prospect. Far better, he held, the present discomfort, if the certainty of ease lay before him. So he gathered his aching members, reached for his stick, whistled on his dogs, and set out.

It was a long climb up the ridges of the Lowe Burn to the stell of fir-trees which marked his boundaries. Then began the gathering of the sheep, and a great scurry of dogs, – black dots on the sleepy, moon-lit hill. With much crying of master and barking of dog the flocks were massed and turned athwart the slopes in the direction of the steading. All the while he limped grumblingly behind, thinking on bed, and leaving everything to his shaggy lieutenants. Then they crossed the Lowe Burn, skirted the bog, and came in a little to the lower meadows, while afar off over the rough crest of the Fairy Knowe twinkled the lights of the farm.

Meanwhile from another point of the hill there came another wayfarer to the same goal. The Sentimentalist was a picturesque figure on holiday, enjoying the summer in the way that still remains the best. Three weeks before he had flung the burden of work from his shoulders, and gone with his rod to the Callowa-foot, whence he fished far and near even to the utmost recesses of the hills. On this evening the soft airs and the triumphant moon had brought him out of doors. He had a dim memory of a fragrant hazelled knoll above the rocky Gled, which looked up and down three valleys. The place drew him, as it lived in his memory, and he must needs get his plaid and cross the miles of heather to the wished-for sleeping-place. There he would bide the night and see the sunrise, and haply the next morning make a raid into the near village to receive letters delayed for weeks.

He crossed the hill when the full white glory of the moon was already apparent in the valleys. The air was so still and mild that one might have slept there and then on the bare hillside and been no penny the worse. The heart of the Sentimentalist was cheered, and he scanned the prospect with a glad thankfulness. To think that three weeks ago he had been living in sultriness and dreary over-work, with a head as dazed as a spinning-top and a ruin of nerves. Now every faculty was alive and keen, he had no thought of nerves, and his old Norfolk jacket, torn and easy, now stained with peat-water and now bleached with weather, was an index to his immediate past. In a little it would be all over, and then once more the dust and worry and heat. But meantime he was in fairyland, where there was little need for dreary prognostication.

And in truth it was a fairyland which dawned on his sight at the crest of the hill. A valley filled with hazy light, and in the middle darkly banded by the stream. All things, village, knoll, bog, and coppice, bright with a duskiness which revealed nought in detail, but only hints of form and colour. A noise of distant sheep rose from the sleeping-place, and the single, solitary note of a night-bird far over the glen. At his foot were crushed thickets of little hill-flowers, thyme and pansies and the odorous bog-myrtle.

Beneath him, nor half a mile distant, was a mound with two lone birches on its summit, and he knew the place of his quest. This was the far-famed Fairy Knowe, where at midsummer the little folk danced, and where, so ran the tale, lay the mystic entrance, of which True Thomas spake, to the kingdom of dreams and shadows. Twenty-five miles distant a railway ran, but here there were still simplicity and antique tales. So in a fine spirit he set himself to the tangled meadowland which intervened.

IV

Miss Phyllis looked wonderingly at the tangled, moonlit hill. 'Is this the place?' she asked.

The Earl nodded. 'Do you feel devout, madam,' said he, 'and will you make the experiment?'

Miss Phyllis looked at him gravely. 'Have I not scrambled over miles of bog, and do you think that I have risked my ankles for nothing? Besides I was always a devout believer.'

'Then this is the way of it. You wait here and walk slowly up, while I get to the other side. There is always a wonderful view at least on the top.'

'But I am rather afraid that I . . .'

'Oh, very well,' said the Earl. 'If we don't perform our part, how can we expect a hard-worked goblin to do his?'

'Then,' said Miss Phyllis, with tight lips and a sigh of melodrama, 'lead on, my lord.' And she watched his figure disappear with some misgiving.

For a little she scanned the patched shadow of birk and fern, and listened uneasily to the rustle of grasses. She heard the footsteps cease, and then rise again in the silence. Suddenly it seemed as if the place had come to life. A crackling, the noise of something in lumbering motion, came from every quarter. Then there would be a sound of scampering, and again the echo of heavy breathing. Now Miss Phyllis was not superstitious, and very little of a coward. Moreover, she was a young woman of the world, with a smattering of most things in heaven and earth, and the airs of an infinite experience. But this moonlit knoll, this wide-stretching, fantastic landscape, and the lucid glamour of the night, cast a spell on her, and for once she forgot everything. Miss Phyllis grew undeniably afraid.

She glanced timorously to the left, whence came the sounds, and then with commendable spirit began to climb the slope. If things were so queer she might reasonably carry out the letter of her injunctions, and in any case the Earl would be there to meet her. But the noise grew stranger, the sound of rustling and scrambling and breathing as if in the chase. Then to her amazement a crackle of twigs rose from her right, and as she hastily turned her head to meet the new alarum, she found herself face to face with a tall man in a plaid.

For one moment both stared in frank discomfiture. Miss Phyllis was horribly alarmed and in deepest mystery. But, she began to reflect, spirits have never yet been known to wear Norfolk jackets and knickerbockers, or take the guise of stalwart, brown-faced men. The Sentimentalist, too, after the natural surprise, recovered himself and held out his hand.

'How do you do, Miss Phyllis?' said he.

The girl gasped, and then a light of recognition came into her eyes.

'What are you doing here, Mr Grey?' she asked.

'Surely I have the first right to the question,' the man said, smiling.

'Then, if you must know, I am looking for the customary spirit to tell the future. I thought you were the thing, and was fearfully scared.'

'But who told you that story, Miss Phyllis? I did not think you would have been so credulous. Your part was always the acute critic's.'

'Then you were wrong,' said the girl, with emphasis. 'Besides, it was Charlie Erskine's doing. He brought me here, and is faithfully keeping his compact at the other side of the hill.'

'Well, well, Callowa had always a queer way of entertaining his guests. But there, Miss Phyllis, I have not seen civilisation for weeks, and am half inclined to believe in things myself. Never again shall you taunt me with "boyish enthusiasm". Was not that your phrase?'

'I have sinned,' said the girl, 'but don't talk of it. Henceforth I belong to the sentimentalists. But you must not spoil my plans. I must get to the top and wait devoutly on the *tertium quid*. You can wait here or go round the foot and meet us at the other side. You have made me feel sceptical already.'

'I am at your service, my lady, and I hope you will get good news from the fairy-folk when . . .'

But at this juncture something held the speech and eyes of both. A figure came wildly over the brow of the hill, as if running for dear life, and took the slope in great bounds through brake and bramble and heather-tussock. Onward it came with frantic arms and ineffectual cries. Suddenly it caught sight of the two as they stood at the hill-foot, the girl in white which showed dimly beneath her cloak, and the square figure of the man. It drew itself up in a spasm, stood one moment in uncomprehending terror, and then flung itself whimpering at their feet.

v

The full history of the events of these minutes has yet to be written. But such in the rough outline of the process of disaster.

It appears that the farmer of the Lowe Moss was driving his sheep in comfort with the aid of his collies, and had just crossed the meadowland and come to the edge of the Knowe. He was not more than half a mile from home, and he was wearied utterly. There still remained the maze of tree-roots and heaps of stones known as the Broken Dykes, and here it was hard to drive beasts even in the clear moonlight. So as he looked to the far lights of his home his temper began to break, and he vehemently abused his dogs.

Just at the foot of the slope there is a nick in the dyke, and far on either side stretches the hazel tangle. If once sheep get there it is hard for the best of collies to recover them in short time. But the flock was heading right, narrow in front, marshalled by vigilant four-footed watchmen, with the leaders making straight for the narrow pass. Then suddenly something happened beyond human expectation. In front of the drove the figure of a man arose as if from the ground. It was enough for the wild hill-sheep. To right and left they scattered, flanked in their race by the worn-out dogs, and in two minutes were far and wide among the bushes.

For a moment in the extremity of his disgust the farmer's power of thought and speech forsook him. Then he looked at the cause of all the trouble. He knew the figure for that of a wandering dealer with whom he had long fought bitter warfare. Doubtless the man had come there by night to spy out the nakedness of his flock and report accordingly. In any case he had been warned off the land before, and the farmer had many old grudges against him. The memory of all overtook him at the moment and turned his brain. He rubbed his eyes. No, there could be no mistaking that yellow top-coat and that scraggy figure. So with stick upraised he ran for the intruder.

When the Earl saw the sheep fleeing wide and an irate man rushing toward him, his first impulse was to run. What possible cause could lead a man to drive sheep at night among rough meadows? But the next instant all hope of escape was at an end, for the foe was upon him. He had just time to leap aside and escape a great blow from a stick, and then he found himself in a fierce grapple with a thick-set, murderous ruffian.

Meanwhile the shepherd of the Redswirehead and the tailor of Callowa had left the high-road and tramped over the moss to the Knowe-foot. The tailor's wine-begotten bravery was somewhat lessened by the still spaces of country and the silent eye of night. His companion had no thought in the matter save to get home, and if his way lay over the crest of the Fairy Knowe it mattered little to him. But when they left the high-road it became necessary to separate, if the correct fashion of the thing were to be observed. The shepherd must slacken pace and make for the near side of the hill, while the tailor would hasten to the other, and the twain would meet at the top.

The shepherd had no objection to going slowly. He lit his pipe and marched with measured tread over the bracken-covered meadows. The tailor set out gaily for the farther side, but ere he had gone far his spirits sank. Fairy tales and old wives' fables had still a measure of credence with him, and this was the sort of errand on which he had never before embarked. He was flying straight in the face of all his most cherished traditions in company with a godless shepherd who believed in nothing but his own worthiness. He began to grow nervous and wish that he were safe in the Callowa Inn instead of scrambling on a desert hill. Yet the man had a vestige of pluck which kept him from turning back, and a fragment of the sceptical which gave him hope.

At the Broken Dyke he halted and listened. Some noise came floating over the tangle other than the fitful bleat of sheep or the twitter of birds. He listened again, and there it came, a crashing and swaying, and a confused sound as of a man muttering. Every several hair bristled on his unhappy head, till he reflected that it must be merely a bullock astray among the bushes, and with some perturbation hastened on his way. He fought through the clinging hazels, knee-deep in bracken, and stumbling ever and again over a rock of heather. The excitement of the climb for a moment drove out his terrors, and with purple face and shortened breath he gained the open. And there he was rooted still, for in the middle a desperate fight was being fought by two unearthly combatants.

He had the power left to recognise that both had the semblance of men and the dress of mortals. But never for a moment was he deceived. He knew of tales without end which told of unearthly visitants meeting at midnight on the lone hillside to settle their ghostly feuds. And even as he looked the mantle of one blew apart, and a glimpse of something strange and white appeared beneath. This was sufficient for the tailor. With a gasp he turned to the hill and climbed it like a deer, moaning to himself in his terror. Over the crest he went and down the other slope, flying wildly over little craigs, diving headlong every now and again into tussocks of bent, or struggling in a maze of birches. Then, or ever he knew, he was again among horrors. A woman with a fluttering white robe stood before him, and by her a man of strange appearance and uncanny height. He had no time to think, but his vague impression was of sheeted ghosts and awful terrors. His legs failed, his breath gave out at last, and he was floundering helplessly at Miss Phyllis' feet.

Meantime, as the young man and the girl gazed mutely at this new visitant, there entered from the left another intruder, clad in homespun, with a mighty crook in his hand and a short black pipe between his teeth. He raised his eyes slightly at the vision of the two, but heaven and earth did not contain what might disturb his composure. But at the sight of the prostate tailor he stopped short, and stared. Slowly the thing dawned upon his brain. The sense of the ludicrous, which dwelled far down in his heart, was stirred to liveliness, and with legs apart he woke the echoes in boisterous mirth.

'God, but it's guid,' and he wiped his eyes on his sleeve. 'That man,' and again the humour of the situation shook him, 'that man thocht to frichten me wi' his ghaists and bogles, and look at him!'

The tailor raised his scared eyes to the newcomer. 'Dinna blaspheme, Jock Rorison,' he moaned with solemn unction. 'I hae seen it, the awfu' thing – twae men fechtin' a ghaistly battle, and yin o' them wi' the licht shinin' through his breistbane.'

'Hearken to him,' said the shepherd, jocularly. 'The wicked have digged a pit,' he began with dignity, and then farcically ended with 'and tumbled in 't themsel'.'

But Miss Phyllis thought fit to seek a clue to the mystery.

'Please tell me what is the meaning of all this,' she asked her companion.

'Why, the man has seen Callowa, and fled.'

'But he speaks of two and a "ghaistly combat".'

'Then Callowa with his usual luck has met the spirit of the place and fallen out with him. I think we had better go and see.'

But the tailor only shivered at the thought, till the long shepherd forcibly pulled him to his feet, and dragged his reluctant steps up the side of the hill.

The combat at the back of the knowe had gone on merrily enough till the advent of the tailor. Both were men of muscle, well-matched in height and years, and they wrestled with vigour and skill. The farmer was weary at the start, and his weariness was less fatigue than drowsiness, and as he warmed to his work he felt his strength returning. The Earl knew nothing of the game; he had not wrestled in his youth with strong out-of-door labourers, and his only resources were a vigorous frame and uncommon agility. But as the minutes passed and both breathed hard, the younger man began to feel that he was losing ground. He could scarce stand out against the strain on his arms, and his ankles ached with the weight which pressed on them.

Now it fell out that just as the tailor arrived on the scene the farmer made a mighty effort and all but swung his opponent from his feet. In the wrench that followed, the buttons on the Earl's light overcoat gave way, and to the farmer's astonished gaze an expanse of white shirt-front was displayed. For a second he relaxed his hold, while the other freed himself and leaped back to recover breath.

Slowly it dawned upon the farmer's intelligence that this was no cattle-dealer with whom he contended. Cattle-dealers do not habitually wear evening clothes when they have any work of guile on hand. And then gradually the flushed features before him awoke recognition. The next moment he could have sunk beneath the ground with confusion, for in this nightly marauder who had turned his sheep he saw no other than the figure of his master, the laird of all the countryside.

For a little the power of speech was denied him, and he stared blankly and shamefacedly while the Earl recovered his scattered wits. Then he murmured hoarsely, –

'I hope your lordship will forgi'e me. I never thocht it was yoursel', for I wad dae onything rather than lift up my hand against ye. I thocht it was an ill-daein' dealer frae east the country, whae has cheated me often, and I was vexed at his turnin' the sheep, seein' that I've had a lang day's wander.' Then he stopped, for he was a man of few words and he could go no further in apology.

Then the Earl, who had entered into the fight in a haphazard spirit, without troubling to enquire its cause, put the fitting end to the strained relations. He was convulsed with laughter, deep and overpowering. Little by little the farmer's grieved face relaxed, and he joined in the mirth, till these two made the silent place echo with unwonted sounds.

To them thus engaged entered a company of four, Miss Phyllis, the Sentimentalist, the shepherd, and the tailor. Six astonished human beings stood exchanging scrutinies under the soft moon. With the tailor the mood was still terror, with the shepherd careless amazement, and with the other two unquenchable mirth. For the one recognised the irate, and now apologetic, farmer of the Lowe Moss and the straggling sheep which told a tale to the observant; while both saw in the other of the dishevelled and ruddy combatants the once respectable form of a friend.

Then spoke the farmer:-

'What's ta'en a' the folk? This knowe's like a kirk skailin'. And, dod, there's Jock Rorison. Is this your best road to the Redswirehead, Jock?'

But the shepherd and his friend were speechless for they had recognised their laird, and the whole matter was beyond their understanding.

'Now,' said Miss Phyllis, 'here's a merry meeting. I have seen more wonders tonight than I can quite comprehend. First, there comes Mr Grey from nowhere in particular with a plaid on his shoulders; then a man with a scared face tumbles at our feet; then another comes to look for him; and now here you are, and you seem to have been fighting. These hills of yours are worse than any fairyland, and, do you know, they are rather exhausting.'

Meantime the Earl was solemnly mopping his brow and smiling on the assembly. 'By George,' he muttered, and then his breath failed him and he could only chuckle. He looked at the tailor, and the sight of that care-ridden face again choked him with laughter.

'I think we have all come across too many spirits tonight,' he said, 'and they have been of rather substantial flesh and bone. At least so I found it. Have you learned much about the future, Miss Phyllis?'

The girl looked shyly at her side. 'Mr Grey has been trying to teach me,' said she.

The Earl laughed with great good-nature. 'Midsummer madness,' he said. 'The moon has touched us all.' And he glanced respectfully upward, where the White Huntress urged her course over the steeps of heaven.

The Earlier Affection

Throughout his life Buchan remained fascinated by Bonnie Prince Charlie and the Jacobites. One story, 'The Company of the Marjolaine', is specifically about the Young Pretender and several of his non-fiction books and novels, such as *Midwinter* (1923) touch on the subject. Arthur Townshend, a Cameron, just down from Oxford and a 'scholar gipsy', becomes caught up in the events following the Young Pretender's defeat. The title comes from St Paul in Colossians, 'Set your affection on things above' and the story was first published in *Grey Weather* (1899).

My host accompanied me to the foot of the fine avenue which looks from Portnacroish to the steely sea-loch. The smoke of the clachan was clear in the air, and the morn was sweet with young leaves and fresh salt breezes. For all about us were woods, till the moor dipped to the water, and then came the great shining spaces straight to the edge of Morven and the stony Ardgower Hills.

'You will understand, Mr Townshend,' said my entertainer, 'that I do not fall in with your errand. It is meet that youth should be wild, but you had been better playing your pranks about Oxford than risking your neck on our Hieland hills, and this but two year come Whitsuntide since the late grievous troubles. It had been better to forget your mother and give your Cameron kin the go-by, than run your craig into the same tow as Ewan's by seeking him on Brae Mamore. Stewart though I be, and proud of my name, I would think twice before I set out on such a ploy. It's likely that Ewan will be blithe to see you and no less to get your guineas, but there are easier ways of helping a friend than just to go to his hidy-hole.'

But I would have none of Mr Stewart's arguments, for my heart was hot on this fool's journey. My cousin Ewan was in the heather, with his head well-priced by his enemies and his friends dead or broken. I was little more than a boy let loose from college, and it seemed paradise itself to thus adventure my person among the wilds.

'Then if you will no take an old man's telling, here's a word for you to keep mind of on the road. There are more that have a grudge against the Cameron than King George's soldiers. Be sure there will be pickings going up Lochaber-ways, and all the Glasgow pack-men and low-country trading-bodies that have ever had their knife in Lochiel will be down on the broken house like a pack of kites. It's not impossible that ye may meet a wheen on the road, for I heard news of some going north from the Campbell country, and it bodes ill for any honest gentleman who may foregather with the black clan. Forbye, there'll be them that will come from Glenurchy-side and Breadalbin, so see you keep a quiet tongue and a watchful eye if ye happen on strangers.'

And with this last word I had shaken his hand, turned my horse to the north, and ridden out among the trees.

The sound of sea-water was ever in my ears, for the road twined in the links of coast and crooks of hill, now dipping to the tide's edge, and now rising to a great altitude amid the heather. The morn was so fresh and shining that I fell in love with myself and my errand, and when I turned a corner and saw a wall of blue hill rise gleaming to the heavens with snow-filled corries, I cried out for the fair land I had come to, and my fine adventure.

By the time I came to Duror it was mid-day, and I stopped for refreshment. There is an inn in Duror, where cheese and bread and usquebagh were to be had – fare enough for a hungry traveller. But when I was on the road again, as I turned the crook of hill by the Heugh of Ardsheal, lo! I was in the thick of a party of men.

They were five in all, dressed soberly in black and brown and grey, and riding the soberest of beasts. Mr Stewart's word rose in my memory, and I shut my mouth and composed my face to secrecy. They would not trouble me long, this covey of merchant-folk, for they would get the ferry at Ballachulish, which was not my road to Brae Mamore.

So I gave them a civil greeting, and would have ridden by, had not Fate stepped in my way. My horse shied at a stick by the roadside, and ere I knew I was jostling and scattering them, trying to curb the accursed tricks of my beast.

After this there was nothing for it but to apologise, and what with my hurry and chagrin I was profuse enough. They looked at me with startled eyes, and one had drawn a pistol from his holster, but when they found I was no reiver they took the thing in decent part.

'It's a sma' maitter,' said one with a thick burr in his voice. 'The hert o' a man and the hoofs o' a horse are controlled by nane but our Maker, as my father aye said. Ye're no to blame, young sir.'

I fell into line with the odd man – for they rode in pairs, and in common civility. I could not push on through them. As I rode behind I had leisure to look at my company. All were elderly men, their ages lying perhaps between five and thirty and twoscore, and all rode with the air of townsmen out on a holiday. They talked gravely among themselves, now looking at the sky (which was clouding over, as is the fashion in a Highland April), and now casting inquiring glances towards my place at the back. The man with whom I rode was a little fellow, younger than the rest and more ruddy and frank of face. He was willing to talk, which he did in a very vile Scots accent which I had hard work to follow. His name he said was Macneil, but he knew nothing of the Highlands, for his abode was Paisley. He questioned me of myself with some curiosity.

'Oh, my name is Townshend,' said I, speaking the truth at random, 'and I have come up from England to see if the report of your mountains be true. It is a better way of seeing the world, say I, than to philander through Italy and France. I am a quiet man of modest means with a taste for the picturesque.'

'So, so,' said the little man. 'But I could show you corn-rigs by the Cart side which are better and bonnier than a wheen muckle stony hills. But every man to his taste, and doubtless, since ye're an Englander, ye'll no hae seen mony brae-faces?'

Then he fell to giving me biographies of each of the
travellers, and as we were some way behind the others he
could speak without fear. 'The lang man in the grey coat is
the Deacon o' the Glesca Fleshers, a man o' great substance and good repute. He's lang had trouble wi' thae
Hieland bodies, for when he bocht nowt frae them they wad
seek a loan of maybe mair than the price, and he wad get
caution on some o' their lands and cot-houses. 'Deed,
we're a' in that line, as ye micht say'; and he raked the
horizon with his hand.

'Then ye go north to recover monies?' said I, inadver-
tently.

He looked cunningly into my face, and, for a second,
suspicion was large in his eyes. 'Ye're a gleg yin,
Mr Townds, and maybe our errand is just no that far
frae what ye mean. But, speaking o' the Deacon, he has a
grand-gaun business in the Trongate, and he has been
elder this sax year in the Barony, and him no forty year
auld. Laidly's his name, and nane mair respeckit among
the merchants o' the city. Yon ither man wi' him is a
Maister Graham, whae comes frae the Menteith way, a
kind o' Hielander by bluid, but wi' nae Hieland tricks in
his heid. He's a sober wud-merchant at the Broomielaw,
and he has come up here on a job about some fir-wuds.
Losh, there's a walth o' timmer in this bit,' and he scanned
greedily the shady hills.

'The twae lang red-heided men are Campbells, brithers,
whae deal in yairn and wabs o' a' kind in the Saltmarket.
Gin ye were wantin' the guid hamespun or the fine tartan in
a' the clan colours ye wad be wise to gang there. But I'm
forgetting ye dinna belang to thae pairts ava'.'

By this time the heavens had darkened to a storm and
the great rain-drops were already plashing on my face.
We were now round the ribs of the hill they call Sgor-
dhonuill and close to the edge of the Leven loch. It was a
desolate, wild place, and yet on the very brink of the
shore amid the birk-woods we came on the inn and the
ferry.

I must needs go in with the others, and if the place was
better than certain hostels I had lodged in on my road –

notably in the accursed land of Lorne – it was far short of
the South. And yet I dare not deny the comfort, for there
was a peat-fire glowing on the hearth and the odour of
cooking meat was rich for hungry nostrils. Forbye, the out-
of-doors was now one pour of hail-water, which darkened
the evening to a murky twilight.

The men sat round the glow after supper and there was
no more talk of going further. The loch was a chaos of white
billows, so the ferry was out of the question; and as for me,
who should have been that night on Glen Leven-side, there
was never a thought of stirring in my head, but I fell into a
deep contentment with the warmth and a full meal, and
never cast a look to the blurred window. I had not yet
spoken to the others, but comfort loosened their tongues,
and soon we were all on terms of gossip. They set themselves to find out every point in my career and my intentions, and I, mindful of Mr Stewart's warning, grew as
austere in manner as the Deacon himself.

'And ye say ye traivel to see the world?' said one of the
Campbells. 'Man, ye've little to dae. Ye maunna be thrang
at hame. If I had a son who was a drone like you, he wad
never finger siller o' mine.'

'But I will shortly have a trade,' said I, 'for I shall be
cutting French throats in a year, Mr Campbell, if luck
favours me.'

'Hear to him,' said the grave Campbell. 'He talks of war,
bloody war, as a man wad talk of a penny-wedding. Know
well, young man, that I value a sodger's trade lower than a
flesher-lad's, and have no respect for a bright sword and a
red coat. I am for peace, but when I speak, for battle they
are strong,' said he, finishing with a line from one of his
Psalms.

I sat rebuked, wishing myself well rid of this company.
But I was not to be let alone, for the Deacon would play the
inquisitor on the matter of my family.

'What brought ye here of a' places? There are mony
pairts in the Hielands better worth seeing. Ye'll hae some
freends, belike, hereaways?'

I told him, 'No,' that I had few friends above the
Border; but the persistent man would not be pacified.

He took upon himself, as the elder, to admonish me on the faults of youth.

'Ye are but a lad,' said he with unction, 'and I wad see no ill come to ye. But the Hielands are an unsafe bit, given up to malignants and papists and black cattle. Tak your ways back, and tell your freends to thank the Lord that they see ye again.' And then he broke into a most violent abuse of the whole place, notably the parts of Appin and Lochaber. It was, he said, the last refuge of all that was vicious and wasteful in the land.

'It is at least a place of some beauty,' I broke in with.

'Beauty,' he cried scornfully, 'd'ye see beauty in black rocks and a grummly sea? Gie me the lown fields about Lanerick, and a' the kind canty south country, and I wad let your bens and corries alane.'

And then Graham launched forth in a denunciation of the people. It was strange to hear one who bore his race writ large in his name talk of the inhabitants of these parts as liars and thieves and good-for-nothings. 'What have your Hielands done,' he cried, 'for the well-being of this land? They stir up rebellions wi' papists and the French, and harry the lands o' the god-fearing. They look down on us merchants, and turn up their hungry noses at decent men, as if cheatry were mair gentrice than honest wark. God, I wad have the lot o' them shipped to the Indies and set to earn a decent living.'

I sat still during the torrent, raging at the dull company I had fallen in with, for I was hot with youth and had little admiration for the decencies. Then the Deacon, taking a Bible from his valise, declared his intention of conducting private worship ere we retired to rest. It was a ceremony I had never dreamed of before, and in truth I cannot fancy a stranger. First the company sang a psalm with vast unction and no melody. Then the Deacon read from some prophet or other, and finally we were all on our knees while a Campbell offered up a prayer.

After that there was no thought of sitting longer, for it seemed that it was the rule of these people to make their prayers the last article in the day. They lay and snored in their comfortless beds, while I, who preferred the safety of a chair to the unknown dangers of such bedding, dozed uneasily before the peats till the grey April morning.

Dawn came in with a tempest, and when the household was stirring and we had broken our fast, a storm from the north-west was all but tearing the roof from above our heads. Without, the loch was a chasm of mist and white foam, and waves broke hoarsely over the shore-road. The landlord, who was also the ferryman, ran about, crying the impossibility of travel. No boat could live a moment in that water, and unless our honours would go round the loch-head into Mamore there was nothing for it but to kick our heels in the public.

The merchants conferred darkly among themselves, and there was much shaking of heads. Then the Deacon came up to me with a long face.

'There's nothing for't,' said he, 'but to risk the loch-head and try Wade's road to Fort William. I dinna mind if that was to be your way, Mr Townds, but it maun be ours, for our business winna wait; so if you're so inclined, we'll be glad o' your company.'

Heaven knows I had no further desire for theirs, but I dared not evade. Once in the heart of Brae Mamore I would find means to give them the slip and find the herd's shieling I had been apprised of, where I might get shelter and news of Ewan. I accepted with as cordial a tone as I could muster, and we set out into the blinding weather.

The road runs up the loch by the clachan of Ballachulish, fords the small stream of Coe which runs down from monstrous precipices, and then, winding round the base of the hill they call Pap of Glencoe, comes fairly into Glen Levin. A more desert place I have not seen. On all sides rose scarred and ragged hills; below, the loch gleamed dully like lead; and the howling storm shook the lone fir-trees and dazed our eyes with wrack. The merchants pulled their cloak-capes over their heads and set themselves manfully to the toil, but it was clearly not to their stomach, for they said scarcely a word to themselves or me. Only Macneil kept a good temper, but his words were whistled away into the wind.

All the way along that dreary brae-face we were slipping and stumbling cruelly. The men had poor skill in guiding a horse, for though they were all well-grown fellows they had the look of those who are better used to bare-leg, rough-foot walking than to stirrup and saddle. Once I had to catch the Deacon's rein and pull him up on the path, or without doubt he would soon have been feeding the ravens at the foot of Corrynakeigh. He thanked me with a grumble, and I saw how tight-drawn were his lips and eyebrows. The mist seemed to get into my brain, and I wandered befogged and foolish in this unknown land. It was the most fantastic misery: underfoot wet rock and heather, on all sides grey dripping veils of rain, and no sound to cheer save a hawk's scream or the crying of an old blackcock from the height, while down in the glen-bottom there was the hoarse roaring of torrents.

And then all of a sudden from the darkness there sprang out a gleam of scarlet, and we had stumbled on a party of soldiers. Some twenty in all, they were marching slowly down the valley, and at the sight of us they grew at once alert. We were seized and questioned till they had assured themselves of our credentials. The merchants they let go at once, but I seemed to stick in their throat.

'What are you after, sir, wandering at such a season north of the Highland line?' the captain of them kept asking.

When I told him my tale of seeking the picturesque he would not believe it, till I lost all patience under the treatment.

'Confound it, sir,' I cried, 'is my speech like that of a renegade Scots Jacobite? I thought my English tongue sufficient surety. And if you ask for a better you have but to find some decent military headquarters where they will tell you that Arthur Townshend is gazetted ensign in the King's own regiment and will proceed within six months to service abroad.'

When I had talked him over, the man made an apology of a sort, but he still looked dissatisfied. Then he turned roundly on us. 'Do you know young Fassiefern?' he asked.

My companions disclaimed any knowledge save by repute, and even I had the grace to lie stoutly.

'If I thought you were friends of Ewan Cameron,' said he, 'you should go no further. It's well known that he lies in hiding in these hills, and this day he is to be routed out and sent to the place he deserves. If you meet a dark man of the middle size with two-three ragged Highlanders at his back, you will know that you have foregathered with Ewan Cameron and that King George's men will not be far behind him.'

Then the Deacon unloosed the bands of his tongue and spoke a homily. 'What have I to dae,' he cried, 'with the graceless breed of the Camerons? If I saw this Ewan of Fassiefern on the bent then I wad be as hot to pursue him as any redcoat. Have I no suffered from him and his clan, and wad I no gladly see every yin o' them clapped in the Tolbooth?' And with the word he turned to a Campbell for approval and received a fierce nod of his red head.

'I must let you pass, sirs,' said the captain, 'but if you would keep out of harm's way you will go back to the Levin shore. Ewan's days of freedom are past, and he will be hemmed in by my men here and a like party from Fort William in front, and outflanked on both sides by other companies. I speak to you as honest gentlemen, and I bid you keep a good watch for the Cameron, if you would be in good grace with the King.' And without more ado he bade his men march.

Our company after this meeting was very glum for a mile or two. The Deacon's ire had been roused by the hint of suspicion, and he grumbled to himself till his anger found vent in a free cursing of the whole neighbourhood and its people. 'Deil take them,' he cried, 'and shame that I should say it, but it's a queer bit where an honest man canna gang his ways without a red-coated sodger casting een at him.' And Graham joined his plaint, till the whole gang lamented like a tinker's funeral.

It was now about mid-day, and the weather, if aught, had grown fiercer. The mist was clearing, but blasts of chill snow drove down on our ears, and the strait pass before us was grey with the fall. In front lay the sheer mountains, the tangle of loch and broken rocks where Ewan lay hid, and into the wilderness ran our bridle-path. Somewhere on the hillside were sentries, somewhere on the road before us was a troop of soldiers, and between them my poor cousin was fairly enclosed. I felt a sort of madness in my brain, as I thought of his fate. Here was I in the company of Whig traders, with no power to warn him, but going forward to see his capture.

A desperate thought struck me, and I slipped from my horse and made to rush into the bowels of the glen. Once there I might climb unseen up the pass, and get far enough in advance to warn him of his danger. My seeing him would be the wildest chance, yet I might take it. But as I left the path I caught a tree-root and felt my heels dangle in the void. That way lay sheer precipice. With a quaking heart I pulled myself up, and made my excuse of an accident as best I could to my staring companions.

Yet the whole pass was traversed without a sight of a human being. I watched every moment to see the troop of redcoats with Ewan in their grip. But no redcoats came; only fresh gusts of snow and the same dreary ribs of hill. Soon we had left the pass and were out on a windy neck of mountain where hags and lochans gloomed among the heather.

And then suddenly as if from the earth there sprang up three men. Even in the mist I saw the red Cameron tartan, and my heart leapt to my mouth. Two were great stalwart men, their clothes drenched and ragged, and the rust on their weapons. But the third was clearly the gentleman – of the middle size, slim, dressed well though also in some raggedness. At the sight the six of us stopped short and gazed dumbly at the three on the path.

I rushed forward and gripped my cousin's hand. 'Ewan,' I cried, 'I am your cousin Townshend come north to put his back to yours. Thank God you are still unharmed'; and what with weariness and anxiety I had almost wept on his neck.

At my first step my cousin had raised his pistol, but when he saw my friendliness he put it back in his belt. When he heard of my cousinship his eyes shone with kindliness, and he bade me welcome to his own sorry country. 'My dear cousin,' he said, 'you have found me in a perilous case and ill-fitted to play the host. But I bid you welcome for a most honest gentleman and kinsman to these few acres of heather that are all now left to me.'

And then before the gaping faces of my comrades I stammered out my story. 'Oh, Ewan, there's death before and behind you and on all sides. There's a troop waiting down the road and there are dragoons coming at your back. You cannot escape, and these men with me are Whigs and Glasgow traders, and no friends to the Cameron name.'

The three men straightened themselves like startled deer.

'How many passed you?' cried Ewan.

'May be a score,' said I.

He stopped for a while in deep thought.

'Then there's not above a dozen behind me. There are four of us here, true men, and five who are no. We must go back or forward, for a goat could not climb these craigs. Well-a-day, my cousin, if we had your five whiggishly-inclined gentlemen with us we might yet make a fight for it.' And he bit his lip and looked doubtfully at the company.

'We will fight nane,' said the Deacon. 'We are men o' peace, traivelling to further our lawful calling. Are we to dip our hands in bluid to please a Hieland Jaicobite?' The two Campbells groaned in acquiescence, but I thought I saw a glint of something not peaceful in Graham's eye.

'But ye are Scots folk,' said Ewan, with a soft, wheedling note in his voice. 'Ye will never see a countryman fall into the hands of redcoat English soldiers?'

'It's the law o' the land,' said a Campbell, 'and what for should we resist it to pleesure you? Besides, we are merchants and no fechtin' tinklers.'

I saw Ewan turn his head and look down the road. Far off in the stillness of the grey weather one could hear the sound of feet on the hill-gravel.

'Gentlemen,' he cried, turning to them with a last appeal, 'you see I have no way of escape. You are all proper men, and I beseech you in God's name to help a poor gentleman in his last extremity. If I could win past the gentry in front, there would be the sea-coast straight before, where even now there lies a vessel to take me to a kinder country. I cannot think that loyalty to my clan and kin should be counted an offence in the eyes of honest men. I do not know whether you are Highland or Lowland, but you are at least men, and may God do to you as you do to me this day. Who will stand with me?'

I sprang to his side, and the four of us stood looking down the road, where afar off came into sight the moving shapes of the foe.

Then he turned again to the others, crying out a word in Gaelic. I do not know what it was, but it must have gone to their hearts' core, for the little man Macneil with a sob came running toward us, and Graham took one step forward and then stopped.

I whispered their names in Ewan's ear and he smiled. Again he spoke in Gaelic, and this time Graham could forbear no more, but with an answering word in the same tongue he flung himself from his horse and came to our side. The two red-headed Campbells stared in some perplexity, their eyes bright with emotion and their hands twitching towards their belts.

Meantime the sound of men came nearer and the game grew desperate. Again Ewan cried in Gaelic, and this time it was low entreaty, which to my ignorant ears sounded with great pathos. The men looked at the Deacon and at us, and then with scarlet faces they too dropped to the ground and stepped to our backs.

Out of the mist came a line of dark weather-browned faces and the gleam of bright coats. 'Will you not come?' Ewan cried to the Deacon.

'I will see no blood shed,' said the man, with set lips.

And then there was the sharp word of command, and ere ever I knew, the rattle of shots; and the next moment we were rushing madly down on the enemy.

I have no clear mind of what happened. I know that the first bullet passed through my coat-collar and a second grazed my boot. I heard one of the Highlanders cry out and clap his hand to his ear, and then we were at death-grips. I used my sword as I could, but I had better have had a dirk, for we were wrestling for dear life, and there was no room for fine play. I saw dimly the steel of Ewan and the Highlanders gleam in the rain; I heard Graham roaring like a bull as he caught at the throat of an opponent. And then all was mist and madness and a great horror. I fell over a little brink of rock with a man a-top of me, and there we struggled till I choked the life out of him. After that I remember nothing till I saw the air clear and the road vacant before us.

Two bodies lay on the heath, besides the one I had accounted for in the hollow. The rest of the soldiers had fled down the pass, and Ewan had his way of escape plain to see. But never have I seen such a change in men. My cousin's coat was red and torn, his shoes all but cut from his feet. A little line of blood trickled over his flushed brow, but he never heeded it, for his eyes burned with the glory of battle. So, too, with his followers, save that one had a hole in his ear and the other a broken arm, which they minded as little as midge-bites. But how shall I tell of my companions? The two Campbells sat on the ground nursing wounds, with wild red hair dishevelled and hoarse blasphemy on their lips. Every now and then one would raise his head and cry some fierce word of triumph. Graham had a gash on his cheek, but he was bending his sword-point on the ground and calling Ewan his blood-brother. The little man Macneil, who had fought like a Trojan, was whimpering with excitement, rubbing his eyes, and staring doubtfully at the heavens. But the Deacon, that man of peace – what shall I say of him? He stood some fifty yards down the pass, peering through the mist at the routed fugitives, his naked sword red in his hand, his whole apparel a ruin of blood and mire, his neatly-dressed hair flying like a beldame's. There he stood hurling the maddest oaths. 'Hell!' he cried. 'Come back and I'll learn ye, my lads. Wait on, and I'll thraw every neck and give the gleds a feed this day.'

Ewan came up and embraced me. 'Your Whigamores are the very devil, cousin, and have been the saving of me. But now we are all in the same boat, so we had better improve our time. Come, lads!' he cried, 'is it for the seashore and a kinder land?'

And all except the Deacon cried out in Gaelic the word of consent, which, being interpreted, is 'Lead, and we follow.'

The Black Fishers

When Simon Hay is killed crossing a drystone dyke his two sons are placed in a predicament. Do they go for help and lose money on a pre-arranged financial transaction or continue with their work and come back to recover him later? This sophisticated black comedy, which first appeared in *Grey Weather* (1899), reveals the influence of Maupassant and Ibsen.

Once upon a time, as the story goes, there lived a man in Gledsmuir, called Simon Hay, who had born to him two sons. They were all very proper men, tall, black-avised, formed after the right model of stalwart folk, and by the account of the place in fear of neither God nor devil. He himself had tried many trades before he found the one which suited his talent; but in the various professions of herd, gamekeeper, drover, butcher, and carrier he had not met with the success he deserved. Some makeshift for a conscience is demanded sooner or later in all, and this Simon could not supply. So he flitted from one to the other with decent haste, till his sons came to manhood and settled the matter for themselves. Henceforth all three lived by their wits in defiance of the law, snaring game, poaching salmon, and working evil over the green earth. Hard drinkers and quick fighters, all men knew them and loved them not. But with it all they kept up a tincture of reputability, foreseeing their best interest. Ostensibly their trade was the modest one of the small crofter, and their occasional attendance at the kirk kept within bounds the verdict of an uncensorious parish.

It chanced that in spring, when the streams come down steely-blue and lipping over their brims, there came the most halcyon weather that ever man heard of. The air was mild as June, the nights soft and clear, and winter fled hotfoot in dismay. Then these three girded themselves and went to the salmon-poaching in the long shining pools of the Callowa in the haughlands below the Dun Craigs. The place was far enough and yet not too far from the town, so that an active walker could go there, have four hours' fishing, and return, all well within the confines of the dark.

On this night their sport was good, and soon the sacks were filled with glittering backs. Then, being drowsy from many nights out o' bed, they bethought them of returning. It would be well to get some hours of sleep before the morning, for they must be up betimes to dispose of their fish. The hardship of such pursuits lies not in the toil but the fate which hardens expediency into necessity.

At the strath which leads from the Callowa vale to Gled they halted. By crossing the ridge of hill they would save three good miles and find a less frequented path. The argument was irresistible; without delay they left the high-way and struck over the bent and heather. The road was rough, but they were near its end, and a serene glow of conscious labour began to steal over their minds.

Near the summit is a drystone dyke which girdles the breast of the hill. It was a hard task to cross with a great load of fish, even for the young men. The father, a man of corpulent humours and maturing years, was nigh choked with his burden. He mounted slowly and painfully on the loose stones, and prepared to jump. But his foothold was insecure, and a stone slipped from its place. Then something terrible followed. The sack swung round from his neck, and brought him headlong to the ground. When the sons ran forward he was dead as a herring, with a broken neck.

The two men stood staring at one another in hopeless bewilderment. Here was something new in their experi-ence, a disturbing element in their plans. They had just the atom of affection for the fellow-worker to make them feel the practical loss acutely. If they went for help to the nearest town, time would be lost and the salmon wasted; and indeed, it was not unlikely that some grave suspicion would attach to their honourable selves.

They held a hurried debate. At first they took refuge in mutual recriminations and well-worn regrets. They felt that

some such sentiments were due to the modicum of respect-
ability in their reputations. But their minds were too practical
to linger long in such barren ground. It was demanded by
common feeling of decency that they should have their
father's body taken home. But were there any grounds for
such feeling? None. It could not matter much to their father,
who was the only one really concerned, whether he was
removed early or late. On the other hand, they had trysted
to meet a man seven miles down the water at five in the
morning. Should he be disappointed? Money was money; it
was a hard world, where one had to work for beer and skittles;
death was a misfortune, but not exactly a deterrent. So
picking up the old man's sack, they set out on their errand.

It chanced that the shepherd of the Lowe Moss returned
late that night from a neighbour's house, and in crossing
the march dyke came on the body. He was much shocked
for he recognised it well as the mortal remains of one who
had once been a friend. The shepherd was a dull man and
had been drinking; so as the subject was beyond his special
domain he dismissed its consideration till some more
convenient season. He did not trouble to inquire into
causes – there were better heads than his for the work –
but set out with all speed for the town.

The Procurator-fiscal had been sitting up late reading in
the works of M. de Maupassant, when he was aroused by a
constable, who told him that a shepherd had come from the
Callowa with news that a man lay dead at the back of a
dyke. The Procurator-fiscal rose with much grumbling,
and wrapped himself up for the night errand. Really, he
reflected with Hedda Gabler, people should not do these
things nowadays. But, once without, his feelings changed.
The clear high space of the sky and the whistling airs of
night were strange and beautiful to a town-bred man. The
round hills and grey whispering river touched his poetic
soul. He began to feel some pride in his vocation.

When he came to the spot he was just in the mood for
high sentiment. The sight gave him a shudder. The full-
blown face ashen with the grip of death jarred on his finer
sensibilities. He remembered to have read of just such a

thing in the works of M. Guy. He felt a spice of anger at fate and her cruel ways.

'How sad!' he said; 'this old man, still hale and fit to enjoy life, goes out into the hills to visit a friend. On returning he falls in with those accursed dykes of yours; there is a slip in the darkness, a cry, and then – he can taste of life no more. Ah, Fate, to men how bitter a task-mistress,' he quoted with a far-off classical reminiscence.

The constable said nothing. He knew Simon Hay well, and guessed shrewdly how he had come by his death, but he kept his own counsel. He did not like to disturb fine sentiment, being a philosopher in a small way.

The two fishers met their man and did their business all in the most pleasant fashion. On their way they had discussed their father's demise. It would interfere little with their profits, for of late he had grown less strong and more exacting. Also, since death must come to all, it was better that it should have taken their father unawares. Otherwise he might have seen fit to make trouble about the cottage which was his, and which he had talked of leaving else-where. On the whole, the night's events were good; it only remained to account for them.

It was with some considerable trepidation that they returned to the town in the soft spring dawning. As they entered, one or two people looked out and pointed to them, and nodded significantly to one another. The two men grew hotly uncomfortable. Could it be possible? No. All must have happened as they expected. Even now they would be bringing their father home. His finding would prove the manner of his death. Their only task was to give some reason for its possibility.

At the bridge-end a man came out and stood before them.

'Stop,' he cried. 'Tam and Andra Hay, prepare to hear bad news. Your auld faither was fund this morning on the back o' Callowa hill wi' a broken neck. It's a sair affliction. Try and thole it like men.'

The two grew pale and faltering. 'My auld faither,' said the chorus. 'Oh ye dinna mean it. Say it's no true. I canna believe it, and him aye sae guid to us. What'll we dae wi'oot him?'

'Bear up, my poor fellows,' and the minister laid a hand on the shoulder of one. 'The Lord gave and the Lord has taken away.' He had a talent for inappropriate quotation.

But for the two there was no comfort. With dazed eyes and drawn faces, they asked every detail, fervently, feverishly. Then with faltering voices they told of how their father had gone the night before to the Harehope shepherd's, who was his cousin, and proposed returning in the morn. They bemoaned their remissness, they bewailed his kindness; and then, attended by condoling friends, these stricken men went down the street, accepting sympathy in every public.

Summer Weather

This tale of possession from *Grey Weather* (1899) looks forward to Buchan's story 'The Green Wilde-beeste'. John Dean becomes so annoyed with his sheep-collie that he kills the dog, an act that comes back to haunt him.

In a certain year the prices of sheep at Gledsmuir sank so low that the hearts of the farmers were troubled; and one – he of Clachlands – sought at once to retrieve his fortunes and accepted an understudy. This was the son of a neighbouring laird, a certain John Anthony Dean, who by way of preparing himself for the possession of a great moorland estate thought it well to learn something of the life of the place. He was an amiable and idyllic young man, whom I once had the pleasure of knowing well. His interest was centred upon the composition of elegant verses, and all that savoured of the poetic was endeared to his soul. Therefore he had long admired the shepherd's life from afar; the word 'pastoral' conjured up a fragrant old-time world; so in a mood pleasantly sentimental he embarked upon the unknown. I need not describe his attainments as sheep-farmer or shepherd; he scarcely learned the barest rudiments; and the sage master of Clachlands trusted him only when he wrought under his own vigilant eye. Most of his friends had already labelled him a good-natured fool, and on the whole I do not feel ready to dispute the verdict. But that on one occasion he was not a fool, that once at least Mr John Anthony Dean rose out of his little world into the air of the heroic, this tale is written to show.

It was a warm afternoon in late June, and, his dog running at heel, he went leisurely forth to the long brown ridges of moor. The whole valley lay sweltering in torrid heat; even there, on the crest of a ridge, there was little coolness. The hills shimmered blue and indeterminate through the haze, and the waters of a little loch not a mile away seemed part of the colourless benty upland. He was dressed in light flannels and reasonable shoes – vastly unlike the professional home-spuns and hob-nailed boots; but even he felt the airless drought and the flinty, dusty earth underfoot, and moderated his pace accordingly.

He was in a highly cheerful frame of mind, and tranquil enjoyment shone in his guileless face. On this afternoon certain cousins were walking over from his father's lodge to visit him at his labours. He contemplated gaily the prospect of showing them this upland Arcady, himself its high-priest and guardian. Of all times afternoon was the season when its charm was most dominant, when the mellow light lay on the far lines of mountain, and the streams were golden and russet in the pools. Then was the hour when ancient peace filled all the land, and the bleat of sheep and the calling of birds were but parts of a primeval silence. Even this dried-up noon-day moor had the charm of an elder poetry. The hot smell of earth, the glare of the sun from the rocks, were all incidents in pastoral. Even thus, he mused, must the shepherds of Theocritus have lived in that land of downs where the sun-burnt cicala hummed under the brown grass.

Some two miles from home he came to the edge of a shallow dale in whose midst a line of baked pebbles and tepid pools broke the monotonous grey. The heat was overpowering, and a vague longing for cool woods and waters stole into his mind. But the thought that this would but add to the tan of his complexion gave him comfort. He pictured the scene of his meeting with his frends; how he would confront them as the bronzed and seasoned uplander with an indescribable glamour of the poetic in his air. He was the man who lived with nature amid the endless moors, who carried always with him the romance of the inexplicable and the remote.

Such pleasing thoughts were roughly broken in on by the sight of his dog. It was a finely-bred sheep-collie, a prizetaker, and not the least costly part of his equipment. Already once in that burning summer the animal had gone into convulsions and come out of them weak and foolish. Now it lay stiffened in exactly the same way, its tongue lolling feebly, and flecks of white on its parched jaw. His sensibilities were affected, and he turned from the pitiable sight.

When he looked again it was creeping after him with tail between legs and its coat damp with sweat. Then at the crossing of a gate he missed the sound of it and looked back. There it lay again, this time more rigid than before, apparently not far from the extremities of death. His face grew grave, for he had come to like the creature and he would regret its loss.

But even as he looked the scene changed utterly. The stiffness relaxed, and before he knew the dog was on its feet and coming towards him. He rubbed his eyes with sheer amazement; for the thing looked like an incarnate devil. Its eyes glowered like coals, and its red cavern of a mouth was lined with a sickening froth. Twice its teeth met with a horrid snap as it rushed straight for him at an incredible swiftness. His mind was all but numbed, but some instinct warned him against suffering the beast to cut him off from home. The far dyke was the nearer, but he chose to make rather for the one he had already crossed. By a hairbreadth he managed to elude the rush and let the thing pass, – then with a very white face and a beating heart he ran for his life.

By a kind chance the thing had run many yards ere it saw his flight. Then it turned and with great leaps like a greyhound made after him. He heard it turn, heard every bound, with the distinctness of uttermost fear. His terror was lest it should gain on him unknown, and overpower him before he had chance to strike. Now he was almost at the dyke; he glanced round, saw the thing not five yards from him, and waited. The great scarlet jaws seemed to rise in the air before him, and with all his power he brought his thick crook down full athwart them. There was something dead and unearthly about these mad jaws; he seemed to be striking lifeless yet murderous flesh, and even as his stick crashed on the teeth his heart was sick with loathing. But he had won his end; for a second the brute fell back, and he leaped on the dyke.

It was a place built of loose moor stones, and on one larger than the rest he took his stand. He dare not trust a further chase; here he must weary the thing out, or miserably perish. Meantime it was rising again, its eyes two blazing pools of fire. Two yards forward it dragged itself, then sprang clear at his throat. He struck with all his might, but the blow missed its forehead, and, hitting the gums, sufficed only to turn it slightly aside, so that it fell on the wall two feet on his left. He lashed at it with frenzied strength, till groaning miserably it rolled off and lay panting on the turf.

The sun blazed straight on his bare head (for he had lost his cap in the chase), and sweat blinded his eyes. He felt ill, giddy, and hopelessly sick of heart. He had seen nothing of madness before in man or animal; the thing was an awful mystery, a voiceless, incredible horror. What not two hours before had been a friendly, sensible collie now lay blinking at him with devouring eyes and jaws where foam was beginning to be dyed with blood. He calculated mechanically on each jump, and as the beast neared him his stick fell with stiff, nerveless force. To tell the truth, the man was numb with terror; his impulse was to sink to the ground; had death faced him in any form less repulsive than this assuredly he would not have striven against it.

It is a weak figure of speech to say that to him each minute seemed of an hour's length. He had no clear sense of time at all. His one sensation was an overmastering horror which directed his aim almost without his knowledge. Three times the thing leaped on him; three times he struck, and it slipped with claws grating on the stone. Then it turned and raced round a circle of heather, with its head between its forepaws like a runaway horse. The man dropped on his knees to rest, looking intently at the circling speck, now far away, now not a dozen yards distant. He vainly hoped that it would tire or leave him; vainly, for of a sudden it made for the wall and he had barely time to get to his feet before it was upon him. This time he struck it down without difficulty, for it was somewhat exhausted; but he noted with new terror that instead of leaping and falling back with open jaws, its teeth had shut with a snap as it neared him. Henceforth he must ward more closely, or the teeth might graze his flesh.

But his strength was failing, and the accursed brute seemed to grow more active and incessant. His knees ached with the attitude, and his arm still trembled with utter fear. From what he told me himself, and from the known hours of his starting and returning, he must have remained not less than two hours perched on that scorching dyke. It is probable that the heat made him somewhat light-headed and that his feet shuffled on the granite. At any rate as the thing came on him with new force he felt the whole fabric crumble beneath him, and the next second was sprawling on his back amid a ruin of stones.

He was aware of a black body hurling on the top of him as he struck feebly in the air. For a moment of agony he waited to be torn, feeling himself beyond resistance. But no savage teeth touched him, and slowly and painfully he raised his head. To his amazement he saw the dog tearing across the moorland in the direction of home.

He was conscious at once of relief, safety, a sort of weak, hysterical joy. Then his delight ceased abruptly, and he scrambled to his feet with all haste. The thing was clearly running for the farm-town, and there in the stack-yard labourers were busied with building hay-ricks, – the result of a premature summer. In the yard women would be going to and fro, and some of the Clachlands children playing. What if the mad brute should find its way thither! There could be no issue but the most dismal tragedy.

Now Mr John Anthony Dean was, speaking generally, a fool, but for one short afternoon he proved himself something more. For he turned and ran at his utmost speed after the fleeing dog. His legs were cramped and tottering, he was weak with fear, and his head was giddy with the sun; but he strained every muscle as if he ran for his own life and not for the life of others. His wind was poor at the best, and soon he was panting miserably, with a parched throat and aching chest; but with set teeth he kept up the chase, seeing only a black dot vanishing across the green moorland.

By some strange freak of madness the brute stopped for a second, looked round and waited. Its pursuer was all but helpless, labouring many yards behind; and had it attacked, it could have met little resistance. The man's heart leaped to his mouth, but – and to his glory I tell it – he never slackened pace. The thing suffered him to approach it, he had already conjured up the awful prospect of that final struggle, when by another freak it turned and set off once more for home.

To me it seems a miracle that under that blazing sun he ever reached the farm; but the fact remains that when the dog three minutes later dashed into an empty yard, the man followed some seconds behind it. By the grace of God the place was void; only a stray hen cackled in the summer stillness. Without swerving an inch it ran for the stable and entered the open door. With a last effort the man came up on its heels, shut the bolt, and left it secure.

He scarcely felt that his toil was ended, so painful was his bodily exhaustion. He had never been a strong man in the common sense, and now his heart seemed bursting, his temples throbbed with pain, and all the earth seemed to dance topsy-turvy. But an unknown hardiness of will seemed to drive him on to see this tragic business to an end. It was his part to shoot the dog there and then, to put himself out of anxiety and the world out of danger. So he staggered to the house, found it deserted, – one and all being busy in the stack-yard, – took down the gun from above the mantelpiece, and, slipping a cartridge in each barrel, hurried out with shambling legs.

He looked in through the stable-window, but no dog was there. Cautiously he opened the door, and peered into the blackness of the stalls, but he could see nothing; then, lifting his eyes by chance to the other window, he saw a sash in fragments and the marks of a sudden leap. With a wild horror he realised that the dog was gone.

He rushed to the hill-road, but the place was vacant of life. Then with a desperate surmise he ran to the path which led to the highway. At first he saw nothing, so unsettled was his vision; then something grew upon his sight, – a black object moving swiftly amid the white dust.

There was but one course for him. He summoned his
strength for a hopeless effort, and set off down the long
dazzling roadway in mad pursuit. By this path his cousins
were coming; even now the brute might be on them, and in
one moment of horror he saw the lady to whom he was
devoted the prey of this nameless thing of dread. At this
point he lost all control of his nerves; tears of weakness and
terror ran over his face; but still he ran as fast as his failing
strength suffered – faster, for an overmastering fear put a
false speed into his limbs and a deceptive ease in his breast.
He cried aloud that the beast might turn on him, for he felt
that in any case his duration was but a thing of seconds. But
he cried in vain, for the thing heeded him not but vanished
into the wood, as he rounded the turn of hill.

Half-way down the descent is a place shaded with thick
trees, cool, green, and mossy, a hermitage from the fiercest
sun. The grass is like a shorn lawn, and a little stream
tinkles in a bed of grey stones. Into this cold dell the man
passed from the glare without, and the shock refreshed him.
This, as it chanced, was his salvation. He increased his
speed, still crying hoarsely the animal's name. When he
came once more into the white dust the brute was not fifty
yards from him, and as he yelled more desperately, it
stopped, turned, saw him, and rushed back to the attack.

He fell on his knees from extreme weakness, and waited
with his gun quivering at shoulder. Now it raked the high
heavens, now it was pointed to the distant hills. His hand
shook like a child's, and in his blindness he crushed the
stock almost against his throat. Up the highway meantime
came those ravening jaws, nearer and ever nearer. Like a
flash the whole picture of the future lay before him, –
himself torn and dying, the wild thing leaving him and
keeping its old course till it met his friends, and then – more
horror and death. And all hung on two cartridges and his
uncertain aim.

His nervousness made him draw the trigger when the
brute was still many yards away. The shot went clear over
its head to spend itself in the empty air. In desperation he
nuzzled the stock below his chin, holding it tight till he was
all but choked, and waited blindly. The thing loomed up

before him in proportions almost gigantic; it seemed to leap to and fro, and blot out the summer heavens. He knew he was crazy; he knew, too, that life was in the balance, and that a random aim would mean a short passage to another world. Two glaring eyes shone out of the black mass, the centre, as it were, of its revolutions. With all his strength he drew the point to them and fired. Suddenly the fire seemed to go out, and the twin lights were darkened.

When the party of pretty young women in summer raiment came up the path a minute later, they saw something dark in the mid-road, and on coming nearer found that it was their cousin. But he presented a strange appearance, for in place of the elegant, bronzed young man they knew, they found a broken-down creature with a bleeding throat and a ghastly face, sitting clutching a gun and weeping hysterically beside a hideous, eyeless dog with a shattered jaw which lay dead on the ground.

Such is the tale of Mr John Anthony Dean and his doings on that afternoon of summer. Yet it must be told – and for human nature's sake I regret it – that his sudden flash into the heroic worked no appreciable difference on his ways. He fled the hill country that very month, and during the next winter published a book of very minor poetry (dedicated to his cousin, Miss Phyllis), which contained an execrable rondeau on his adventure, with the refrain – 'From Canine Jaws', wherein the author likened the dog to Cerberus, himself to 'strong Amphitryon's son', and wound up with grateful thanksgiving to the 'Muse' for his rescue. As I said before, it is not my business to apologise for Mr Dean; but it is my privilege to note this proof of the heroic inconsistency of man.

The Oasis in the Snow

Another tale from *Grey Weather* (1899) about possession and *temenos*, here the oasis in the snow.

This tale was told to me by the shepherd of Callowa, when I sheltered once in his house against an April snowstorm – for he who would fish Gled in spring must fear neither wind nor weather. The shepherd was a man of great height, with the slow, swinging gait, the bent carriage, the honest eyes, and the weather-tanned face which are the marks of his class. He talked little, for life is too lonely or too serious in these uplands for idle conversation; but when once his tongue was loosened, under the influence of friendship or drink, he could speak as I have heard few men ever talk, for his mind was a storehouse of forty years' experience, the harvest of an eye shrewd and observant. This story he told me as we sat by the fire, and looked forth every now and then drearily on the weather.

They crack about snaw-storms nowadays, and ken naucht about them. Maybe there's a wee pickle driftin' and a road blockit, and there's a great cry about the terrible storm. But, lord, if they had kenned o' the storms I've kenned o' they would speak a wee thing mair serious and respectfu'. And bodies come here i' the simmer and gang daft about the bonny green hills, as they ca' them, and think life here sae quate and peacefu', as if the folk here had nocht to dae but daunder roond their hills and follow their wark as trig and easy as if they were i' the holms o' Clyde and no i' the muirs o' Gled. But they dinna ken, and weel for them, how cauld and hungry and cruel are the hills, how easy a man gangs to his death i' thae braw glens, how the wind stings i' the morn and the frost bites at nicht, o' the bogs and sklidders and dreich hillsides, where there's life neither for man nor beast.

Weel, about this story, it was yince in a Februar' mony year syne that it a' happened, when I was younger and lichter on my feet and mair gleg i' the seein'.

Ye mind Doctor Crichton – he's deid thae ten 'ear, but he was a braw doctor in his time. He could cure when anither was helpless, and the man didna leeve whae wad ride further on less errand.

Now the doctor was terrible keen on fishin' and shootin' and a' manner o' sport. I've heard him say that there were three things he likit weel abune ithers. Yin was the back o' a guid horse, anither a guid water and a clear wast wind, and the third a snawy day and a shot at the white hares. He had been crakin' on me for mony a day to gang wi' him, but I was thrang that 'ear wi' cairtin' up hay for the sheep frae lower doon the glens and couldna dae't. But this day I had trystit to gang wi' him, for there had been a hard frost a' the week, and the hares on the hills wad be in graund fettle. Ye ken the way o' the thing. Yae man keeps yae side o' the hill and the ither the ither, and the beasts gang atween them, back and forrit. Whiles ye'll see them pop round the back o' a dyke and aff again afore ye can get a shot. It's no easy wark, for the skins o' the craturs are ill to tell frae the snawy grund, and a man taks to hae a gleg ee afore he can pick them oot, and a quick hand ere he can shoot. But the doctor was rale skilfu' at it and verra proud, so we set aff brisk-like wi' our guns.

It was snawin' lichtly when we startit, and ere we had gone far it begood to snaw mair. And the air was terrible keen, and cut like a scythe-blade. We were weel wrappit up and walkit a' our pith, but our fingers were soon like to come off, and it was nane sae easy to handle the gun. We tried the Wildshaw Hichts first, and got nane there, though we beat up and doon, and were near smoored wi' snaw i' the gullies. I didna half like the look o' things, for it wasna canny that there should be nae hares, and, forbye, the air was gettin' like a rusty saw to the face. But the doctor wad hear naething o' turnin' back, for he had plenty o' speerit, had the man, and said if we didna get hares on yae hill we wad get them on the ither.

At that time ye'll mind that I had twae dowgs, baith guid but verra contrar' in natur'. There was yin ca'ed Tweed, a fine, canty sort o' beast, very freendly to the bairns, and gien to followin' me to kirk and things o' that sort. But he was nae guid for the shootin', for he was mortal feared at the sound o' a gun, and wad rin hame as he were shot. The ither I ca'ed Voltaire, because he was terrible against releegion. On Sabbath day about kirk-time he gaed aff to the hills, and never lookit near the hoose till I cam back. But he was a guid sheep dowg and, forbye, he was broken till the gun, and verra near as guid 's a retriever. He wadna miss a day's shootin' for the warld, and mony a day he's gane wi'oot his meat ower the heid o't. Weel, on this day he had startit wi' us and said nae words about it; but noo he began to fa' ahint, and I saw fine he didna like the business. I kenned the dowg never did onything wi'oot a guid reason, and that he was no easy to fricht, so I began to feel uneasy. I stopped for a meenute to try him, and pretended I was gaun to turn hame. He cam rinnin' up and barkit about my legs as pleased as ye like, and when I turned again he looked awfu' dowie.

I pointed this oot to the doctor, but he paid nae attention. 'Tut, tut,' says he, 'if ye're gaun to heed a dowg's havers, we micht gie a' thing up at yince.'

'It's nae havers,' I said, hot-like, for I didna like to hear my dowg misca'ed. 'There's mair sense in that beast than what's in a heap o' men's heids.'

'Weel, weel,' he says, 'sae let it be. But I'm gaun on, and ye can come or no, just as ye like.'

'Doctor,' says I again, 'ye dinna ken the risk ye're rinnin'. I'm a better juidge o' the wather than you, and I tell ye that I'm feared at this day. Ye see that the air is as cauld 's steel, and yet there's mist a' in front o' ye and ahint. Ye ken the auld owercome, "Rouk is snaw's wraith," and if we dinna see a fearsome snaw afore this day's dune, I'll own my time's been wastit.'

But naething wad move him, and I had to follow him for fair shame. Sune after, too, we startit some hares, and though we didna get ony, it set the excitement o' the sport on us. I sune got as keen as himsel', and sae we trampit on, gettin' farther intil the hills wi' every step, and thinkin' naething about the snaw.

We tried the Gledscleuch and got naething, and syne we gaed on to the Allercleuch, and no anither beast did we see. Then we struck straucht for the Cauldhope Loch, which lies weel hoddit in hills miles frae ony man. But there we cam nae better speed, for a' we saw was the frozen loch and the dowie threshes and snaw, snaw everywhere, lyin' and fa'in'. The day had grown waur, and still that dour man wadna turn back. 'Come on,' says he, 'the drift's clearin', and in a wee we'll be on clear grund'; and he steppit oot as he were on the laigh road. The air wasna half as cauld, but thick just like a nicht in hairst; and though there wasna muckle snaw fa'in' yet, it felt as though there were miles o' 't abune in the cluds and pressin' doun to the yirth. Forbye, it was terrible sair walkin', for though the snaw on the grund wasna deep, it was thick and cloggin'. So on we gaed, the yin o' us in high fettle, the ither no verra carin', till we cam to the herd's shielin' o' the Lanely Bield, whilk lies in the very centre o' the hills, whaur I had never been afore.

We chappit at the door and they took us in. The herd was a dacent man, yin Simon Trumbull, and I had seen him aften at kirk and market. So he bade us welcome, and telled us to get our claes dried, for we wadna gang anither step that nicht. Syne his wife made us tea, and it helpit us michtily, for we had drank a' our whisky lang syne. They had a great fire roarin' up the lum, and I was sweired, I can tell ye, to gang oot o' the warm place again into the ill wather.

But I must needs be aff if I was to be hame that nicht, and keep my wife from gaun oot o' her mind. So I gets up and buttons to my coat.

'Losh, man,' says the herd, 'ye're never thinkin' o' leavin'. It'll be the awfu'est nicht that ever man heard tell o'. I've herdit thae hills this mony 'ear, and I never saw sic tokens o' death i' the air. I've my sheep fauldit lang syne, and my hoose weel stockit, or I wadna bide here wi' an easy hert.'

'A' the mair need that I should gang,' says I, 'me that has naething dune. Ye ken fine my wife. She wad die wi' fricht, if I didna come hame.'

Simon went to the door and opened it. It blew back on the wa', and a solid mass o' snaw fell on the floor. 'See that,' he says. 'If ye dinna believe me, believe your ain een. Ye need never think o' seein' Callowa the nicht.'

'See it or no,' said I, 'I'll hae to try 't. Ye'd better bide, doctor; there's nae cause for you to come wi' me.'

'I'll gang wi' you,' he said. 'I brocht ye intil this, and I'll see ye oot o't.' And I never liked the man sae weel as at the word.

When the twae o' us walkit frae that hoose it was like walkin' intil a drift o' snaw. The air was sae thick that we couldna richt see the separate flakes. It was just a great solid mass sinkin' ever doun, and as heavy as a thousand ton o' leid. The breath went frae me at the verra outset. Something clappit on my chest, and I had nocht to dae but warstle on wi' nae mair fushion than a kittlin'. I had a grip o' the doctor's hand, and muckle we needit it, for we wad sune hae been separate and never mair heard o'. My dowg Voltaire, whae was gien for ordinar' to rinnin' wide and playin' himsel', kept close rubbin' against my heels. We were miles frae hame, and unless the thing cleared there was sma' chance o' us winnin' there. Yae guid thing, there was little wind, but just a saft, even fa'; so it wasna so bad as though it had been a fierce driftin'. I had a general kind o' glimmer o' the road, though I had never been in thae hills afore. If we held doun by the Lanely Bield Burn we wad come to the tap o' the Stark Water, whilk cam into Gled no a mile abune Callowa. So on we warstled, prayin' and greetin' like bairns, wi' scarce a thocht o' what we were daein'.

'Whaur are we?' says the doctor in a wee, and his voice sounded as though he had a naipkin roond his mouth.

'I think we should be somewhere near the Stark heid,' said I. 'We're gaun doun, and there's nae burn hereaways but it.'

'But I aye thocht the Stark Glen was a' sklidders at the heid,' said he; 'and this is as saft a slope as a hoose riggin'.'

'I canna help that,' says I. 'It maun e'en be it, or we've clean missed the airt.'

So on we gaed again, and the snaw aye got deeper. It wasna awfu' saft, so we didna sink far as we walkit, but it was terrible wearin'. I sune was sae tired that I could scarce drag mysel'; forbye being frichtit oot o' my senses. But the doctor was still stoot and hopefu', and I just followed him.

Suddenly, ere ever we kenned, the slope ceased, and we were walkin' on flat grund. I could scarce believe my een, but there it was at my feet, as laigh as a kitchen floor. But the queer thing was that while a' around was deep snaw, this place was a' but bare, and here and there rigs o' green land stuck oot.

'What in the warld's this?' says I, as I steppit oot boldly, and I turned to my companion. When I saw him I was fair astonished. For his face was white as the snaw, and he was tremblin' to his fingers.

'Ye're no feared, are ye?' I asked. 'D' ye no ken guid land when ye see 't?'

His teeth were chattering in his heid. 'You hae na sense to be feared. The Almichty help us, but I believe we're daein' what nae man ever did afore.'

I never saw sae queer a place. The great wecht o' snaw was still fa'in' on us, but it seemed to disappear when it cam to the grund. And our feet when we steppit aye sank a wee bit, but no in snaw. The feel i' the air wasna cauld, but if onything 't was het and damp. The sweat began to rin doon aff my broo, and I could hear the man ahint me pantin' like a broken-winded horse. I lookit roond me for the dowg, but nae dowg was to be seen; for at the first step we took on the queer land he had ta'en himsel' aff. I didna like the look o't, for it wad hae ta'en muckle to drive the beast frae my side.

Every now and then we cam on a wee hillock whaur the snaw lay deeper, but the spaces atween were black and saft, and crunkled aneath the feet. Ye ken i' the spring about the burn-heids how the water rins oot o' the grund, and a' the colour o' the place is a sodden grey. Weel, 't was the same here. There was a seepin', dreepin' feel i' the grund whilk made it awesome to the eye. Had I been i' my clear senses, I wad hae been rale puzzled about the maitter, but I was donnered wi' the drifts and the weariness, and thocht only o' gettin' by 't. But sune a kind o' terror o' the thing took me. Every time my feet touched the grund, as I walkit, a groo gae'd through my body. I grat wi' the fair hate o' the

place, and when I lookit at my neebor it didna mak me
better. For there he was gaun along shakin' like a tree-tap,
and as white 's a clout. It made it waur that the snaw was sae
thick i' the air that we couldna see a foot in front. It was like
walkin' blindfold roond the tap o' a linn.

Then a' of a sudden the bare grund stopped, and we were
flounderin' among deep drifts up to the middle. And yet it
was a relief, and my hert was strengthened. By this time I
had clean lost coont o' the road, but we keepit aye to the
laigh land, whiles dippin' intil a glen and whiles warstlin' up
a brae face. I had learned frae mony days in hill mists to
keep frae gaun roond about. We focht our way like fair
deevils, for the terror o' the place ahint had grippit us like a
vice. We ne'er spak a word, but wrocht till our herts were
like to burst and our een felt fou o' bluid. It got caulder and
caulder, and thicker and ever thicker. Hope had lang syne
gane frae us, and fricht had ta'en its place. It was just a
maitter o' keepin' up till we fell down, and then . . .

It wasna lang ere they fund us, for find us they did, by
God's grace and the help o' the dowg. For the beast went
hame and made sic a steer that my wife roused the nearest
neebor and got folk startit oot to seek us. And wad ye
believe it, the dowg took them to the verra bit. They fund
the doctor last, and he lay in his bed for a month and mair
wi' the effects. But for mysel', I was nane the waur. When
they took me hame, I was put to bed, and sleepit on for
twenty hoor, as if I had been streikit oot. They waukened
me every six hoor, and put a spoonfu' o' brandy doon my
throat, and when a' was feenished, I rase as weel as ever.

It was about fower months after that I had to gang ower
to Annandale wi' sheep, and cam back by the hills. It was a
road I had never been afore, and I think it was the wildest
that ever man trod. I mind it was a warm, bricht day, verra
het and wearisome for the walkin'. Bye and bye I cam to a
place I seemed to ken, though I had never been there to my
mind, and I thocht hoo I could hae seen it afore. Then I
mindit that it was abune the heid o' the Stark, and though
the snaw had been in my een when I last saw it, I minded
the lie o' the land and the saft slope. I turned verra keen to

ken what the place was whaur me and the doctor had had sic a fricht. So I went oot o' my way, and climbed yae hill and gaed doun anither, till I cam to a wee rig, and lookit doun on the verra bit.

I just lookit yince, and then turned awa' wi' my hert i' my mooth.

For there below was a great green bog, oozing and blinking in the sun.

Gideon Scott

This story was recently discovered in Buchan's private
papers in the National Library of Scotland. As he travels
to Edinburgh, Gideon Scott, landlord of the Crook Inn,
is held up by a highwayman, a man he discovers he has
met before.

If anyone should travel up the pleasant valley of Tweed from
Peebles, some distance up on the right hand bank of the river
he would see a green spur on the side of a dark heath-clad hill.
And if he were inclined to examine it further, he would find on
the summit the ruins of what was once a castle. Across the
river, among the trees, he would see a grey ivy-covered wall.
These few stones are all that remain of two famous castles, the
abode of a still more remarkable family. The Tweedies of
Tinnis and Drumelzier were one of the oldest families in
Scotland. They derived their name and origin from the
genius, or water spirit of Tweed. For centuries they lorded
over the whole district of Upper Tweeddale. But in more
civilised times, like many other noble families, they got into
debt, and in the beginning of the seventeenth century we find
the last of the clan in a debtors' prison in Edinburgh. The
estates passed into other hands, and the place where once they
were now knows them no more.

I

One of these spring days in which winter had completely
got the predominance of summer was merging into darkness and the light of day was gradually leaving the kitchen
of the Crook Inn to make way for the more cheerful light of
the fire. The Crook Inn, as all travellers between Edinburgh

and Dumfries know, is situated on the top of the high bank
of the Tweed, a few miles below its junction with the Talla.
It was the haunt of all the drovers who came from the south
to the Scottish fairs, and every other day the mail coach
stopped to change horses. Now and then a shepherd or a
farmer dropped in or a belated traveller in that stormy
region. On this particular night several shepherds from the
hills, a sprinkling of drovers and two men, who by their
dress appeared to be travelling chapmen, thronged around
the ample fireplace in the inn kitchen. The great black oak
rafters were plentifully adorned with smoked hams,
shoulders of beef and white hares, as beseemed the season
of the year. One of the shepherds got up and opened the
door. A great blast blew in with a few raindrops.

'What kind o' nicht is it, shepherd?' said one of the
packmen.

'Nae nicht for me to get back to the Hopehead in,' was
the surly answer. The great black clouds were coming thick
over the sky, while on the horizon a grey vapour was slowly
arising. The hills looked near and black. The roar of the
Tweed, swollen high by recent rains, came up above the
noise of the wind. The shepherd slammed the door, let
down the bar which closed it, and returned once more to
his seat at the fire.

'There's nae lack o' wet weather in the air,' said he. 'There'll
be nae crossing Tweed the nicht, and less the morn. It's a guid
thing Biggar fair is past, and I have my stock sell't.'

'It will be a bad look out for us,' said one of the drovers,
'we'll never see Dumfries this week.'

'It's a providence for me,' said the landlord of the inn,
Gideon Scott by name, a big burly man of about forty, with
a shrewd, quiet face, 'it's a clear godsend that I havena' to
go to Edinburgh this month. Ye ken I have to go in every
month in the way of business. But who should be going in
this week but Jamie Hislop my wife's brother, so he got my
commission, and, being a man of his word, I can lippen to
him. It's an awful time this to travel in. Just in this week last
year the coach fell over the Blyth Bridge and killed two
passengers. And the driver of the mail told me that there is a
tale of terrible robberies in the Lothians, and even hinted

that the Dumfries coach hersel wasna over safe. Lord preserve Jamie Hislop and my commission.'

By this time the candles had been brought in and set down on the high oak dressser. At this period the shepherd of Kingledores rose to go, and a tall dark man, who stood by the fireplace and was evidently a shepherd, rose to follow him. The latter man was by far the most striking-looking in the company. He was dressed in rough home-spuns, marked here and there with spots of tar and tufts of wool from his recent operations with sheep at Biggar fair. His face was tanned brown with the weather but there was a certain nobility, not so often found among shepherds, in his clear cut features and proud bearing. He must have been considerably over six feet high, and his brawny legs, broad shoulders, and muscular arms showed that he possessed great bodily strength. As he rose to go he picked up his stout horn-handled stick and whistled on his dog which was lying below the table.

'Yeddie, Yeddie,' cried the host in astonishment, 'guid-sakes, man, you're no going to try to get to Talla the nicht. No mortal man could get halfway.'

'Psa, what's a blast o' rain to me, Gidden, it's no' the first time I been out in it.'

'Sit down, ye loon,' said the host angrily, 'I'll let no man go away frae my hoose the nicht. It wisna' half sic an ill nicht last Martinmas when Tam Laidlaw, the herd of Stanhope, was drowned trying to cross the ford down there. Ye ken the bridge was washed away wi' the last flood and ye'll never ford the river when it is like this.'

'It maun be done,' said Yeddie, as without another word he wrapped his plaid around his shoulders and went out into the night.

'An obstinate mule if ever there was one,' said the land-lord. 'Aweel, he'll wish he had taen my advice when he finds himself in the Black Linn.' Supper, which two centuries ago was taken at a much earlier hour than in our times, was now set on the table. The company took their seats before viands which were admirably adapted to satisfy hungry men – a salmon from the Tweed, a piece of black-faced mutton from the hills, and a large bowl of porridge, which stood at one end of the table and from which platefuls were ladled out to each man. When the supper was finished, a large china bowl, a number of glasses and a silver ladle were brought in and the landlord proceeded to brew a bowl of toddy. It was served round to the guests and, as their glasses were replenished pretty frequently, their spirits became somewhat exuberant. One of the packmen entered upon a lengthy tale, stopping every now and then to laugh loudly at some joke, which the company invariably failed to appreciate. As a diversion a drover sang a bacchanalian song very popular in that part of the country, and the rest took up the chorus, which emphatically declared that they had hitherto trusted to Providence and would still continue to do it. Then a draught board was produced and one of the shepherds and the sober packman played a game. The other drovers produced a dirty pack of cards and began to play for money. The rest of the shepherds, who cared for none of these things, sat down round the fire with the host and discussed the prices of sheep and the prospects of the weather. Gideon had been somewhat gloomy all the evening. He had failed to enter heartily into the mirth at the supper table, and had talked to his guests with the air of a man performing a disagreeable duty. Now he broke in upon the conversation with an abrupt question:

'What in the world made Yeddie tak' the road for Talla the nicht?'

'I'm sure I dinna ken, Gidden,' said one of the shepherds who hailed from Moffat Water, 'he's a queer body, is Yeddie, but when once he's set his heart on onything, I'd like to see the man that wad stop him.'

'There's ower mony o' his kind in the country the noo, and we could weel be rid o' half o' them. Restless, peppery chiels, wha canna bide to hear a word against them. I saw a better man hang't in the Grass-market afore I left Edinburgh.'

'I am no caring what he is, but I wish he hadna' tried the Tweed the nicht.'

There was silence for a while, broken only by the crackling of the wood in the fire and the howling of the storm outside. Then came a gust of wind stronger than the rest and with a crash the door was blown open. Up jumped

Gideon to shut the door, while the candles were almost blown out by the violence of the blast.

'Guidsakes, come and look at the water!' roared the astonished landlord.

One or two shepherds came, the rest being either too drunk or too busy to attend. They looked out from the door porch and a wonderful sight met their eyes. The Tweed had burst the barriers of its banks and was bearing down the valley a wilderness of swirling yellow water. The roar was like that of the North Sea in the winter storms. Trunks of trees and broken fragments of wooden bridges floated on the surface. Far down the glen a line of white foam marked where the river plunged over the Black Linn. The air was almost free from rain, but the murky blackness in the southern sky told of a terrible rainfall further up the stream. Broad Law on the other side of the river was almost wholly enveloped in mist, the which stood out in peculiar contrast to the blackness of the moorlands beneath. They looked on for a few minutes in silence, then Gideon went into the kitchen again. He took down his bonnet from a peg, wrapped a plaid round his shoulders and took a large ash stick which stood in the corner. He then put a flask of brandy in his pocket and rejoined his comrades at the door.

'I'm going doon to the ford to see if I can see onything o' Yeddie. Will ony o' ye come with me?'

Two shepherds, Wat Fletcher from Drumelzier and Robert Senton of Fruid, went out with him. Down the rough hillside they went for a few paces and then turned down the valley for about half a mile, gradually approaching nearer the river till they came to where a small cart track led down to the water's edge. Here was the ford, though on this night, ford there was none. A small rowan tree marked where the road began on the other side. Between them and this tree lay many yards of brown, unpassable water.

'If Yeddie tried the ford, he was drowned,' said Gideon in a mournful tone. For a considerable time they waited there scanning the stream and shouting the name of the lost shepherd. Then they began sadly to go away when a dog's barking came on their ear. They listened and waited. Again it was heard further down the river.

'I could swear onywhere that that was Maisie's bark,' said Fletcher.

'If that's Yeddie's dog, Yeddie's no' far off,' said Rob Senton. Quickly, with Gideon in front, they rushed down the bank of the Tweed, guided by the barking of the dog. They were now close upon that terrible fall, known all over the district as the Black Linn. The waters of the Tweed rush into a narrow channel, with high precipitous rocks on both sides. Then the river dashes over a linn some thirty feet high, into a deep black pool, from which the fall gets its name. The pool is thickly fringed with hazel and rowan trees, many bending far over the water. On the banks they found a small collie, black and tan in colour, rushing up and down the grass, barking wildly. When it saw the three men, it immediately made for them and, crouching at their feet, whined and moaned in the most piteous manner. Then it sprang up again and rushed along the bank, every now and then looking back to see that it was followed. At last it reached a gap in the trees above where the river made a turn. An old oak, knotted and gnarled with very age ran out into the water, bending its boughs close to the stream. Here the collie stopped and with one long-drawn howl attempted to crawl along a bough of the oak. Gideon caught it by the tail and swung it back, for he had caught a glimpse of something at the end of the branch which moved him to rapid action. The current had washed down a large wooden plank, probably from some ruined bridge, against an arm of the oak. Wedged in between the tree and the plank, with his legs in the water, was the unconscious form of Yeddie. Knowing that there was not a moment to lose, since at any moment the stream might wash away the plank, Gideon flung off his plaid, and prepared to crawl along the bough. Slowly and painfully he made his way, with the wood creaking at every movement. Sometimes he lost his footing and clutched the branch to save himself. Sometimes a larger wave than usual washed over his legs. At last he was within reach, and was able to grip the shepherd's coat. But now a new difficulty faced him. He could not re-cross the branch with such a burden in his arms. There was no alternative but to leap into the flood and carry Yeddie with him. The tide was running hard, but he saw that it would carry him close to the bank which a strong man might catch. With a cry to the men to run for the turning he clutched Yeddie more tightly and slipped off the branch. The water surged over his head and he felt as if he would never rise again. But up he came and struck out boldly. The weight of his burden was a sad hindrance to him; without it he felt that he might have saved himself. Once more he sank and once more he rose. The bank loomed black before, and he saw that now was his chance or never. With one great effort he clutched a tree root which projected, and felt himself being washed in towards the side: then two pairs of strong hands gripped him and he and his burden were lifted into safety.

Gideon was soon restored to himself by a mouthful of brandy, and then he turned to the man he had rescued. To bring him back to consciousness was a much more difficult task. He had abandoned the idea of crossing at the ford and attempted the river below the linn, where the breadth is not so great but that a strong man might leap over it. The attempt had failed and he had been carried down by the current. His head had been badly cut by a sharp rock and after being borne along for about a hundred yards he had been caught by the tree. Here, weak with fatigue and the loss of blood, he had been exposed for more than three hours with the water dashing over him.

At first, the treatment of Gideon and his men had no effect. But, after a time, through vigorous rubbing and repeated doses of brandy, their patient showed signs of consciousness. Then he opened his eyes and recovered so far as to be able to speak and thank his preservers. Weak and faint he was conveyed to the inn by the strong arms of the three men and there put to bed. But Yeddie was blessed with an iron constitution, and, though the night's adventures might have killed most men, they had little or no effect on him. In a week his cut was almost healed and he was able to proceed to his house at Talla.

II

The springtime had passed into the summer and the time of the long, hot days had come, when Gideon Scott made preparations for his journey to Edinburgh. This was always a great event to the household at the moorland inn. The night before the appointed day few of the inmates got any sleep, for the coach passed at three o'clock in the morning. On this occasion Gideon's journey was more important than usual, for he had to receive a sum of money which was owing him from a cattle dealer in Edinburgh, and had also resolved to buy an additional horse, on which he might make his journey home. Accordingly, early on Tuesday morning, when the fleecy mist had not yet lifted from the hilltops, and the sun was beginning to make himself seen over the hills of Kingledores, Gideon stood on the doorstep of the Crook Inn, accoutred for his journey. He had not waited long, when the lumbering, crazy old coach came round the turn of the hill, and drew up at the inn door. Gideon hoisted himself into it along with what little luggage he had, and soon was carried out of sight of his home. With what transpired till he reached Edinburgh we have little to do. Suffice it to say that he had an uneventful journey, unattended by any of the usual accidents which befell the unhappy coach; that he transacted his business in Edinburgh, bought his horse, and set out on his return journey. His purchase, which was a fine brown mare, had been warranted by Jock Scott, his cousin from whom he had bought it, to be able to outrun any animal in the Lothians. Gideon took his road through the village of Liberton and thence out into the pleasant valley of the Esk. Ere nightfall he arrived at Leadburn, where he put up for the night. Next morning he remembered an old friend of his who lived at Bordlands, whom he resolved to visit. Accordingly, he pushed on, and about midday arrived at Bordlands. His friend was of a sociable character, and prevailed upon him to stay longer than his better judgment required. Thus it came about that it was nearly six o'clock when he left Bordlands with the intention of reaching Broughton that night.

All went well until he passed through the little village of Kirkurd, and reached the wild moorland, which extends without a human dwelling to the village of Broughton, twelve miles away. Gideon rode on for a considerable distance until he became aware of three men riding at right angles to the highway. Whether it was the influence of the farmer of Bordlands' ale or not, I do not know, but Gideon instantly conceived the idea that these men intended to block the road. They might be highwaymen or they might not but he had heard of daring attacks lately and he had a large sum of money in his pocket, so he clapped spurs to his horse and rode at full speed along the highway. Now the three horsemen did a still more suspicious thing; they directed their horses for a point in the road where it made a sharp turn. Gideon felt that if he did not get to this place first he was a lost man, for he dare not trust himself to the bogs on the side of the road. He knew that his mare could hold her own on the highway, so he strained every nerve to get the lead. She responded gallantly to his calls, everything seemed to dance before Gideon's eyes; he saw only the white spot which marked where the bend was, and the black forms of his pursuers. Now to his joy he saw that he was gaining ground; the three horsemen saw this also and endeavoured with might and main to recover it. At last the turn was reached and with one great bound the mare swept round it with the three men about twelve yards behind her. Then began a race grim and long. The horses of the highwaymen though inferior in quality to Gideon's mare were very much fresher. The road from this point leads in an almost straight line down the valley of a small stream to the village of Broughton. It was now about nine o'clock and the dusk was creeping up the sky. Gideon felt faint and giddy; the landscape swam before his eyes, he dared not look behind him but he knew his pursuers were near. He wondered that no shot had been fired, but he concluded that they had no firearms. Now he could see the lights of Broughton twinkling through the gathering gloom six miles ahead. New courage grew up within him. He stood up in his stirrups and coaxed and patted his mare. She made one gallant effort more and gained other ten yards. Then she fell back again to her old pace. But now the highwaymen made a fresh effort also and Gideon felt with a sickening sense of terror that they were gaining on him. On and on they swept, gaining at every step. Now he could feel their horses' breath on the back of his neck. One more gallant effort the mare made, and increased the distance between them by a few yards. But it was her last; her breath came up in great pants; the gallop was changed to a canter, the canter to a trot, and the trot to a walk. Then, with a rush, the three horsemen dashed past the terror-stricken Gideon and caught his mare's bridle. The unhappy man gave himself up for lost, and thought woefully of the fate of his money, when an extraordinary thing happened. As soon as the leader cast his eyes on Gideon's face,

'Stand back,' he roared in a voice of thunder, 'and let him past.'

The highwaymen wheeled their horses round and galloped away, leaving the astonished Gideon to proceed on his way in safety. But by the dim light that remained, he had recognised in the leader of the three the saturnine features of Yeddie.

III

Gideon, one afternoon in the month of October, might be seen mounting his mare in the courtyard of the Cross Keys Inn at Peebles. He had come down from the hills for the autumn fair; for Gideon was a versatile man in his way, and in addition to his occupation of inn-keeper, he was a small sheep farmer. The day was one of those fine clear autumn days, with just a touch of frost in the air. As he rode along through the pleasant woods of Neidpath, his heart was glad within him, and he felt at peace with all men, that is with the exception of Robin the drover who had cheated him out of thirty pounds, at the last fair, at Biggar. Gideon was one of these men who remember an injury for about two months, and then forget it entirely. At first he had thought he would have liked to kill Robin, now he simply wished to make him pay back. On this special afternoon the air was the air of spring, and had it not been for the withered leaves one might have thought it March. Gideon crossed the bridge over the Lyne Water, then but newly erected, and remembered how he had to swim his horse over the stream the last time he came this road. Then he rode along through the rich meadows which make the valley of the Tweed at this point like a nobleman's estate. One would hardly have thought it the same river here gliding slowly through among high reeds and between banks as smooth as a lawn, as that which half a dozen miles further up tumbles and rushes among desolate brown moors, and rocky hills. About five o'clock in the afternoon he bethought himself that he was thirsty, and being near the little village of Stobo, he resolved to pay a visit to the inn and taste its ale. He alighted from his horse at the inn door and marched in and called loudly for the master, Sandilands. The master appeared, a tall stout man, renowned in his younger days for his feats at hammer throwing.

'Well, Gidden, how have ye come't on at Peebles?'

'Very weel, very weel, Jamie, considering the folk that were there,' said Gideon.

'Are ye bidin' here a' nicht? Come awa' in, come awa' in,' said the host.

'No, no man, I just want a glass o' ale; I've to be at the Crook the nicht.'

'Ye should hae been sooner on the road then, Gidden.'

Gideon looked out at the gathering dusk and reflected that the landlord's observation was true.

'What in the world's that noise, Jamie? I thocht ye kept a quieter hoose.'

'It's a party o' dragoons frae Embro', Gidden. I wish folk like them came oftener. It would be a blessing for this inn. Lord save us, but they've drunk an awfu' quantity o' yale the day.'

'What do ye think they're here for, lad? I've heard o' naething lately.'

'Oh, they winna tell that. But there's something brewing up the muirs, that we'll hear tell o' afore long.' The ale had meantime been brought, and Gideon quenched his thirst.

'Well, guid day, Jamie. I maun off, if I've to get to the Crook the nicht.'

He mounted his horse and rode slowly down the village street. He crossed the bridge of Tweed and turned up the river. No sooner had he got out of sight of the village than he changed his slow walk into a gallop. The mention of soldiers had brought the name of Yeddie before his mind. Since his adventure on the Edinburgh road, he had heard little about Yeddie. He kept the events of that night a profound secret, but on making enquiries in a way which would excite no suspicion he found that Yeddie was but little at home. Moreover he had heard of great robberies in the Lothians and Clydesdale, and from the descriptions which he got of the chief actors in them he had but little doubt that Yeddie was one. Now when he heard of the dragoons' expedition into so remote a part of the country, he instinctively guessed that they had traced him nearer home. With that thought a resolution was formed in his mind. He would get the start of them and warn their victims. How to do it he did not know but he had an idea that if he once got up into the moors he would meet Yeddie. There was only one road up the river and at this time of the year, in a wild part of the country the dragoons would likely keep to it. There is no analysing the motives of some men. What could induce a sober respectable man like Gideon to strain every nerve and even risk his own life to shield a notorious highwayman, is a mystery. But in the most prosaic of men there is always some strain of the romantic. Here in this sober inn-keeper, the Border strain derived from his reiving ancestors, the tendency to defend any breaker of the law at the risk of his own neck, comes out.

The night was now getting darker, and he was some four miles up the water from Stobo. Still he had not met a soul, not even a shepherd or a ploughman, everything was as quiet as a Sabbath morning.

In a little while he saw a great dark mass looming before him, which he knew was the spur of the hill on which Tinnis castle stands, formerly the home of the Tweedies. Here the road for the Crook left the main path, so here Gideon came to a standstill. Perhaps the soldiers had no thought of Yeddie. Perhaps they meant to go to Broughton or

Biggar; or perhaps their expectations were wrong, and the object of their pursuit was not there. At any rate he would go home, he couldn't do anything more. Just then far down the valley he heard the sound of horses' feet; 'these were the soldiers,' thought he, he would wait for them and watch them pass before he went home. Up the brown hillside along the rocky pathway he directed his horse's steps, till he came to a small plateau from which he could command a full view of the valley. Here he dismounted from his mare and let her graze while he himself sat down on a boulder close by. From the road they could not have been distinguished from boulders, although on account of the moonlight they could see up and down the valley almost to Stobo. The night grew chilly, and Gideon began to feel cold perched up on that hillside. He remembered that he had left his plaid at Stobo, and he called himself a fool for his madcap haste.

From his watch-tower he saw the soldiers moving like snails along the road. 'Ah,' thought Gideon, 'they are near somebody, they are going cautiously.' Now they were not half a mile distant but still they kept at the same slow pace. Sometimes when the mind of a man is most intent upon anything, some trivial thing or other comes in and distracts his attention. Gideon happened to look up at the sky and there he saw a flock of birds flying, which he knew by their flight to be wild geese. Then he fell to wondering why so few wild geese had come to the moors this year. He remembered the sport he had had in his younger days, stalking these same birds in the marshy ground beside the Tweed at three o'clock on a frosty winter morning. He remembered the peculiar cry with which they rose; but at this point his ornithological memories were rudely interrupted by a gunshot from the valley. Up he sprang and looked down; he saw a confused mass of men standing in different attitudes on the road; another man fleeing on foot towards Stobo, and another man on horseback galloping up in the opposite direction. Gideon's attention was divided between watching this man and soothing his horse, now terrified by the number of shots. He saw several men ride in pursuit of him; then the fugitive's riding began to get peculiar; he swayed backwards in his saddle, and finally dropped off at the point where the mountain path left the main road while his horse galloped on. 'He kens the path,' said Gideon to himself, 'he'll be up here in five minutes.' He watched the pursuers ride after the riderless horse and then looked down among the brackens through which the footway ran. For some minutes he saw and heard nothing except the cries of troopers, and the sound of their horses' feet. Then he heard the brackens in front of him rustle and Yeddie's head and shoulders emerged from among them. The look of fear which crossed his face when he saw a man, was immediately changed to one of joy as he recognised Gideon.

The latter bent over and grasped his arms and pulled him up beside him. The thin stream of blood which trickled down from below Yeddie's left shoulder, together with his slow and painful breathing, showed that he was badly wounded.

'O, Gidden,' he gasped, 'we saw ye pass and let ye go on. But, fules that we were, we took the dragoons for drovers, and – I doubt they've done for me.'

'Na, na, Yeddie, I'll get ye off yet. But ye see the end your ill doings hae brocht ye to. Man, man, could ye no hae bidden at hame, instead of ridin' and reivin' ower a' the country?'

A groan from the wounded man was the only answer.

'I'll no preach to ye my puir lad; ye're punished enuch.'

By this time the soldiers had discovered the ruse and were retracing their steps. Gideon felt that there was no time to be lost. Carefully he placed Yeddie on his mare's back, and mounted behind him, putting one arm around his body to support him. Then he rode slowly up the path till he reached the brow of the hill overhanging Drumelzier Burn. Up that glen and over the back of Glenheurie Rig lay Talla. If once he got there he knew that no trooper could reach them. But the way was long and dangerous and the burden was heavy for his mare. Now a shout arose from below, which told that his pursuers had discovered the track. This renewed his resolution. He rode quickly down the broken pathway into the glen. Thus began the ride which is famous in Upper Tweeddale. The country people still speak of Gideon Scott's Ride as something uncanny. The mare also, which carried two men ten miles over a rough country, still enjoys a reputation in the stories of the district.

Gideon knew that if the mare could but keep up, he would never be overtaken, for the dragoons must needs ride very slow, since they had no knowledge of the windings of the road. Moreover, he felt that if he could not get to Talla, and dress Yeddie's wound, Yeddie would die. On the crest of the hill ere he started he had wrapped a portion of his plaid over the wound, but the blood kept coming through the cloth and dropping on his hand. No sound came from the wounded man except an occasional groan when the motion of the mare hurt him.

It was about nine o'clock at night when he started on his ride; ere they reached Talla the light was beginning to appear over the grey hills of Holmes Water. Many times the mare had stumbled, twice she had sunk in a bog and was extricated by Gideon with great difficulty. Her knees and legs were bleeding from contact with sharp rocks, her wind was almost gone and her eyes shone like blood in her head. Gideon also was sore spent between the labour of supporting his burden and assisting the horse. As for Yeddie, he had fallen into a sort of stupor; he lay resting on Gideon's arm, with a face as pale as death in strange contrast to his blood-drenched plaid. The troopers had long since fallen off. Weary, jaded and well nigh dead, the horse and its two riders stopped at the door of the small shepherd's hut at Talla. Gideon, though scarce able to stand from fatigue, managed to undo the door and carry Yeddie in. He placed him on the bed and tottered out to see to his horse. But the mare had looked after herself. She had dragged herself to the stream's edge and was now lying drinking great draughts of water and resting her weary limbs. Then he went back and sat down in a chair by Yeddie's bed. A great sleep came over him and completely overpowered him. For five hours he slept and then he was wakened by the mare, who had come in to the hut in search of food. He arose and found some oats for her. Then he rummaged about and got some cold mutton for himself. Then and not till then he remembered Yeddie. He found a flask of brandy on a shelf, and succeeded in forcing some of it between his lips. In time Gideon succeeded in getting him out of the death-like stupor into which he had fallen. He went down to the stream for water, and dressed his wound, which had now stopped bleeding, as well as he could. Yeddie lay perfectly still watching Gideon's operations.

'I doubt I'm done for, Gidden,' said he.

'Na, na, I saved your life afore and I think I'll get ye roond this time.'

'I've a bullet in my breast, Gidden; there's nae hope for me, lad. I'm done for this time.' Then he burst out, 'O, I'll never dae't noo, I'll never dae't noo. I dinna care a whistle for death, if I just had finished it.'

'Whisht, man, whisht,' said Gideon, but he saw with a sinking heart the signs on Yeddie's face which told too clearly of death.

Then Yeddie spoke, 'Gideon, ye've been a guid friend to me, and I have just one mair thing to ask ye. I am going to tell ye something which you'll promise me never to tell to anyone.' (Gideon noticed that Yeddie had dropped the Tweeddale dialect and spoke, as he thought, more like a gentleman than a shepherd.) He promised what he required.

'Ye've heard,' said the dying man, 'of the Tweedies of Drumelzier, who used to be great folk in this countryside?'

'Ay, ay,' said Gideon. 'They were awfu' folk, they keepit a' Tweedside under their feet.'

'Well, my name is Adam Tweedie, and I am the last of the line. My grandfather had to sell the estates, and my father was a lawyer in Edinburgh. I was brought up to succeed him, but I had little love for the work. I had heard of the doings of my ancestors, and I resolved to do my best to get back the family possessions. When my father died I kept on his business, for my first idea was to make a fortune as a lawyer. But when I saw that I was not fitted to do anything of the kind, I gave up the idea and looked out for something else. Then I fell in with some wild fellows of my own age who first put the idea into my head of taking to the road. The upshot was that I sold the business and came up to Talla, where I had still this sheep farm belonging to me. I stayed in this cottage and with three other companions whose names I cannot tell, I became a —, call it highwayman, it was no better. Jamie Morrison, the lawyer in Edinburgh, was my banker; he thought I made the money from my farms. If I had lived another year, I would have accomplished my work; but it will never be done now.'

Yeddie's voice now became faint and his breathing more difficult. 'I can trust you to tell no one, Gideon. I would'na' like folk to know that the last of the clan came so low, though it was the trade of my forebears. Ye might do me the last favour of carrying news of my death to the laird of Mossfennan; he'll tell the others.' His voice failed him and he was silent.

Gideon sat in silence by his bed till the short day faded into night and then Yeddie died. Gideon arose and went down the valley to Mossfennan. Along with the laird he returned next morning and buried the dead man and then rode home alone with a heavy heart.

No-Man's Land

In the autumn of 1898 Buchan submitted to *Blackwood's Magazine* what he described as 'a story of a primitive survival among Scottish moorlands'. After a few changes it was published the following January as 'No-Man's Land' and became the first story in his collection, *The Watcher by the Threshold* (1902). It bears certain similarities to Conan Doyle's *The Lost World* and looks forward to several Buchan novels, most notably *The Dancing Floor* (1926). It is a good example of how Buchan's imagination invested a familiar countryside with mysterious properties. Graves, a young academic not unlike Buchan himself, is captured by a tribe of Picts while walking in Galloway and though he escapes his experience has tragic ramifications.

I THE SHIELING OF FARAWA

It was with a light heart and a pleasing consciousness of holiday that I set out from the inn at Allermuir to tramp my fifteen miles into the unknown. I walked slowly, for I carried my equipment on my back – my basket, fly-books and rods, my plaid of Grant tartan (for I boast myself a distant kinsman of that house), and my great staff, which had tried ere then the front of the steeper Alps. A small valise with books and some changes of linen clothing had been sent on ahead in the shepherd's own hands. It was yet early April, and before me lay four weeks of freedom – twenty-eight blessed days in which to take fish and smoke the pipe of idleness. The Lent term had pulled me down, a week of modest enjoyment thereafter in town had finished the work; and I drank in the sharp moorish air like a thirsty man who has been forwandered among deserts.

I am a man of varied tastes and a score of interests. As an undergraduate I had been filled with the old mania for the complete life. I distinguished myself in the Schools, rowed in my college eight, and reached the distinction of practising for three weeks in the Trials. I had dabbled in a score of learned activities, and when the time came that I won the inevitable St Chad's fellowship on my chaotic acquirements, and I found myself compelled to select if I would pursue a scholar's life, I had some toil in finding my vocation. In the end I resolved that the ancient life of the North, of the Celts and the Northmen and the unknown Pictish tribes, held for me the chief fascination. I had acquired a smattering of Gaelic, having been brought up as a boy in Lochaber, and now I set myself to increase my store of languages. I mastered Erse and Icelandic, and my first book – a monograph on the probable Celtic elements in the Eddic songs – brought me the praise of scholars and the deputy-professor's chair of Northern Antiquities. So much for Oxford. My vacations had been spent mainly in the North – in Ireland, Scotland, and the Isles, in Scandinavia and Iceland, once even in the far limits of Finland. I was a keen sportsman of a sort, an old-experienced fisher, a fair shot with gun and rifle, and in my hillcraft I might well stand comparison with most men. April has ever seemed to me the finest season of the year even in our cold northern altitudes, and the memory of many bright Aprils had brought me up from the South on the night before to Allerfoot, whence a dogcart had taken me up Glen Aller to the inn at Allermuir; and now the same desire had set me on the heather with my face to the cold brown hills.

You are to picture a sort of plateau, benty and rock-strewn, running ridge-wise above a chain of little peaty lochs and a vast tract of inexorable bog. In a mile the ridge ceased in a shoulder of hill, and over this lay the head of another glen, with the same doleful accompaniment of sunless lochs, mosses, and a shining and resolute water. East and west and north, in every direction save the south, rose walls of gashed and serrated hills. It was a grey day with blinks of sun, and when a ray chanced to fall on one of the great dark faces, lines of light and colour sprang into being which told of mica and granite. I was in high spirits, as on the eve of holiday; I had breakfasted excellently on eggs and salmon-steaks; I had no cares to speak of, and my prospects were not uninviting. But in spite of myself the landscape began to take me in thrall and crush me. The silent vanished peoples of the hills seemed to be stirring; dark primeval faces seemed to stare at me from behind boulders and jags of rock. The place was so still, so free from the cheerful clamour of nesting birds, that it seemed a *temenos* sacred to some old-world god. At my feet the lochs lapped ceaselessly; but the waters were so dark that one could not see bottom a foot from the edge. On my right the links of green told of snake-like mires waiting to crush the unwary wanderer. It seemed to me for the moment a land of death, where the tongues of the dead cried aloud for recognition.

My whole morning's walk was full of such fancies. I lit a pipe to cheer me, but the things would not be got rid of. I thought of the Gaels who had held those fastnesses; I thought of the Britons before them, who yielded to their advent. They were all strong peoples in their day, and now they had gone the way of the earth. They had left their mark on the levels of the glens and on the more habitable uplands, both in names and in actual forts, and graves where men might still dig curios. But the hills – that black stony amphitheatre before me – it seemed strange that the hills bore no traces of them. And then with some uneasiness I reflected on that older and stranger race who were said to have held the hill-tops. The Picts, the Picti – what in the name of goodness were they? They had troubled me in all my studies, a sort of blank wall to put an end to speculation. We knew nothing of them save certain strange names which men called Pictish, the names of those hills in front of me – the Muneraw, the Yirnie, the Calmarton. They were the *corpus vile* for learned experiment; but Heaven alone knew what dark abyss of savagery once yawned in the midst of this desert.

And then I remembered the crazy theories of a pupil of mine at St Chad's, the son of a small landowner on the Aller, a young gentleman who had spent his substance too freely at Oxford, and was now dreeing his weird in the

Backwoods. He had been no scholar; but a certain imagination marked all his doings, and of a Sunday night he would come and talk to me of the North. The Picts were his special subject, and his ideas were mad. 'Listen to me,' he would say, when I had mixed him toddy and given him one of my cigars; 'I believe there are traces – ay, and more than traces – of an old culture lurking in those hills and waiting to be discovered. We never hear of the Picts being driven from the hills. The Britons drove them from the lowlands, the Gaels from Ireland did the same for the Britons; but the hills were left unmolested. We hear of no one going near them except outlaws and tinklers. And in that very place you have the strangest mythology. Take the story of the Brownie. What is that but the story of a little swart man of uncommon strength and cleverness, who does good and ill indiscriminately, and then disappears? There are many scholars, as you yourself confess, who think that the origin of the Brownie was in some mad belief in the old race of the Picts, which still survived somewhere in the hills. And do we not hear of the Brownie in authentic records right down to the year 1756? After that, when people grew more incredulous, it is natural that the belief should have begun to die out; but I do not see why stray traces should not have survived till late.'

'Do you not see what that means?' I had said in mock gravity. 'Those same hills are, if anything, less known now than they were a hundred years ago. Why should not your Picts or Brownies be living to this day?'

'Why not, indeed?' he had rejoined, in all seriousness.

I laughed, and he went to his rooms and returned with a large leather-bound book. It was lettered, in the rococo style of a young man's taste, 'Glimpses of the Unknown', and some of the said glimpses he proceeded to impart to me. It was not pleasant reading; indeed, I had rarely heard anything so well fitted to shatter sensitive nerves. The early part consisted of folk-tales and folk-sayings, some of them wholly obscure, some of them with a glint of meaning, but all of them with some hint of a mystery in the hills. I heard the Brownie story in countless versions. Now the thing was a friendly little man, who wore grey breeches and lived on brose; now he was a twisted being, the sight of which made the ewes miscarry in the lambing-time. But the second part was the stranger, for it was made up of actual tales, most of them with date and place appended. It was a most Bedlamite catalogue of horrors, which, if true, made the wholesome moors a place instinct with tragedy. Some told of children carried away from villages, even from towns, on the verge of the uplands. In almost every case they were girls, and the strange fact was their utter disappearance. Two little girls would be coming home from school, would be seen last by a neighbour just where the road crossed a patch of heath or entered a wood and then – no human eye ever saw them again. Children's cries had startled outlying shepherds in the night, and when they had rushed to the door they could hear nothing but the night wind. The instances of such disappearances were not very common – perhaps once in twenty years – but they were confined to this one tract of country, and came in a sort of fixed progression from the middle of the last century, when the record began. But this was only one side of the history. The latter part was all devoted to a chronicle of crimes which had gone unpunished, seeing that no hand had ever been traced. The list was fuller in last century;[1] in the earlier years of the present it had dwindled; then came a revival about the 'Fifties; and now again in our own time it had sunk low. At the little cottage of Auchterbrean, on the roadside in Glen Aller, a labourer's wife had been found pierced to the heart. It was thought to be a case of a woman's jealousy, and her neighbour was accused, convicted, and hanged. The woman, to be sure, denied the charge with her last breath; but circumstantial evidence seemed sufficiently strong against her. Yet some people in the glen believed her guiltless. In particular, the carrier who had found the dead woman declared that the way in which her neighbour received the news was a sufficient proof of innocence; and the doctor who was first

1. The narrative of Mr Graves was written in the year 1898.

summoned professed himself unable to tell with what instrument the wound had been given. But this was all before the days of expert evidence, so the woman had been hanged without scruple. Then there had been another story of peculiar horror, telling of the death of an old man at some little lonely shieling called Carrickfey. But at this point I had risen in protest, and made to drive the young idiot from my room.

'It was my grandfather who collected most of them,' he said. 'He had theories,[1] but people called him mad, so he was wise enough to hold his tongue. My father declares the whole thing mania; but I rescued the book, had it bound, and added to the collection. It is a queer hobby; but, as I say, I have theories, and there are more things in heaven and earth—'

But at this he heard a friend's voice in the Quad., and dived out, leaving the banal quotation unfinished.

Strange though it may seem, this madness kept coming back to me as I crossed the last few miles of moor. I was now on a rough tableland, the watershed between two lochs, and beyond and above me rose the stony backs of

1. In the light of subsequent events I have jotted down the materials to which I refer. The last authentic record of the Brownie is in the narrative of the shepherd of Clachlands, taken down towards the close of last century by the Reverend Mr Gillespie, minister of Allerkirk, and included by him in his 'Songs and Legends of Glen Aller'. The authorities on the strange carrying-away of children are to be found in a series of articles in a local paper, the *Allerfoot Advertiser*, September and October 1878, and a curious book published anonymously at Edinburgh in 1848, entitled *The Weathergaw*. The records of the unexplained murders in the same neighbourhood are all contained in Mr Fordoun's 'Theory of Expert Evidence', and an attack on the book in the *Law Review* for June 1881. The Carrickfey case has a pamphlet to itself – now extremely rare – a copy of which was recently obtained in a bookseller's shop in Dumfries by a well-known antiquary, and presented to the library of the Supreme Court in Edinburgh.

the hills. The burns fell down in a chaos of granite boulders, and huge slabs of grey stone lay flat and tumbled in the heather. The full waters looked prosperously for my fishing, and I began to forget all fancies in anticipation of sport.

Then suddenly in a hollow of land I came on a ruined cottage. It had been a very small place, but the walls were still half-erect, and the little moorland garden was outlined on the turf. A lonely apple-tree, twisted and gnarled with winds, stood in the midst.

From higher up on the hill I heard a loud roar, and I knew my excellent friend the shepherd of Farawa, who had come thus far to meet me. He greeted me with the boisterous embarrassment which was his way of prefacing hospitality. A grave reserved man at other times, on such occasions he thought it proper to relapse into hilarity. I fell into step with him, and we set off for his dwelling. But first I had the curiosity to look back to the tumble-down cottage and ask him its name.

A queer look came into his eyes. 'They ca' the place Carrickfey,' he said. 'Naebody has daured to bide there this twenty year sin' – but I see ye ken the story.' And, as if glad to leave the subject, he hastened to discourse on fishing.

II TELLS OF AN EVENING'S TALK

The shepherd was a masterful man; tall, save for the stoop which belongs to all moorland folk, and active as a wild goat. He was not a new importation, nor did he belong to the place; for his people had lived in the remote Borders, and he had come as a boy to this shieling of Farawa. He was unmarried, but an elderly sister lived with him and cooked his meals. He was reputed to be extraordinarily skilful in his trade; I know for a fact that he was in his way a keen sportsman; and his few neighbours gave him credit for a sincere piety. Doubtless this last report was due in part to his silence, for after his first greeting he was wont to relapse into a singular taciturnity. As we strode across the heather he gave me a short outline of his year's lambing. 'Five pairs o' twins yestreen, twae this morn; that makes thirty-five yowes that hae lambed since the Sabbath. I'll dae weel if God's willin'.' Then, as I looked towards the hill-tops whence the thin mist of morn was trailing, he followed my gaze. 'See,' he said with uplifted crook – 'see that sicht. Is that no what is written of in the Bible when it says, "The mountains do smoke."' And with this piece of exegesis he finished his talk, and in a little we were at the cottage.

It was a small enough dwelling in truth, and yet large for a moorland house, for it had a garret below the thatch, which was given up to my sole enjoyment. Below was the wide kitchen with box-beds, and next to it the inevitable second room, also with its cupboard sleeping-places. The interior was very clean, and yet I remember to have been struck with the faint musty smell which is inseparable from moorland dwellings. The kitchen pleased me best, for there the great rafters were black with peat-reek, and the uncovered stone floor, on which the fire gleamed dully, gave an air of primeval simplicity. But the walls spoiled all, for tawdry things of to-day had penetrated even there. Some grocers' almanacs – years old – hung in places of honour, and an extraordinary lithograph of the Royal Family in its youth. And this, mind you, between crooks and fishing-rods and old guns, and horns of sheep and deer.

The life for the first day or two was regular and placid. I was up early, breakfasted on porridge (a dish which I detest), and then off to the lochs and streams. At first my sport prospered mightily. With a drake-wing I killed a salmon of seventeen pounds, and the next day had a fine basket of trout from a hill-burn. Then for no earthly reason the weather changed. A bitter wind came out of the north-east, bringing showers of snow and stinging hail, and lashing the waters into storm. It was now farewell to fly-fishing. For a day or two I tried trolling with the minnow on the lochs, but it was poor sport, for I had no boat, and the edges were soft and mossy. Then in disgust I gave up the attempt, went back to the cottage, lit my biggest pipe, and sat down with a book to await the turn of the weather.

The shepherd was out from morning till night at his work, and when he came in at last, dog-tired, his face would be set and hard, and his eyes heavy with sleep. The strangeness of the man grew upon me. He had a shrewd brain beneath his thatch of hair, for I had tried him once or twice, and found him abundantly intelligent. He had some smattering of an education, like all Scottish peasants, and, as I have said, he was deeply religious. I set him down as a fine type of his class, sober, serious, keenly critical, free from the bondage of superstition. But I rarely saw him, and our talk was chiefly in monosyllables – short interjected accounts of the number of lambs dead or alive on the hill. Then he would produce a pencil and note-book, and be immersed in some calculation; and finally he would be revealed sleeping heavily in his chair, till his sister wakened him, and he stumbled off to bed.

So much for the ordinary course of life; but one day – the second I think of the bad weather – the extraordinary happened. The storm had passed in the afternoon into a resolute and blinding snow, and the shepherd, finding it hopeless on the hill, came home about three o'clock. I could make out from his way of entering that he was in a great temper. He kicked his feet savagely against the door-post. Then he swore at his dogs, a thing I had never heard him do before. 'Hell!' he cried, 'can ye no keep out o' my road, ye britts?' Then he came sullenly into the kitchen, thawed his numbed hands at the fire, and sat down to his meal.

I made some aimless remark about the weather.

'Death to man and beast,' he grunted. 'I hae got the sheep doun frae the hill, but the lambs will never thole this. We maun pray that it will no last.'

His sister came in with some dish. 'Margit,' he cried, 'three lambs away this morning, and three deid wi' the hole in the throat.'

The woman's face visibly paled. 'Guid help us, Adam; that hasna happened this three year.'

'It has happened noo,' he said, surlily. 'But, by God! if it happens again I'll gang mysel' to the Scarts o' the Muneraw.'

'O Adam!' the woman cried shrilly, 'haud your tongue. Ye kenna wha hears ye.' And with a frightened glance at me she left the room.

I asked no questions, but waited till the shepherd's anger should cool. But the cloud did not pass so lightly. When he had finished his dinner he pulled his chair to the fire and sat staring moodily. He made some sort of apology to me for his conduct. 'I'm sore troubled, sir; but I'm vexed ye should see me like this. Maybe things will be better the morn.' And then, lighting his short black pipe, he resigned himself to his meditations.

But he could not keep quiet. Some nervous unrest seemed to have possessed the man. He got up with a start and went to the window, where the snow was drifting unsteadily past. As he stared out into the storm I heard him mutter to himself, 'Three away, God help me, and three wi' the hole in the throat.'

Then he turned round to me abruptly. I was jotting down notes for an article I contemplated in the *Revue Celtique*, so my thoughts were far away from the present. The man recalled me by demanding fiercely, 'Do ye believe in God?'

I gave him some sort of answer in the affirmative.

'Then do ye believe in the Devil?' he asked.

The reply must have been less satisfactory, for he came forward and flung himself violently into the chair before me.

'What do ye ken about it?' he cried. 'You that bides in a southern toun, what can ye ken o' the God that works in thae hills and the Devil – ay, the manifold devils – that He suffers to bide here? I tell ye, man, that if ye had seen what I have seen ye wad be on your knees at this moment praying to God to pardon your unbelief. There are devils at the back o' every stane and hidin' in every cleuch, and it's by the grace o' God alone that a man is alive upon the earth.' His voice had risen high and shrill, and then suddenly he cast a frightened glance towards the window and was silent.

I began to think that the man's wits were unhinged, and the thought did not give me satisfaction. I had no relish for the prospect of being left alone in this moorland dwelling with the cheerful company of a maniac. But his next

movements reassured me. He was clearly only dead-
tired, for he fell sound asleep in his chair, and by the time
his sister brought tea and wakened him, he seemed to have
got the better of his excitement.

When the window was shuttered and the lamp lit, I set
myself again to the completion of my notes. The shepherd
had got out his Bible, and was solemnly reading with one
great finger travelling down the lines. He was smoking, and
whenever some text came home to him with power he
would make pretence to underline it with the end of the
stem. Soon I had finished the work I desired, and, my mind
being full of my pet hobby, I fell into an inquisitive mood,
and began to question the solemn man opposite on the
antiquities of the place.

He stared stupidly at me when I asked him concerning
monuments or ancient weapons.

'I kenna,' said he. 'There's a heap o' queer things in the
hills.'

'This place should be a centre for such relics. You know
that the name of the hill behind the house, as far as I can
make it out, means the "Place of the Little Men". It is a
good Gaelic word, though there is some doubt about its
exact interpretation. But clearly the Gaelic peoples did not
speak of themselves when they gave the name; they must
have referred to some older and stranger population.'

The shepherd looked at me dully, as not understanding.

'It is partly this fact – besides the fishing, of course –
which interests me in this countryside,' said I, gaily.

Again he cast the same queer frightened glance towards the
window. 'If ye'll tak the advice of an aulder man,' he said,
slowly, 'ye'll let well alane and no meddle wi' uncanny things.'

I laughed pleasantly, for at last I had found out my hard-
headed host in a piece of childishness. 'Why, I thought that
you of all men would be free from superstition.'

'What do ye call supersteetion?' he asked.

'A belief in old wives' tales,' said I, 'a trust in the crude
supernatural and the patently impossible.'

He looked at me beneath his shaggy brows. 'How do ye
ken what is impossible? Mind ye, sir, ye're no in the toun
just now, but in the thick of the wild hills.'

'But, hang it all, man,' I cried, 'you don't mean to say that you believe in that sort of thing? I am prepared for many things up here, but not for the Brownie, – though, to be sure, if one could meet him in the flesh, it would be rather pleasant than otherwise, for he was a companionable sort of fellow.'

'When a thing pits the fear o' death on a man he aye speaks well of it.'

It was true – the Eumenides and the Good Folk over again; and I awoke with interest to the fact that the conversation was getting into strange channels.

The shepherd moved uneasily in his chair. 'I am a man that fears God, and has nae time for daft stories; but I havena traivelled the hills for twenty years wi' my een shut. If I say that I could tell ye stories o' faces seen in the mist, and queer things that have knocked against me in the snaw, wad ye believe me? I wager ye wadna. Ye wad say I had been drunk, and yet I am a God-fearing temperate man.'

He rose and went to a cupboard, unlocked it, and brought out something in his hand, which he held out to me. I took it with some curiosity, and found that it was a flint arrow-head.

Clearly a flint arrow-head, and yet like none that I had ever seen in any collection. For one thing it was larger, and the barb less clumsily thick. More, the chipping was new, or comparatively so; this thing had not stood the wear of fifteen hundred years among the stones of the hillside. Now there are, I regret to say, institutions which manufacture primitive relics; but it is not hard for a practised eye to see the difference. The chipping has either a regularity and a balance which is unknown in the real thing, or the rudeness has been overdone, and the result is an implement incapable of harming a mortal creature. But this was the real thing if it ever existed; and yet – I was prepared to swear on my reputation that it was not half a century old.

'Where did you get this? I asked with some nervousness.

'I hae a story about that,' said the shepherd. 'Outside the door there ye can see a muckle flat stane aside the buchts. One simmer nicht I was sitting there smoking till the dark, and I wager there was naething on the stane then. But that same nicht I awoke wi' a queer thocht, as if there were folk moving around the house – folk that didna mak' muckle noise. I mind o' lookin' out o' the windy, and I could hae sworn I saw something black movin' amang the heather and intil the buchts. Now I had maybe threescore o' lambs there that nicht, for I had to tak' them many miles off in the early morning. Weel, when I gets up about four o'clock and gangs out, as I am passing the muckle stane I finds this bit errow. "That's come here in the nicht," says I, and I wunnered a wee and put it in my pouch. But when I came to my faulds what did I see? Five o' my best hoggs were away, and three mair were lying deid wi' a hole in their throat.'

'Who in the world—?' I began.

'Dinna ask,' said he. 'If I aince sterted to speir about thae maitters. I wadna keep my reason.'

'Then that was what happened on the hill this morning?'

'Even sae, and it has happened mair than aince sin' that time. It's the most uncanny slaughter, for sheep-stealing I can understand, but no this pricking o' the puir beasts' wizands. I kenna how they dae't either, for it's no wi' a knife or ony common tool.'

'Have you never tried to follow the thieves?'

'Have I no?' he asked, grimly. 'If it had been common sheep-stealers I wad hae had them by the heels, though I had followed them a hundred miles. But this is no common. I've tracked them, and it's ill they are to track; but I never got beyond ae place, and that was the Scarts o' the Muneraw that ye've heard me speak o'.'

'But who in Heaven's name are the people? Tinklers or poachers or what?'

'Ay,' said he, drily. 'Even so. Tinklers and poachers whae wark wi' stane errows and kill sheep by a hole in their throat. Lord, I kenna what they are, unless the Muckle Deil himsel'.'

The conversation had passed beyond my comprehension. In this prosaic hard-headed man I had come on the dead-rock of superstition and blind fear.

'That is only the story of the Brownie over again, and he is an exploded myth,' I said, laughing.

'Are ye the man that exploded it?' said the shepherd, rudely. 'I trow no, neither you nor ony ither. My bonny man, if ye lived a twalmonth in thae hills, ye wad sing safter about exploded myths, as ye call them.'

'I tell you what I would do,' said I. 'If I lost sheep as you lose them, I would go up the Scarts of the Muneraw and never rest till I had settled the question once and for all.' I spoke hotly, for I was vexed by the man's childish fear.

'I daresay ye wad,' he said, slowly. 'But then I am no you, and maybe I ken mair o' what is in the Scarts o' the Muneraw. Maybe I ken that whilk, if ye kenned it, wad send ye back to the South Country wi' your hert in your mouth. But, as I say, I am no sae brave as you, for I saw something in the first year o' my herding here which put the terror o' God on me, and makes me a fearfu' man to this day. Ye ken the story o' the gudeman o' Carrickfey?'

I nodded.

'Weel, I was the man that fand him. I had seen the deid afore and I've seen them since. But never have I seen aucht like the look in that man's een. What he saw at his death I may see the morn, so I walk before the Lord in fear.'

Then he rose and stretched himself. 'It's bedding-time, for I maun be up at three,' and with a short good night he left the room.

III THE SCARTS OF THE MUNERAW

The next morning was fine, for the snow had been intermittent, and had soon melted except in the high corries. True, it was deceptive weather, for the wind had gone to the rainy south-west, and the masses of cloud on that horizon boded ill for the afternoon. But some days' inaction had made me keen for a chance of sport, so I rose with the shepherd and set out for the day.

He asked me where I proposed to begin.

I told him the tarn called the Loch o' the Threshes, which lies over the back of the Muneraw on another watershed. It is on the ground of the Rhynns Forest, and I had fished it of old from the Forest House. I knew the merits of the trout, and I knew its virtues in a south-west wind, so I had resolved to go thus far afield.

The shepherd heard the name in silence. 'Your best road will be ower that rig, and syne on to the water o' Caulds. Keep abune the moss till ye come to the place they ca' the Nick o' the Threshes. That will take ye to the very lochside, but it's a lang road and a sair.'

The morning was breaking over the bleak hills. Little clouds drifted athwart the corries, and wisps of haze fluttered from the peaks. A great rosy flush lay over one side of the glen, which caught the edge of the sluggish bog-pools and turned them to fire. Never before had I seen the mountain-land so clear, for far back into the east and west I saw mountain-tops set as close as flowers in a border, black crags seamed with silver lines which I knew for mighty waterfalls, and below at my feet the lower slopes fresh with the dewy green of spring. A name stuck in my memory from the last night's talk.

'Where are the Scarts of the Muneraw?' I asked.

The shepherd pointed to the great hill which bears the name, and which lies, a huge mass, above the watershed.

'D'ye see yon corrie at the east that runs straucht up the side? It looks a bit scart, but it's sae deep that it's aye derk at the bottom o't. Weel, at the tap o' the rig it meets anither corrie that runs doun the ither side, and that one they ca' the Scarts. There is a sort o' burn in it that flows intil the Dule and sae intil the Aller, and, indeed, if ye were gaun there it wad be from Aller Glen that your best road wad lie. But it's an ill bit, and ye'll be sair guidit if ye try't.'

There he left me and went across the glen, while I struck upwards over the ridge. At the top I halted and looked down on the wide glen of the Caulds, which there is little better than a bog, but lower down grows into a green pastoral valley. The great Muneraw still dominated the landscape, and the black scaur on its side seemed blacker than before. The place fascinated me, for in that fresh morning air the shepherd's fears seemed monstrous. 'Some day,' said I to myself, 'I will go and explore the whole of that mighty hill.' Then I descended and struggled over the moss, found the Nick, and in two hours' time was on the loch's edge.

I have little in the way of good to report of the fishing. For perhaps one hour the trout took well; after that they sulked steadily for the day. The promise, too, of fine weather had been deceptive. By mid-day the rain was falling in that soft soaking fashion which gives no hope of clearing. The mist was down to the edge of the water, and I cast my flies into a blind sea of white. It was hopeless work, and yet from a sort of ill-temper I stuck to it long after my better judgment had warned me of its folly. At last, about three in the afternoon, I struck my camp, and prepared myself for a long and toilsome retreat.

And long and toilsome it was beyond anything I had ever encountered. Had I had a vestige of sense I would have followed the burn from the loch down to the Forest House. The place was shut up, but the keeper would gladly have given me shelter for the night. But foolish pride was too strong in me. I had found my road in mist before, and could do it again.

Before I got to the top of the hill I had repented my decision; when I got there I repented it more. For below me was a dizzy chaos of grey; there was no landmark visible; and before me I knew was the bog through which the Caulds Water twined. I had crossed it with some trouble in the morning, but then I had light to pick my steps. Now I could only stumble on, and in five minutes I might be in a bog-hole, and in five more in a better world.

But there was no help to be got from hesitation, so with a rueful courage I set off. The place was if possible worse than I had feared. Wading up to the knees with nothing before you but a blank wall of mist and the cheerful consciousness that your next step may be your last – such was my state for one weary mile. The stream itself was high, and rose to my armpits, and once and again I only saved myself by a violent leap backwards from a pitiless green slough. But at last it was past, and I was once more on the solid ground of the hillside.

Now, in the thick weather I had crossed the glen much lower down than in the morning, and the result was that the hill on which I stood was one of the giants which, with the Muneraw for centre, guard the watershed. Had I taken the proper way, the Nick o' the Threshes would have led me to the Caulds, and then once over the bog a little ridge was all that stood between me and the glen of Farawa. But instead I had come a wild cross-country road, and was now, though I did not know it, nearly as far from my destination as at the start.

Well for me that I did not know, for I was wet and dispirited, and had I not fancied myself all but home, I should scarcely have had the energy to make this last ascent. But soon I found it was not the little ridge I had expected. I looked at my watch and saw that it was five o'clock. When, after the weariest climb, I lay on a piece of level ground which seemed the top, I was not surprised to find that it was now seven. The darkening must be at hand, and sure enough the mist seemed to be deepening into a greyish black. I began to grow desperate. Here was I on the summit of some infernal mountain, without any certainty where my road lay. I was lost with a vengeance, and at the thought I began to be acutely afraid.

I took what seemed to me the way I had come, and began to descend steeply. Then something made me halt, and the next instant I was lying on my face trying painfully to retrace my steps. For I had found myself slipping, and before I could stop, my feet were dangling over a precipice with Heaven alone knows how many yards of sheer mist between me and the bottom. Then I tried keeping the ridge, and took that to the right, which I thought would bring me nearer home. It was no good trying to think out a direction, for in the fog my brain was running round, and I seemed to stand on a pin-point of space where the laws of the compass had ceased to hold.

It was the roughest sort of walking, now stepping warily over acres of loose stones, now crawling down the face of some battered rock, and now wading in the long dripping heather. The soft rain had begun to fall again, which completed my discomfort. I was now seriously tired, and, like all men who in their day have bent too much over books, I began to feel it in my back. My spine ached, and my breath came in short broken pants. It was a pitiable state of affairs for an honest man who had never encountered much grave discomfort. To ease myself I was compelled to leave my basket behind me, trusting to return and find it, if I should ever reach safety and discover on what pathless hill I had been strayed. My rod I used as a staff, but it was of little use, for my fingers were getting too numb to hold it.

Suddenly from the blankness I heard a sound as of human speech. At first I thought it mere craziness – the cry of a weasel or a hill-bird distorted by my ears. But again it came, thick and faint, as through acres of mist, and yet clearly the sound of 'articulate-speaking men'. In a moment I lost my despair and cried out in answer. This was some forwandered traveller like myself, and between us we could surely find some road to safety. So I yelled back at the pitch of my voice and waited intently.

But the sound ceased, and there was utter silence again. Still I waited, and then from some place much nearer came the same soft mumbling speech. I could make nothing of it. Heard in that drear place it made the nerves tense and the heart timorous. It was the strangest jumble of vowels and consonants I had ever met.

A dozen solutions flashed through my brain. It was some maniac talking Jabberwock to himself. It was some belated traveller whose wits had given out in fear. Perhaps it was only some shepherd who was amusing himself thus, and whiling the way with nonsense. Once again I cried out and waited.

Then suddenly in the hollow trough of mist before me, where things could still be half discerned, there appeared a figure. It was little and squat and dark; naked, apparently, but so rough with hair that it wore the appearance of a skin-covered being. It crossed my line of vision, not staying for a moment, but in its face and eyes there seemed to lurk an elder world of mystery and barbarism, a troll-like life which was too horrible for words.

The shepherd's fear came back on me like a thunderclap. For one awful instant my legs failed me, and I had almost fallen. The next I had turned and ran shrieking up the hill.

If he who may read this narrative has never felt the force of an overmastering terror, then let him thank his Maker and pray that he never may. I am no weak child, but a strong grown man, accredited in general with sound sense and little suspected of hysterics. And yet I went up that brae-face with my heart fluttering like a bird and my throat aching with fear. I screamed in short dry gasps; involuntarily, for my mind was beyond any purpose. I felt that beast-like clutch at my throat; those red eyes seemed to be staring at me from the mist; I heard ever behind and before and on all sides the patter of those inhuman feet.

Before I knew I was down, slipping over a rock and falling some dozen feet into a soft marshy hollow. I was conscious of lying still for a second and whimpering like a child. But as I lay there I awoke to the silence of the place. There was no sound of pursuit; perhaps they had lost my track and given up. My courage began to return, and from this it was an easy step to hope. Perhaps after all it had been merely an illusion, for folk do not see clearly in the mist, and I was already done with weariness.

But even as I lay in the green moss and began to hope, the faces of my pursuers grew up through the mist. I stumbled madly to my feet; but I was hemmed in, the rock behind and my enemies before. With a cry I rushed forward, and struck wildly with my rod at the first dark body. It was as if I had struck an animal, and the next second the thing was wrenched from my grasp. But still they came no nearer. I stood trembling there in the centre of those malignant devils, my brain a mere weathercock, and my heart crushed shapeless with horror. At last the end came, for with the vigour of madness I flung myself on the nearest, and we rolled on the ground. Then the monstrous things seemed to close over me, and with a choking cry I passed into unconsciousness.

IV THE DARKNESS THAT IS UNDER THE EARTH

There is an unconsciousness that is not wholly dead, where a man feels numbly and the body lives without the brain. I was beyond speech or thought, and yet I felt the upward or downward motion as the way lay in hill or glen, and I most assuredly knew when the open air was changed for the close underground. I could feel dimly that lights were flared in

my face, and that I was laid in some bed on the earth. Then
with the stopping of movement the real sleep of weakness
seized me, and for long I knew nothing of this mad world.

Morning came over the moors with birdsong and the glory
of fine weather. The streams were still rolling in spate, but
the hill-pastures were alight with dawn, and the little seams
of snow were glistening like white fire. A ray from the
sunrise cleft its path somehow into the abyss, and danced
on the wall above my couch. It caught my eye as I wakened,
and for long I lay crazily wondering what it meant. My head
was splitting with pain, and in my heart was the same
fluttering nameless fear. I did not wake to full consciousness; not till the twinkle of sun from the clean bright out-of-
doors caught my senses did I realise that I lay in a great dark
place with a glow of dull firelight in the middle.

In time things rose and moved around me, a few ragged
shapes of men, without clothing, shambling with their huge
feet and looking towards me with curved beast-like glances.
I tried to marshal my thoughts, and slowly, bit by bit, I built
up the present. There was no question to my mind of
dreaming; the past hours had scored reality upon my brain.
Yet I cannot say that fear was my chief feeling. The first
crazy terror had subsided, and now I felt mainly a sickened
disgust with just a tinge of curiosity. I found that my knife,
watch, flask, and money had gone, but they had left me a
map of the countryside. It seemed strange to look at the
calico, with the name of a London printer stamped on the
back, and lines of railway and highroad running through
every shire. Decent and comfortable civilisation! And here
was I a prisoner in this den of nameless folk, and in the
midst of a life which history knew not.

Courage is a virtue which grows with reflection and the
absence of the immediate peril. I thought myself into some
sort of resolution, and lo! when the Folk approached me
and bound my feet I was back at once in the most miserable
terror. They tied me, all but my hands, with some strong
cord, and carried me to the centre, where the fire was
glowing. Their soft touch was the acutest torture to my
nerves, but I stifled my cries lest some one should lay his

hand on my mouth. Had that happened, I am convinced my reason would have failed me.

So there I lay in the shine of the fire, with the circle of unknown things around me. There seemed but three or four, but I took no note of number. They talked huskily among themselves in a tongue which sounded all gutturals. Slowly my fear became less an emotion than a habit, and I had room for the smallest shade of curiosity. I strained my ear to catch a word, but it was a mere chaos of sound. The thing ran and thundered in my brain as I stared dumbly into the vacant air. Then I thought that unless I spoke I should certainly go crazy, for my head was beginning to swim at the strange cooing noise.

I spoke a word or two in my best Gaelic, and they closed round me inquiringly. Then I was sorry I had spoken, for my words had brought them nearer, and I shrank at the thought. But as the faint echoes of my speech hummed in the rock-chamber, I was struck by a curious kinship of sound. Mine was sharper, more distinct, and staccato; theirs was blurred, formless, but still with a certain root-resemblance.

Then from the back there came an older being, who seemed to have heard my words. He was like some foul grey badger, his red eyes sightless, and his hands trembling on a stump of bog-oak. The others made way for him with such deference as they were capable of, and the thing squatted down by me and spoke.

To my amazement his words were familiar. It was some manner of speech akin to the Gaelic, but broadened, lengthened, coarsened. I remembered an old book-tongue, commonly supposed to be an impure dialect once used in Brittany, which I had met in the course of my researches. The words recalled it, and as far as I could remember the thing, I asked him who he was and where the place might be.

He answered me in the same speech – still more broadened, lengthened, coarsened. I lay back with sheer amazement. I had found the key to this unearthly life.

For a little an insatiable curiosity, the ardour of the scholar, prevailed. I forgot the horror of the place, and

thought only of the fact that here before me was the greatest
find that scholarship had ever made. I was precipitated into
the heart of the past. Here must be the fountainhead of all
legends, the chrysalis of all beliefs. I actually grew light-
hearted. This strange folk around me were now no more
shapeless things of terror, but objects of research and
experiment. I almost came to think them not unfriendly.

For an hour I enjoyed the highest of earthly pleasures. In
that strange conversation I heard – in fragments and
suggestions – the history of the craziest survival the world
has ever seen. I heard of the struggles with invaders,
preserved as it were in a sort of shapeless poetry. There
were bitter words against the Gaelic oppressor, bitterer
words against the Saxon stranger, and for a moment
ancient hatreds flared into life. Then there came the tale
of the hill-refuge, the morbid hideous existence preserved
for centuries amid a changing world. I heard fragments of
old religions, primeval names of god and goddess, half-
understood by the Folk, but to me the key to a hundred
puzzles. Tales which survive to us in broken disjointed
riddles were intact here in living form. I lay on my elbow
and questioned feverishly. At any moment they might
become morose and refuse to speak. Clearly it was my
duty to make the most of a brief good fortune.

And then the tale they told me grew more hideous. I
heard of the circumstances of the life itself and their daily
shifts for existence. It was a murderous chronicle – a history
of lust and rapine and unmentionable deeds in the darkness. One thing they had early recognised – that the race
could not be maintained within itself; so that ghoulish
carrying away of little girls from the lowlands began, which
I had heard of but never credited. Shut up in those dismal
holes, the girls soon died, and when the new race had
grown up the plunder had been repeated. Then there were
bestial murders in lonely cottages, done for God knows
what purpose. Sometimes the occupant had seen more
than was safe, sometimes the deed was the mere exuberance of a lust of slaying. As they gabbled their tales my
heart's blood froze, and I lay back in the agonies of fear. If
they had used the others thus, what way of escape was open

for myself? I had been brought to this place, and not
murdered on the spot. Clearly there was torture before
death in store for me, and I confess I quailed at the thought.

But none molested me. The elders continued to jabber
out their stories, while I lay tense and deaf. Then to my
amazement food was brought and placed beside me –
almost with respect. Clearly my murder was not a thing
of the immediate future. The meal was some form of
mutton – perhaps the shepherd's lost ewes – and a little
smoking was all the cooking it had got. I strove to eat, but
the tasteless morsels choked me. Then they set drink before
me in a curious cup, which I seized on eagerly, for my
mouth was dry with thirst. The vessel was of gold, rudely
formed, but of the pure metal, and a coarse design in circles
ran round the middle. This surprised me enough, but a
greater wonder awaited me. The liquor was not water, as I
had guessed, but a sort of sweet ale, a miracle of flavour.
The taste was curious, but somehow familiar; it was like no
wine I had ever drunk, and yet I had known that flavour all
my life. I sniffed at the brim, and there rose a faint fragrance
of thyme and heather honey and the sweet things of the
moorland. I almost dropped it in my surprise; for here in
this rude place I had stumbled upon that lost delicacy of the
North, the heather ale.

For a second I was entranced with my discovery, and
then the wonder of the cup claimed my attention. Was it a
mere relic of pillage, or had this folk some hidden mine of
the precious metal? Gold had once been common in these
hills. There were the traces of mines on Cairnsmore;
shepherds had found it in the gravel of the Gled Water;
and the name of a house at the head of the Clachlands
meant the 'Home of Gold'.

Once more I began my questions, and they answered
them willingly. There and then I heard that secret for which
many had died in old time, the secret of the heather ale.
They told of the gold in the hills, of corries where the sand
gleamed and abysses where the rocks were veined. All this
they told me, freely, without a scruple. And then, like a
clap, came the awful thought that this, too, spelled death.
These were secrets which this race aforetime had guarded

with their lives; they told them generously to me because
there was no fear of betrayal. I should go no more out from
this place.

The thought put me into a new sweat of terror – not at
death, mind you, but at the unknown horrors which might
precede the final suffering. I lay silent, and after binding my
hands they began to leave me and go off to other parts of the
cave. I dozed in the horrible half-swoon of fear, conscious
only of my shaking limbs, and the great dull glow of the fire
in the centre. Then I became calmer. After all, they had
treated me with tolerable kindness: I had spoken their
language, which few of their victims could have done for
many a century; it might be that I had found favour in their
eyes. For a little I comforted myself with this delusion, till I
caught sight of a wooden box in a corner. It was of modern
make, one such as grocers use to pack provisions in. It had
some address nailed on it, and an aimless curiosity compelled me to creep thither and read it. A torn and weather-
stained scrap of paper, with the nails at the corner rusty
with age; but something of the address might still be made
out. Amid the stains my feverish eyes read, 'To Mr M—,
Carrickfey, by Allerfoot Station.'

The ruined cottage in the hollow of the waste with the
single gnarled apple-tree was before me in a twinkling. I
remembered the shepherd's shrinking from the place and
the name, and his wild eyes when he told me of the thing
that had happened there. I seemed to see the old man in his
moorland cottage, thinking no evil; the sudden entry of the
nameless things; and then the eyes glazed in unspeakable
terror. I felt my lips dry and burning. Above me was the
vault of rock; in the distance I saw the fire-glow and the
shadows of shapes moving around it. My fright was too
great for inaction, so I crept from the couch, and silently,
stealthily, with tottering steps and bursting heart, I began to
reconnoitre.

But I was still bound, my arms tightly, my legs more
loosely, but yet firm enough to hinder flight. I could not get
my hands at my leg-straps, still less could I undo the
manacles. I rolled on the floor, seeking some sharp edge
of rock, but all had been worn smooth by the use of

centuries. Then suddenly an idea came upon me like an
inspiration. The sounds from the fire seemed to have
ceased, and I could hear them repeated from another
and more distant part of the cave. The Folk had left their
orgy round the blaze, and at the end of the long tunnel I saw
its glow fall unimpeded upon the floor. Once there, I might
burn off my fetters and be free to turn my thoughts to
escape.

I crawled a little way with much labour. Then suddenly I
came abreast an opening in the wall, through which a path
went. It was a long straight rock-cutting, and at the end I
saw a gleam of pale light. It must be the open air; the way of
escape was prepared for me; and with a prayer I made what
speed I could towards the fire.

I rolled on the verge, but the fuel was peat, and the warm
ashes would not burn the cords. In desperation I went
farther, and my clothes began to singe, while my face ached
beyond endurance. But yet I got no nearer my object. The
strips of hide warped and cracked, but did not burn. Then
in a last effort I thrust my wrists bodily into the glow and
held them there. In an instant I drew them out with a groan
of pain, scarred and sore, but to my joy with the band
snapped in one place. Weak as I was, it was now easy to free
myself, and then came the untying of my legs. My hands
trembled, my eyes were dazed with hurry, and I was longer
over the job than need have been. But at length I had loosed
my cramped knees and stood on my feet, a free man once
more.

I kicked off my boots, and fled noiselessly down the
passage to the tunnel mouth. Apparently it was close on
evening, for the white light had faded to a pale yellow. But it
was daylight, and that was all I sought, and I ran for it as
eagerly as ever runner ran to a goal. I came out on a rock-
shelf, beneath which a moraine of boulders fell away in a
chasm to a dark loch. It was all but night, but I could see the
gnarled and fortressed rocks rise in ramparts above, and
below the unknown screes and cliffs which make the side of
the Muneraw a place only for foxes and the fowls of the air.

The first taste of liberty is an intoxication, and assuredly I
was mad when I leaped down among the boulders. Happily

at the top of the gully the stones were large and stable, else the noise would certainly have discovered me. Down I went, slipping, praying, my charred wrists aching, and my stockinged feet wet with blood. Soon I was in the jaws of the cleft, and a pale star rose before me. I have always been timid in the face of great rocks, and now, had not an awful terror been dogging my footsteps, no power on earth could have driven me to that descent. Soon I left the boulders behind, and came to long spouts of little stones, which moved with me till the hillside seemed sinking under my feet. Sometimes I was face downwards, once and again I must have fallen for yards. Had there been a cliff at the foot, I should have gone over it without resistance; but by the providence of God the spout ended in a long curve into the heather of the bog.

When I found my feet once more on soft boggy earth, my strength was renewed within me. A great hope of escape sprang up in my heart. For a second I looked back. There was a great line of shingle with the cliffs beyond, and above all the unknown blackness of the cleft. There lay my terror, and I set off running across the bog for dear life. My mind was clear enough to know my road. If I held round the loch in front I should come to a burn which fed the Farawa stream, on whose banks stood the shepherd's cottage. The loch could not be far; once at the Farawa I would have the light of the shieling clear before me.

Suddenly I heard behind me, as if coming from the hillside, the patter of feet. It was the sound which white hares make in the winter-time on a noiseless frosty day as they patter over the snow. I have heard the same soft noise from a herd of deer when they changed their pastures. Strange that so kindly a sound should put the very fear of death in my heart. I ran madly, blindly, yet thinking shrewdly. The loch was before me. Somewhere I had read or heard, I do not know where, that the brutish aboriginal races of the North could not swim. I myself swam powerfully; could I but cross the loch I should save two miles of a desperate country.

There was no time to lose, for the patter was coming nearer, and I was almost at the loch's edge. I tore off my coat and rushed in. The bottom was mossy, and I had to struggle far before I found any depth. Something plashed in the water before me, and then something else a little behind. The thought that I was a mark for unknown missiles made me crazy with fright, and I struck fiercely out for the other shore. A gleam of moonlight was on the water at the burn's exit, and thither I guided myself. I found the thing difficult enough in itself, for my hands ached, and I was numb from my bonds. But my fancy raised a thousand phantoms to vex me. Swimming in that black bog water, pursued by those nameless things, I seemed to be in a world of horror far removed from the kindly world of men. My strength seemed inexhaustible from my terror. Monsters at the bottom of the water seemed to bite at my feet, and the pain of my wrists made me believe that the loch was boiling hot, and that I was in some hellish place of torment.

I came out on a spit of gravel above the burn mouth, and set off down the ravine of the burn. It was a strait place, strewn with rocks; but now and then the hill turf came in stretches, and eased my wounded feet. Soon the fall became more abrupt, and I was slipping down a hillside, with the water on my left making great cascades in the granite. And then I was out in the wider vale where the Farawa water flowed among links of moss.

Far in front, a speck in the blue darkness, shone the light of the cottage. I panted forward, my breath coming in gasps and my back shot with fiery pains. Happily the land was easier for the feet as long as I kept on the skirts of the bog. My ears were sharp as a wild beast's with fear, as I listened for the noise of pursuit. Nothing came but the rustle of the gentlest hill-wind and the chatter of the falling streams.

Then suddenly the light began to waver and move athwart the window. I knew what it meant. In a minute or two the household at the cottage would retire to rest, and the lamp would be put out. True, I might find the place in the dark, for there was a moon of sorts and the road was not desperate. But somehow in that hour the lamplight gave a promise of safety which I clung to despairingly.

And then the last straw was added to my misery. Behind me came the pad of feet, the pat-patter, soft, eerie, incredibly swift. I choked with fear, and flung myself forward in a last effort. I give my word it was sheer mechanical shrinking that drove me on. God knows I would have lain down to die in the heather, had the things behind me been a common terror of life.

I ran as man never ran before, leaping hags, scrambling through green well-heads, straining towards the fast-dying light. A quarter of a mile and the patter sounded nearer. Soon I was not two hundred yards off, and the noise seemed almost at my elbow. The light went out, and the black mass of the cottage loomed in the dark.

Then, before I knew, I was at the door, battering it wearily and yelling for help. I heard steps within and a hand on the bolt. Then something shot past me with lighting force and buried itself in the wood. The dreadful hands were almost at my throat, when the door was opened and I stumbled in, hearing with a gulp of joy the key turn and the bar fall behind me.

V THE TROUBLES OF A CONSCIENCE

My body and senses slept, for I was utterly tired, but my brain all the night was on fire with horrid fancies. Again I was in that accursed cave; I was torturing my hands in the fire; I was slipping barefoot among jagged boulders; and then with bursting heart I was toiling the last mile with the cottage light – now grown to a great fire in the heavens – blazing before me.

It was broad daylight when I awoke, and I thanked God for the comfortable rays of the sun. I had been laid in a box-bed off the inner room, and my first sight was the shepherd sitting with folded arms in a chair regarding me solemnly. I rose and began to dress, feeling my legs and arms still tremble with weariness. The shepherd's sister bound up my scarred wrists and put an ointment on my burns; and, limping like an old man, I went into the kitchen.

I could eat little breakfast, for my throat seemed dry and narrow; but they gave me some brandy-and-milk, which put strength into my body. All the time the brother and sister sat in silence, regarding me with covert glances.

'Ye have been delivered from the jaws o' the Pit,' said the man at length. 'See that,' and he held out to me a thin shaft of flint. 'I fand that in the door this morning.'

I took it, let it drop, and stated vacantly at the window. My nerves had been too much tried to be roused by any new terror. Out of doors it was fair weather, flying gleams of April sunlight and the soft colours of spring. I felt dazed, isolated, cut off from my easy past and pleasing future, a companion of horrors and the sport of nameless things. Then suddenly my eye fell on my books heaped on a table, and the old distant civilisation seemed for the moment inexpressibly dear.

'I must go – at once. And you must come too. You cannot stay here. I tell you it is death. If you knew what I know you would be crying out with fear. How far is it to Allermuir? Eight, fifteen miles; and then ten down Glen Aller to Allerfoot, and then the railway. We must go together while it is daylight, and perhaps we may be untouched. But quick, there is not a moment to lose.' And I was on my shaky feet, and bustling among my possessions.

'I'll gang wi' ye to the station,' said the shepherd, 'for ye're clearly no fit to look after yourself. My sister will bide and keep the house. If naething has touched us this ten year, naething will touch us the day.'

'But you cannot stay. You are mad,' I began; but he cut me short with the words, 'I trust in God.'

'In any case let your sister come with us. I dare not think of a woman alone in this place.'

'I'll bide,' said she. 'I'm no feared as lang as I'm indoors and there's steeks on the windies.'

So I packed my few belongings as best I could, tumbled my books into a haversack, and, gripping the shepherd's arm nervously, crossed the threshold. The glen was full of sunlight. There lay the long shining links of the Farawa burn, the rough hills tumbled beyond, and far over all the scarred and distant forehead of the Muneraw. I had always looked on moorland country as the freshest on earth –

clean, wholesome, and homely. But now the fresh uplands
seemed like a horrible pit. When I looked to the hills my
breath choked in my throat, and the feel of soft heather
below my feet set my heart trembling.

It was a slow journey to the inn at Allermuir. For one
thing, no power on earth would draw me within sight of the
shieling of Carrickfey, so we had to cross a shoulder of hill
and make our way down a difficult glen, and then over a
treacherous moss. The lochs were now gleaming like
fretted silver; but to me, in my dreadful knowledge, they
seemed more eerie than on that grey day when I came. At
last my eyes were cheered by the sight of a meadow and a
fence; then we were on a little byroad; and soon the fir-
woods and corn-lands of Allercleuch were plain before us.

The shepherd came no farther, but with brief good-bye
turned his solemn face hillwards. I hired a trap and a man
to drive, and down the ten miles of Glen Aller I struggled to
keep my thoughts from the past. I thought of the kindly
South Country, of Oxford, of anything comfortable and
civilised. My driver pointed out the objects of interest as in
duty bound, but his words fell on unheeding ears. At last he
said something which roused me indeed to interest – the
interest of the man who hears the word he fears most in the
world. On the left side of the river there suddenly sprang
into view a long gloomy cleft in the hills, with a vista of dark
mountains behind, down which a stream of considerable
size poured its waters.

'That is the Water o' Dule,' said the man in a reverent
voice. 'A graund water to fish, but dangerous to life, for it's
a' linns. Awa' at the heid they say there's a terrible wild
place called the Scarts o' Muneraw, – that's a shouther o'
the muckle hill itsel' that ye see, – but I've never been there,
and I never kent ony man that had either.'

At the station, which is a mile from the village of Allerfoot, I found I had some hours to wait on my train for the
south. I dared not trust myself for one moment alone, so I
hung about the goods-shed, talked vacantly to the porters,
and when one went to the village for tea I accompanied
him, and to his wonder entertained him at the inn. When I
returned I found on the platform a stray bagman who was

that evening going to London. If there is one class of men in the world which I heartily detest it is this; but such was my state that I hailed him as a brother, and besought his company. I paid the difference for a first-class fare, and had him in the carriage with me. He must have thought me an amiable maniac, for I talked in fits and starts, and when he fell asleep I would wake him up and beseech him to speak to me. At wayside stations I would pull down the blinds in case of recognition, for to my unquiet mind the world seemed full of spies sent by that terrible Folk of the Hills. When the train crossed a stretch of moor I would lie down on the seat in case of shafts fired from the heather. And then at last with utter weariness I fell asleep, and woke screaming about midnight to find myself well down in the cheerful English midlands, and red blast-furnaces blinking by the railway-side.

In the morning I breakfasted in my rooms at St Chad's with a dawning sense of safety. I was in a different and calmer world. The lawn-like quadrangles, the great trees, the cawing of rooks, and the homely twitter of sparrows – all seemed decent and settled and pleasing. Indoors the oak-panelled walls, the shelves of books, the pictures, the faint fragrance of tobacco, were very different from the gimcrack adornments and the accursed smell of peat and heather in that deplorable cottage. It was still vacation-time, so most of my friends were down; but I spent the day hunting out the few cheerful pedants to whom term and vacation were the same. It delighted me to hear again their precise talk, to hear them make a boast of their work, and narrate the childish little accidents of their life. I yearned for the childish once more; I craved for women's drawing-rooms, and women's chatter, and everything which makes life an elegant game. God knows I had had enough of the other thing for a lifetime!

That night I shut myself in my rooms, barred my windows, drew my curtains, and made a great destruction. All books or pictures which recalled to me the moorlands were ruthlessly doomed. Novels, poems, treatises I flung into an old box, for sale to the second-hand bookseller. Some prints and water-colour sketches I tore to pieces with my own hands. I ransacked my fishing-book, and condemned all tackle for moorland waters to the flames. I wrote a letter to my solicitors, bidding them go no further in the purchase of a place in Lorn I had long been thinking of. Then, and not till then, did I feel the bondage of the past a little loosed from my shoulders. I made myself a night-cap of rum-punch instead of my usual whisky-toddy, that all associations with that dismal land might be forgotten, and to complete the renunciation I returned to cigars and flung my pipe into a drawer.

But when I woke in the morning I found that it is hard to get rid of memories. My feet were still sore and wounded, and when I felt my arms cramped and reflected on the causes, there was that black memory always near to vex me.

In a little term began, and my duties – as deputy-professor of Northern Antiquities – were once more clamorous. I can well believe that my hearers found my lectures strange, for instead of dealing with my favourite subjects and matters, which I might modestly say I had made my own, I confined myself to recondite and distant themes, treating even these cursorily and dully. For the truth is, my heart was no more in my subject. I hated – or I thought I hated – all things Northern with the virulence of utter fear. My reading was confined to science of the most recent kind, to abstruse philosophy, and to foreign classics. Anything which savoured of romance or mystery was abhorrent; I pined for sharp outlines and the tangibility of a high civilisation.

All the term I threw myself into the most frivolous life of the place. My Harrow schooldays seemed to have come back to me. I had once been a fair cricketer, so I played again for my college, and made decent scores. I coached an indifferent crew on the river. I fell into the slang of the place, which I had hitherto detested. My former friends looked on me askance, as if some freakish changeling had possessed me. Formerly I had been ready for pedantic discussion, I had been absorbed in my work, men had spoken of me as a rising scholar. Now I fled the very mention of things I had once delighted in. The Professor of Northern Antiquities, a scholar of European reputation, meeting me once in the Parks, embarked on an account of certain novel rings recently found in Scotland, and to his horror found that, when he had got well under weigh, I had slipped off unnoticed. I heard afterwards that the good old man was found by a friend walking disconsolately with bowed head in the middle of the High Street. Being rescued from among the horses' feet, he could only murmur, 'I am thinking of Graves, poor man! And a year ago he was as sane as I am!'

But a man may not long deceive himself. I kept up the illusion valiantly for the term; but I felt instinctively that the fresh schoolboy life, which seemed to me the extreme opposite to the ghoulish North, and as such the most desirable of things, was eternally cut off from me. No cunning affectation could ever dispel my real nature or efface the memory of a week. I realised miserably that sooner or later I must fight it out with my conscience. I began to call myself a coward. The chief thoughts of my mind began to centre themselves more and more round that unknown life waiting to be explored among the wilds.

One day I met a friend – an official in the British Museum – who was full of some new theory about primitive habitations. To me it seemed inconceivably absurd; but he was strong in his confidence, and without flaw in his evidence. The man irritated me, and I burned to prove him wrong, but I could think of no argument which was final against his. Then it flashed upon me that my own experience held the disproof; and without more words I left him, hot, angry with myself, and tantalised by the unattainable.

I might relate my *bona-fide* experience, but would men believe me? I must bring proofs, I must complete my researches, so as to make them incapable of disbelief. And there in those deserts was waiting the key. There lay the greatest discovery of the century – nay, of the millennium. There, too, lay the road to wealth such as I had never dreamed of. Could I succeed, I should be famous for ever. I would revolutionise history and anthropology; I would systematise folklore; I would show the world of men the pit whence they were digged and the rock whence they were hewn.

And then began a game of battledore between myself and my conscience.

'You are a coward,' said my conscience.

'I am sufficiently brave,' I would answer. 'I have seen things and yet lived. The terror is more than mortal, and I cannot face it.'

'You are a coward,' said my conscience.

'I am not bound to go there again. It would be purely for my own aggrandisement if I went, and not for any matter of duty.'

'Nevertheless you are a coward,' said my conscience.

'In any case the matter can wait.'

'You are a coward.'

Then came one awful midsummer night, when I lay sleepless and fought the thing out with myself. I knew that the strife was hopeless, that I should have no peace in this world again unless I made the attempt. The dawn was breaking when I came to the final resolution; and when I rose and looked at my face in a mirror, lo! it was white and lined and drawn like a man of sixty.

VI SUMMER ON THE MOORS

The next morning I packed a bag with some changes of clothing and a collection of notebooks, and went up to town. The first thing I did was to pay a visit to my solicitors. 'I am about to travel,' said I, 'and I wish to have all things settled in case any accident should happen to me.' So I arranged for the disposal of my property in case of death, and added a codicil which puzzled the lawyers. If I did not return within six months, communications were to be entered into with the shepherd at the shieling of Farawa – post-town Allerfoot. If he could produce any papers, they were to be put into the hands of certain friends, published, and the cost charged to my estate. From my solicitors I went to a gunmaker's in Regent Street and bought an ordinary six-chambered revolver, feeling much as a man must feel who proposed to cross the Atlantic in a skiff and purchased a small life-belt as a precaution.

I took the night express to the North, and, for a marvel, I slept. When I awoke about four we were on the verge of Westmoreland, and stony hills blocked the horizon. At first I hailed the mountain-land gladly; sleep for the moment had caused forgetfulness of my terrors. But soon a turn of the line brought me in full view of a heathery moor, running far to a confusion of distant peaks. I remembered my mission and my fate, and if ever condemned criminal felt a more bitter regret I pity his case. Why should I alone among the millions of this happy isle be singled out at the repository of a ghastly secret, and be cursed by a conscience which would not let it rest?

I came to Allerfoot early in the forenoon, and got a trap to drive me up the valley. It was a lowering grey day, hot and yet sunless. A sort of heat-haze cloaked the hills, and every now and then a smurr of rain would meet us on the road, and in a minute be over. I felt wretchedly dispirited; and when at last the white-washed kirk of Allermuir came into sight and the broken-backed bridge of Aller, man's eyes seemed to have looked on no drearier scene since time began.

I ate what meal I could get, for, fears or no, I was voraciously hungry. Then I asked the landlord to find me some man who would show me the road to Farawa. I demanded company, not for protection – for what could two men do against such brutish strength? – but to keep my mind from its own thoughts.

The man looked at me anxiously.

'Are ye acquaint wi' the folks, then?' he asked.

I said I was, that I had often stayed in the cottage.

'Ye ken that they've a name for being queer. The man never comes here forbye once or twice a-year, and he has few dealings wi' other herds. He's got an ill name, too, for losing sheep. I dinna like the country ava. Up by yon Muneraw – no that I've ever been there, but I've seen it afar off – is enough to put a man daft for the rest o' his days. What's taking ye thereaways? It's no the time for the fishing?'

I told him that I was a botanist going to explore certain hill-crevices for rare ferns. He shook his head, and then after some delay found me an ostler who would accompany me to the cottage.

The man was a shock-headed, long-limbed fellow, with fierce red hair and a humorous eye. He talked sociably about his life, answered my hasty questions with deftness, and beguiled me for the moment out of myself. I passed the melancholy lochs, and came in sight of the great stony hills without the trepidation I had expected. Here at my side was one who found some humour even in those uplands. But one thing I noted which brought back the old uneasiness. He took the road which led us farthest from Carrickfey, and when to try him I proposed the other, he vetoed it with emphasis.

After this his good spirits departed, and he grew distrustful.

'What mak's ye a freend o' the herd at Farawa?' he demanded a dozen times.

Finally, I asked him if he knew the man, and had seen him lately.

'I dinna ken him, and I hadna seen him for years till a fortnicht syne, when a' Allermuir saw him. He cam doun one afternoon to the public-hoose, and begood to drink. He had aye been kenned for a terrible godly kind o' a man, so ye may believe folk wondered at this. But when he had stuck to the drink for twae days, and filled himsel' blind-fou half-a-dozen o' times, he took a fit o' repentance, and raved and blethered about siccan a life as he led in the muirs. There was some said he was speakin' serious, but maist thocht it was juist daftness.'

'And what did he speak about?' I asked sharply.

'I canna verra weel tell ye. It was about some kind o' bogle that lived in the Muneraw – that's the shouthers o't ye see yonder – and it seems that the bogle killed his sheep and frichted himsel'. He was aye bletherin', too, about something or somebody ca'd Grave; but oh! the man wasna wise.' And my companion shook a contemptuous head.

And then below us in the valley we saw the shieling, with a thin shaft of smoke rising into the rainy grey weather. The man left me, sturdily refusing any fee. 'I wantit my legs stretched as weel as you. A walk in the hills is neither here nor there to a stoot man. When will ye be back, sir?'

The question was well-timed. 'To-morrow fortnight,' I said, 'and I want somebody from Allermuir to come out here in the morning and carry some baggage. Will you see to that?'

He said 'Ay,' and went off, while I scrambled down the hill to the cottage. Nervousness possessed me, and though it was broad daylight and the whole place lay plain before me, I ran pell-mell, and did not stop till I reached the door.

The place was utterly empty. Unmade beds, unwashed dishes, a hearth strewn with the ashes of peat, and dust thick on everything, proclaimed the absence of inmates. I began to be horribly frightened. Had the shepherd and his sister, also, disappeared? Was I left alone in this bleak place, with a dozen lonely miles between me and human dwellings? I could not return alone; better this horrible place than the unknown perils of the out-of-doors. Hastily I barricaded the door, and to the best of my power shuttered the windows; and then with dreary forebodings I sat down to wait on fortune.

In a little I heard a long swinging step outside and the sound of dogs. Joyfully I opened the latch, and there was the shepherd's grim face waiting stolidly on what might appear.

At the sight of me he stepped back. 'What in the Lord's name are ye daein' here?' he asked. 'Didna ye get enough afore?'

'Come in,' I said, sharply. 'I want to talk.'

In he came with those blessed dogs, – what a comfort it was to look on their great honest faces! He sat down on the untidy bed and waited.

'I came because I could not stay away. I saw too much to give me any peace elsewhere. I must go back, even though I risk my life for it. The cause of scholarship demands it as well as the cause of humanity.'

'Is that a' the news ye hae?' he said. 'Weel, I've mair to tell ye. Three weeks syne my sister Margit was lost, and I've never seen her mair.'

My jaw fell, and I could only stare at him.

'I cam hame from the hill at nightfa' and she was gone. I lookit for her up hill and doun, but I couldna find her. Syne I think I went daft. I went to the Scarts and huntit them up and doun, but no sign could I see. The Folk can bide quiet enough when they want. Syne I went to Allermuir and drank mysel' blind, – me, that's a God-fearing man and a saved soul; but the Lord help me, I didna ken what I was at. That's my news, and day and night I wander thae hills, seekin' for what I canna find.'

'But, man, are you mad?' I cried. 'Surely there are neighbours to help you. There is a law in the land, and you had only to find the nearest police-office and compel them to assist you.'

'What guid can man dae?' he asked. 'An army o' sodgers couldna find that hidy-hole. Forby, when I went into Allermuir wi' my story the folk thocht me daft. It was that set me drinking, for – the Lord forgive me! – I wasna my ain maister. I threepit till I was hairse, but the bodies just lauch'd.' And he lay back on the bed like a man mortally tired.

Grim though the tidings were, I can only say that my chief feeling was of comfort. Pity for the new tragedy had swallowed up my fear. I had now a purpose, and a purpose, too, not of curiosity but of mercy.

'I go to-morrow morning to the Muneraw. But first I want to give you something to do.' And I drew roughly a chart of the place on the back of a letter. 'Go into Allermuir to-morrow, and give this paper to the landlord at the inn. The letter will tell him what to do. He is to raise at once all the men he can get, and come to the place on the chart marked with a cross. Tell him life depends on his hurry.'

The shepherd nodded. 'D'ye ken the Folk are watching for you? They let me pass without trouble, for they've nae use for me, but I see fine they're seeking you. Ye'll no gang half a mile the morn afore they grip ye.'

'So much the better,' I said. 'That will take me quicker to the place I want to be at.'

'And I'm to gang to Allermuir the morn,' he repeated, with the air of a child conning a lesson. 'But what if they'll no believe me?'

'They'll believe the letter.'

'Maybe,' he said, and relapsed into a doze.

I set myself to put that house in order, to rouse the fire, and prepare some food. It was dismal work; and meantime outside the night darkened, and a great wind rose, which howled round the walls and lashed the rain on the windows.

VII *IN TUAS MANUS, DOMINE!*

I had not gone twenty yards from the cottage door ere I knew I was watched. I had left the shepherd still dozing, in the half-conscious state of a dazed and broken man. All night the wind had wakened me at intervals, and now in the half-light of morn the weather seemed more vicious than ever. The wind cut my ears, the whole firmament was full of the rendings and thunders of the storm. Rain fell in blinding sheets, the heath was a marsh, and it was the most I could do to struggle against the hurricane which stopped my breath. And all the while I knew I was not alone in the desert.

All men know – in imagination or in experience – the sensation of being spied on. The nerves tingle, the skin grows hot and prickly, and there is a queer sinking of the heart. Intensify this common feeling a hundredfold, and you get a tenth part of what I suffered. I am telling a plain tale, and record bare physical facts. My lips stood out from my teeth as I heard, or felt, a rustle in the heather, a scraping among stones. Some subtle magnetic link seemed established between my body and the mysterious world around. I became sick – acutely sick – with the ceaseless apprehension.

My fright became so complete that when I turned a corner of rock, or stepped in deep heather, I seemed to feel a body rub against mine. This continued all the way up the Farawa water, and then up its feeder to the little lonely loch. It kept me from looking forward; but it likewise kept me in such a sweat of fright that I was ready to faint. Then the notion came upon me to test this fancy of mine. If I was tracked thus closely, clearly the trackers would bar my way if I turned back. So I wheeled round and walked a dozen paces down the glen.

Nothing stopped me. I was about to turn again, when something made me take six more paces. At the fourth something rustled in the heather, and my neck was gripped as in a vice. I had already made up my mind on what I would do. I would be perfectly still, I would conquer my fear, and let them do as they pleased with me so long as they took me to their dwelling. But at the touch of the hands my resolutions fled. I struggled and screamed. Then something was clapped on my mouth, speech and strength went from me, and once more I was back in the maudlin childhood of terror.

In the cave it was always a dusky twilight. I seemed to be lying in the same place, with the same dull glare of firelight far off, and the same close stupefying smell. One of the creatures was standing silently at my side, and I asked him some trivial question. He turned and shambled down the passage, leaving me alone.

Then he returned with another, and they talked their guttural talk to me. I scarcely listened till I remembered that in a sense I was here of my own accord, and on a definite mission. The purport of their speech seemed to be that, now I had returned, I must beware of a second flight. Once I had been spared; a second time I should be killed without mercy.

I assented gladly. The Folk, then, had some use for me. I felt my errand prospering.

Then the old creature which I had seen before crept out of some corner and squatted beside me. He put a claw on my shoulder, a horrible, corrugated, skeleton thing, hairy to the finger-tips and nailless. He grinned, too, with toothless gums, and his hideous old voice was like a file on sandstone.

I asked questions, but he would only grin and jabber, looking now and then furtively over his shoulder towards the fire.

I coaxed and humoured him, till he launched into a narrative of which I could make nothing. It seemed a mere string of names, with certain words repeated at fixed intervals. Then it flashed on me that this might be a religious incantation. I had discovered remnants of a ritual and a mythology among them. It was possible that these were sacred days, and that I had stumbled upon some rude celebration.

I caught a word or two and repeated them. He looked at me curiously. Then I asked him some leading question, and he replied with clearness. My guess was right. The midsummer week was the holy season of the year, when sacrifices were offered to the gods.

The notion of sacrifices disquieted me, and I would fain have asked further. But the creature would speak no more. He hobbled off, and left me alone in the rock-chamber to listen to a strange sound which hung ceaselessly about me. It must be the storm without, like a park of artillery rattling among the crags. A storm of storms surely, for the place echoed and hummed, and to my unquiet eye the very rock of the roof seemed to shake!

Apparently my existence was forgotten, for I lay long before any one returned. Then it was merely one who brought food, the same strange meal as before, and left hastily. When I had eaten I rose and stretched myself. My hands and knees still quivered nervously; but I was strong and perfectly well in body. The empty, desolate, tomb-like place was eerie enough to scare any one; but its emptiness was comfort when I thought of its inmates. Then I wandered down the passage towards the fire which was burning in loneliness. Where had the Folk gone? I puzzled over their disappearance.

Suddenly sounds began to break on my ear, coming from some inner chamber at the end of that in which the fire burned. I could scarcely see for the smoke; but I began to make my way towards the noise, feeling along the sides of rock. Then a second gleam of light seemed to rise before me, and I came to an aperture in the wall which gave entrance to another room.

This in turn was full of smoke and glow – a murky orange glow, as if from some strange flame of roots. There were the squat moving figures, running in wild antics round the fire. I crouched in the entrance, terrified and yet curious, till I saw something beyond the blaze which held me dumb.

Apart from the others and tied to some stake in the wall was a woman's figure, and the face was the face of the shepherd's sister.

My first impulse was flight. I must get away and think, – plan, achieve some desperate way of escape. I sped back to the silent chamber as if the gang were at my heels. It was still empty, and I stood helplessly in the centre, looking at the impassable walls of rock as a wearied beast may look at the walls of its cage. I bethought me of the way I had escaped before and rushed thither, only to find it blocked by a huge contrivance of stone. Yards and yards of solid rock were between me and the upper air, and yet through it all came the crash and whistle of the storm. If I were at my wits' end in this inner darkness, there was also high commotion among the powers of the air in that upper world.

As I stood I heard the soft steps of my tormentors. They seemed to think I was meditating escape, for they flung themselves on me and bore me to the ground. I did not struggle, and when they saw me quiet, they squatted round and began to speak. They told me of the holy season and its sacrifices. At first I could not follow them; then when I caught familiar words I found some clue, and they became intelligible. They spoke of a woman, and I asked, 'What woman?' With all frankness they told me of the custom which prevailed – how every twentieth summer a woman was sacrificed to some devilish god, and by the hand of one of the stranger race. I said nothing, but my whitening face must have told them a tale, though I strove hard to keep my composure. I asked if they had found the victims. 'She is in this place,' they said: 'and as for the man, thou art he.' And with this they left me.

I had still some hours; so much I gathered from their talk, for the sacrifice was at sunset. Escape was cut off for ever. I have always been something of a fatalist, and at the prospect of the irrevocable end my cheerfulness returned. I had my pistol, for they had taken nothing from me. I took out the little weapon and fingered it lovingly. Hope of the lost, refuge of the vanquished, ease to the coward, – blessed be he who first conceived it!

The time dragged on, the minutes grew to hours, and still I was left solitary. Only the mad violence of the storm broke the quiet. It had increased in fury, for the stones at the mouth of the exit by which I had formerly escaped seemed to rock with some external pressure, and cutting shafts of wind slipped past and cleft the heat of the passage. What a sight the ravine outside must be, I thought, set in the forehead of a great hill, and swept clean by every breeze! Then came a crashing, and the long hollow echo of a fall. The rocks are splitting, said I; the road down the corrie will be impassable now and for evermore.

I began to grow weak with the nervousness of the waiting, and by-and-by I lay down and fell into a sort of doze. When I next knew consciousness I was being roused by two of the Folk, and bidden get ready. I stumbled to my feet, felt for the pistol in the hollow of my sleeve, and prepared to follow.

When we came out into the wider chamber the noise of the storm was deafening. The roof rang like a shield which has been struck. I noticed, perturbed as I was, that my guards cast anxious eyes around them, alarmed, like myself, at the murderous din. Nor was the world quieter when we entered the last chamber, where the fire burned and the remnant of the Folk waited. Wind had found an entrance from somewhere or other, and the flames blew here and there, and the smoke gyrated in odd circles. At the back, and apart from the rest, I saw the dazed eyes and the white old drawn face of the woman.

They led me up beside her to a place where there was a rude flat stone, hollowed in the centre, and on it a rusty iron knife, which seemed once to have formed part of a scythe-blade. Then I saw the ceremonial which was marked out for me. It was the very rite which I had dimly figured as current among a rude people, and even in that moment of horror I had something of the scholar's satisfaction.

The oldest of the Folk, who seemed to be a sort of priest, came to my side and mumbled a form of words. His fetid breath sickened me; his dull eyes, glassy like a brute's with age, brought my knees together. He put the knife in my hands, dragged the terror-stricken woman forward to the altar, and bade me begin.

I began by sawing her bonds through. When she felt herself free she would have fled back, but stopped when I bade her. At that moment there came a noise of rending and crashing as if the hills were falling, and for one second the eyes of the Folk were averted from the frustrated sacrifice.

Only for a moment. The next they saw what I had done, and with one impulse rushed towards me. Then began the last scene in the play. I sent a bullet through the right eye of the first thing that came on. The second shot went wide; but the third shattered the hand of an elderly ruffian with a club. Never for an instant did they stop, and now they were clutching at me. I pushed the woman behind, and fired three rapid shots in blind panic, and then, clutching the scythe, I struck right and left like a madman.

Suddenly I saw the foreground sink before my eyes. The roof sloped down, and with a sickening hiss a mountain of rock and earth seemed to precipitate itself on the foremost of my assailants. One, nipped in the middle by a rock, caught my eye by his hideous writhings. Two only remained in what was now a little suffocating chamber, with embers from the fire still smoking on the floor.

The woman caught me by the hand and drew me with her, while the two seemed mute with fear. 'There's a road at the back,' she screamed. 'I ken it. I fand it out.' And she pulled me up a narrow hole in the rock.

How long we climbed I do not know. We were both fighting for air, with the tightness of throat and chest, and the craziness of limb which mean suffocation. I cannot tell when we first came to the surface, but I remember the woman, who seemed to have the strength of extreme terror, pulling me from the edge of a crevasse and laying me on a flat rock. It seemed to be the depth of winter, with sheer-falling rain and a wind that shook the hills.

Then I was once more myself and could look about me. From my feet yawned a sheer abyss, where once had been a

hill-shoulder. Some great mass of rock on the brow of the
mountain had been loosened by the storm, and in its fall
had caught the lips of the ravine and blocked the upper
outlet from the nest of dwellings. For a moment I feared
that all had been destroyed.

My feeling – Heaven help me! – was not thankfulness for
God's mercy and my escape, but a bitter mad regret. I
rushed frantically to the edge, and when I saw only the
blackness of darkness I wept weak tears. All the time the
storm was tearing at my body, and I had to grip hard by
hand and foot to keep my place.

Suddenly on the brink of the ravine I saw a third figure.
We two were not the only fugitives. One of the Folk had
escaped.

I ran to it, and to my surprise the thing as soon as it saw
me rushed to meet me. At first I thought it was with some
instinct of self-preservation, but when I saw its eyes I knew
the purpose of fight. Clearly one or other should go no
more from the place.

We were some ten yards from the brink when I grappled
with it. Dimly I heard the woman scream with fright, and
saw her scramble across the hillside. Then we were tugging
in a death-throe, the hideous smell of the thing in my face,
its red eyes burning into mine, and its hoarse voice
muttering. Its strength seemed incredible; but I, too, am
no weakling. We tugged and strained, its nails biting into
my flesh, while I choked its throat unsparingly. Every
second I dreaded lest we should plunge together over
the ledge, for it was thither my adversary tried to draw
me. I caught my heel in a nick of rock, and pulled madly
against it.

And then, while I was beginning to glory with the pride of
conquest, my hope was dashed in pieces. The thing seemed
to break from my arms, and, as if in despair, cast itself
headlong into the impenetrable darkness. I stumbled
blindly after it, saved myself on the brink, and fell back,
sick and ill, into a merciful swoon.

VIII NOTE IN CONCLUSION BY THE EDITOR

At this point the narrative of my unfortunate friend, Mr Graves of St Chad's, breaks off abruptly. He wrote it shortly before his death, and was prevented from completing it by the attack of heart failure which carried him off. In accordance with the instructions in his will, I have prepared it for publication, and now in much fear and hesitation give it to the world. First, however, I must supplement it by such facts as fall within my knowledge.

The shepherd seems to have gone to Allemuir and by the help of the letter convinced the inhabitants. A body of men was collected under the landlord, and during the afternoon set out for the hills. But unfortunately the great midsummer storm – the most terrible of recent climatic disturbances – had filled the mosses and streams, and they found themselves unable to proceed by any direct road. Ultimately late in the evening they arrived at the cottage of Farawa, only to find there a raving woman, the shepherd's sister, who seemed crazy with brain-fever. She told some rambling story about her escape, but her narrative said nothing of Mr Graves. So they treated her with what skill they possessed, and sheltered for the night in and around the cottage. Next morning the storm had abated a little, and the woman had recovered something of her wits. From her they learned that Mr Graves was lying in a ravine on the side of the Muneraw in imminent danger of his life. A body set out to find him; but so immense was the landslip, and so dangerous the whole mountain, that it was nearly evening when they recovered him from the ledge of rock. He was alive, but unconscious, and on bringing him back to the cottage it was clear that he was, indeed, very ill. There he lay for three months, while the best skill that could be got was procured for him. By dint of an uncommon toughness of constitution he survived; but it was an old and feeble man who returned to Oxford in the early winter.

The shepherd and his sister immediately left the countryside, and were never more heard of, unless they are the pair of unfortunates who are at present in a

Scottish pauper asylum, incapable of remembering even their names. The people who last spoke with them declared that their minds seemed weakened by a great shock, and that it was hopeless to try to get any connected or rational statement.

The career of my poor friend from that hour was little short of a tragedy. He awoke from his illness to find the world incredulous; even the country-folk of Allermuir set down the story to the shephered's craziness and my friend's credulity. In Oxford his argument was received with polite scorn. An account of his experiences which he drew up for *The Times* was refused by the editor; and an article on 'Primitive Peoples of the North', embodying what he believed to be the result of his discoveries, was unanimously rejected by every responsible journal in Europe. At first he bore the treatment bravely. Reflection convinced him that the colony had not been destroyed. Proofs were still awaiting his hand, and with courage and caution he might yet triumph over his enemies. But unfortunately, though the ardour of the scholar burned more fiercely than ever and all fear seemed to have been purged from his soul, the last adventure had grievously sapped his bodily strength. In the spring following his accident he made an effort to reach the spot – alone, for no one could be persuaded to follow him in what was regarded as a childish madness. He slept at the now deserted cottage of Farawa, but in the morning found himself unable to continue, and with difficulty struggled back to the shepherd's cottage at Allercleuch, where he was confined to bed for a fortnight. Then it became necessary for him to seek health abroad, and it was not till the following autumn that he attempted the journey again. He fell sick a second time at the inn of Allermuir, and during his convalescence had himself carried to a knoll in the inn garden, whence a glimpse can be obtained of the shoulder of the Muneraw. There he would sit for hours with his eyes fixed on the horizon, and at times he would be found weeping with weakness and vexation. The last attempt was made but two months before his last illness. On this occasion he got no farther than Carlisle, where he was taken ill with what proved to be a premonition of death. After that he shut his lips tightly, as though recognising the futility of his hopes. Whether he had been soured by the treatment he received, or whether his brain had already been weakened, he had become a morose silent man, and for the two years before his death had few friends and no society. From the obituary notice in *The Times* I take the following paragraph, which shows in what light the world had come to look upon him:–

'At the outset of his career he was regarded as a rising scholar in one department of archæology, and his Taffert lectures were a real contribution to an obscure subject. But in after-life he was led into fantastic speculations; and when he found himself unable to convince his colleagues, he gradually retired into himself, and lived practically a hermit's life till his death. His career, thus broken short, is a sad instance of the fascination which the recondite and the quack can exercise even over men of approved ability.'

And now his own narrative is published, and the world can judge as it pleases about the amazing romance. The view which will doubtless find general acceptance is that the whole is a figment of the brain, begotten of some harmless moorland adventure and the company of such religious maniacs as the shepherd and his sister. But some who knew the former sobriety and calmness of my friend's mind may be disposed timorously and with deep hesitation to another verdict. They may accept the narrative, and believe that somewhere in those moorlands he met with a horrible primitive survival, passed through the strangest adventure, and had his fingers on an epoch-making discovery. In this case they will be inclined to sympathise with the loneliness and misunderstanding of his latter days. It is not for me to decide the question. Though a fellow-historian, the Picts are outside my period, and I dare not advance an opinion on a matter with which I am not fully familiar. But I would point out that the means of settling the question are still extant, and I would call upon some young archæologist, with a reputation to make, to seize upon the chance of the century. Most of the expresses for the North stop at Allerfoot; a ten-miles' drive will bring him to Allermuir; and then with a fifteen-miles' walk he is at Farawa and on the threshold of discovery. Let him follow the burn and cross the ridge and ascend the Scarts of the Muneraw, and, if he return at all, it may be with a more charitable judgment of my unfortunate friend.

The Far Islands

The second story in *The Watcher by the Threshold* (1902) was first published in *Blackwood's Magazine* in November 1899 and has since been anthologised several times. It introduces the Raden family, later to figure in *John Macnab* (1925), and is an important story in that it reveals so many of the preoccupations that Buchan would explore throughout his writing career such as the power of place, the way the mystical impinges on the ordinary world, the tension between a person's primitive and civilised sides, the relationship between Scotland and England and how certain feelings can be passed on from generation to generation, the premise of *The Path of the King* (1921). Adam Melfort's dream in *A Prince of the Captivity* (1933) about the Scottish island, Eilean Ban, is reminiscent of Colin Raden's here.

Lady Alice, Lady Louise,
Between the wash of the tumbling seas—

I

When Bran the Blessed, as the story goes, followed the white bird on the Last Questing, knowing that return was not for him, he gave gifts to his followers. To Heliodorus he gave the gift of winning speech, and straightaway the man went south to the Italian seas, and, becoming a scholar, left many descendants who sat in the high places of the Church. To Raymond he gave his steel battle-axe, and bade him go out to the warrior's path and hew his way to a throne; which the man forthwith accomplished, and became an ancestor in the fourth degree of the first king of Scots. But to Colin, the youngest and the dearest, he gave no gift, whispering only a word in his ear and laying a finger on his eyelids. Yet

Colin was satisfied, and he alone of the three, after their master's going, remained on that coast of rock and heather.

In the third generation from Colin, as our elders counted years, came one Colin the Red, who built his keep on the cliffs of Acharra and was a mighty sea-rover in his day. Five times he sailed to the rich parts of France, and a good score of times he carried his flag of three stars against the easterly Vikings. A mere name in story, but a sounding piece of nomenclature well garnished with tales. A mastermind by all accounts, but cursed with a habit of fantasy; for, hearing in his old age of a land to the westward, he forthwith sailed into the sunset, but three days later was washed up, a twisted body, on one of the outer isles.

So far it is but legend, but with his grandson, Colin the Red, we fall into the safer hands of the chroniclers. To him God gave the unnumbered sorrows of story-telling, for he was a bard, cursed with a bard's fervours, and none the less a mighty warrior among his own folk. He it was who wrote the lament called 'The White Waters of Usna', and the exquisite chain of romances, 'Glede-red Gold and Grey Silver'. His tales were told by many fires, down to our grandfathers' time, and you will find them still pounded at by the folklorists. But his airs – they are eternal. On harp and pipe they have lived through the centuries; twisted and tortured, they survive in many song-books; and I declare that the other day I heard the most beautiful of them all murdered by a band at a German watering-place. This Colin led the wanderer's life, for he disappeared at middle-age, no one knew whither, and his return was long looked for by his people. Some thought that he became a Christian monk, the holy man living in the sea-girt isle of Cuna, who was found dead in extreme old age, kneeling on the beach, with his arms, contrary to the fashion of the Church, stretched to the westward.

As history narrowed into bonds and forms the descendants of Colin took Raden for their surname, and settled more firmly on their lands in the long peninsula of crag and inlets which runs west to the Atlantic. Under Donald of the Isles they harried the Kings of Scots, or, on their own authority, made war on Macleans and Macranalds, till their flag of the three stars, their badge of the grey-goose feather, and their on-cry of 'Cuna' were feared from Lochalsh to

Cantire. Later they made a truce with the King, and entered into the royal councils. For years they warded the western coast, and as king's lieutenants smoked out the inferior pirates of Eigg and Torosay. A Raden was made a Lord of Sleat, another was given lands in the low country and the name Baron of Strathyre, but their honours were transitory and short as their lives. Rarely one of the house saw middle-age. A bold, handsome, and stirring race, it was their fate to be cut off in the rude warfare of the times, or, if peace had them in its clutches, to man vessel and set off once more on those mad western voyages which were the weird of the family. Three of the name were found drowned on the far shore of Cuna; more than one sailed straight out of the ken of mortals. One rode with the Good Lord James on the pilgrimage of the Heart of Bruce, and died by his leader's side in the Saracen battle. Long afterwards a Raden led the western men against the Cheshire archers at Flodden, and was slain himself in the steel circle around the king.

But the years brought peace and a greater wealth, and soon the cold stone tower was left solitary on the headland, and the new house of Kinlochuna rose by the green links of the stream. The family changed its faith, and an Episcopal chaplain took the place of the old mass-priest in the tutoring of the sons. Radens were in the '15 and the '45. They rose with Bute to power, and they long disputed the pride of Dundas in the northern capital. They intermarried with great English houses till the sons of the family were Scots only in name, living much abroad or in London, many of them English landowners by virtue of a mother's blood. Soon the race was of the common over-civilised type, graceful, well-mannered, with abundant good looks, but only once in a generation reverting to the rugged northern strength. Eton and Oxford had in turn displaced the family chaplain, and the house by the windy headland grew emptier and emptier save when grouse and deer brought home its fickle masters.

II

A childish illness brought Colin to Kinlochuna when he had reached the mature age of five, and delicate health kept

him there for the greater part of the next six years. During
the winter he lived in London, but from the late northern
spring, through all the long bright summers, he lived in the
great tenantless place without company – for he was an only
child. A French nurse had the charge of his doings, and
when he had passed through the formality of lessons there
were the long pinewoods at his disposal, the rough moor,
the wonderful black holes with the rich black mud in them,
and best of all the bay of Acharra, below the headland, with
Cuna lying in the waves a mile to the west. At such times his
father was busy elsewhere; his mother was dead; the family
had few near relatives; so he passed a solitary childhood in
the company of seagulls and the birds of the moor.

His time for the beach was the afternoon. On the left as
you go down through the woods from the house there runs
out the great headland of Acharra, red and grey with
mosses, and with a nimbus always of screaming seafowl. To the right runs a low beach of sand, passing into
rough limestone boulders and then into the heather of the
wood. This in turn is bounded by a reef of low rocks falling
by gentle breaks to the water's edge. It is crowned with a
tangle of heath and fern, bright at most seasons with
flowers, and dwarf pine-trees straggle on its crest till one
sees the meaning of its Gaelic name, 'The Ragged Cock's-
Comb'. This place was Colin's playground in fine weather.
When it blew rain or snow from the north he dwelt indoors
among dogs and books, puzzling his way through great
volumes from his father's shelves. But when the mild west-
wind weather fell on the sea, then he would lie on the hot
sand – Amèlie the nurse reading a novel on the nearest rock
– and kick his small heels as he followed his fancy. He built
great sand castles to the shape of Acharra old tower, and
peopled them with preposterous knights and ladies; he
drew great moats and rivers for the tide to fill; he fought
battles innumerable with crackling seaweed, till Amèlie,
with her sharp cry of 'Colin, Colin', would carry him
houseward for tea.

Two fancies remained in his mind through those boyish
years. One was about the mysterious shining sea before
him. In certain weathers it seemed to him a solid pathway.

Cuna, the little ragged isle, ceased to block the horizon, and his own white road ran away down into the west, till suddenly it stopped and he saw no farther. He knew he ought to see more, but always at one place, just when his thoughts were pacing the white road most gallantly, there came a baffling mist to his sight, and he found himself looking at a commonplace sea with Cuna lying very real and palpable in the offing. It was a vexatious limitation, for all his dreams were about this pathway. One day in June, when the waters slept in a deep heat, he came down the sands barefoot, and lo! there was his pathway. For one moment things seemed clear, the mist had not gathered on the road, and with a cry he ran down to the tide's edge and waded in. The touch of water dispelled the illusion, and almost in tears he saw the cruel back of Cuna blotting out his own magic way.

The other fancy was about the low ridge of rocks which bounded the bay on the right. His walks had never extended beyond it, either on the sands or inland, for that way lay a steep hillside and a perilous bog. But often on the sands he had come to its foot and wondered what country lay beyond. He made many efforts to explore it, difficult efforts, for the vigilant Amèlie had first to be avoided. Once he was almost at the top when some sea-weed to which he clung gave way, and he rolled back again to the soft warm sand. By-and-by he found that he knew what was beyond. A clear picture had built itself up in his brain of a mile of reefs, with sand in bars between them, and beyond all a sea-wood of alders slipping from the hill's skirts to the water's edge. This was not what he wanted in his explorations, so he stopped, till one day it struck him that the westward view might reveal something beyond the hog-backed Cuna. One day, pioneering alone, he scaled the steepest heights of the sea-weed and pulled his chin over the crest of the ridge. There, sure enough, was his picture – a mile of reefs and the tattered sea-wood. He turned eagerly seawards. Cuna still lay humped on the waters, but beyond it he seemed to see his shining pathway running far to a speck which might be an island. Crazy with pleasure he stared at the vision, till slowly it melted into the waves, and Cuna the inexorable once more blocked the skyline. He climbed down, his heart in a doubt between despondency and hope.

It was the last day of such fancies, for on the morrow he had to face the new world of school.

At Cecil's Colin found a new life and a thousand new interests. His early delicacy had been driven away by the sea-winds of Acharra, and he was rapidly growing up a tall, strong child, straight of limb like all his house, but sinewy and alert beyond his years. He learned new games with astonishing facility, became a fast bowler with a genius for twists, and a Rugby three-quarters full of pluck and cunning. He soon attained to the modified popularity of a private school, and, being essentially clean, strong, and healthy, found himself a mark for his juniors' worship and a favourite with masters. The homage did not spoil him, for no boy was ever less self-possessed. On the cricket-ground and the football-field he was a leader, but in private he had the nervous, sensitive manners of the would-be recluse. No one ever accused him of 'side' – his polite, halting address was the same to junior and senior; and the result was that wild affection which simplicity in the great is wont to inspire. He spoke with a pure accent, in which lurked no northern trace; in a little he had forgotten all about his birthplace and his origin. His name had at first acquired for him the sobriquet of 'Scottie', but the title was soon dropped from its manifest inaptness.

In his second year at Cecil's he caught a prevalent fever, and for days lay very near the brink of death. At his worst he was wildly delirious, crying ceaselessly for Acharra and the beach at Kinlochuna. But as he grew convalescent the absorption remained, and for the moment he seemed to have forgotten his southern life. He found himself playing on the sands, always with the boundary ridge before him, and the hump of Cuna rising in the sea. When dragged back to his environment by the inquiries of Bellew, his special friend, who came to sit with him, he was so abstracted and forgetful that the good Bellew was seriously grieved. 'The chap's a bit cracked, you know,' he announced in hall. 'Didn't know me. Asked me what "footer" meant when I told him about the Bayswick match, and talked about nothing but a lot of heathen Scotch names.'

One dream haunted Colin throughout the days of his recovery. He was tormented with a furious thirst, poorly assuaged at long intervals by watered milk. So when he crossed the borders of dreamland his first search was always for a well. He tried the brushwood inland from the beach, but it was dry as stone. Then he climbed with difficulty the boundary ridge, and found little pools of salt water, while far on the other side gleamed the dark black bog-holes. Here was not what he sought, and he was in deep despair, till suddenly over the sea he caught a glimpse of his old path running beyond Cuna to a bank of mist. He rushed down to the tide's edge, and to his amazement found solid ground. Now was the chance for which he had long looked, and he ran happily westwards, till of a sudden the solid earth seemed to sink with him, and he was in the waters struggling. But two curious things he noted. One was that the far bank of mist seemed to open for a pin-point of time, and he had a gleam of land. He saw nothing distinctly, only a line which was not mist and was not water. The second was that the water was fresh, and as he was drinking from this curious new fresh sea he awoke. The dream was repeated three times before he left the sick-room. Always he wakened at the same place, always he quenched his thirst in the fresh sea, but never again did the mist open for him and show him the strange country.

From Cecil's he went to the famous school which was the tradition in his family. The Head spoke to his house-master of his coming. 'We are to have another Raden here,' he said, 'and I am glad of it, if the young one turns out to be anything like the others. There's a good deal of dry-rot among the boys just now. They are all too old for their years and too wise in the wrong way. They haven't anything like the enthusiasm in games they had twenty years ago when I first came here. I hope this young Raden will stir them up.' The house-master agreed, and when he first caught sight of Colin's slim, well-knit figure, looked into the handsome kindly eyes, and heard his curiously diffident speech, his doubts vanished. 'We have got the right stuff now,' he told himself, and the senior for whom the new boy fagged made the same comment.

From the anomalous insignificance of fagdom Colin climbed up the School, leaving everywhere a record of honest good-nature. He was allowed to forget his cricket and football, but in return he was initiated into the mysteries of the river. Water had always been his delight, so he went through the dreary preliminaries of being coached in a tub-pair till he learned to swing steadily and get his arms quickly forward. Then came the stages of scratch fours and scratch eights, till after a long apprenticeship he was promoted to the dignity of a thwart in the Eight itself. In his last year he was Captain of Boats, a position which joins the responsibility of a Cabinet Minister to the rapturous popular applause of a successful warrior. Nor was he the least distinguished of a great band. With Colin at seven the School won the Ladies' after the closest race on record.

The Head's prophecy fell true, for Colin was a born leader. For all his good-humour and diffidence of speech, he had a trick of shutting his teeth which all respected. As captain he was the idol of the school, and he ruled it well and justly. For the rest, he was a curious boy with none of the ordinary young enthusiasms, reserved for all his kindliness. At house 'shouters' his was not the voice which led the stirring strains of 'Stroke out all you know,' though his position demanded it. He cared little about work, and the School-house scholar, who fancied him from his manner a devotee of things intellectual, found in Colin but an affected interest. He read a certain amount of modern poetry with considerable boredom; fiction he never opened. The truth was that he had a romance in his own brain which, willy nilly, would play itself out, and which left him small relish for the pale second-hand inanities of art. Often, when with others he would lie in the deep meadows by the river on some hot summer's day, his fancies would take a curious colour. He adored the soft English landscape, the lush grasses, the slow streams, the

ancient secular trees. But as he looked into the hazy green
distance a colder air would blow on his cheek, a pungent
smell of salt and pines would be for a moment in his
nostrils, and he would be gazing at a line of waves on a
beach, a ridge of low rocks, and a shining sea-path running
out to – ah, that he could not tell! The envious Cuna would
suddenly block all the vistas. He had constantly the vision
before his eyes, and he strove to strain into the distance
before Cuna should intervene. Once or twice he seemed
almost to achieve it. He found that by keeping on the top of
the low rock-ridge he could cheat Cuna by a second or two,
and get a glimpse of a misty something out in the west. The
vision took odd times for recurring, – once or twice in
lecture, once on the cricket-ground, many times in the
fields of a Sunday, and once while he paddled down to the
start in a Trials race. It gave him a keen pleasure: it was his
private domain, where at any moment he might make some
enchanting discovery.

As this time he began to spend his vacations at Kinlochuna. His father, an elderly ex-diplomat, had perma-
nently taken up his abode there, and was rapidly settling
into the easy life of the Scots laird. Colin returned to his
native place without enthusiasm. His childhood there had
been full of lonely hours, and he had come to like the warm
south country. He found the house full of people, for his
father entertained hugely, and the talk was of sport and
sport alone. As a rule, your very great athlete is bored by
Scots shooting. Long hours of tramping and crouching
among heather cramp without fully exercising the body;
and unless he has the love of the thing ingrained in him, the
odds are that he will wish himself home. The father, in his
new-found admiration for his lot, was content to face all
weathers; the son found it an effort to keep pace with such
vigour. He thought upon the sunlit fields and reedy water-
courses with regret, and saw little in the hills but a rough
waste scarred with rock and sour with mosses.

He read widely throughout these days, for his father had
a taste for modern letters, and new books lay littered about
the rooms. He read queer Celtic tales which he thought
'sickening rot', and mild Celtic poetry which he failed to

understand. Among the guests was a noted manufacturer
of fiction, whom the elder Raden had met somewhere and
bidden to Kinlochuna. He had heard the tale of Colin's
ancestors and the sea headland of Acharra, and one day he
asked the boy to show him the place, as he wished to make a
story of it. Colin assented unwillingly, for he had been slow
to visit this place of memories, and he did not care to make
his first experiment in such company. But the gentleman
would not be gainsaid, so the two scrambled through the
sea-wood and climbed the low ridge which looked over the
bay. The weather was mist and drizzle; Cuna had wholly
hidden herself, and the bluff Acharra loomed hazy and far.
Colin was oddly disappointed: this reality was a poor place
compared with his fancies. His companion stroked his
peaked beard, talked nonsense about Colin the Red and
rhetoric about 'the spirit of the misty grey weather having
entered into the old tale'. 'Think,' he cried; 'to those old
warriors beyond that bank of mist was the whole desire of
life, the Golden City, the Far Islands, whatever you care to
call it.' Colin shivered, as if his holy places had been
profaned, set down the man in his mind most unjustly
as an 'awful little cad', and hurried him back to the house.

Oxford received the boy with open arms, for his reputation
had long preceded him. To the majority of men he was the
one freshman of his year, and gossip was busy with his
prospects. Nor was gossip disappointed. In his first year he
rowed seven in the Eight. The next year he was captain of
his college boats, and a year later the O.U.B.C. made him
its president. For three years he rowed in the winning
Eight, and old coaches agreed that in him the perfect
seven had been found. It was he who in the famous race
of 18— caught up in the last three hundred yards the
quickened stroke which gave Oxford victory. As he grew
to his full strength he became a splendid figure of a man –
tall, supple, deep-chested for all his elegance. His quick
dark eyes and his kindly hesitating manners made people
think his face extraordinarily handsome, when really it was
in no way above the common. But his whole figure, as he
stood in his shorts and sweater on the raft at Putney, was so

full of youth and strength that people involuntarily smiled when they saw him – a smile of pleasure in so proper a piece of manhood.

Colin enjoyed life hugely at Oxford, for to one so frank and well equipped the place gave of its best. He was the most distinguished personage of his day there, but, save to school friends and the men he met officially on the river, he was little known. His diffidence and his very real exclusiveness kept him from being the centre of a host of friends. His own countrymen in the place were utterly nonplussed by him. They claimed him eagerly as a fellow, but he had none of the ordinary characteristics of the race. There were Scots of every description around him – pale-faced Scots who worked incessantly, metaphysical Scots who talked in the Union, robustious Scots who played football. They were all men of hearty manners and many enthusiasms, – who quoted Burns and dined to the immortal bard's honour every 25th of January; who told interminable Scotch stories, and fell into fervours over national sports, dishes, drinks, and religions. To the poor Colin it was all inexplicable. At the remote house of Kinlochuna he had never heard of a Free Kirk or a haggis. He had never read a line of Burns, Scott bored him exceedingly, and in all honesty he thought Scots games inferior to southern sports. He had no great love for the bleak country, he cared nothing for the traditions of his house, so he was promptly set down by his compatriots as 'denationalised and degenerate'.

He was idle, too, during these years as far as his 'schools' were concerned, but he was always very intent upon his own private business. Whenever he sat down to read, when he sprawled on the grass at river picnics, in chapel, in lecture – in short, at any moment when his body was at rest and his mind at leisure – his fancies were off on the same old path. Things had changed, however, in that country. The boyish device of a hard road running over the waters had gone, and now it was invariably a boat which he saw beached on the shingle. It differed in shape. At first it was an ugly salmon-coble, such as the fishermen used for the nets at Kinlochuna. Then it passed, by rapid transitions, through a canvas skiff which it took good watermanship to sit, a whiff, an ordinary dinghey, till at last it settled itself into a long rough boat, pointed at both ends, with oar-holes in the sides instead of row-locks. It was the devil's own business to launch it, and launch it anew he was compelled to for every journey; for though he left it bound in a little rock hollow below the ridge after landing, yet when he returned, lo! there was the clumsy thing high and dry upon the beach.

The odd point about the new venture was that Cuna had ceased to trouble him. As soon as he had pulled his first stroke the island disappeared, and nothing lay before him but the sea-fog. Yet, try as he might, he could come little nearer. The shores behind him might sink and lessen, but the impenetrable mist was still miles to the westward. Sometimes he rowed so far that the shore was a thin line upon the horizon, but when he turned the boat it seemed to ground in a second on the beach. The long laboured journey out and the instantaneous return, puzzled him at first, but soon he became used to them. His one grief was the mist, which seemed to grow denser as he neared it. The sudden glimpse of land which he had got from the ridge of rock in the old boyish days was now denied him, and with the denial came a keener exultation in the quest. Somewhere in the west, he knew, must be land, and in this land a well of sweet water – for so he had interpreted his feverish dream. Sometimes, when the wind blew against him, he caught scents from it – generally the scent of pines, as on the little ridge on the shore behind him.

One day on his college barge, while he was waiting for a picnic party to start, he seemed to get nearer than before. Out on that western sea, as he saw it, it was fresh, blowing weather, with a clear hot sky above. It was hard work rowing, for the wind was against him, and the sun scorched his forehead. The air seemed full of scents – and sounds, too, sounds of far-away surf and wind in trees. He rested for a moment on his oars and turned his head. His heart beat quickly, for there was a rift in the mist, and far through a line of sand ringed with snow-white foam.

Somebody shook him roughly, – 'Come on, Colin, old man. They're all waiting for you. Do you know you've been half asleep?'

Colin rose and followed silently, with drowsy eyes. His mind was curiously excited. He had looked inside the veil of mist. Now he knew what was the land he sought.

He made the voyage often, now that the spell was broken. It was short work to launch the boat, and, whereas it had been a long pull formerly, now it needed only a few strokes to bring him to the Rim of the Mist. There was no chance of getting farther, and he scarcely tried. He was content to rest there, in a world of curious scents and sounds, till the mist drew down and he was driven back to shore.

The change in his environment troubled him little. For a man who has been an idol at the University to fall suddenly into the comparative insignificance of Town is often a bitter experience; but Colin, whose thoughts were not ambitious, scarcely noticed it. He found that he was less his own master than before, but he humbled himself to his new duties without complaint. Many of his old friends were about him; he had plenty of acquaintances; and, being 'sufficient unto himself', he was unaccustomed to ennui. Invitations showered upon him thick and fast. Match-making mothers, knowing his birth and his father's income, and reflecting that he was the only child of his house, desired him as a son-in-law. He was bidden welcome everywhere, and the young girls, for whose sake he was thus courted, found in him an attractive mystery. The tall good-looking athlete, with the kind eyes and the prepos-terously nervous manner, wakened their maidenly sympa-thies. As they danced with him or sat next to him at dinner, they talked fervently of Oxford, of the north, of the army, of his friends. 'Stupid, but nice, my dear,' was Lady Afflint's comment; and Miss Clara Etheridge, the beauty of the year, declared to her friends that he was a 'dear boy, but so awkward'. He was always forgetful, and ever apologetic; and when he forgot the Shandwicks' theatre-party, the Herapaths' dance, and at least a dozen minor matters, he began to acquire the reputation of a cynic and a recluse.

'You're a queer chap, Col,' Lieutenant Bellew said in expostulation.

Colin shrugged his shoulders; he was used to the description.

'Do you know that Clara Etheridge was trying all she knew to please you this afternoon, and you looked as if you weren't listening? Most men would have given their ears to be in your place.'

'I'm awfully sorry, but I thought I was very polite to her.'

'And why weren't you at the Marshams' show?'

'Oh, I went to polo with Collinson and another man. And, I say, old chap, I'm not coming to the Logans tomorrow. I've got a fence on with Adair at the school.'

Little Bellew, who was a tremendous mirror of fashion and chevalier in general, looked up curiously at his tall friend.

'Why don't you like the women, Col, when they're so fond of you?'

'They aren't,' said Colin hotly, 'and I don't dislike 'em. But, Lord! they bore me. I might be doing twenty things when I talk nonsense to one of 'em for an hour. I come back as stupid as an owl, and besides there's heaps of things better sport.'

The truth was that, while among men he was a leader and at his ease, among women his psychic balance was so oddly upset that he grew nervous and returned unhappy. The boat on the beach, ready in general to appear at the slightest call, would delay long after such experiences, and its place would be taken by some woman's face for which he cared not a straw. For the boat, on the other hand, he cared a very great deal. In all his frank wholesome existence there was this enchanting background, this pleasure-garden which he cherished more than anything in life. He had come of late to look at it with somewhat different eyes. The eager desire to search behind the mist was ever with him, but now he had also some curiosity about the details of the picture. As he pulled out to the Rim of the Mist sounds seemed to shape themselves on his lips, which by-and-by grew into actual words in his memory. He wrote them down in scraps, and after some sorting they seemed to him a kind

of Latin. He remembered a college friend of his, one
Medway, now reading for the Bar, who had been the
foremost scholar of his acquaintance; so with the scrap
of paper in his pocket he climbed one evening to Medway's
rooms in the Temple.

The man read the words curiously, and puzzled for a bit.
'What's made you take to Latin comps so late in life, Colin?
It's baddish, you know, even for you. I thought they'd have
licked more into you at Eton.'

Colin grinned with amusement. 'I'll tell you about it
later,' he said. 'Can you make out what it means?'

'It seems to be a kind of dog-Latin or monkish Latin or
something of the sort,' said Medway. 'It reads like this:
"*Soles occidere solent*" (that's cribbed from Catullus, and
besides it's the regular monkish pun) . . . *qua* . . . then
blandula something. Then there's a lot of Choctaw, and
then *illæ insulæ dilectæ in quas festinant somnia animulæ
gaudia*. That's pretty fair rot. Hullo, by George! here's
something better – *Insula pomorum insula vitæ*. That's
Geoffrey of Monmouth.'

He made a dive to a bookcase and pulled out a battered little
calf-bound duodecimo. 'Here's all about your Isle of Apple-
trees. Listen. "Situate far out in the Western ocean, beyond
the Utmost Islands, beyond even the little Isle of Sheep where
the cairns of dead men are, lies the Island of Apple-trees where
the heroes and princes of the nations live their second life."'
He closed the book and put it back. 'It's the old ancient story,
the Greek Hesperides, the British Avilion, and this Apple-tree
Island is the northern equivalent.'

Colin sat entranced, his memory busy with a problem.
Could he distinguish the scents of apple-trees among the
perfumes of the Rim of the Mist. For the moment he
thought he could. He was roused by Medway's voice
asking the story of the writing.

'Oh, it's just some nonsense that was running in my
head, so I wrote it down to see what it was.'

'But you must have been reading. A new exercise for you,
Colin!'

'No, I wasn't reading. Look here. You know the sort of
pictures you make for yourself of places you like.'

'Rather! Mine is a Yorkshire moor with a little red shooting-box in the heart of it.'

'Well, mine is different. Mine is a sort of beach with a sea and a lot of islands somewhere far out. It is a jolly place, fresh, you know, and blowing, and smells good. 'Pon my word, now I think of it, there's always been a scent of apples.'

'Sort of cider-press? Well, I must be off. You'd better come round to the club and see the telegrams about the war. *You* should be keen about it.'

One evening, a week later, Medway met a friend called Tillotson at the club, and, being lonely, they dined together. Tillotson was a man of some note in science, a dabbler in psychology, an amateur historian, a ripe genealogist. They talked of politics and the war, of a new book, of Mrs Runnymede, and finally of their hobbies.

'I am writing an article,' said Tillotson. 'Craikes asked me to do it for the *Monthly*. It's on a nice point in psychics. I call it "The Transmission of Fallacies," but I do not mean the logical kind. The question is, Can a particular form of hallucination run in a family for generations? The proof must, of course, come from my genealogical studies. I maintain it can. I instance the Douglas-Ernotts, not one of whom can see straight with the left eye. That is one side. In another class of examples I take the Drapiers, who hate salt water and never go on board ship if they can help it. Then you remember the Durwards? Old Lady Balcrynie used to tell me that no one of the lot could ever stand the sight of a green frock. There's a chance for the romancer. The Manorwaters have the same madness, only their colour is red.'

A vague remembrance haunted Medway's brain.

'I know a man who might give you points from his own case. Did you ever meet a chap Raden – Colin Raden?'

Tillotson nodded. 'Long chap – in the Guards? 'Varsity oar, and used to be a crack bowler? No, I don't know him. I know him well by sight, and I should like to meet him tremendously – as a genealogist, of course.'

'Why?' asked Medway.

'Why? Because the man's family is unique. You never hear much about them nowadays, but away up in that

north-west corner of Scotland they have ruled since the
days of Noah. Why, man, they were aristocrats when our
Howards and Nevilles were greengrocers. I wish you would
get this Raden to meet me some night.'

'I am afraid there's no chance of it just at present,' said
Medway, taking up an evening paper. 'I see that his
regiment has gone to the front. But remind me when he
comes back, and I'll be delighted.'

III

And now there began for Colin a curious divided life, –
without, a constant shifting of scene, days of heat and
bustle and toil, – within, a slow, tantalising, yet exquisite
adventure. The Rim of the Mist was now no more the goal
of his journeys, but the starting-point. Lying there, amid
cool, fragrant sea-winds, his fanciful ear was subtly alert for
the sounds of the dim land before him. Sleeping and
waking the quest haunted him. As he flung himself on
his bed the kerosene-filled air would change to an ocean
freshness, the old boat would rock beneath him, and with
clear eye and a boyish hope he would be waiting and
watching. And then suddenly he would be back on
shore, Cuna and the Acharra headland shining grey in
the morning light, and with gritty mouth and sand-filled
eyes he would awaken to the heat of the desert camp.

He was kept busy, for his good-humour and energy
made him a willing slave, and he was ready enough for
volunteer work when others were weak with heat and
despair. A thirty-mile ride left him untired; more, he
followed the campaign with a sharp intelligence and
found a new enthusiasm for his profession. Discomforts
there might be, but the days were happy; and then – the
cool land, the bright land, which was his for the thinking
of it.

Soon they gave him reconnoitring work to do, and his
wits were put to the trial. He came well out of the thing, and
earned golden praise from the silent colonel in command.
He enjoyed it as he had enjoyed a hard race on the river or a
good cricket match, and when his worried companions

marvelled at his zeal he stammered and grew uncomfortable.

'How the deuce do you keep it up, Colin?' the major asked him. 'I'm an old hand at the job, and yet I've got a temper like devilled bones. You seem as chirpy as if you were going out to fish a chalkstream on a June morning.'

'Well, the fact is—' and Colin pulled himself up short, knowing that he could never explain. He felt miserably that he had an unfair advantage of the others. Poor Bellew, who groaned and swore in the heat at his side, knew nothing of the Rim of the Mist. It was really rough luck on the poor beggars, and who but himself was the fortunate man?

As the days passed a curious thing happened. He found fragments of the Other world straying into his common life. The barriers of the two domains were falling, and more than once he caught himself looking at a steel-blue sea when his eyes should have found a mustard-coloured desert. One day, on a reconnoitring expedition, they stopped for a little on a hillock above a jungle of scrub, and, being hot and tired, scanned listlessly the endless yellow distances.

'I suppose yon hill is about ten miles off,' said Bellew with dry lips.

Colin looked vaguely. 'I should say five.'

'And what's that below it – the black patch? Stones or scrub?'

Colin was in a day-dream. 'Why do you call it black? It's blue, quite blue.'

'Rot,' said the other. 'It's grey-black.'

'No, it's water with the sun shining on it. It's blue, but just at the edges it's very near sea-green.'

Bellew rose excitedly. 'Hullo, Col, you're seeing the mirage! And you the fittest of the lot of us! You've got the sun in your head, old man!'

'Mirage!' Colin cried in contempt. He was awake now, but the thought of confusing his own bright western sea with a mirage gave him a curious pain. For a moment he felt the gulf of separation between his two worlds, but only for a moment. As the party remounted he gave his fancies the rein, and ere he reached camp he had felt the oars in his hand and sniffed the apple-tree blossom from the distant beaches.

The major came to him after supper.

'Bellew told me you were a bit odd to-day, Colin,' he said. 'I expect your eyes are getting baddish. Better get your sand-spectacles out.'

Colin laughed. 'Thanks. It's awfully good of you to bother, but I think Bellew took me up wrong. I never was fitter in my life.'

By-and-by the turn came for pride to be humbled. A low desert fever took him, and though he went through the day as usual, it was with dreary lassitude; and at night, with hot hands clasped above his damp hair, he found sleep a hard goddess to conquer.

It was the normal condition of the others, so he had small cause to complain, but it worked havoc with his fancies. He had never been ill since his childish days, and this little fever meant much to one whose nature was poised on a needle-point. He found himself confronted with a hard bare world, with the gilt rubbed from its corners. The Rim of the Mist seemed a place of vague horrors; when he reached it his soul was consumed with terror; he struggled impotently to advance; behind him Cuna and the Acharra coast seemed a place of evil dreams. Again, as in his old fever, he was tormented with a devouring thirst, but the sea beside him was not fresh, but brackish as a rock-pool. He yearned for the apple-tree beaches in front; there, he knew, were cold springs of water; the fresh smell of it was blown towards him in his nightmare.

But as the days passed and the misery for all grew more intense, an odd hope began to rise in his mind. It could not last, coolness and health were waiting near, and his reason for the hope came from the odd events at the Rim of the Mist. The haze was clearing from the foreground, the surf-lined coast seemed nearer, and though all was obscure save the milk-white sand and the foam, yet here was earnest enough for him. Once more he became cheerful; weak and lightheaded he rode out again; and the major, who was recovering from sun-stroke, found envy take the place of pity in his soul.

The hope was near fulfilment. One evening when the heat was changing into the cooler twilight, Colin and Bellew were sent with a small picked body to scour the foot-hills above the river in case of a flank attack during the night-march. It was work they had done regularly for weeks, and it is possible that precautions were relaxed. At any rate, as they turned a corner of hill, in a sandy pass where barren rocks looked down on more barren thorn thickets, a couple of rifle-shots rang out from the scarp, and above them appeared a line of dark faces and white steel. A mere handful, taken at a disadvantage, they could not hope to disperse numbers, so Colin gave the word to wheel about and return. Again shots rang out, and little Bellew had only time to catch at his friend's arm to save him from falling from the saddle.

The word of command had scarcely left Colin's mouth when a sharp pain went through his chest, and his breath seemed to catch and stop. He felt as in a condensed moment of time the heat, the desert smell, the dust in his eyes and throat, while he leaned helplessly forward on his horse's mane. Then the world vanished for him . . . The boat was rocking under him, the oars in his hand. He pulled and it moved, straight, arrow-like towards the forbidden shore. As if under a great wind the mist furled up and fled. Scents of pines, of apple-trees, of great fields of thyme and heather, hung about him; the sound of wind in a forest, of cool waters falling in showers, of old moorland music, came thin and faint with an exquisite clearness. A second and the boat was among the surf, its gunwale ringed with white foam, as it leaped to the still waters beyond. Clear and deep and still the water lay, and then the white beaches shelved downward, and the boat grated on the sand. He turned, every limb alert with a strange new life, crying out words which had shaped themselves on his lips and which an echo seemed to catch and answer. There was the green forest before him, the hills of peace, the cold white waters. With a passionate joy he leaped on the beach, his arms outstretched to this new earth, this light of the world, this old desire of the heart – youth, rapture, immortality.

Bellew brought the body back to camp, himself half-dead with fatigue and whimpering like a child. He almost fell from his horse, and when others took his burden from him and laid it reverently in his tent, he stood beside it, rubbing sand and sweat from his poor purblind eyes, his teeth chattering with fever. He was given something to drink, but he swallowed barely a mouthful.

'It was some d-d-damned sharpshooter,' he said. 'Right through the breast, and he never spoke to me again. My poor old Col! He was the best chap God ever created, and I do-don't care a dash what becomes of me now. I was at school with him, you know, you men.'

'Was he killed outright?' asked the major hoarsely.

'N-no. He lived for about five minutes. But I think the sun had got into his head or he was mad with pain, for he d-d-didn't know where he was. He kept crying out about the smell of pine-trees and heather and a lot of pure nonsense about water.'

'*Et dulces reminiscitur Argos*,' somebody quoted mournfully, as they went out to the desert evening.

The Watcher by the Threshold

'The Watcher by the Threshold', the title story of Buchan's 1902 short story collection, was first published in
Blackwood's Magazine and then in a shorter version in *The
Atlantic Monthly* in December 1900. It was partly inspired
by Bulwer Lytton's 'Dweller of the Threshold' in his
novel *Zanoni* (1842) and with its theme of the survival of
pagan rites in a supposedly Christian society, is an early
working of *The Dancing Floor* (1926) and *Witch Wood*
(1927). The narrator Henry, a prototype for Edward
Leithen, is summoned by Sybil Ladlaw, whose husband
Robert has become possessed by a Devil. Together with
the local minister, Henry tries to help his friend.

A chill evening in the early October of the year 189— found
me driving in a dogcart through the belts of antique
woodland which form the lowland limits of the hilly parish
of More. The Highland express, which brought me from
the north, took me no farther than Perth. Thence it had
been a slow journey in a disjointed local train, till I emerged
on the platform at Morefoot, with a bleak prospect of pot
stalks, coal heaps, certain sour corn lands, and far to the
west a line of moor where the sun was setting. A neat groom
and a respectable trap took the edge off my discomfort, and
soon I had forgotten my sacrifice and found eyes for the
darkening landscape. We were driving through a land of
thick woods, cut at rare intervals by old long-frequented
highways. The More, which at Morefoot is an open sewer,
became a sullen woodland stream, where the brown leaves
of the season drifted. At times we would pass an ancient
lodge, and through a gap in the trees would come a glimpse
of chipped crowstep gable. The names of such houses, as
told me by my companion, were all famous. This one had

been the home of a drunken Jacobite laird, and a king of north country Medmenham. Unholy revels had waked the old halls, and the devil had been toasted at many a hell-fire dinner. The next was the property of a great Scots law family, and there the old Lord of Session, who built the place, in his frouzy wig and carpet slippers, had laid down the canons of Taste for his day and society. The whole country had the air of faded and bygone gentility. The mossy roadside walls had stood for two hundred years; the few wayside houses were toll bars or defunct hostelries. The names, too, were great: Scots baronial with a smack of France, – Chatelray and Riverslaw, Black Holm and Fountainblue. The place had a cunning charm, mystery dwelt in every cranny, and yet it did not please me. The earth smelt heavy and raw; the roads were red underfoot; all was old, sorrowful, and uncanny. Compared with the fresh Highland glen I had left, where wind and sun and flying showers were never absent, all was chilly and dull and dead. Even when the sun sent a shiver of crimson over the crests of certain firs, I felt no delight in the prospect. I admitted shamefacedly to myself that I was in a very bad temper.

I had been staying at Glenaicill with the Clanroydens, and for a week had found the proper pleasure in life. You know the house with its old rooms and gardens, and the miles of heather which defend it from the world. The shooting had been extraordinary for a wild place late in the season; for there are few partridges, and the woodcock are notoriously late. I had done respectably in my stalking, more than respectably on the river, and creditably on the moors. Moreover, there were pleasant people in the house – and there were the Clanroydens. I had had a hard year's work, sustained to the last moment of term, and a fortnight in Norway had been disastrous. It was therefore with real comfort that I had settled myself down for another ten days in Glenaicill, when all my plans were shattered by Sibyl's letter. Sibyl is my cousin and my very good friend, and in old days when I was briefless I had fallen in love with her many times. But she very sensibly chose otherwise, and married a man Ladlaw – Robert John Ladlaw, who had been at school with me. He was a cheery, good-humoured fellow, a great sportsman, a justice of the peace, and deputy lieutenant for his county, and something of an antiquary in a mild way. He had a box in Leicestershire to which he went in the hunting season, but from February till October he lived in his moorland home. The place was called the House of More, and I had shot at it once or twice in recent years. I remembered its loneliness and its comfort, the charming diffident Sibyl, and Ladlaw's genial welcome. And my recollections set me puzzling again over the letter which that morning had broken into my comfort. 'You promised us a visit this autumn,' Sibyl had written, 'and I wish you would come as soon as you can.' So far common politeness. But she had gone on to reveal the fact that Ladlaw was ill; she did not know how, exactly, but something, she thought, about his heart. Then she had signed herself my affectionate cousin, and then had come a short, violent post-script, in which, as it were, the fences of convention had been laid low. 'For Heaven's sake, come and see us,' she scrawled below. 'Bob is terribly ill, and I am crazy. Come at once.' To cap it she finished with an afterthought: 'Don't bother about bringing doctors. It is not their business.'

She had assumed that I would come, and dutifully I set out. I could not regret my decision, but I took leave to upbraid my luck. The thought of Glenaicill, with the woodcock beginning to arrive and the Clanroydens imploring me to stay, saddened my journey in the morning, and the murky, coaly, midland country of the afternoon completed my depression. The drive through the woodlands of More failed to raise my spirits. I was anxious about Sibyl and Ladlaw, and this accursed country had always given me a certain eeriness on my first approaching it. You may call it silly, but I have no nerves and am little susceptible to vague sentiment. It was sheer physical dislike of the rich deep soil, the woody and antique smells, the melancholy roads and trees, and the flavour of old mystery. I am aggressively healthy and wholly Philistine. I love clear outlines and strong colours, and More with its half tints and hazy distances depressed me miserably. Even when the road crept uphill and the trees ended, I found nothing to hearten me in the moorland which succeeded. It was genuine moorland, close on eight hundred feet above the sea, and through it ran this old grass-grown coach road. Low hills rose to the left, and to the right, after some miles of peat, flared the chimneys of pits and oil works. Straight in front the moor ran out into the horizon, and there in the centre was the last dying spark of the sun. The place was as still as the grave save for the crunch of our wheels on the grassy road, but the flaring lights to the north seemed to endow it with life. I have rarely had so keenly the feeling of movement in the inanimate world. It was an unquiet place, and I shivered nervously. Little gleams of loch came from the hollows, the burns were brown with peat, and every now and then there rose in the moor jags of sickening red stone. I remembered that Ladlaw had talked about the place as the old Manann, the holy land of the ancient races. I had paid little attention at the time, but now it struck me that the old peoples had been wise in their choice. There was something uncanny in this soil and air. Framed in dank mysterious woods and a country of coal and ironstone, at no great distance from the capital city, it was a sullen relic of a lost barbarism. Over the low hills lay a green pastoral country with bright streams and valleys, but here, in this peaty desert, there were few sheep and little cultivation. The House of More was the only dwelling, and, save for the ragged village, the wilderness was given over to the wild things of the hills. The shooting was good, but the best shooting on earth would not persuade me to make my abode in such a place. Ladlaw was ill; well, I did not wonder. You can have uplands without air, moors that are not health-giving, and a country life which is more arduous than a townsman's. I shivered again, for I seemed to have passed in a few hours from the open noon to a kind of dank twilight.

We passed the village and entered the lodge gates. Here there were trees again – little innocent new-planted firs, which flourished ill. Some large plane trees grew near the house, and there were thickets upon thickets of the ugly elderberry. Even in the half darkness I could see that the lawns were trim and the flower beds respectable for the season; doubtless Sibyl looked after the gardeners. The oblong whitewashed house, more like a barrack than ever, opened suddenly on my sight, and I experienced my first sense of comfort since I left Glenaicill. Here I should find warmth and company; and sure enough, the hall door was wide open, and in the great flood of light which poured from it Sibyl stood to welcome me.

She ran down the steps as I dismounted, and, with a word to the groom, caught my arm and drew me into the shadow. 'Oh, Henry, it was so good of you to come. You mustn't let Bob think that you know he is ill. We don't talk about it. I'll tell you afterwards. I want you to cheer him up. Now we must go in, for he is in the hall expecting you.'

While I stood blinking in the light, Ladlaw came forward with outstretched hand and his usual cheery greeting. I looked at him and saw nothing unusual in his appearance; a little drawn at the lips, perhaps, and heavy below the eyes, but still fresh-colored and healthy. It was Sibyl who showed change. She was very pale, her pretty eyes were deplorably mournful, and in place of her delightful shyness there were the self-confidence and composure of pain. I was honestly shocked, and as I dressed my heart was full of hard thoughts about Ladlaw. What could his illness mean? He seemed well and cheerful, while Sibyl was pale; and yet it was Sibyl who had written the postscript. As I warmed myself by the fire, I resolved that this particular family difficulty was my proper business.

The Ladlaws were waiting for me in the drawing-room. I noticed something new and strange in Sibyl's demeanour. She looked to her husband with a motherly, protective air, while Ladlaw, who had been the extreme of masculine independence, seemed to cling to his wife with a curious appealing fidelity. In conversation he did little more than echo her words. Till dinner was announced he spoke of the weather, the shooting, and Mabel Clanroyden. Then he did a queer thing; for when I was about to offer my arm to Sibyl he forestalled me, and clutching her right arm with his left hand led the way to the dining room, leaving me to follow in some bewilderment.

I have rarely taken part in a more dismal meal. The House of More has a pretty Georgian panelling through most of the rooms, but in the dining room the walls are level and painted a dull stone color. Abraham offered up Isaac in a ghastly picture in front of me. Some photographs of the Quorn hung over the mantelpiece, and five or six drab ancestors filled up the remaining space. But one thing was new and startling. A great marble bust, a genuine antique, frowned on me from a pedestal. The head was in the late Roman style, clearly of some emperor, and in its commonplace environment the great brows, the massive neck, and the mysterious solemn lips had a surprising effect. I nodded toward the thing, and asked what it represented.

Ladlaw grunted something which I took for 'Justinian', but he never raised his eyes from his plate. By accident I caught Sibyl's glance. She looked toward the bust, and laid a finger on her lips.

The meal grew more doleful as it advanced. Sibyl scarcely touched a dish, but her husband ate ravenously of everything. He was a strong, thickset man, with a square kindly face burned brown by the sun. Now he seemed to have suddenly coarsened. He gobbled with undignified haste, and his eye was extraordinarily vacant. A question made him start, and he would turn on me a face so strange and inert that I repented the interruption.

I asked him about the autumn's sport. He collected his wits with difficulty. He thought it had been good, on the whole, but he had shot badly. He had not been quite so fit as usual. No, he had had nobody staying with him. Sibyl had wanted to be alone. He was afraid the moor might have been undershot, but he would make a big day with keepers and farmers before the winter.

'Bob has done pretty well,' Sibyl said. 'He hasn't been out often, for the weather has been very bad here. You can have no idea, Henry, how horrible this moorland place of ours can be when it tries. It is one great sponge sometimes, with ugly red burns and mud to the ankles.'

'I don't think it's healthy,' said I.

Ladlaw lifted his face. 'Nor do I. I think it's intolerable, but I am so busy I can't get away.'

Once again I caught Sibyl's warning eye as I was about to question him on his business.

Clearly the man's brain had received a shock, and he was beginning to suffer from hallucinations. This could be the only explanation, for he had always led a temperate life. The distrait, wandering manner was the only sign of his malady, for otherwise he seemed normal and mediocre as ever. My heart grieved for Sibyl, alone with him in this wilderness.

Then he broke the silence. He lifted his head and looked nervously around till his eye fell on the Roman bust.

'Do you know that this countryside is the old Manann?' he said.

It was an odd turn to the conversation, but I was glad of a sign of intelligence. I answered that I had heard so.

'It's a queer name,' he said oracularly, 'but the thing it stood for was queerer, Manann, Manaw,' he repeated, rolling the words on his tongue. As he spoke, he glanced sharply, and, as it seemed to me, fearfully, at his left side.

The movement of his body made his napkin slip from his left knee and fall on the floor. It leaned against his leg, and he started from its touch as if he had been bitten by a snake. I have never seen a more sheer and transparent terror on a man's face. He got to his feet, his strong frame shaking like a rush. Sibyl ran round to his side, picked up the napkin and flung it on a sideboard. Then she stroked his hair as one would stroke a frightened horse. She called him by his old boy's name of Robin, and at her touch and voice he became quiet. But the particular course then in progress was removed, untasted.

In a few minutes he seemed to have forgotten his behaviour, for he took up the former conversation. For a time he spoke well and briskly. 'You lawyers,' he said, 'understand only the dry framework of the past. You cannot conceive the rapture, which only the antiquary can feel, of constructing in every detail an old culture. Take this Manann. If I could explore the secret of these moors, I would write the world's greatest book. I would

write of that prehistoric life when man was knit close to
nature. I would describe the people who were brothers of
the red earth and the red rock and the red streams of the
hills. Oh, it would be horrible, but superb, tremendous! It
would be more than a piece of history; it would be a new
gospel, a new theory of life. It would kill materialism once
and for all. Why, man, all the poets who have deified and
personified nature would not do an eighth part of my work.
I would show you the unknown, the hideous, shrieking
mystery at the back of this simple nature. Men would see
the profundity of the old crude faiths which they affect to
despise. I would make a picture of our shaggy, sombre-eyed
forefather, who heard strange things in the hill silences. I
would show him brutal and terror-stricken, but wise, wise,
God alone knows how wise! The Romans knew it, and they
learned what they could from him, though he did not tell
them much. But we have some of his blood in us, and we
may go deeper. Manann! A queer land nowadays! I sometimes love it and sometimes hate it, but I always fear it. It is
like that statue, inscrutable.'

I would have told him that he was talking mystical
nonsense, but I had looked toward the bust, and my
rudeness was checked on my lips. The moor might be
a common piece of ugly waste land, but the statue was
inscrutable, – of that there was no doubt. I hate your cruel
heavy-mouthed Roman busts; to me they have none of the
beauty of life, and little of the interest of art. But my eyes
were fastened on this as they had never before looked on
marble. The oppression of the heavy woodlands, the
mystery of the silent moor, seemed to be caught and
held in this face. It was the intangible mystery of culture
on the verge of savagery – a cruel, lustful wisdom, and yet
a kind of bitter austerity which laughed at the game of life
and stood aloof. There was no weakness in the heavy-
veined brow and slumbrous eyelids. It was the face of one
who had conquered the world, and found it dust and
ashes; one who had eaten of the tree of the knowledge of
good and evil, and scorned human wisdom. And at the
same time, it was the face of one who knew uncanny
things, a man who was the intimate of the half-world and

the dim background of life. Why on earth I should connect the Roman grandee[1] with the moorland parish of More I cannot say, but the fact remains that there was that in the face which I knew had haunted me through the woodlands and bogs of the place – a sleepless, dismal, incoherent melancholy.

'I bought that at Colenzo's,' Ladlaw said, 'because it took my fancy. It matches well with this place?'

I thought it matched very ill with his drab walls and Quorn photographs, but I held my peace.

'Do you know who it is?' he asked. 'It is the head of the greatest man the world has ever seen. You are a lawyer and know your Justinian.'

The Pandects are scarcely part of the daily work of a common-law barrister. I had not looked into them since I left college.

'I know that he married an actress,' I said, 'and was a sort of all-round genius. He made law, and fought battles, and had rows with the Church. A curious man! And wasn't there some story about his selling his soul to the devil, and getting law in exchange? Rather a poor bargain!'

I chattered away, sillily enough, to dispel the gloom of that dinner table. The result of my words was unhappy. Ladlaw gasped and caught at his left side, as if in pain. Sibyl, with tragic eyes, had been making signs to me to hold my peace. Now she ran round to her husband's side and comforted him like a child. As she passed me, she managed to whisper in my ear to talk to her only, and let her husband alone.

For the rest of dinner I obeyed my orders to the letter. Ladlaw ate his food in gloomy silence, while I spoke to Sibyl of our relatives and friends, of London, Glenaicill,

1. I have identified the bust, which, when seen under other circumstances, had little power to affect me. It was a copy of the head of Justinian in the Tesci Museum at Venice, and several duplicates exist, dating apparently from the seventh century, and showing traces of Byzantine decadence in the scroll work on the hair. It is engraved in M. Delacroix's *Byzantium*, and, I think, in Windscheid's *Pandektenlehrbuch*.

and any random subject. The poor girl was dismally forgetful, and her eye would wander to her husband with wifely anxiety. I remember being suddenly overcome by the comic aspect of it all. Here were we three fools alone in the dank upland: one of us sick and nervous, talking out-of-the-way nonsense about Manann and Justinian, gobbling his food and getting scared at his napkin; another gravely anxious; and myself at my wits' end for a solution. It was a Mad Tea-Party with a vengeance: Sibyl the melancholy little Dormouse, and Ladlaw the incomprehensible Hatter. I laughed aloud, but checked myself when I caught my cousin's eye. It was really no case for finding humour. Ladlaw was very ill, and Sibyl's face was getting deplorably thin.

I welcomed the end of that meal with unmannerly joy, for I wanted to speak seriously with my host. Sibyl told the butler to have the lamps lighted in the library. Then she leaned over toward me and spoke low and rapidly: 'I want you to talk with Bob. I'm sure you can do him good. You'll have to be very patient with him, and very gentle. Oh, please try to find out what is wrong with him. He won't tell me, and I can only guess.'

The butler returned with word that the library was ready to receive us, and Sibyl rose to go. Ladlaw half rose, protesting, making the most curious feeble clutches to his side. His wife quieted him. 'Henry will look after you, dear,' she said. 'You are going into the library to smoke.' Then she slipped from the room, and we were left alone.

He caught my arm fiercely with his left hand, and his grip nearly made me cry out. As we walked down the hall, I could feel his arm twitching from the elbow to the shoulder. Clearly he was in pain, and I set it down to some form of cardiac affection, which might possibly issue in paralysis.

I settled him in the biggest armchair, and took one of his cigars. The library is the pleasantest room in the house, and at night, when a peat fire burned on the old hearth and the great red curtains were drawn, it used to be the place for comfort and good talk. Now I noticed changes. Ladlaw's

bookshelves had been filled with the Proceedings of anti-
quarian societies and many light-hearted works on sport.
But now the Badminton library had been cleared out of a
shelf where it stood most convenient to the hand, and its
place taken by an old Leyden reprint of Justinian. There
were books on Byzantine subjects of which I never dreamed
he had heard the names; there were volumes of history and
speculation, all of a slightly bizarre kind; and to crown
everything, there were several bulky medical works with
gaudily coloured plates. The old atmosphere of sport and
travel had gone from the room with the medley of rods,
whips, and gun cases which used to cumber the tables.
Now the place was moderately tidy and somewhat learned,
and I did not like it.

Ladlaw refused to smoke, and sat for a little while in
silence. Then of his own accord he broke the tension.

'It was devilish good of you to come, Harry. This is a
lonely place for a man who is a bit seedy.'

'I thought you might be alone,' I said, 'so I looked you up
on my way down from Glenaicill. I'm sorry to find you
feeling ill.'

'Do you notice it?' he asked sharply.

'It's tolerably patent,' I said. 'Have you seen a doctor?'

He said something uncomplimentary about doctors, and
kept looking at me with his curious dull eyes.

I remarked the strange posture in which he sat, his head
screwed round to his right shoulder, and his whole body a
protest against something at his left hand.

'It looks like a heart,' I said. 'You seem to have pains in
your left side.'

Again a spasm of fear. I went over to him and stood at the
back of his chair.

'Now for goodness' sake, my dear fellow, tell me what is
wrong. You're scaring Sibyl to death. It's lonely work for
the poor girl, and I wish you would let me help you.'

He was lying back in his chair now, with his eyes half
shut, and shivering like a frightened colt. The extraordinary
change in one who had been the strongest of the strong kept
me from realising his gravity. I put a hand on his shoulder,
but he flung it off.

'For God's sake, sit down!' he said hoarsely. 'I'm going to tell you, but I'll never make you understand.'

I sat down promptly opposite him.

'It's the devil,' he said very solemnly.

I am afraid that I was rude enough to laugh. He took no notice, but sat, with the same tense, miserable air, staring over my head.

'Right,' said I. 'Then it is the devil. It's a new complaint, so it's as well I did not bring a doctor. How does it affect you?'

He made the old impotent clutch at the air with his left hand. I had the sense to become grave at once. Clearly this was some serious mental affection, some hallucination born of physical pain.

Then he began to talk in a low voice, very rapidly, with his head bent forward like a hunted animal's. I am not going to set down what he told me in his own words, for they were incoherent often, and there was much repetition. But I am going to write the gist of the odd story which took my sleep away on that autumn night, with such explanations and additions I think needful. The fire died down, the wind arose, the hour grew late, and still he went on in his mumbling recitative. I forgot to smoke, forgot my comfort – everything but the odd figure of my friend and his inconceivable romance. And the night before I had been in cheerful Glenaicill!

He had returned to the House of More, he said, in the latter part of May, and shortly after he fell ill. It was a trifling sickness, – influenza or something, – but he had never quite recovered. The rainy weather of June depressed him, and the extreme heat of July made him listless and weary. A kind of insistent sleepiness hung over him, and he suffered much from nightmare. Toward the end of July his former health returned, but he was haunted with a curious oppression. He seemed to himself to have lost the art of being alone. There was a perpetual sound in his left ear, a kind of moving and rustling at his left side, which never left him by night or day. In addition, he had become the prey of nerves and an insensate dread of the unknown.

Ladlaw, as I have explained, was a commonplace man, with fair talents, a mediocre culture, honest instincts, and the beliefs and incredulities of his class. On abstract grounds, I should have declared him an unlikely man to be the victim of an hallucination. He had a kind of dull bourgeois rationalism, which used to find reasons for all things in heaven and earth. At first he controlled his dread with proverbs. He told himself it was the sequel of his illness or the light-headedness of summer heat on the moors. But it soon outgrew his comfort. It became a living second presence, an *alter ego* which dogged his footsteps. He grew acutely afraid of it. He dared not be alone for a moment, and clung to Sibyl's company despairingly. She went off for a week's visit in the beginning of August, and he endured for seven days the tortures of the lost. The malady advanced upon him with swift steps. The presence became more real daily. In the early dawning, in the twilight, and in the first hour of the morning it seemed at times to take a visible bodily form. A kind of amorphous featureless shadow would run from his side into the darkness, and he would sit palsied with terror. Sometimes, in lonely places, his footsteps sounded double, and something would brush elbows with him. Human society alone exorcised it. With Sibyl at his side he was happy; but as soon as she left him, the thing came slinking back from the unknown to watch by him. Company might have saved him, but joined to his affliction was a crazy dread of his fellows. He would not leave his moorland home, but must bear his burden alone among the wild streams and mosses of that dismal place.

The 12th came, and he shot wretchedly, for his nerve had gone to pieces. He stood exhaustion badly, and became a dweller about the doors. But with this bodily inertness came an extraordinary intellectual revival. He read widely in a blundering way, and he speculated unceasingly. It was characteristic of the man that as soon as he left the paths of the prosaic he should seek his supernatural in a very concrete form. He assumed that he was haunted by the devil – the visible personal devil in whom our fathers believed. He waited hourly for the shape at his side to speak, but no words came. The Accuser of the Brethren in all but tangible form was his ever present companion. He felt, he declared, the spirit of old evil entering subtly into his blood. He sold his soul many times over, and yet there was no possibility of resistance. It was a Visitation more undeserved than Job's, and a thousandfold more awful.

For a week or more he was tortured with a kind of religious mania. When a man of a healthy secular mind finds himself adrift on the terrible ocean of religious troubles he is peculiarly helpless, for he has not the most rudimentary knowledge of the winds and tides. It was useless to call up his old carelessness; he had suddenly dropped into a new world where old proverbs did not apply. And all the while, mind you, there was the shrinking terror of it – an intellect all alive to the torture and the most unceasing physical fear. For a little he was on the far edge of idiocy.

Then by accident it took a new form. While sitting with Sibyl one day in the library, he began listlessly to turn over the leaves of an old book. He read a few pages, and found the hint to a story like his own. It was some French Life of Justinian, one of the unscholarly productions of last century, made up of stories from Procopius and tags of Roman law. Here was his own case written down in black and white; and the man had been a king of kings. This was a new comfort, and for a little – strange though it may seem – he took a sort of pride in his affliction. He worshipped the great Emperor, and read every scrap he could find on him, not excepting the Pandects and the Digest. He sent for the bust in the dining room, paying a fabulous price. Then he settled himself to study his imperial prototype, and the study became an idolatry. As I have said, Ladlaw was a man of ordinary talents, and certainly of meagre imaginative power. And yet from the lies of the Secret History and the crudities of German legalists he had constructed a marvelous portrait of a man. Sitting there in the half-lighted room, he drew the picture: the quiet cold man with his inheritance of Dacian mysticism, holding the great world in fee, giving it law and religion, fighting its wars, building its churches, and yet all the while intent upon his own private work of making his peace with his soul – the churchman and warrior whom all the world worshipped, and yet one going through life with his lip quivering. He Watched by the Threshold ever at the left side. Sometimes at night, in the great Brazen Palace, warders heard the Emperor walking in the dark corridors, alone, and yet not alone; for once, when a servant entered with a lamp, he saw his master with a face as of another world, and something beside him which had no face or shape, but which he knew to be that hoary Evil which is older than the stars.

Crazy nonsense! I had to rub my eyes to assure myself that I was not sleeping. No! There was my friend with his suffering face, and it was the library of More.

And then he spoke of Theodora, – actress, harlot, *dévote*, empress. For him the lady was but another part of the uttermost horror, a form of the shapeless thing at his side. I felt myself falling under the fascination. I have no nerves and little imagination, but in a flash I seemed to realise something of that awful featureless face, crouching ever at a man's hand, till darkness and loneliness come, and it rises to its mastery. I shivered as I looked at the man in the chair before me. These dull eyes of his were looking upon things I could not see, and I saw their terror. I realised that it was grim earnest for him. Nonsense or no, some devilish fancy had usurped the place of his sanity, and he was being slowly broken upon the wheel. And then, when his left hand twitched, I almost cried out. I had thought it comic before; now it seemed the last proof of tragedy.

He stopped, and I got up with loose knees and went to the window. Better the black night than the intangible horror within. I flung up the sash and looked out across the moor. There was no light; nothing but an inky darkness and the uncanny rustle of elder bushes. The sound chilled me, and I closed the window.

'The land is the old Manann,' Ladlaw was saying. 'We are beyond the pale here. Do you hear the wind?'

I forced myself back into sanity and looked at my watch. It was nearly one o'clock.

'What ghastly idiots we are!' I said. 'I am off to bed.'

Ladlaw looked at me helplessly. 'For God's sake, don't leave me alone!' he moaned. 'Get Sibyl.'

We went together back to the hall, while he kept the same feverish grasp on my arm. Some one was sleeping in a chair by the hall fire, and to my distress I recognised my hostess. The poor child must have been sadly wearied. She came forward with her anxious face.

'I'm afraid Bob has kept you very late, Henry,' she said. 'I hope you will sleep well. Breakfast at nine, you know.' And then I left them.

Over my bed there was a little picture, a reproduction of some Italian work, of Christ and the Demoniac. Some impulse made me hold my candle up to it. The madman's face was torn with passion and suffering, and his eye had the pained furtive expression which I had come to know. And by his left side there was a dim shape crouching.

I got into bed hastily, but not to sleep. I felt that my reason must be going. I had been pitchforked from our clear and cheerful modern life into the mists of old superstition. Old tragic stories of my Calvinist upbringing returned to haunt me. The man dwelt in by a devil was no new fancy, but I believed that science had docketed and analysed and explained the devil out of the world. I remembered my dabblings in the occult before I settled down to law – the story of Donisarius, the monk of Padua, the unholy legend of the Face of Proserpine, the tales of *succubi* and *incubi*, the Leannain Sith and the Hidden Presence. But here was something stranger still. I had stumbled upon that very possession which fifteen hundred years ago had made the monks of New Rome tremble and cross themselves. Some devilish occult force, lingering through the ages, had come to life after a long sleep. God knows what earthly connection there was between the splendid Emperor of the World and my prosaic friend, or between the glittering shores of the Bosporus and this moorland parish! But the land was the old Manann! The spirit may have lingered in the earth and air, a deadly legacy from Pict and Roman. I had felt the uncanniness of the place; I had augured ill of it from the first. And then in sheer disgust I rose and splashed my face with cold water.

I lay down again, laughing miserably at my credulity. That I, the sober and rational, should believe in this crazy fable was too palpably absurd. I would steel my mind resolutely against such harebrained theories. It was a mere bodily ailment – liver out of order, weak heart, bad circulation, or something of that sort. At the worst it might be some affection of the brain, to be treated by a specialist. I vowed to myself that next morning the best doctor in Edinburgh should be brought to More.

The worst of it was that my duty compelled me to stand my ground. I foresaw the few remaining weeks of my holiday blighted. I should be tied to this moorland prison, a sort of keeper and nurse in one, tormented by silly fancies. It was a charming prospect, and the thought of Glenaicill and the woodcock made me bitter against Ladlaw. But there was no way out of it. I might do Ladlaw good, and I could not have Sibyl worn to death by his vagaries.

My ill nature comforted me, and I forgot the horror of the thing in its vexation. After that I think I fell asleep and dozed uneasily till morning. When I woke I was in a better frame of mind. The early sun had worked wonders with the moorland. The low hills stood out fresh-coloured and clear against a pale October sky; the elders sparkled with frost; the raw film of morn was rising from the little loch in tiny clouds. It was a cold, rousing day, and I dressed in good spirits and went down to breakfast.

I found Ladlaw looking ruddy and well; very different from the broken man I remembered of the night before. We were alone, for Sibyl was breakfasting in bed. I remarked on his ravenous appetite, and he smiled cheerily. He made two jokes during the meal; he laughed often, and I began to forget the events of the previous day. It seemed to me that I might still flee from More with a clear conscience. He had forgotten about his illness. When I touched distantly upon the matter he showed a blank face.

It might be that the affection had passed; on the other hand, it might return to him at the darkening. I had no means to decide. His manner was still a trifle distrait and peculiar, and I did not like the dullness in his eye. At any rate, I should spend the day in his company, and the evening would decide the question.

I proposed shooting, which he promptly vetoed. He was no good at walking, he said, and the birds were wild. This seriously limited the possible occupations. Fishing there was none, and hill-climbing was out of the question. He proposed a game at billiards, and I pointed to the glory of the morning. It would have been sacrilege to waste such sunshine in knocking balls about. Finally we agreed to drive somewhere and have lunch, and he ordered the dogcart.

In spite of all forebodings I enjoyed the day. We drove in the opposite direction from the woodland parts, right away across the moor to the coal country beyond. We lunched at the little mining town of Borrowmuir, in a small and noisy public house. The roads made bad going, the country was far from pretty, and yet the drive did not bore me. Ladlaw talked incessantly – talked as I had never heard man talk before. There was something indescribable in all he said, a different point of view, a lost groove of thought, a kind of innocence and archaic shrewdness in one. I can only give you a hint of it, by saying that it was like the mind of an early ancestor placed suddenly among modern surroundings. It was wise with a remote wisdom, and silly (now and then) with a quite antique and distant silliness.

I will give instances of both. He provided me with a theory of certain early fortifications, which must be true, which commends itself to the mind with overwhelming conviction, and yet which is so out of the way of common speculation that no man could have guessed it. I do not propose to set down the details, for I am working at it on my own account. Again, he told me the story of an old marriage custom, which till recently survived in this district – told it with full circumstantial detail and constant allusions to other customs which he could not possibly have known of. Now for the other side. He explained why well water is in winter warmer than a running stream, and this was his explanation: at the antipodes our winter is summer, consequently, the water of a well which comes through from the other side of the earth must be warm in winter and cold in summer, since in our summer it is winter there. You perceive what this is. It is no mere silliness, but a genuine effort of an early mind, which had just grasped the fact of the antipodes, to use it in explanation.

Gradually I was forced to the belief that it was not Ladlaw who was talking to me, but something speaking through him, something at once wiser and simpler. My old fear of the devil began to depart. This spirit, the exhalation, whatever it was, was ingenuous in its way, at least in its daylight aspect. For a moment I had an idea that it was a real reflex of Byzantine thought, and that by cross-examining I might make marvellous discoveries. The ardour of the scholar began to rise in me, and I asked a question about that much-debated point, the legal status of the *apocrisiarii*. To my vexation he gave no response. Clearly the intelligence of this familiar had its limits.

It was about three in the afternoon, and we had gone half of our homeward journey, when signs of the old terror began to appear. I was driving, and Ladlaw sat on my left. I noticed him growing nervous and silent, shivering at the flick of the whip, and turning halfway round toward me. Then he asked me to change places, and I had the unpleasant work of driving from the wrong side. After that I do not think he spoke once till we arrived at More, but sat huddled together, with the driving rug almost up to his chin – an eccentric figure of a man.

I foresaw another such night as the last, and I confess my heart sank. I had no stomach for more mysteries, and somehow with the approach of twilight the confidence of the day departed. The thing appeared in darker colours, and I found it in my mind to turn coward. Sibyl alone deterred me. I could not bear to think of her alone with this demented being. I remembered her shy timidity, her innocence. It was monstrous that the poor thing should be called on thus to fight alone with phantoms.

When we came to the House it was almost sunset. Ladlaw got out very carefully on the right side, and for a second stood by the horse. The sun was making our shadows long, and as I stood beyond him it seemed for a moment that his shadow was double. It may have been mere fancy, for I had not time to look twice. He was standing, as I have said, with his left side next the horse. Suddenly the harmless elderly cob fell into a very panic of fright, reared upright, and all but succeeded in killing its master. I was in time to pluck Ladlaw from under its feet, but the beast had become perfectly unmanageable, and we left a groom struggling to quiet it.

In the hall the butler gave me a telegram. It was from my clerk, summoning me back at once to an important consultation.

Here was a prompt removal of my scruples. There could be no question of my remaining, for the case was one of the first importance, which I had feared might break off my holiday. The consultation fell in vacation time to meet the convenience of certain people who were going abroad, and there was the most instant demand for my presence. I must go, and at once; and, as I hunted in the time-table, I found that in three hours' time a night train for the south would pass Borrowmuir which might be stopped by special wire.

But I had no pleasure in my freedom. I was in despair about Sibyl, and I hated myself for my cowardly relief. The dreary dining room, the sinister bust, and Ladlaw crouching and quivering – the recollection, now that escape was before me, came back on my mind with the terror of a nightmare. My first thought was to persuade the Ladlaws to come away with me. I found them both in the drawing-room – Sibyl very fragile and pale, and her husband sitting as usual like a frightened child in the shadow of her skirts. A sight of him was enough to dispel my hope. The man was fatally ill, mentally, bodily; and who was I to attempt to minister to a mind diseased?

But Sibyl – she might be saved from the martyrdom. The servants would take care of him, and, if need be, a doctor might be got from Edinburgh to live in the house. So while he sat with vacant eyes staring into the twilight, I tried to persuade Sibyl to think of herself. I am frankly a sun worshipper. I have no taste for arduous duty, and the quixotic is my abhorrence. I laboured to bring my cousin to this frame of mind. I told her that her first duty was to herself, and that this vigil of hers was beyond human endurance. But she had no ears for my arguments.

'While Bob is ill I must stay with him,' she said always in answer, and then she thanked me for my visit, till I felt a brute and a coward. I strove to quiet my conscience, but it told me always that I was fleeing from my duty; and then, when I was on the brink of a nobler resolution, a sudden overmastering terror would take hold of me, and I would listen hysterically for the sound of the dogcart on the gravel.

At last it came, and in a sort of fever I tried to say the conventional farewells. I shook hands with Ladlaw, and when I dropped his hand it fell numbly on his knee. Then I took my leave, muttering hoarse nonsense about having had a 'charming visit', and 'hoping soon to see them both in town'. As I backed to the door, I knocked over a lamp on a small table. It crashed on the floor and went out, and at the sound Ladlaw gave a curious childish cry. I turned like a coward, and ran across the hall to the front door, and scrambled into the dogcart.

The groom would have driven me sedately through the park, but I must have speed or go mad. I took the reins from him and put the horse into a canter. We swung through the gates and out into the moor road, for I could have no peace till the ghoulish elder world was exchanged for the homely ugliness of civilisation. Once only I looked back, and there against the sky line, with a solitary lit window, the House of More stood lonely in the red desert.

Fountainblue

Alec Maitland, forty, famous and rich, returns to his Scottish childhood haunts to seek the hand of Clara Etheridge. He is contrasted with another suitor, Despencer, in scenes reminiscent of Buchan's novel, *The Half-Hearted* (1900), written shortly before this *Blackwood's Magazine* story of August 1901. Like other stories in *The Watcher by the Threshold*, 'Fountainblue' is, as the Buchan scholar David Daniell has pointed out, 'about the hidden, primitive influence exerted by the topography of Lowland or Western Scotland', but it is also 'about a special sort of medieval romanticism in which the hero is ultimately more concerned to "make" his soul than to achieve the pinnacle of worldly success and have the desirable girl'. The adventurer who devoted himself to the service of Britain, but was unable to settle there, was a familiar theme in the fiction of the period, most obviously demonstrated in Somerset Maugham's *The Explorer* (1907), but Buchan gives the story much greater psychological depth with his portrayal of a man who turns his back on conventional success in order to find his more primitive self.

I

Once upon a time, as the story-books say, a boy came over a ridge of hill, from which a shallow vale ran out into the sunset. It was a high, wind-blown country, where the pines had a crook in their backs and the rocks were scarred and bitten with winter storms. But below was the beginning of pastoral. Soft birch-woods, shady beeches, meadows where cattle had browsed for generations, fringed the little brown river as it twined to the sea. Farther, and the waves broke on white sands, the wonderful billows of the West which cannot bear to be silent. And between, in a garden wilderness, with the evening flaming in its windows, stood Fountainblue, my little four-square castle which guards the valley and the beaches.

The boy had torn his clothes, scratched his face, cut one finger deeply, and soaked himself with bog-water, but he whistled cheerfully and his eyes were happy. He had had an afternoon of adventure, startling emprises achieved in solitude; assuredly a day to remember and mark with a white stone. And the beginning had been most unpromising. After lunch he had been attired in his best raiment, and, in the misery of a broad white collar, despatched with his cousins to take tea with the small lady who domineered in Fountainblue. The prospect had pleased him greatly, the gardens fed his fancy, the hostess was an old confederate, and there were sure to be excellent things to eat. But his curious temper had arisen to torment him. On the way he quarrelled with his party, and in a moment found himself out of sympathy with the future. The enjoyment crept out of the prospect. He knew that he did not shine in society, he foresaw an afternoon when he would be left out in the cold and his hilarious cousins treated as the favoured guests. He reflected that tea was a short meal at the best, and that games on a lawn were a poor form of sport. Above all, he felt the torture of his collar and the straitness of his clothes. He pictured the dreary return in the twilight, when the afternoon, which had proved, after all, such a dismal failure, had come to a weary end. So, being a person of impulses, he mutinied at the gates of Fountainblue and made for the hills. He knew he should get into trouble, but trouble, he had long ago found out, was his destiny, and he scorned to avoid it. And now, having cast off the fear of God and man, he would for some short hours do exactly as he pleased.

Half-crying with regret for the delights he had forsworn, he ran over the moor to the craggy hills which had always been forbidden him. When he had climbed among the rocks awe fell upon the desolate little adventurer, and he bewailed his choice. But soon he found a blue hawk's nest, and the possession of a coveted egg inspired him to advance. By-and-by he had climbed so high that he could not return, but must needs scale Stob Ghabhar itself. With a quaking heart he achieved it, and then, in the pride of his heroism, he must venture down the Grey Correi where the wild goats lived. He saw a bearded ruffian, and pursued him with stones, stalking him cunningly till he was out of breath. Then he found odd little spleenwort ferns, which he pocketed, and high up in the rocks a friendly raven croaked his encouragement. And then, when the shadows length-ened, he set off cheerily homewards, hungry, triumphant, and very weary.

All the way home he flattered his soul. In one afternoon he had been hunter and trapper, and what to him were girls' games and pleasant things to eat? He pictured himself the hardy outlaw, feeding on oatmeal and goat's-flesh, the terror and pride of his neighbourhood. Could the little mistress of Fountainblue but see him now, how she would despise his prosaic cousins! And then, as he descended on the highway, he fell in with his forsaken party.

For a wonder they were in good spirits – so good that they forgot to remind him, in their usual way, of the domestic terrors awaiting him. A man had been there who had told them stories and shown them tricks, and there had been coconut cake, and Sylvia had a new pony on which they had ridden races. The children were breathless with excitement, very much in love with each other as common sharers in past joys. And as they talked all the colour went out of his afternoon. The blue hawk's egg was cracked, and it looked a stupid, dingy object as it lay in his cap. His rare ferns were crumpled and withered, and who was to believe his stories of Stob Ghabhar and the Grey Correi? He had been a fool to barter ponies and tea and a man who knew tricks for the barren glories of following his own fancy. But at any rate he would show no sign. If he was to be an outlaw, he would carry his outlawry well; so with a catch in his voice and tears in his eyes he jeered at his inattentive companions, upbraid-ing himself all the while for his folly.

II

The sun was dipping behind Stob Ghabhar when Maitland drove over the ridge of hill, whence the moor-road dips to Fountainblue. Twenty long miles from the last outpost of railway to the western sea-loch, and twenty of the barest, steepest miles in the bleak north. And all the way he had been puzzling himself with the half-painful, half-pleasing memories of a childhood which to the lonely man still overtopped the present. Every wayside bush was the home of recollection. In every burn he had paddled and fished; here he had found the jack-snipe's nest, there he had hidden when the shepherds sought him for burning the heather in May. He lost for a little the burden of his years and cares, and lived again in that old fresh world which had no boundaries, where sleep and food were all his thought at night, and adventure the sole outlook of the morning. The western sea lay like a thin line of gold beyond the moorland, and down in the valley in a bower of trees lights began to twinkle from the little castle. The remote mountains, hiding deep corries and woods in their bosom, were blurred by twilight to a single wall of hazy purple, which shut off this fairy glen impenetrably from the world. Fountainblue – the name rang witchingly in his ears. Fountainblue, the last home of the Good Folk, the last hold of the vanished kings, where the last wolf in Scotland was slain, and, as stories go, the last saint of the Great Ages taught the people – what had Fountainblue to do with his hard world of facts and figures? The thought woke him to a sense of the present, and for a little he relished the paradox. He had left it long ago, an adventurous child; now he was returning with success behind him and a portion of life's good things his own. He was rich, very rich and famous. Few men of forty had his power, and he had won it all in fair struggle with enemies and rivals and a niggardly world. He had been feared and hated, as he had been extravagantly admired; he had been rudely buffeted by fortune, and had met the blows with a fighter's joy. And out of it all something hard and austere had shaped itself, something very much a man, but a man with little heart and a lack of kindly human failings. He was master of himself in a curious degree, but the mastery absorbed his interests. Nor had he ever regretted it, when suddenly in this outlandish place the past swept over him, and he had a vision of a long avenue of vanished hopes. It pleased and disquieted him, and as the road dipped into the valley he remembered the prime cause of this mood of vagaries.

He had come up into the north with one purpose in view, he frankly told himself. The Etheridges were in Fountain-blue, and ever since, eight months before, he had met Clara Etheridge, he had forgotten his ambitions. A casual neigh-bour at a dinner-party, a chance partner at a ball – and then he had to confess that this slim, dark, bright-eyed girl had broken in irrevocably upon his contentment. At first he hated it for a weakness, then he welcomed the weakness with feverish ecstasy. He did nothing by halves, so he sought her company eagerly, and, being a great man in his way, found things made easy for him. But the girl remained shy and distant, flattered doubtless by his atten-tion, but watching him curiously as an intruder from an alien world. It was characteristic of the man that he never thought of a rival. His whole aim was to win her love; for rivalry with other men he had the contempt of a habitual conqueror. And so the uneasy wooing went on till the Etheridges left town, and he found himself a fortnight later with his work done and a visit before him to which he looked forward with all the vehemence of a nature whose strong point had always been its hope. As the road wound among the fir-trees, he tried to forecast the life at Foun-tainblue, and map out the future in his usual business-like way. But now the future refused to be thus shorn and parcelled: there was an unknown quantity in it which defied his efforts.

The house-party were sitting round the hall-fire when he entered. The high-roofed place, the flagged floor strewn with rugs, and the walls bright with the glow of fire on armour, gave him a boyish sense of comfort. Two men in knickerbockers were lounging on a settle, and at his entrance came forward to greet him. One was Sir Hugh Clanroyden, a follower of his own; the other he recognised as a lawyer named Durward. From the circle of women Miss Etheridge rose and welcomed him. Her mother was out, but would be back for dinner; meantime he should be shown his room. He noticed that her face was browner, her hair a little less neat, and there seemed something franker

and kindlier in her smile. So in a very good humour he went
to rid himself of the dust of the roads.

Durward watched him curiously, and then turned,
laughing, to his companion, as the girl came back to her
friends with a heightened colour in her cheeks.

'Romeo the second,' he said. 'We are going to be
spectators of a comedy. And yet, heaven knows! Maitland
is not cast for comedy.'

The other shook his head. 'It will never come off. I've
known Clara Etheridge most of my life, and I would as
soon think of marrying a dancing-girl to a bishop. She is
a delightful person, and my very good friend, but how
on earth is she ever to understand Maitland? And how
on earth can he see anything in her? Besides, there's
another man.'

Durward laughed. 'Despencer! I suppose he will be a
serious rival with a woman; but imagine him Maitland's
rival in anything else! He'd break him like a rotten stick in
half an hour. I like little Despencer, and I don't care about
Maitland; but all the same it is absurd to compare the two,
except in love-making.'

'Lord, it will be comic,' and Clanroyden stretched his
long legs and lay back on a cushion. The girls were still
chattering beside the fire, and the twilight was fast darkening into evening.

'You dislike Maitland?' he asked, looking up. 'Now, I
wonder why?'

Durward smiled comically at the ceiling. 'Oh, I know I
oughtn't to. I know he's supposed to be a man's man, and
that it's bad form for a man to say he dislikes him. But I'm
honest enough to own to detesting him. I suppose he's
great, but he's not great enough yet to compel one to fall
down and worship him, and I hate greatness in the making.
He goes through the world with his infernal arrogance and
expects everybody to clear out of his way. I am told we live
in an age of reason, but that fellow has burked reason. He
never gives a reason for a thing he does, and if you try to
argue he crushes you. He has killed good talk for ever with
his confounded rudeness. All the little sophistries and
conventions which make life tolerable are so much rubbish

to him, and he shows it. The plague of him is that he can
never make-believe. He is as hard as iron, and as fierce as
the devil, and about as unpleasant. You may respect the
sledge-hammer type, but it's confoundedly dull. Why, the
man has not the imagination of a rabbit, except in his
description of people he dislikes. I liked him when he said
that Layden reminded him of a dissipated dove, because I
disliked Layden; but when Freddy Alton played the fool
and people forgave him, because he was a good sort,
Maitland sent him about his business, saying he had no
further use for weaklings. He is so abominably cold-
blooded and implacable that everyone must fear him,
and yet most people can afford to despise him. All the
kind simple things of life are shut out of his knowledge. He
has no nature, only a heart of stone and an iron will and a
terribly subtle brain. Of course he is a great man – in a way,
but at the best he is only half a man. And to think that he
should have fallen in love, and be in danger of losing to
Despencer! It's enough to make one forgive him.'

Clanroyden laughed. 'I can't think of Despencer. It's too
absurd. But, seriously, I wish I saw Maitland well rid of this
mood, married or cured. That sort of man doesn't take
things easily.'

'It reminds one of Theocritus and the Cyclops in love.
Who would have thought to see him up in this moorland
place, running after a girl? He doesn't care for sport.'

'Do you know that he spent most of his childhood in this
glen, and that he *is* keen about sport? He is too busy for
many holidays, but he once went with Burton to the
Caucasus, and Burton said the experience nearly killed
him. He said that the fellow was tireless, and as mad and
reckless as a boy with nothing to lose.'

'Well, that simply bears out what I say of him. He does
not understand the meaning of sport. When he gets keen
about anything he pursues it as carefully and relentlessly as
if it were something on the Stock Exchange. Now little
Despencer is a genuine sportsman in his canary-like way.
He loves the art of the thing and the being out of doors.
Maitland, I don't suppose, ever thinks whether it is a ceiling
or the sky above his august head, Despencer—'

BUT at the moment Clanroyden uncrossed his legs, bringing his right foot down heavily upon his companion's left. Durward looked up and saw a young man coming towards him, smiling.

The newcomer turned aside to say something to the girls round the fire, and then came and sat on an arm of the settle. He was a straight, elegant person, with a well-tanned, regular face, and very pleasant brown eyes.

'I've had such an afternoon,' he said. 'You never saw a place like Cairnlora. It's quite a little stone tower all alone in a firwood, and nothing else between the moor and the sea. It is furnished as barely as a prison, except for the chairs, which are priceless old Dutch things. Oh, and the silver at tea was the sort of thing that only Americans can buy nowadays. Mrs Etheridge is devoured with envy. But the wonder of the house is old Miss Elphinstone. She must be nearly seventy, and she looks forty-five, except for her hair. She speaks broad Scots, and she has the manners of a *marquise*. I would give a lot to have had Raeburn paint her. She reminded me of nothing so much as a hill-wind with her keen high-coloured old face. Yes, I have enjoyed the afternoon.'

'Jack has got a new enthusiasm,' said Durward. 'I wish I were like you to have a new one once a week. By the way, Maitland has arrived at last.'

'Really!' said Despencer. 'Oh, I forgot to tell you something which you would never have guessed. Miss Elphinstone is Maitland's aunt, and he was brought up a good deal at Cairnlora. He doesn't take his manners from her, but I suppose he gets his cleverness from that side of the family. She disapproves of him strongly, so of course I had to defend him. And what do you think she said? "He has betrayed his tradition. He has sold his birthright for a mess of pottage, and I wish him joy of his bargain!" Nice one for your party, Hugh.'

Miss Etheridge had left the group at the fire and was standing at Despencer's side. She listened to him with a curious air of solicitude, like an affectionate sister. At the mention of Maitland's name Clanroyden had watched her narrowly, but her face did not change. And when

Despencer asked, 'Where is the new arrival?' she talked
of him with the utmost nonchalance.

Maitland came down to dinner, ravenously hungry and in
high spirits. Nothing was changed in this house since he
had stared at the pictures and imagined terrible things
about the armour and broken teacups with childish im-
partiality. His own favourite seat was still there, where,
hidden by a tapestry screen, he had quarrelled with Sylvia
while their elders gossiped. This sudden flood of memories
mellowed him towards the world. He was cordial to
Despencer, forbore to think Durward a fool, and answered
every one of Mr Etheridge's many questions. For the first
time he felt the success of his life. The old house recalled
his childhood, and the sight of Clanroyden, his devoted
follower, reminded him of his power. Somehow the weariful crying for the moon, which had always tortured him,
was exchanged for a glow of comfort, a shade of complacency in his haggard soul . . . And then the sight of Clara
dispelled his satisfaction.

Here in this cheerful homely party of friends he found
himself out of place. On state occasions he could acquit
himself with credit, for the man had a mind. He could make
the world listen to him when he chose, and the choice was
habitual. But now his loneliness claimed its lawful con-
sequences, and he longed for the little friendly graces which
he had so often despised. Despencer talked of scenery and
weather with a tenderness to which this man, who loved
nature as he loved little else, was an utter stranger. This
elegant and appropriate sentiment would have worried him
past endurance, if Miss Clara had not shared it. It was she
who told some folk-tale about the Grey Correi with the
prettiest hesitancy which showed her feeling. And then the
talk drifted to books and people, flitting airily about their
petty world. Maitland felt himself choked by their accom-
plishments. Most of the subjects were ones no sane man
would trouble to think of, and yet here were men talking
keenly about trifles and disputing with nimble-witted
cleverness on the niceties of the trivial. Feeling miserably
that he was the only silent one, he plunged desperately into

the stream, found himself pulled up by Despencer and deftly turned. The event gave him the feeling of having been foiled by a kitten.

Angry with the world, angrier with his own angularity, he waited for the end of the meal. Times had not changed in this house since he had been saved by Sylvia from social disgrace. But when the women left the room he found life easier. His host talked of sport, and he could tell him more about Stob Ghabhar than any keeper. Despencer, victorious at dinner, now listened like a docile pupil. Durward asked a political question, and the answer came sharp and definite. Despencer demurred gently, after his fashion. 'Well, but surely—' and a grimly smiling 'What do you know about it?' closed the discussion. The old Maitland had returned for the moment.

The night was mild and impenetrably dark, and the fall of waters close at hand sounded like a remote echo. An open hall-door showed that some of the party had gone out to the garden, and the men followed at random. A glimmer of white frocks betrayed the women on the lawn, standing by the little river which slipped by cascade and glide from the glen to the low pasture-lands. In the featureless dark there was no clue to locality. The place might have been Berkshire or a suburban garden.

Suddenly the scream of some animal came from the near thicket. The women started and asked what it was.

'It was a hill-fox,' said Maitland to Clara. 'They used to keep me awake at nights on the hill. They come and bark close to your ear and give you nightmare.'

The lady shivered. 'Thank Heaven for the indoors,' she said. 'Now, if I had been the daughter of one of your old Donalds of the Isles, I should have known that cry only too well. Wild nature is an excellent background, but give me civilisation in front.'

Maitland was looking into the wood. 'You will find it creeps far into civilisation if you look for it. There is a very narrow line between the warm room and the savage out-of-doors.'

'There are miles of luxuries,' the girl cried, laughing. 'People who are born in the wrong country have to hunt

over half the world before they find their savagery. It is all
very tame, but I love the tameness. You may call yourself
primitive, Mr Maitland, but you are the most complex and
modern of us all. What would Donald of the Isles have said
to politics and the Stock Exchange?'

They had strolled back to the house. 'Nevertheless I
maintain my belief,' said the man. 'You call it miles of
rampart; I call the division a line, a thread, a sheet of glass.
But then, you see, you only know one side, and I only know
the other.'

'What preposterous affectation!' the girl said, as with a
pretty shiver she ran indoors. Maitland stood for a moment
looking back at the darkness. Within the firelit hall, with its
rugs and little tables and soft chairs, he had caught a
glimpse of Despencer smoking a cigarette. As he looked
towards the hills he heard the fox's bark a second time, and
then somewhere from the black distance came a hawk's
scream, hoarse, lonely, and pitiless. The thought struck
him that the sad elemental world of wood and mountain
was far more truly his own than this cosy and elegant
civilisation. And, oddly enough, the thought pained him.

III

The day following was wet and windy, when a fire was
grateful, and the hills, shrouded in grey mist, had no
attractions. The party read idly in armchairs during the
morning, and in the afternoon Maitland and Clanroyden
went down to the stream mouth after sea-trout. So
Despencer remained to talk to Clara, and, having
played many games of picquet and grown heartily tired
of each other, as tea-time approached they fell to
desultory comments on their friends. Maitland was
beginning to interest the girl in a new way. Formerly
he had been a great person who was sensible enough to
admire her, but something remote and unattractive, for
whom friendship (much less love) was impossible. But
now she had begun to feel his power, his manhood. The
way in which other men spoke of him impressed her
unconsciously, and she began to ask Despencer ques-

tions which were gall and wormwood to that young man.
But he answered honestly, after his fashion.

'Isn't he very rich?' she asked. 'And I suppose he lives
very plainly?'

'Rich as Crœsus, and he sticks in his ugly rooms in the
Albany because he never thinks enough about the thing to
change. I've been in them once, and you never saw such a
place. He's a maniac for fresh air, so they're large enough,
but they're littered like a stable with odds and ends of
belongings. He must have several thousand books, and yet
he hasn't a decent binding among them. He hasn't a
photograph of a single soul, and only one picture,
which, I believe, was his father. But you never saw such
a collection of whips and spurs and bits. It smells like a
harness-room, and there you find Maitland, when by any
chance he is at home, working half the night and up to the
eyes in papers. I don't think the man has any expenses
except food and rent, for he wears the same clothes for
years. And he has given up horses.'

'Was he fond of horses?' Miss Clara asked.

'Oh, you had better ask him. I really can't tell you any
more about him.'

'But how do his friends get on with him?'

'He has hardly any, but his acquaintances, who are all the
world, say he is the one great man of the future. If you want
to read what people think of him, you had better look at the
"Monthly".'

Under cover of this one ungenerous word Despencer
made his escape, for he hated the business, but made it the
rule of his life 'never to crab a fellow'. Miss Clara promptly
sought out the 'Monthly', and found twenty pages of super-
fine analysis and bitter, grudging praise. She read it with
interest, and then lay back in her chair and tried to fix her
thoughts. It is only your unhealthy young woman who
worships strength in the abstract, and the girl tried to
determine whether she admired the man as a power or
disliked him as a brute. She chose a compromise, and the
feeling which survived was chiefly curiosity.

The result of the afternoon was that when the fishermen
returned, and Maitland, in dry clothes, appeared for tea,

she settled herself beside him and prepared to talk. Maitland, being healthily tired, was in an excellent temper, and he found himself enticed into what for him was a rare performance – talk about himself. They were sitting apart from the others, and, ere ever he knew, he was answering the girl's questions with an absent-minded frankness. In a little she had drawn from him the curious history of his life, which most men knew, but never from his own lips.

'I was at school for a year,' he said, 'and then my father died and our affairs went to pieces. I had to come back and go into an office, a sort of bank. I hated it, but it was good for me, for it taught me something, and my discontent made me ambitious. I had about eighty pounds a year, and I saved from that. I worked too at books incessantly, and by-and-by I got an Oxford scholarship, at an obscure college. I went up there, and found myself in a place where everyone seemed well-off, while I was a pauper. However, it didn't trouble me much, for I had no ambition to play the fool. I only cared about two things – horses and metaphysics. I hated all games, which I thought only fit for children. I daresay it was foolish, but then you see I had had a queer upbringing. I managed to save a little money, and one vacation when I was wandering about in Norfolk, sleeping under haystacks and working in harvest-fields when my supplies ran down, I came across a farmer. He was a good fellow and a sort of sportsman, and I took a fancy to him. He had a colt to sell which I fancied more, for I saw it had blood in it. So I bought it for what seemed a huge sum to me in those days, but I kept it at his farm and I superintended its education. I broke it myself and taught it to jump, and by-and-by in my third year I brought it to Oxford and entered for the Grind on it. People laughed at me, but I knew my own business. The little boys who rode in the thing knew nothing about horses, and not one in ten could ride; so I entered and won. It was all I wanted, for I could sell my horse then, and the fellow who rode second bought it. It was decent of him, for I asked a big figure, and I think he had an idea of doing me a kindness. I made him my private secretary the other day.'

'You mean Lord Drapier?' she asked.

'Yes – Drapier. That gave me money to finish off and begin in town. Oh, and I had got a first in my schools. I knew very little about anything except metaphysics, and I never went to tutors. I suppose I knew a good deal more than the examiners in my own subject, and anyhow they felt obliged to give me my first after some grumbling. Then I came up to town with just sixty pounds in my pocket, but I had had the education of a gentleman.'

Maitland looked out of the window, and the sight of the mist-clad hills recalled him to himself. He wondered why he was telling the girl this story, and he stopped suddenly.

'And what did you do in town?' she asked, with interest.

'I hung round and kept my eyes open. I nearly starved, for I put half my capital on a horse which I thought was safe, and lost it. By-and-by, quite by accident, I came across a curious fellow, Ransome – you probably have heard his name. I met him in some stables where he was buying a mare, and he took a liking to me. He made me his secretary, and then, because I liked hard work, he let me see his business. It was enormous, for the man was a genius after a fashion; and I slaved away in his office and down at the docks for about three years. He paid me just enough to keep body and soul together and cover them with clothes; but I didn't grumble, for I had a sort of idea that I was on my probation. And then my apprenticeship came to an end.'

'Yes,' said the girl.

'Yes; for you see Ransome was an odd character. He had a sort of genius for finance, and within his limits he was even a great administrator. But in everything else he was as simple as a child. His soul was idyllic: he loved green fields and Herrick and sheep. So it had always been his fancy to back out some day and retire with his huge fortune to some country place and live as he pleased. It seemed that he had been training me from the first day I went into the business, and now he cut the rope and left the whole enormous concern in my hands. I needed every atom of my wits, and the first years were a hard struggle. I became of course very rich; but I had to do more, I had to keep the thing at its old level. I had no natural turn for the work, and I had to acquire capacity by sheer grind. However, I managed it, and then, when I felt my position sure, I indulged myself with a hobby and went into politics.'

'You call it a hobby?'

'Certainly. The ordinary political career is simply a form of trifling. There's no trade on earth where a man has to fear so few able competitors. Of course it's very public and honourable and that sort of thing, and I like it; but sometimes it wearies me to death.'

The girl was looking at him with curious interest. 'Do you always get what you want?' she asked.

'Never,' he said.

'Then is your success all disappointment?'

'Oh, I generally get a bit of my ambitions, which is all one can hope for in this world.'

'I suppose your ambitions are not idyllic, like Mr Ransome's?'

He laughed. 'No, I suppose not. I never could stand your Corot meadows and ivied cottages and village church bells. But I am at home in this glen, or used to be.'

'You said that last night, and I thought it was affectation,' said the girl; 'but perhaps you are right. I'm not at home in this scenery, at any rate in this weather. Ugh, look at that mist driving and that spur of Stob Ghabhar! I really must go and sit by the fire.'

IV

The next day dawned clear and chill, with a little frost to whiten the heather; but by midday the sun had turned August to June, and sea and land drowsed in a mellow heat. Maitland was roused from his meditations with a pipe on a garden-seat by the appearance of Miss Clara, her eyes bright with news. He had taken her in to dinner the night before, and for the first time in his life had found himself talking easily to a woman. Her interest of the afternoon had not departed; and Despencer in futile disgust shunned the drawing-room, his particular paradise, and played billiards with Clanroyden in the spirit of an unwilling martyr.

'We are going out in the yacht,' Miss Clara cried, as she emerged from the shadow of a fuchsia-hedge, 'to the Isles of the Waves, away beyond the Seal's Headland. Do you know the place, Mr Maitland?'

'Eilean na Cille? Yes. It used to be dangerous for currents, but a steam-yacht does not require to fear them.'

'Well, we'll be ready to start at twelve, and I must go in to give orders about lunch.'

A little later she came out with a bundle of letters in her hands. 'Here are your letters, Mr Maitland; but you mustn't try to answer them, or you'll be late.' He put the lot in his jacket pocket and looked up at the laughing girl. 'My work is six hundred miles behind me,' he said, 'and today I have only the Eilean na Cille to think of.' And, as she passed by, another name took the place of the Eilean, and it seemed to him that at last he had found the link which was to bind together the two natures – his boyhood and his prime.

Out on the loch the sun was beating with that steady August blaze which is more torrid than midsummer. But as the yacht slipped between the horns of the land, it came into a broken green sea with rollers to the north where the tireless Atlantic fretted on the reefs. In a world of cool salt winds and the golden weather of afternoon, with the cries of tern and gull about the bows and the foam and ripple of green water in the wake, the party fell into a mood of supreme contentment. The restless Miss Clara was stricken into a figure of contemplation, which sat in the bows and watched the hazy blue horizon and the craggy mainland hills in silent delight. Maitland was revelling in the loss of his isolation. He had ceased to be alone, a leader, and for the moment felt himself one of the herd, a devotee of humble pleasures. His mind was blank, his eyes filled only with the sea, and the lady of his devotion, in that happy moment of romance, seemed to have come at last within the compass of his hopes.

The Islands of the Waves are low green ridges which rise little above the highest tide-mark. The grass is stiff with salt, the sparse heather and rushes are crooked with the winds, but there are innumerable little dells where a light wild scrub flourishes, and in one a spring of sweet water sends a tiny stream to the sea. The yacht's company came ashore in boats; and tea was made with a great bustle beside the well, while the men lay idly in the bent and smoked. All wind seemed to have died down, a soft, cool, airless peace like a June evening was abroad, and the heavy surging of the tides had sunk to a distant whisper. Maitland lifted his head, sniffed the air, and looked uneasily to the west, meeting the eye of one of the sailors engaged in the same scrutiny. He beckoned the man to him.

'What do you make of the weather?' he asked.

The sailor, an East-coast man from Arbroath, shook his head. 'It's ower lown a' of a sudden,' he said. 'It looks like mair wind nor we want, but I think it'll haud till the morn.'

Maitland nodded and lay down again. He smiled at the return of his old sea craft and weather-lore, on which he had prided himself in his boyhood; and when Miss Clara came up to him with tea she found him grinning vacantly at the sky.

'What a wonderful lull in the wind,' she said. 'When I was here last these were real isles of the waves, with spray flying over them and a great business to land. But now they might be the island in Fountainblue lake.'

'Did you ever hear of the Ocean Quiet?' he asked. 'I believe it to be a translation of a Gaelic word which is a synonym for death, but it is also a kind of natural phenomenon. Old people at Cairnlora used to talk of it. They said that sometimes fishermen far out at sea in blowing weather came into a place of extraordinary peace, where the whole world was utterly still and they could hear their own hearts beating.'

'What a pretty fancy!' said the girl.

'Yes; but it had its other side. The fishermen rarely came home alive, and if they did they were queer to the end of their days. Another name for the thing was the Breathing of God. It is an odd idea, the passing from the wholesome turmoil of nature to the uncanny place where God crushes you by His silence.'

'All the things to eat are down by the fire,' she said, laughing. 'Do you know, if you weren't what you are, people might think you a poet, Mr Maitland. I thought you cared for none of these things.'

'What things?' he asked. 'I don't care for poetry. I am merely repeating the nonsense I was brought up on. Shall I talk to you about politics?'

'Heaven forbid! And now I will tell you my own story about these isles. There is a hermit's cell on one of them and crosses, like Iona. The hermit lived alone all winter, and was fed by boats from the shore when the weather was calm. When one hermit died another took his place, and no one knew where he came from. Now one day a great lord in Scotland disappeared from his castle. He was the King's Warden of the Marches and the greatest soldier of his day, but he disappeared utterly out of men's sight, and people forgot about him. Long years after the Northmen in a great fleet came down upon these isles, and the little chiefs fled before them. But suddenly among them there appeared an old man, the hermit of the Wave Islands, who organised resistance and gathered a strong army. No one dared oppose him, and the quarrelsome petty chiefs forgot their quarrels under his banner, for he had the air of one born to command. At last he met the invaders in the valley of Fountainblue, and beat them so utterly that few escaped to their ships. He fell himself in the first charge, but not before his followers had heard his battle-cry of "Saint Bride", and known the Hermit of the Isles and the great King's Warden were the same.'

'That was a common enough thing in wild times. Men grew tired of murder and glory and waving banners, and wanted quiet to make their peace with their own souls. I should have thought the craving scarcely extinct yet.'

'Then here is your chance, Mr Maitland,' said the girl, laughing. 'A little trouble would make the hut habitable, and you could simply disappear, leaving no address to forward your letters to. Think of the sensation, "Disappearance of a Secretary of State", and the wild theories and the obituaries. Then some day when the land question became urgent on the mainland, you would turn up suddenly, settle it with extraordinary wisdom, and die after confiding your life-story to some country reporter. But I am afraid it would scarcely do, for you would be discovered by Scotland Yard, which would be ignominious.'

'It is a sound idea, but the old device is too crude. However, it could be managed differently. Some day, when civilisation grows oppressive, Miss Clara, I will remember your advice.'

The afternoon shadows were beginning to lengthen, and from the west a light sharp wind was crisping the sea. The yacht was getting up steam, and boats were coming ashore for the party. The deep blue waters were flushing rose-pink as the level westering sun smote them from the summit of a cloudbank. The stillness had gone, and the air was now full of sounds and colour. Miss Clara, with an eye on the trim yacht, declared her disapproval. 'It is an evening for the cutter,' she cried, and in spite of Mrs Etheridge's protests she gave orders for it to be made ready. Then the self-willed young woman looked round for company. 'Will you come, Mr Maitland?' she said. 'You can sail a boat, can't you? And Mr Despencer, I shall want you to talk to me when Mr Maitland is busy. We shall race the yacht, for we ought to be able to get through the Scart's Neck with this wind.'

'I am not sure if you are wise, Miss Clara,' and Maitland pulled down his brows as he looked to the west. 'It will be wind – in a very little, and you stand the chance of a wetting.'

'I don't mind. I want to get the full good of such an evening. You want to be near the water to understand one of our sunsets. I can be a barbarian too, you know.'

It was not for Maitland to grumble at this friendliness; so he followed her into the cutter with Despencer, who had no love for the orders but much for her who gave them. He took the helm and steered, with directions from the lady, from his memory of the intricate coast. Despencer with many rugs looked to Miss Clara's comfort, and, having assured his own, was instantly entranced with the glories of the evening.

The boat tripped along for a little in a dazzle of light into the silvery grey of the open water. Far in front lay the narrow gut called the Scart's Neck, which was the by-way to the loch of Fountainblue. Then Maitland at the helm felt the sheets suddenly begin to strain, and, looking behind, saw that the Isles of the Waves were almost lost in the gloom, and that the roseate heavens were quickly darkening behind. The wind which he had feared was upon them; a few seconds more and it was sending the cutter staggering among billows. He could hardly make himself heard in the din, as he roared directions to Despencer about disposing of his person in another part of the boat. The girl with flushed face was laughing in pure joy of the storm. She caught a glimpse of Maitland's serious eye and looked over the gunwale at the threatening west. Then she too became quiet, and meekly sat down on the thwart to which he motioned her.

The gale made the Scart's Neck impossible, and the murky sky seemed to promise greater fury ere the morning. Twilight was falling, and the other entrance to the quiet loch meant the rounding of a headland and a difficult course through a little archipelago. It was the only way, for return was out of the question, and it seemed vain to risk the narrow chances of the short-cut. Maitland looked down at his two companions, and reflected with pleasure that he was the controller of their fates. He had sailed much as a boy, and he found in this moment of necessity that his old lore returned to him. He felt no mistrust of his powers: whatever the gale he could land them at Fountainblue, though it might take hours and involve much discomfort. He remembered the coast like his own name; he relished the grim rage of the elements, and he kept the cutter's head out to sea with a delight in the primeval conflict.

The last flickering rays of light, coming from the screen of cloud, illumined the girl's pale face, and the sight disquieted him. There was a hint of tragedy in this game. Despencer, nervously self-controlled, was reassuring Clara. Ploughing onward in the blackening night in a frail boat on a wind-threshed sea was no work for a girl. But it was Despencer who was comforting her! Well, it was his proper work. He was made for the business of talking soft things to women. Maitland, his face hard with spray, looked into the darkness with a kind of humour in his heart. And then, as the boat shore and dipped into the

storm, its human occupants seemed to pass out of the
picture, and it was only a shell tossed on great waters in
the unfathomable night. The evening had come, moonless
and starless, and Maitland steered as best he could by the
deeper blackness which was the configuration of the
shore. Something loomed up that he knew for the headland, and they were drifting in a quieter stretch of sea,
with the breakers grumbling ahead from the little tangle
of islands.

Suddenly he fell into one of the abstractions which had
always dogged him through his strenuous life. His mind
was clear, he chose his course with a certain precision, but
the winds and waves had become to him echoes of echoes.
Wet with spray and shifting his body constantly with the
movement of the boat, it yet was all a phantasmal existence,
while his thoughts were following an airy morrice in a
fairyland world. The motto of his house, the canting motto
of old reivers, danced in his brain – '*Parmi ceu haut bois
conduyrai m'amie*' – 'Through the high wood I will conduct
my love' – and in a land of green forests, dragon-haunted,
he was piloting Clara robed in a quaint medieval gown,
himself in speckless plate-armour. His fancy fled through a
score of scenes, sometimes on a dark heath, or by a lonely
river, or among great mountains, but always the lady and
her protector. Clara, looking up from Despencer's side,
saw his lips moving, noted that his eyes were glad, and for a
moment hoped better things of their chances.

Then suddenly she was dumb with alarm, for the cutter
heeled over, and but that Maitland woke to clear consciousness and swung the sheet loose, all would have been
past. The adventure nerved him and quickened his senses.
The boat seemed to move more violently than the wind
drove her, and in the utter blackness he felt for the first time
the grip of the waters. The ugly cruel monster had wakened, and was about to wreak its anger on the toy. And
then he remembered the currents which raced round
Eilean Righ and the scattered isles. Dim shapes loomed
up, shapes strange and unfriendly, and he felt miserably
that he was as helpless now as Despencer. To the left night
had wholly shut out the coast; his one chance was to run for

one of the isles and risk a landing. It would be a dreary
waiting for the dawn, but safety had come before any
comfort. And yet, he remembered, the little islands were
rock-bound and unfriendly, and he was hurrying forward in
the grip of a black current with a gale behind and unknown
reefs before.

And then he seemed to remember something of this
current which swept along the isles. In a little – so he
recalled a boyish voyage in clear weather – they would
come to a place where the sea ran swift and dark beside a
kind of natural wharf. Here he had landed once upon a
time, but it was a difficult enterprise, needing a quick and
a far leap at the proper moment, for the stream ran very
fast. But if this leap were missed there was still a chance.
The isle was the great Eilean Righ, and the current swung
round its southern end, and then, joining with another
stream, turned up its far side, and for a moment washed
the shore. But if this second chance were missed, then
nothing remained but to fall into the great sea-going
stream and be carried out to death in the wide Atlantic.
He strained his eyes to the right for Eilean Righ. Something seemed to approach, as they bent under an access of
the gale. They bore down upon it, and he struggled to
keep the boat's head away, for at this pace to grate upon
rock would mean upsetting. The sail was down, fluttering
ar..idships like a captive bird, and the gaunt mast
bowed with the wind. A horrible fascination, the inertia
of nightmare, seized him. The motion was so swift and
beautiful; why not go on and onward, listlessly?
And then, conquering the weakness, he leaned forward
and called to Clara. She caught his arm like a child, and he
pulled her up beside him. Then he beckoned Despencer,
and, shrieking against the din, told him to follow him
when he jumped. Despencer nodded, his teeth chattering
with cold and the novel business. Suddenly out of the
darkness, a yard on their right, loomed a great flat rock
along which the current raced like a mill-lade. The boat
made to strike, but Maitland forced her nose out to sea,
and then as the stern swung round he seized his chance.
Holding Clara with his left arm he stood up, balanced

himself for a moment on the gunwale, and jumped. He
landed sprawling on his side on some wet seaweed, over
which the sea was lipping, but undeniably on land. As he
pulled himself up he had a vision of the cutter, dancing
like a cork, vanishing down the current into the darkness.

Holding the girl in his arms he picked his way across the
rock pools to the edge of the island heather. For a moment
he thought Clara had fainted. She lay still the inert, her eyes
shut, her hair falling foolishly over her brow. He sprinkled
some water on her face, and she revived sufficiently to ask
her whereabouts. He was crossing the island to find
Despencer, but he did not tell her. 'You are safe,' he
said, and he carried her over the rough ground as lightly
as a child. An intense exhilaration had seized him. He ran
over the flats and strode up the low hillocks with one
thought possessing his brain. To save Despencer, that of
course was the far-off aim on his mind's horizon, but all the
foreground was filled with the lady. '*Parmi ceu haut bois*' –
the old poetry of the world had penetrated to his heart. The
black night and the wild wind and the sea were the
ministrants of love. The hollow shams of life with their
mincing conventions had departed, and in this savage out-
world a man stood for a man. The girl's light tweed jacket
was no match for this chill gale, so he stopped for a
moment, took off his own shooting-coat and put it round
her. And then, as he came over a little ridge, he was aware
of a grumbling of waters and the sea.

The beach was hidden in a veil of surf which sprinkled
the very edge of the bracken. Beyond, the dark waters were
boiling like a caldron, for the tides in this little bay ran with
the fury of a river in spate. A moon was beginning to
struggle through the windy clouds, and surf, rock, and
wave began to shape themselves out of the night. Clara
stood on the sand, a slim, desolate figure, and clung to
Maitland's arm. She was still dazed with the storm and the
baffling suddenness of change. Maitland, straining his eyes
out to sea, was in a waking dream. With the lady no toil was
too great, no darkness terrible; for her he would scale the
blue air and plough the hills and do all the lover's feats of
romance. And then suddenly he shook her hand roughly

from his arm and ran forward, for he saw something coming down the tide.

Before he left the boat he had lowered the sail, and the cutter swung to the current, an odd amorphous thing, now heeling over with a sudden gust and now pulled back to balance by the strong grip of the water. A figure seemed to sit in the stern, making feeble efforts to steer. Maitland knew the coast and the ways of the sea. He ran through the surf-ring into the oily-black eddies, shouting to Despencer to come overboard. Soon he was not ten yards from the cutter's line, where the current made a turn towards the shore before it washed the iron rocks to the right. He found deep water, and in two strokes was in the grip of the tides and borne wildly towards the reef. He prepared himself for what was coming, raising his feet and turning his right shoulder to the front. And then with a shock he was pinned against the rock-wall, with the tides tugging at his legs, while his hands clung desperately to a shelf. Here he remained, yelling directions to the coming boat. Surf was in his eyes, so that at first he could not see, but at last in a dip of the waves he saw the cutter, a man's form in the stern, plunging not twenty yards away. Now was his chance or never, for while the tide would take a boat far from his present place of vantage, it would carry a lighter thing, such as a man's body, in a circle nearer to the shore. He yelled again, and the world seemed to him quiet for a moment, while his voice echoed eerily in the void. Despencer must have heard it, for the next moment he saw him slip pluckily overboard, making the cutter heel desperately with his weight. And then – it seemed an age – a man, choking and struggling weakly, came down the current, and, pushing his right arm out against the rush of water, he had caught the swimmer by the collar and drawn him in to the side of the rock.

Then came the harder struggle. Maitland's left hand was numbing, and though he had a foothold, it was too slight to lean on with full weight. A second lassitude oppressed him, a supreme desire to slip into those racing tides and rest. He was in no panic about death, but he had the practical man's love of an accomplished task, and it nerved him to the extreme toil. Slowly by inches he drew himself up the edge of the reef, cherishing jealously each grip and foothold, with Despencer, half-choked and all but fainting, hanging heavily on his right arm. Blind with spray, sick with sea-water, and aching with his labours, he gripped at last the tangles of seaweed, which meant the flat surface, and with one final effort raised himself and Despencer to the top. There he lay for a few minutes with his head in a rock-pool till the first weariness had passed.

He staggered with his burden in his arms along the ragged reef to the strip of sand where Clara was weeping hysterically. The sight of her restored Maitland to vigour, the appeal of her lonely figure there in the wet brackens. She must think them all dead, he reflected, and herself desolate, for she could not have interpreted rightly his own wild rush into the waves. When she heard his voice she started, as if at a ghost, and then seeing his burden, ran towards him. 'Oh, he is dead!' she cried. 'Tell me! tell me!' and she clasped the inert figure so that her arm crossed Maitland's. Despencer, stupefied and faint, was roused to consciousness by a woman's kisses on his cheek, and still more by his bearer abruptly laying him on the heather. Clara hung over him like a mother, calling him by soft names, pushing his hair from his brow, forgetful of her own wet and sorry plight. And meanwhile Maitland stood watching, while his palace of glass was being shivered about his ears.

Aforetime his arrogance had kept him from any thought of jealousy; now the time and place were too solemn for trifling, and facts were laid bare before him. Sentiment does not bloom readily in a hard nature, but if it once comes to flower it does not die without tears and agonies. The wearied man, who stood quietly beside the hysterical pair, had a moment of peculiar anguish. Then he conquered sentiment, as he had conquered all other feelings of whose vanity he was assured. He was now, as he was used to be, a man among children; and as a man he had his work. He bent over Clara. 'I know a hollow in the middle of the island,' he said, 'where we can camp the night. I'll carry Despencer, for his ankle is twisted. Do you think you could try to walk?'

The girl followed obediently, her eyes only on her lover. Her trust in the other was infinite, her indifference to him impenetrable; while he, hopelessly conscious of his fate, saw in the slim dishevelled figure at his side the lost lady, the mistress for him of all romance and generous ambitions. The new springs in his life were choked; he had still his work, his power, and, thank God, his courage; but the career which ran out to the horizon of his vision was black and loveless. And he held in his arms the thing which had frustrated him, the thing he had pulled out of the deep in peril of his body; and at the thought life for a moment seemed to be only a comic opera with tragedy to shift the scenes.

He found a cleft between two rocks with a soft floor of heather. There had been no rain, so the bracken was dry, and he gathered great armfuls and driftwood logs from the shore. Soon he had a respectable pile of timber, and then in the nick of the cleft he built a fire. His matches, being in his jacket pocket, had escaped the drenchings of salt water, and soon with a smoke and crackling and sweet scent of burning wood, a fire was going cheerily in the darkness. Then he made a couch of bracken, and laid there the still feeble Despencer. The man was more weak than ill; but for his ankle he was unhurt; and a little brandy would have brought him to himself. But this could not be provided, and Clara saw in his condition only the sign of mortal sickness. With haggard eyes she watched by him, easing his head, speaking soft kind words, forgetful of her own cold and soaking clothes. Maitland drew her gently to the fire, shook down the bracken to make a rest for her head, and left a pile of logs ready for use. 'I am going to the end of the island,' he said, 'to light a fire for a signal. It is the only part which they can see on the mainland, and if they see the blaze they will come off for us as soon as it is light.' The pale girl listened obediently. This man was the master, and in his charge was the safety of her lover and herself.

Maitland turned his back upon the warm nook, and stumbled along the ridge to the northern extremity of the isle. It was not a quarter of a mile away, but the land was so rough with gullies and crags that the journey took him nearly an hour. Just off the extreme point was a flat rock, sloping northward to a considerable height, a place from which a beacon could penetrate far over the mainland. He gathered brackens for kindling, and driftwood which former tides had heaped on the beach; and then with an armful he splashed through the shallow surf to the rock. Scrambling to the top, he found a corner where a fire might be lit, a place conspicuous and yet sheltered. Here he laid his kindling, and then in many wet journeys he carried his stores of firewood from the mainland to the rock. The lighting was nervous work, for he had few matches; but at last the dampish wood had caught, and tongues of flame shot up out of the smoke. Meantime the wind had sunk lower, the breakers seemed to have been left behind, and the eternal surge of the tides became the dominant sound to the watcher by the beacon.

And then, it seemed to him, the great convulsions of the night died away, and a curious peace came down upon the waters. The fire leaped in the air, the one living thing in a hushed and expectant world. It was not the quiet of sleep but of a sudden cessation, like the lull after a great flood or a snowslip. The tides still eddied and swayed, but it was noiselessly; the world moved, yet without sound or friction. The bitter wind which chilled his face and stirred up the red embers was like a phantom blast, without the roughness of a common gale. For a moment he seemed to be set upon a high mountain with the world infinitely remote beneath his feet. To all men there come moments of loneliness of body, and to some few the mingled ectasy and grief of loneliness of soul. The child-tale of the Ocean Quiet came back to him, the hour of the Breathing of God. Surely the great silence was now upon the world. But it was an evil presage, for all who sailed into it were homeless wanderers for ever after. Ah well! he had always been a wanderer, and the last gleam of home had been left behind, where by the firelight in the cold cranny a girl was crooning over her lover.

His past, his monotonous, brilliant past, slipped by with the knotless speed of a vision. He saw a boy, haunted with dreams, chafing at present delights, clutching evermore at the faint things of fancy. He saw a man, playing with the counters which others played with, fighting at first for bare existence and then for power and the pride of life. Success came over his path like a false dawn, but he knew in his heart that he had never sought it. What was that remote inefable thing he had followed? Here in the quiet of the shadowy waters he had the moment of self-revelation which comes to all, and hopes and dim desires seemed to stand out with the clearness of accomplished facts. There had always been something elect and secret at the back of his fiercest ambitions. The ordinary cares of men had been to him but little things to be played with; he had won by despising them; casting them from him, they had fallen into the hollow of his hand. And he had held them at little, finding his reward in his work, and in a certain alertness and freshness of spirit which he had always cherished. There is a story of island-born men who carry into inland places and the streets of cities the noise of sea-water in their ears, and hear continually the tern crying and the surf falling. So from his romantic boyhood this man had borne an arrogance towards the things of the world which had given him a contemptuous empire over a share of them. As he saw the panorama of his life no place or riches entered into it, but only himself, the haggard, striving soul, growing in power, losing, perhaps, in wisdom. And then, at the end of the way, Death, to shrivel the power to dust, and with the might of his sunbeam to waken to life the forgotten world of the spirit.

In the hush he seemed to feel the wheel and the drift of things, the cosmic order of nature. He forgot his weariness and his plashing clothes as he put more wood on the beacon and dreamed into the night. The pitiless sea, infinite, untamable, washing the Poles and hiding Earth's secrets in her breast, spoke to him with a far-remembered voice. The romance of the remote isles, the homes of his people, floating still in a twilight of old story, rose out of the darkness. His life, with its routine and success, seemed in a moment hollow, a child's game, unworthy of a man. The little social round, the manipulation of half-truths, the easy victories over fools – surely this was not the task for him. He was a dreamer, but a dreamer with an iron hand;

he was scarcely in the prime of life; the world was wide and his chances limitless. One castle of cards had already been overthrown; the Ocean Quiet was undermining another. He was sick of domesticity of every sort – of town, of home, of civilisation. The sad elemental world was his, the fury and the tenderness of nature, the peace of the wilds which old folk had called the Breathing of God. '*Parmi ceu haut bois conduyrai m'amie*' – this was still his motto, to carry untarnished to the end an austere and beautiful dream. His little ambitions had been but shreds and echoes and shadows of this supreme reality. And his love had been but another such simulacrum; for what he had sought was no foolish, laughing girl, but the Immortal Shepherdess, who, singing the old songs of youth, drives her flocks to the hill in the first dewy dawn of the world.

Suddenly he started and turned his head. Day was breaking in a red windy sky, and somewhere a boat's oars were plashing in the sea. And then he realised for the first time that he was cold and starving and soaked to the bone.

V MR HENRY DURWARD TO LADY CLAUDIA ETHERIDGE

'. . . Things have happened, my dear Clo, since I last wrote; time has passed; tomorrow I leave this place and go to stalk with Drapier; and yet in the stress of departure I take time to answer the host of questions with which you assailed me. I am able to give you the best of news. You have won your bet. Your prophecy about the conduct of the "other Etheridge girl" has come out right. They are both here, as it happens, having come on from Fountainblue, – both the hero and the heroine, I mean, of this most reasonable romance. You know Jack Despencer, one of the best people in the world, though a trifle given to chirping. But I don't think the grasshopper will become a burden to Miss Clara, for she likes that sort of thing. She must, for there is reason to believe that she refused for its sake the greatest match – I speak with all reverence – which this happy country could offer. I know you like Maitland as little as I do, but we agree in admiring the Colossus from a distance. Well, the Colossus has, so to speak, been laid low by a frivolous member of your sex. It is all a most romantic tale. Probably you have heard the gist of it, but here is the full and circumstantial account.

'We found Maitland beside the fire he had been feeding all night, and I shall never forget his figure alone in the dawn on that rock, drenched and dishevelled, but with his haggard white face set like a Crusader's. He took us to a kind of dell in the centre of the island, where we found Clara and Despencer shivering beside a dying fire. He had a twisted ankle and had got a bad scare, while she was perfectly composed, though she broke down when we got home. It must have been an awful business for both, but Maitland never seems to have turned a hair. I want to know two things. First, how in the presence of great danger he managed to get his dismissal from the lady? – for get it he assuredly did, and Despencer at once appeared in the part of the successful lover; second, what part he played in the night's events? Clara remembered little, Despencer only knew that he had been pulled out of the sea, but over all Maitland seems to have brooded like a fate. As usual he told us nothing. It was always his way to give the world results and leave it to find out his methods for itself . . .

'Despencer overwhelmed him with gratitude. His new happiness made him in love with life, and he included Maitland in the general affection. The night's events seemed to have left their mark on the great man also. He was very quiet, forgot to be rude to anybody, and was kind to both Clara and Despencer. It is his way of acknowledging defeat, the great gentleman's way, for, say what we like about him, he is a tremendous gentleman, one of the last of the breed . . .

'And then he went away – two days later. Just before he went Hugh Clanroyden and myself were talking in the library, which has a window opening on a flower-garden. Despencer was lying in an invalid's chair under a tree and Clara was reading to him. Maitland was saying goodbye, and he asked for Despencer. We told him that he was with Clara in the garden. He smiled one of those odd scarce smiles of his, and went out to them. When I saw his broad shoulders bending over the chair and the strong face looking down at the radiant Jack with his amiable good looks, confound it, Clo, I had to contrast the pair, and admit with Shakespeare the excellent foppery of the world. Well-a-day! "Smooth Jacob still robs homely Esau." And perhaps it is a good thing, for we are most of us Jacobs, and Esau is an uncomfortable fellow in our midst.

'A week later came the surprising, the astounding news that he had taken the African Governorship. A career ruined, everyone said, the finest chance in the world flung away; and then people speculated, and the story came out in bits, and there was only one explanation. It is the right one, as I think you will agree, but it points to some hidden weakness in that iron soul that he could be moved to fling over the ambitions of years because of a girl's choice. He will go and bury himself in the wilds, and our party will have to find another leader. Of course he will do his work well, but it is just as if I were to give up my chances of the Woolsack for a county-court judgeship. He will probably be killed, for he has a million enemies; he is perfectly fearless, and he does not understand the arts of compromise. It was a privilege, I shall always feel, to have known him. He was a great man, and yet – intellect, power, character, were at the mercy of a girl's caprice. As I write, I hear Clara's happy laugh below in the garden, probably at some witticism of the fortunate Jack's. Upon which, with my usual pride in the obvious, I am driven to reflect that the weak things in life may confound the strong, and that, after all, the world is to the young . . .'

VI SIR HUGH CLANROYDEN TO MR HENRY DURWARD
SOME YEARS LATER

'. . . I am writing this on board ship, as you will see from the heading, and shall post it when I get to the Cape. You have heard of my appointment, and I need not tell you how deep were my searchings of heart before I found courage to accept. Partly I felt that I had got my chance; partly I thought – an inconsequent feeling – that Maitland, if he had lived, would have been glad to see me in the place. But I am going to wear the Giant's Robe, and Heaven knows I have not the shoulders to fill it. Yet I am happy in thinking that I am in a small sense faithful to his memory.

'No further news, I suppose, has come of the manner of his death? Perhaps we shall never know, for it was on one of those Northern expeditions with a few men by which he held the frontier. I wonder if anyone will ever write fully the history of all that he did? It must have been a titanic work, but his methods were always so quiet that people accepted his results like a gift from Providence. He was given, one gathers, a practically free hand, and he made the country – four years' work of a man of genius. They wished to bring his body home, but he made them bury him where he fell – a characteristic last testament. And so he has gone out of the world into the world's history.

'I am still broken by his death, but, now that he is away, I begin to see him more clearly. Most people, I think, misunderstood him. I was one of his nearest friends, and I only knew bits of the man. For one thing – and I hate to use the vulgar word – he was the only aristocrat I ever heard of. Our classes are three-fourths of them of yesterday's growth, without the tradition, character, manner, or any trait of an aristocracy. And the few, who are nominally of the blood, have gone to seed in mind, or are spoilt by coarse marriages, or, worst of all, have the little trifling superior airs of incompetence. But he, he had the most transcendent breeding in mind and spirit. He had no need for self-assertion, for his most casual acquaintances put him at once in a different class from all other men. He had never a trace of a vulgar ideal; men's opinions, worldly honour, the common pleasures of life, were merely degrees of the infinitely small. And yet he was no bloodless mystic. If race means anything, he had it to perfection. Dreams and fancies to him were the realities, while facts were the shadows which he made dance as it pleased him.

'The truth is, that he was that rarest of mortals, the iron dreamer. He thought in æons and cosmic cycles, and because of it he could do what he pleased in life. We call a man practical if he is struggling in the crowd with no knowledge of his whereabouts, and yet in our folly we deny the name to the clear-sighted man who can rule the crowd from above. And here I join issue with you and everybody else. You thought it was Miss Clara's refusal which sent him abroad and interrupted his career. I read the thing otherwise. His love for the girl was a mere accident, a survival of the domestic in an austere spirit. Something, I do not know what, showed him his true desires. She may have rejected him; he may never have spoken to her; in any case the renunciation had to come. You must remember that that visit to Fountainblue was the first that he had paid since his boyhood to his boyhood's home. Those revisitings have often a strange trick of self-revelation. I believe that in that night on the island he saw our indoor civilisation and his own destiny in so sharp a contrast that he could not choose but make the severance. He found work where there could be small hope of honour or reward, but many a chance for a hero. And I am sure that he was happy, and that it was the longed-for illumination that dawned on him with the bullet which pierced his heart.

'But, you will say, the fact remains that he was once in love with Miss Clara, and that she would have none of him. I do not deny it. He was never a favourite with women; but, thank heaven, I have better things to do than study their peculiarities . . .'

The Outgoing of the Tide [1]

A draft of 'The Outgoing of the Tide', the last story in
The Watcher by the Threshold (1902), appears in a note-
book dated October 1898 but was published in *The
Atlantic Monthly* only in January 1902. With its theme
of the conflict between witchcraft and religion, it has
certain parallels with one of Buchan's most famous
novels, *Witch Wood* (1927).

'Between the hours of twelve and one, even at the turning
of the tide.'

Men come from distant parts to admire the tides of Solway,
which race in at flood and retreat at ebb with a greater
speed than a horse can follow. But nowhere are there
queerer waters than in our own parish of Caulds, at the
place called the Sker Bay, where between two horns of land
a shallow estuary receives the stream of the Sker. I never
daunder by its shores and see the waters hurrying like
messengers from the great deep without solemn
thoughts, and a memory of Scripture words on the terror
of the sea. The vast Atlantic may be fearful in its wrath, but
with us it is no clean open rage, but the deceit of the
creature, the unholy ways of quicksands when the waters
are gone, and their stealthy return like a thief in the night
watches. But in times of which I write there were more
awful fears than any from the violence of nature. It was
before the day of my ministry in Caulds, for then I was a tot
callant in short clothes in my native parish of Lesmahagow;

1. From the unpublished Remains of the Reverend
   John Dennistoun. Sometime Minister of the Gospel
   in the Parish of Caulds, and Author of Satan's
   Artifices against the Elect.

but the worthy Dr Chrystal, who had charge of spiritual
things, has told me often of the power of Satan and his
emissaries in that lonely place. It was the day of warlocks
and apparitions, now happily driven out by the zeal of the
General Assembly. Witches pursued their wanchancy calling,
bairns were spirited away, young lassies selled their souls to
the Evil One, and the Accuser of the Brethren, in the shape of
a black tyke, was seen about cottage doors in the gloaming.
Many and earnest were the prayers of good Dr Chrystal, but
the evil thing, in spite of his wrestling, grew and flourished in
his midst. The parish stank of idolatry, abominable rites were
practised in secret, and in all the bounds there was no one had
a more evil name for the black traffic than one Alison Sempill,
who bode at the Skerburnfoot.

The cottage stood nigh the burn, in a little garden, with
lilyoaks and grosart bushes lining the pathway. The Sker
ran by in a line among rowand trees, and the noise of its
waters was ever about the place. The highroad on the other
side was frequented by few, for a nearer-hand way to the
west had been made through the lower Moss. Sometimes a
herd from the hills would pass by with sheep, sometimes a
tinkler or a wandering merchant, and once in a long while
the laird of Heriotside on his grey horse riding to Gledsmuir. And they who passed would see Alison hirpling in her
garden, speaking to herself like the ill wife she was, or
sitting on a cutty-stool by the doorside, with her eyes on
other than mortal sights. Where she came from no man
could tell. There were some said she was no woman, but a
ghost haunting some mortal tenement. Others would
threep she was gentrice, come of a persecuting family in
the west, who had been ruined in the Revolution wars. She
never seemed to want for siller; the house was as bright as a
new preen, the yaird better delved than the manse garden;
and there was routh of fowls and doos about the small
steading, forbye a whee sheep and milk-kye in the fields.
No man ever saw Alison at any market in the countryside,
and yet the Skerburnfoot was plenished yearly in all proper
order. One man only worked on the place, a doited lad who
had long been a charge to the parish, and who had not the
sense to fear danger or the wit to understand it. Upon all

others the sight of Alison, were it but for a moment, cast a cold grue, not to be remembered without terror. It seems she was not ordinarily ill-famed, as men use the word. She was maybe sixty years in age, small and trig, with her grey hair folded neatly under her mutch. But the sight of her eyes was not a thing to forget. John Dodds said they were the een of a deer with the Devil ahint them; and, indeed, they would so appal an onlooker that a sudden unreasoning terror came into his heart, while his feet would impel him to flight. Once John, being overtaken in drink on the roadside by the cottage, and dreaming that he was burning in hell, awoke and saw the old wife hobbling toward him. Thereupon he fled soberly to the hills, and from that day became a quiet-living, humble-minded Christian. She moved about the country like a ghost, gathering herbs in dark loanings, lingering in kirkyairds, and casting a blight on innocent bairns. Once Robert Smellie found her in a ruinous kirk on the Lang Muir, where of old the idolatrous rites of Rome were practised. It was a hot day, and in the quiet place the flies buzzed in clouds, and he noted that she sat clothed in them as with a garment, yet suffering no discomfort. Then he, having mind of Beelzebub, the god of flies, fled without a halt homewards; but, falling in the coo's loan, broke two ribs and a collar bone, the whilk misfortune was much blessed to his soul. And there were darker tales in the countryside, of weans stolen, of lassies misguided, of innocent beasts cruelly tortured, and in one and all there came in the name of the wife of the Skerburnfoot. It was noted by them that kenned best that her cantrips were at their worst when the tides in the Sker Bay ebbed between the hours of twelve and one. At this season of the night the tides of mortality run lowest, and when the outgoing of these unco waters fell in with the setting of the current of life, then indeed was the hour for unholy revels. While honest men slept in their beds, the auld rudas carlines took their pleasure. That there is a delight in sin no man denies, but to most it is but a broken glint in the pauses of their conscience. But what must be the hellish joy of those lost beings who have forsworn God, and trysted with the Prince of Darkness, it is not for a Christian to say. Certain it is that it must be great, though their master waits at the end of the road to claim the wizened things they call their souls. Serious men – notably Gidden Scott in the Bach of the Hill, and Simon Wanch in the Sheilin of Chasehope – have seen Alison wandering on the wet sands, dancing to no earthy musick, while the heavens, they said, were full of lights and sounds which betokened the presence of the Prince of the Powers of the Air. It was a season of heart-searching for God's saints in Caulds, and the dispensation was blessed to not a few.

It will seem strange that in all this time the Presbytery was idle, and no effort was made to rid the place of so fell an influence. But there was a reason, and the reason, as in most like cases, was a lassie. Forbye Alison there lived at the Skerburnfoot a young maid, Ailie Sempill, who by all accounts was as good and bonnie as the other was evil. She passed for a daughter of Alison's – whether born in wedlock or not I cannot tell; but there were some said she was no kin to the auld witch wife, but some bairn spirited away from honest parents. She was young and blithe, with a face like an April morning, and a voice in her that put the laverocks to shame. When she sang in the kirk, folk have told me that they had a foretaste of the musick of the New Jerusalem, and when she came in by the village of Caulds old men stottered to their doors to look at her. Moreover, from her earliest days the bairn had some glimmerings of grace. Though no minister would visit the Skerburnfoot, or, if he went, departed quicker than he came, the girl Ailie attended regular at the catechising at the mains of Sker. It may be that Alison thought she would be a better offering for the Devil if she were given the chance of forswearing God, or it may be that she was so occupied in her own dark business that she had no care of the bairn. Meanwhile, the lass grew up in the nurture and admonition of the Lord. I have heard Dr Chrystal say that he never had a communicant more full of the things of the Spirit. From the day when she first declared her wish to come forward to the hour when she broke bread at the table, she walked like one in a dream. The lads of the parish might cast admiring eyes on her bright cheeks and yellow hair, as she sat in her white

gown in the kirk, but well they knew she was not for them.
To be the bride of Christ was the thought that filled her
heart; and when, at the fencing of the table, Dr Chrystal
preached from Matthew nine and fifteen, 'Can the children
of the bridechamber mourn as long as the bridegroom is
with them?' it was remarked by sundry that Ailie's face was
liker the countenance of an angel than of a mortal lass.

It is with the day of her first communion that this
narrative of mine begins. As she walked home, after the
morning table, she communed in secret, and her heart sang
within her. She had mind of God's mercies in the past; how
he had kept her feet from the snares of evil doers which had
been spread around her youth. She had been told unholy
charms like the Seven South Streams and the Nine Rowand
Berries, and it was noted, when she went first to the
catechising, that she prayed, 'Our Father which wert in
heaven', the prayer which the ill wife Alison had taught her;
meaning by it Lucifer, who had been in heaven, and had
been cast out therefrom. But when she had come to years of
discretion, she had freely chosen the better part, and evil
had ever been repelled from her soul like Gled water from
the stones of Gled brig. Now she was in a rapture of holy
content. The Druchen Bell – for the ungodly fashion
lingered in Caulds – was ringing in her ears as she left
the village, but to her it was but a kirk bell and a goodly
sound. As she went through the woods where the primroses
and the whitethorn were blossoming, the place seemed as
the land of Elim, wherein there were twelve wells and
threescore and ten palm trees. And then, as it might be,
another thought came into her head, for it is ordained that
frail mortality cannot long continue in holy joy. In the kirk
she had been only the bride of Christ, but as she came
through the wood, with the birds lilting and the winds of
the world blowing, she had mind of another lover; for this
lass, though so cold to men, had not escaped the common
fate. It seems that the young Heriotside, riding by one day,
stopped to speir something or other, and got a glisk of
Ailie's face which caught his fancy. He passed the road
again many times, and then he would meet her in the
gloaming, or of a morning in the field as she went to fetch

the kye. 'Blue are the hills that are far away', is an owercome in the countryside, and while at first on his side it may have been but a young man's fancy, to her he was like the god Apollo descending from the skies. He was good to look on, brawly dressed, and with a tongue in his head that would have wiled the bird from the tree. Moreover, he was of gentle kin, and she was a poor lass biding in a cot house with an ill-reputed mother. It seems that in time the young man, who had begun the affair with no good intentions, fell honestly in love, while she went singing about the doors as innocent as a bairn, thinking of him when her thoughts were not on higher things. So it came about that long ere Ailie reached home it was on young Heriotside that her mind dwelled, and it was the love of him that made her eyes glow and her cheeks redden.

Now it chanced that at that very hour her master had been with Alison, and the pair of them were preparing a deadly pit. Let no man say that the Devil is not a cruel tyrant. He may give his folk some scrapings of unhallowed pleasure, but he will exact tithes, yea, of anise and cummin, in return, and there is aye the reckoning to pay at the hinder end. It seems that now he was driving Alison hard. She had been remiss of late – fewer souls sent to hell, less zeal in quenching the Spirit, and, above all, the crowning offence that her bairn had communicated in Christ's kirk. She had waited overlong, and now it was like that Ailie would escape her toils. I have no skill of fancy to tell of that dark collogue, but the upshot was that Alison swore by her lost soul and the pride of sin to bring the lass into thrall to her master. The fiend had bare departed when Ailie came over the threshold to find the auld carline glunching over the fire.

It was plain she was in the worst of tempers. She flyted on the lass till the poor thing's cheek paled. 'There you gang,' she cries, 'broking wi' thae wearifu' Pharisees o' Caulds, whae daurna darken your mither's door! A bonnie dutiful child, quotha! Wumman, hae ye nae pride, or even the excuse o' a tinkler-lass?' And then she changed her voice and would be as saft as honey: 'My puir wee Ailie, was I thrawn till ye? Never mind, my bonnie. You and me are a' that's left, and we maunna be ill to ither.' And then the two had their dinner, and all the while the auld wife was crooning over the lass. 'We maun 'gree weel,' she says, 'for we're like to be our lee-lane for the rest o' our days. They tell me Heriotside is seeking Joan o' the Croft, and they're sune to be cried in Gledsmuir's kirk.'

It was the first the lass had heard of it, and you may fancy she was struck dumb. And so with one thing and other the auld witch raised the fiends of jealousy in that innocent heart. She would cry out that Heriotside was an ill-doing wastrel, and had no business to come and flatter honest lassies. And then she would speak of his gentle birth and his leddy mother, and say it was indeed presumption to hope that so great a gentleman could mean all that he said. Before long Ailie was silent and white, while her mother rimed on about men and their ways. And then she could thole it no longer, but must go out and walk by the burn to cool her hot brow and calm her thoughts, while the witch indoors laughed to herself at her devices.

For days Ailie had an absent eye and a sad face, and it so fell out that in all that time young Heriotside, who had scarce missed a day, was laid up with a broken arm and never came near her. So in a week's time she was beginning to hearken to her mother when she spoke of incantations and charms for restoring love. She kenned it was sin, but though not seven days syne she had sat at the Lord's table, so strong is love in a young heart that she was on the very brink of it. But the grace of God was stronger than her weak will. She would have none of her mother's runes and philters, though her soul cried out for them. Always when she was most disposed to listen some merciful power stayed her consent. Alison grew thrawner as the hours passed. She kenned of Heriotside's broken arm, and she feared that any day he might recover and put her stratagems to shame. And then it seems that she collogued with her master and heard word of a subtler device. For it was approaching that uncanny time of year, the festival of Beltane, when the auld pagans were wont to sacrifice to their god Baal. In this season warlocks and carlines have a special dispensation to do evil, and Alison waited on its coming with graceless joy.

As it happened, the tides in the Sker Bay ebbed at this time between the hours of twelve and one, and, as I have said, this was the hour above all others when the Powers of Darkness were most potent. Would the lass but consent to go abroad in the unhallowed place at this awful season and hour of the night, she was as firmly handfasted to the Devil as if she had signed a bond with her own blood; for then, it seemed, the forces of good fled far away, the world for one hour was given over to its ancient prince, and the man or woman who willingly sought the spot was his bondservant forever. There are deadly sins from which God's people may recover. A man may even communicate unworthily, and yet, so be it he sin not against the Holy Ghost, he may find forgiveness. But it seems that for the Beltane sin there could be no pardon, and I can testify from my own knowledge that they who once committed it became lost souls from that day. James Denchar, once a promising professor, fell thus out of sinful bravery and died blaspheming; and of Kate Mallison, who went the same road, no man can tell. Here indeed was the witch wife's chance; and she was the more keen, for her master had warned her that this was her last chance. Either Ailie's soul would be his, or her auld wrunkled body and black heart would be flung from this pleasant world to their apportioned place.

Some days later it happened that young Heriotside was stepping home over the Lang Muir about ten at night, it being his first jaunt from home since his arm had mended. He had been to the supper of the Forest Club at the Cross Keys in Gledsmuir, a clamjamphry of wild young blades who passed the wine and played at cartes once a fortnight. It seems he had drunk well, so that the world ran round about and he was in the best of tempers. The moon came down and bowed to him, and he took off his hat to it. For every step he travelled miles, so that in a little he was beyond Scotland altogether and pacing the Arabian desert. He thought he was the Pope of Rome, so he held out his foot to be kissed, and rolled twenty yards to the bottom of a small brae. Syne he was the king of France, and fought hard with a whin bush till he had banged it to pieces. After that nothing would content him but he must be a bogle, for he found his head dunting on the stars and his legs were knocking the hills together. He thought of the mischief he was doing to the auld earth, and sat down and cried at his wickedness. Then he went on, and maybe the steep road to the Moss Rig helped him, for he began to get soberer and ken his whereabouts.

On a sudden he was aware of a man linking along at his side. He cried a fine night, and the man replied. Syne, being merry from his cups, he tried to slap him on the back. The next he kenned he was rolling on the grass, for his hand had gone clean through the body and found nothing but air.

His head was so thick with wine that he found nothing droll in this. 'Faith, friend,' he says, 'that was a nasty fall for a fellow that has supped weel. Where might your road be gaun to?'

'To the World's End,' said the man, 'but I stop at the Skerburnfoot.'

'Bide the night at Heriotside,' says he. 'It's a thought out of your way, but it's a comfortable bit.'

'There's mair comfort at the Skerburnfoot,' said the dark man.

Now the mention of the Skerburnfoot brought back to him only the thought of Ailie, and not of the witch wife, her mother. So he jaloused no ill, for at the best he was slow in the uptake.

The two of them went on together for a while, Heriotside's fool head filled with the thought of the lass. Then the dark man broke silence. 'Ye 're thinkin' o' the maid Ailie Sempill,' says he.

'How ken ye that?' asked Heriotside.

'It is my business to read the hearts o' men,' said the other.

'And who may ye be?' said Heriotside, growing eerie.

'Just an auld packman,' says he, 'nae name ye wad ken, but kin to mony gentle houses.'

'And what about Ailie, you that ken sae muckle?' asked the young man.

'Naething,' was the answer, – 'naething that concerns you, for ye'll never get the lass.'

'By God and I will!' says Heriotside, for he was a profane swearer.

'That's the wrong name to seek her in, ony way,' said the man.

At this the young laird struck a great blow at him with his stick, but found nothing to resist him but the hill wind.

When they had gone on a bit the dark man spoke again. 'The lassie is thirled to holy things,' says he; 'she has nae care for flesh and blood, – only for devout contemplation.'

'She loves me,' says Heriotside.

'Not you,' says the other, 'but a shadow in your stead.'

At this the young man's heart began to tremble, for it seemed that there was truth in what his companion said, and he was owerdrunk to think gravely.

'I kenna whatna man ye are,' he says, 'but ye have the skill of lassies' hearts. Tell me truly, is there no way to win her to common love?'

'One way there is,' said the man, 'and for our friendship's sake I will tell you it. If ye can ever tryst wi' her on Beltane's E'en on the Sker sands, at the green link o' the burn where the sands begin, on the ebb o' the tide when the midnight is by, but afore cockrow, she'll be yours, body and soul, for this world and forever.'

And then it appeared to the young man that he was walking his love up the grass walk of Heriotside, with the house close by him. He thought no more of the stranger he had met, but the word stuck in his heart.

It seems that about this very time Alison was telling the same tale to poor Ailie. She cast up to her every idle gossip she could think of. 'It's Joan o' the Croft,' was aye her owercome, and she would threep that they were to be cried in kirk on the first Sabbath of May. And then she would rime on about the black cruelty of it, and cry down curses on the lover, so that her daughter's heart grew cauld with fear. It is terrible to think of the power of the world even in a redeemed soul. Here was a maid who had drunk of the well of grace and tasted of God's mercies, and yet there were moments when she was ready to renounce her hope. At those awful seasons God seemed far off and the world very nigh, and to sell her soul for love looked a fair bargain; at other times she would resist the Devil and comfort herself with prayer; but aye when she awoke there was the sore

heart, and when she went to sleep there were the weary
eyes. There was no comfort in the goodliness of spring or
the bright sunshine weather, and she who had been wont to
go about the doors lightfoot and blithe was now as dowie as
a widow woman.

And then one afternoon in the hinder end of April came
young Heriotside riding to the Skerburnfoot. His arm was
healed, he had got him a fine new suit of green, and his
horse was a mettle beast that well set off his figure. Ailie was
standing by the doorstep as he came down the road, and
her heart stood still with joy. But a second thought gave her
anguish. This man, so gallant and braw, would never be for
her; doubtless the fine suit and the capering horse were for
Joan o' the Croft's pleasure. And he, in turn, when he
remarked her wan cheeks and dowie eyes, had mind to
what the dark man said on the muir, and saw in her a maid
sworn to no mortal love. Yet his passion for her had grown
fiercer than ever, and he swore to himself that he would win
her back from her phantasies. She, one may believe, was
ready enough to listen. As she walked with him by the Sker
water his words were like musick to her ears, and Alison
wi.hin doors laughed to herself and saw her devices
prosper.

He spoke to her of love and his own heart, and the girl
hearkened gladly. Syne he rebuked her coldness and cast
scorn upon her piety, and so far was she beguiled that she
had no answer. Then from one thing and another he spoke
of some true token of their love. He said he was jealous, and
craved something to ease his care. 'It's but a small thing I
ask,' says he, 'but it will make me a happy man, and nothing
ever shall come atween us. Tryst wi' me for Beltane's E'en
on the Sker sands, at the green link o' the burn where the
sands begin, on the ebb o' the tide when midnight is by, but
afore cockcrow. For,' said he, 'that was our forbears' tryst
for true lovers, and wherefore no for you and me?'

The lassie had grace given her to refuse, but with a
woeful heart, and Heriotside rode off in black discontent, leaving poor Ailie to sigh her love. He came back
the next day and the next, but aye he got the same answer.
A season of great doubt fell upon her soul. She had no

clearness in her hope, nor any sense of God's promises. The Scriptures were an idle tale to her, prayer brought her no refreshment, and she was convicted in her conscience of the unpardonable sin. Had she been less full of pride, she would have taken her troubles to good Dr Chrystal and got comfort; but her grief made her silent and timorous, and she found no help anywhere. Her mother was ever at her side, seeking with coaxings and evil advice to drive her to the irrevocable step. And all the while there was her love for the man riving in her bosom, and giving her no ease by night or day. She believed she had driven him away, and repented her denial. Only her pride held her back from going to Heriotside and seeking him herself. She watched the road hourly for a sight of his face, and when the darkness came she would sit in a corner brooding over her sorrows.

At last he came, speiring the old question. He sought the same tryst, but now he had a further tale. It seemed he was eager to get her away from the Skerburnside and auld Alison. His aunt, Lady Balerynie, would receive her gladly at his request till the day of their marriage; let her but tryst with him at the hour and place he named, and he would carry her straight to Balerynie, where she would be safe and happy. He named that hour, he said, to escape men's observation for the sake of her own good name. He named that place, for it was near her dwelling, and on the road between Balerynie and Heriotside, which fords the Sker Burn. The temptation was more than mortal heart could resist. She gave him the promise he sought, stifling the voice of conscience; and as she clung to his neck it seemed to her that heaven was a poor thing compared with a man's love.

Three days remained till Beltane's E'en, and throughout this time it was noted that Heriotside behaved like one possessed. It may be that his conscience pricked him, or that he had a glimpse of his sin and its coming punishment. Certain it is that if he had been daft before, he now ran wild in his pranks, and an evil report of him was in every mouth. He drank deep at the Cross Keys, and fought two battles with young lads that had angered him. One he let off with a touch on the shoulder; the other goes lame to this day from a wound he got in the groin. There was word of the procurator fiscal taking note of his doings, and troth, if they had continued long he must have fled the country. For a wager he rode his horse down the Dow Craig, wherefore the name of the place has been the Horseman's Craig ever since. He laid a hundred guineas with the laird of Slofferfield that he would drive four horses through the Slofferfield loch, and in the prank he had his bit chariot dung to pieces and a good mare killed. And all men observed that his eyes were wild and the face grey and thin, and that his hand would twitch, as he held the glass, like one with the palsy.

The Eve of Beltane was lower and hot in the low country, with fire hanging in the clouds and thunder grumbling about the heavens. It seems that up in the hills it had been an awesome deluge of rain, but on the coast it was still dry and lowering. It is a long road from Heriotside to the Skerburnfoot. First you go down the Heriot water, and syne over the Lang Muir to the edge of Mucklewhan. When you pass the steadings of Mirehope and Cockmalane, you turn to the right and ford the Mire Burn. That brings you on to the turnpike road, which you will ride till it bends inland, while you keep on straight over the Whinny Knowes to the Sker Bay. There, if you are in luck, you will find the tide out and the place fordable dryshod for a man on a horse. But if the tide runs, you will do well to sit down on the sands and content yourself till it turn, or it will be the solans and scarts of the Solway that will be seeing the next of you. On this Beltane's E'en, the young man, after supping with some wild young blades, bade his horse be saddled about ten o'clock. The company were eager to ken his errand, but he waved them back. 'Bide here,' he says, 'and boil the wine till I return. This is a ploy of my own on which no man follows me.' And there was that in his face, as he spoke, which chilled the wildest, and left them well content to keep to the good claret and the saft seat, and let the daft laird go his own ways.

Well and on he rode down the bridle path in the wood, along the top of the Heriot glen, and as he rode he was aware of a great noise beneath him. It was not wind, for there was none, and it was not the sound of thunder; and aye as he speired at himself what it was it grew the louder, till he came to a break in the trees. And then he saw the cause, for Heriot was coming down in a furious flood, sixty yards wide, tearing at the roots of the aiks and flinging red waves against the drystone dykes. It was a sight and sound to solemnise a man's mind, deep calling unto deep, the great waters of the hills running to meet with the great waters of the sea. But Heriotside recked nothing of it, for his heart had but one thought and the eye of his fancy one figure. Never had he been so filled with love of the lass; and yet it was not happiness, but a deadly, secret fear.

As he came to the Lang Muir it was gey and dark, though there was a moon somewhere behind the clouds. It was little he could see of the road, and ere long he had tried many moss pools and sloughs, as his braw new coat bare witness. Aye in front of him was the great hill of Mucklewhan, where the road turned down by the Mire. The noise of the Heriot had not long fallen behind him ere another began, the same eerie sound of burns crying to ither in the darkness. It seemed that the whole earth was overrun with waters. Every little runnel in the bay was astir, and yet the land around him was as dry as flax, and no drop of rain had fallen. As he rode on the din grew louder, and as he came over the top of Mirehope he kenned by the mighty rushing noise that something uncommon was happening with the Mire Burn. The light from Mirehope Sheilin twinkled on his left, and had the man not been dozened with his fancies he might have observed that the steading was deserted and men were crying below in the fields. But he rode on, thinking of but one thing, till he came to the cot house of Cockma-lane, which is nigh the fords of the Mire.

John Dodds, the herd who bode in the place, was standing at the door, and he looked to see who was on the road so late.

'Stop!' says he, – 'stop, Laird Heriotside! I kenna what your errand is, but it is to no holy purpose that ye're out on Beltane E'en. D' ye no hear the warring o' the waters?'

And then in the still night came the sound of Mire like the clash of armies.

'I must win over the ford,' says the laird quickly, thinking of another thing.

'Ford!' cried John, in scorn. 'There'll be nae ford for you the nicht unless it was the ford o' the river Jordan. The burns are up and bigger than man ever saw them. It'll be a Beltane's E'en that a' folk will remember. They tell me that Gled valley is like a loch, and that there's an awesome heap o' folk drouned in the hills. Gin ye were ower the Mire, what about crossin' the Caulds and the Sker?' says he, for he jaloused he was going to Gledsmuir.

And then it seemed that that word brought the laird to his senses. He looked the airt the rain was coming from, and he saw it was the airt the Sker flowed. In a second, he has told me, the works of the Devil were revealed to him. He saw himself a tool in Satan's hands; he saw his tryst a device for the destruction of the body as it was assuredly meant for the destruction of the soul; and there came black on his mind the picture of an innocent lass borne down by the waters, with no place for repentance. His heart grew cold in his breast. He had but one thought, – a sinful and reckless one: to get to her side, that the two might go together to their account. He heard the roar of the Mire as in a dream, and when John Dodds laid hands on his bridle he felled him to the earth. And the next seen of it was the laird riding the floods like a man possessed.

The horse was the grey stallion he aye rode, the very beast he had ridden for many a wager with the wild lads of the Cross Keys. No man but himself durst back it, and it had lamed many a hostler lad and broke two necks in its day. But it seems it had the mettle for any flood, and took the Mire with little spurring. The herds on the hillside looked to see man and steed swept into eternity; but though the red waves were breaking about his shoulders, and he was swept far down, he aye held on for the shore. The next thing the watchers saw was the laird struggling up the far bank and casting his coat from him, so that he rode in his sark. And then he set off like a wildfire across the muir toward the turnpike road. Two men saw him on the road, and have recorded their experience. One was a gangrel, by name McNab, who was travelling from Gledsmuir to Allerkirk with a heavy pack on his back and a bowed head. He heard a sound like wind afore him, and, looking up, saw coming down the road a grey horse stretched out to a wild gallop, and a man on its back with a face like a soul in torment. He kenned not whether it was devil or mortal, but flung himself on the roadside and lay like a corp for an hour or more, till the rain aroused him. The other was one Sim Doolittle, the fish hawker from Allerfoot, jogging home in his fish cart from Gledsmuir fair. He had drunk more than was fit for him, and he was singing some light song, when he saw approaching, as he said, the pale horse mentioned in the Revelation, with Death seated as the rider. Thought of his sins came on him like a thunderclap; fear loosened his knees. He leaped from the cart to the road, and from the road to the back of a dyke; thence he flew to the hills, and was found the next morning far up among the Mire Craigs, while his horse and cart were gotten on the Aller sands, the horse lamed and the cart without the wheels.

At the tollhouse the road turns inland to Gledsmuir, and he who goes to the Sker Bay must leave it and cross the wild land called the Whinny Knowes, a place rough with bracken and foxes' holes and old stone cairns. The toll-man, John Gilzean, was opening the window to get a breath of air in the lower night, when he heard or saw the approaching horse. He kenned the beast for Heriotside's, and, being a friend of the laird's, he ran down in all haste to open the yett, wondering to himself about the laird's errand on this night. A voice came down the road to him bidding him hurry; but John's old fingers were slow with the keys, and so it happened that the horse had to stop, and John had time to look up at the gast and woeful face.

'Where away the nicht sae late, laird?' says John.

'I go to save a soul from hell,' was the answer.

And then it seems that through the open door there came the chapping of a clock.

'Whatna hour is that?' asks Heriotside.

'Midnicht,' says John, trembling, for he did not like the look of things.

There was no answer but a groan, and horse and man went racing down the dark hollows of the Whinny Knowes.

How he escaped a broken neck in that dreadful place no human being will ever ken. The sweat, he has told me, stood in cold drops upon his forehead; he scarcely was aware of the saddle in which he sat, and his eyes were stelled in his head so that he saw nothing but the sky ayont him. The night was growing colder, and there was a small sharp wind stirring from the east. But hot or cold, it was all one to him, who was already cold as death. He heard not the sound of the sea nor the peeseweeps startled by his horse, for the sound that ran in his ears was the roaring Sker water and a girl's cry. The thought kept goading him, and he spurred the grey horse till the creature was madder than himself. It leaped the hole which they call the Devil's Mull as I would step over a thristle, and the next he kenned he was on the edge of the Sker Bay.

It lay before him white and ghaistly, with mist blowing in wafts across it and a slow swaying of the tides. It was the better part of a mile wide, but save for some fathoms in the middle, where the Sker current ran, it was no deeper even at flood than a horse's fetlocks. It looks eerie at bright midday, when the sun is shining and whaups are crying among the seaweeds; but think what it was on that awesome night, with the Powers of Darkness brooding over it like a cloud! The rider's heart quailed for a moment in natural fear. He stepped his beast a few feet in, still staring afore him like a daft man. And then something in the sound or the feel of the waters made him look down, and he perceived that the ebb had begun and the tide was flowing out to sea.

He kenned that all was lost, and the knowledge drove him to stark despair. His sins came in his face like birds of night, and his heart shrunk like a pea. He knew himself for a lost soul, and all that he loved in the world was out in the tides. There, at any rate, he could go, too, and give back that gift of life he had so blackly misused. He cried small and saft like a bairn, and drove the grey out into the water. And aye as he spurred it the foam should have been flying as high as his head, but in that uncanny hour there was no foam; only the waves running sleek like oil. It was not long ere he had come to the Sker channel, where the red moss waters were roaring to the sea, – an ill place to ford in midsummer heat, and certain death, as folk reputed it, at the smallest spate. The grey was swimming; but it seemed the Lord had other purposes for him than death, for neither man nor horse could droun. He tried to leave the saddle, but he could not; he flung the bridle from him, but the grey held on as if some strong hand were guiding. He cried out upon the Devil to help his own; he renounced his Maker and his God: but whatever his punishment, he was not to be drouned. And then he was silent, for something was coming down the tide.

It came down as quiet as a sleeping bairn, straight for him as he sat with his horse breasting the waters; and as it came the moon crept out of a cloud, and he saw a glint of yellow hair. And then his madness died away, and he was himself again, a weary and stricken man. He hung down over the tide and caught the body in his arms, and then let the grey make for the shallows. He cared no more for the Devil and all his myrmidons, for he kenned brawly he was damned. It seemed to him that his soul had gone from him, and he was as toom as a hazel shell. His breath rattled in his throat, the tears were dried up in his head, his body had lost its strength, and yet he clung to the drouned maid as to a hope of salvation. And then he noted something at which he marvelled dumbly. Her hair was drookit back from her clay-cold brow, her eyes were shut, but in her face there was the peace of a child; it seemed even that her lips were smiling. Here, certes, was no lost soul, but one who had gone joyfully to meet her Lord. It may be in that dark hour at the burn-foot, before the spate caught her, she had been given grace to resist her adversary and fling herself upon God's mercy. And it would seem that it had been granted; for when he came to the Skerburnfoot, there in the corner sat the weird wife Alison, dead as a stone.

For days Heriotside wandered the country, or sat in his own house with vacant eye and trembling hands. Conviction of sin held him like a vice: he saw the lassie's death laid at his door; her face haunted him by day and night, and the word of the Lord dirled in his ears, telling of wrath and punishment. The greatness of his anguish wore him to a shadow, and at last he was stretched on his bed and like to perish. In his extremity worthy Dr Chrystal went to him unasked, and strove to comfort him. Long, long the good man wrestled, but it seemed as if his ministrations were to be of no avail. The fever left his body, and he rose to stotter about the doors; but he was still in his torments, and the mercy-seat was far from him. At last in the back end of the year came Mungo Muirhead to Caulds to the autumn communion, and nothing would serve him but he must try his hand at the storm-tossed soul. He spoke with power and unction, and a blessing came with his words: the black cloud lifted and showed a glimpse of grace, and in a little the man had some assurance of salvation. He became a pillar of Christ's kirk, prompt to check abominations, notably the sin of witchcraft; foremost in good works, but with it all a humble man who walked contritely till his death. When I came first to Caulds I sought to prevail upon him to accept the eldership, but he aye put me by, and when I heard his tale I saw that he had done wisely. I mind him well as he sat in his chair or daundered through Caulds, a kind word for every one and sage counsel in time of distress, but withal a severe man to himself and a crucifier of the body. It seems that this severity weakened his frame, for three years syne come Martinmas he was taken ill with a fever of the bowels, and after a week's sickness he went to his account, where I trust he is accepted.

The Knees of the Gods

'The Knees of the Gods' is a piece of whimsy that
mixes some political satire and historical speculation
with Buchan's knowledge of climbing in the Alps and
Cuillins. It was published in *The Scottish Mountaineering
Club Journal* in January 1907.

This story was told to me by a friend whom I shall call
Smith, a man of limited imagination and unswerving
veracity. He prefaced his narrative by declaring that never
in his life had he dreamed before or at any rate remembered
the details in the morning, and that in any other case and to
any other man he would have been ashamed to repeat the
nonsense. From which I argued that my friend had been
more than a little scared.

It seemed that Smith had gone to Chamonix in the end of
May for a rest. He had had no thought of climbing, for at
that season it is only by the merest chance that serious
ascents are possible. As it fell out, however, the chance was
given him. A fortnight of uninterrupted sunshine stripped
the snow from the Aiguilles, and Smith, forgetful of the
work he was writing on 'The Metaphysics of the Impossible', was tempted and fell. He began with the Charmoz;
he then did the Blaitière by the northern ridge; and fired
now with intolerable pride, attempted and achieved the
Grèpon. It was on the night following this last ascent that
he dreamed the dream I am about to relate. As I have said,
his pride had become overweening, and he had gone to bed
with his head full of presumptuous plans. He would do the
Dent de Requin; then he might have a try at the Aiguille de
la Republique; after that, perhaps, at the virgin Capuchin.
He would return to England with a record of achievements,

done out of due season, which would make his mountain-eering friends blaspheme.

The slumbers of a climber are usually dreamless. No sooner has tattered cheek been laid to cool pillow than there comes that hammering of the infamous boots on the door which announces three o'clock and time to get up. But on this night Smith had scarcely closed his eyes when he began to dream.

He found himself, he said, in what seemed to be the smoking-room of an hotel. It was winter time, for a large fire was burning on the hearth, and on closer inspection he noticed that the fuel was peat. Clearly this was not Switzerland. And then something about the room struck him as familiar. He went to the window, drew up the blind a little and looked out. Snow lay deep on the ground, and a moon in a patch of open sky showed a line of jagged white hills. The sight brought him at once to his bearings. The ancient barn-like shape had been changed. The well-worn sofa had gone; gone, too, the moth-eaten deer's horn above the fireplace, the rickety writing-tables, the few well-thumbed books. There were some good Della Robbia imitations on the mantelpiece. A Chippendale bureau stood in a corner, and some pretty Turcoman rugs lay on the floor. The place was furnished like a sitting-room at the Ritz, but it was none the less the smoking-room of the Sligachan Inn.

While Smith sat on a spindle-legged chair, wondering what had become of his pipe, and wondering still more how on earth he had got there, a party of men entered, dressed as if for some climbing expedition. It seemed an odd thing to be starting at dead of night in mid-winter for the Coolins, but somehow when he looked at the climbers he did not think their conduct ridiculous. They were all long men and incredibly lean, and about their movement was a nervous strength which Smith remembered to have noticed in one or two great guides of his acquaintance. With them came a man whom he thought he recognised. He rubbed his eyes and stared at him, and then a nod from the other convinced him. It was his friend Brown, a Chancery barrister, longer and thinner than he remembered him, but undoubtedly Brown.

The party talked for a few minutes and drank minute tumblers of milk. Then they departed, leaving Brown behind them. Smith had by this time found his pipe, and walked to the fireplace to get a light.

'My dear good fellow,' said Brown, 'for Heaven's sake throw away that poison!' and he looked darkly at the pipe.

Now Brown had been accustomed to smoke cigars of a peculiar rankness, and Smith was therefore surprised at his tone.

'What do you mean?' he asked. 'You know you smoke like a chimney yourself.'

'I!' cried Brown in horror, 'I never touched the stuff in my life. No one does nowadays, except a few obese Germans.'

Smith would have liked to contradict him, but he had so many questions to ask that he forbore.

'Where are those fellows going?' he said. 'They must be maniacs to set out at this time of night. I suppose they are walking to Glenbrittle or Camasunary?'

Brown stared. 'My dear man, they are not trippers. They are going to do the traverse of the Coolins – Sgurr-nan-Gillean to Garsbheinn. They will breakfast at Glenbrittle about nine o'clock.'

'Now, look here, Brown,' said Smith, 'what is the good of talking rot to me? That traverse has never been done in the longest summer's day, and in a winter night it is unthinkable—'

He stopped, for it seemed to him that everything about his present position was unthinkable. How had he come there, what had happened to the Sligachan Inn, what above all things had happened to Brown, who used to be a tubby little man tired out by a day's grouse shooting? Had he, Smith, gone to sleep like Rip Van Winkle and awakened in a new century? The odd thing was that he felt no alarm, only an insatiable curiosity. He wanted to cross-examine Brown, but he did not know how to begin, for his ignorance would seem to the other to call for an explanation he was unable to give.

'You have been away from mountaineering for some years,' said Brown politely. 'I don't wonder that it all seems odd to you.'

'I wish you'd explain things a bit,' said Smith. 'What do people do nowadays? As you say, I have been out of the world for some time. About Chamonix, for instance?'

'Ah, there you touch upon a sore subject. There has been a great row, but happily it is now settled. There are railways, of course, up Mont Blanc and the Verte and the Grandes Jorasses, but these we did not mind. But last year they proposed to put electric lifts on the Aiguilles, and then we had to draw the line. There are five ex-presidents of the Alpine Club in the Cabinet, including the Foreign Secretary, so we brought pressure to bear on France, and after a little fuss she climbed down. There is not much good climbing left at Chamonix, but the Aiguilles still make a pleasant day.'

'How do you mean?' said Smith. 'A pleasant *day!*'

'Oh, yes. One of the most popular scrambles in Europe is to start from the Montanvert and run over the Charmoz, Grèpon, Blaitière, Plan, and Midi. The best time is nine and a half hours.'

'That,' said Smith excitedly, 'is an infernal lie.'

Brown coloured. 'I beg your pardon,' he said stiffly. 'Do you doubt my word?'

Smith saw that he had made a mistake. 'Forgive me, old man, but it seems so strange to me. I am sorry for being rude, but I feel exactly like some kind of Rip Van Winkle awakening to a more strenuous world. What about Zermatt?'

'Alas,' said Brown, restored to good temper, 'that is a sad tale. No mountaineer goes there now except for exercise. The Dent Blanche still offers interesting snow work for beginners. But the other peaks are festooned with railways, and the Matterhorn, as you have probably heard, is covered in.'

'Covered in,' said Smith in amazement. 'What are you saying?'

'Oh, you go to the Schwarzsee or the Zmutt, and you find a door where you take a ticket – 10 francs it costs. Then you are conducted by housemaids up carpeted stairs heated by electricity. At every third landing or so there is a restaurant where you can lunch, and there are balconies for the view. In the end you come to a little glass cupola, and you raise a skylight and climb out on the top. Or if you like you can do the whole thing in a lift. The summit is a sort of German beer-garden.'

'Then where do people climb nowadays – serious climbers, I mean?' asked Smith with a doleful sinking of heart.

'Mainly in the Himalaya and the Karakoram. Everest and the other great peaks are a little hackneyed, but there are still a good many summits unclimbed. There are one or two places also in the Kuen-lun and the Bolivian Andes where I am told you have a chance of first ascents. Ruwenzori, too, has a good reputation because of the difficulty of equatorial snow.'

'And what about Scotland?' said Smith, looking sadly around the room, filled for him with so many memories wearied and contented evenings.

'Scotland is still fairly good, given the right kind of weather, but the Coolins are almost the only hills which are worth doing. You see all the other places like Coire Mhic Fhearchair and Ben Nevis and the Sutherland hills are a little too much scrambled about on. But some of us combined and had the Coolins made a climbing reserve and we don't allow fancy railways on the peaks. Of course, they are useless in summer, only fit for tourists and artists and people out of training. But given a really good snow storm or a pitch-dark night, and you may get some very far scrambling. I had quite a hard time last Christmas Eve in a blizzard doing the traverse of the range. We nearly got hung up at the Alasdair-Dubh Gap. The best thing here, I think, is the Waterpipe Gully, when there is a real torrent coming down it, provided you keep to the gully all the time, and don't go out on the face. You're half drowned before you finish, but it's excellent fun.'

Smith, having no comment to make adequate to his surprise, disregarded Brown's disapproval and lit his pipe.

'Have some Talisker,' he said hospitably to his companion.

'Good Lord!' said Brown in consternation. 'What are you saying? The thing's forbidden as a beverage, and there's a tremendous penalty on its sale. Unless you're ill and have a doctor's certificate, you can't get it . . . You were asking about Ben Nevis. The last time I was there was when my battalion of the Scottish Mountain Rifles went into camp on the top in December. We had some good practice with ice-axes among the gullies.'

'What in the name of wonder are the Scottish Mountain Rifles?' asked Smith, and then he repented of his question, fearing that Brown might think him a maniac and tell him no more. But Brown seemed to have a love for explaining what to him must have been the obvious, and continued without a sign of surprise.

'In old days they were called the Scottish Horse. But when motors displaced horses in war it was thought best to utilise the advantage Scotland offered, and turn them into a mountain corps. About the same time the deer-forests were made national manœuvre grounds, so they had every chance in training. They are a very fit lot of men, and all of them can climb rocks with heavy baggage, and handle an ice-axe. The officers are *ex-officio* members of the Alpine Club. I should like to have shown you the way the sergeants took their men up the Ben Nevis buttresses.'

A question had long been hovering on Smith's lips. 'But what started all this colossal revolution?' he asked.

Brown stared. 'This is schoolboy history with a vengeance. Every one knows that it began years ago when the Labour Party first came into power, and introduced *geist* into our national life. The first Haldane Ministry nationalised the great landed estates, introduced conscription, made the phonetic spelling of Gaelic names compulsory, and united the Empire. After that, of course, it was a short step to physical training and the reform of diet and the reconstruction of the individual life. Now, thank Heaven, we are on the road to national health – some way off it yet, but still on the road.'

'What the devil do you mean by *geist*?' asked Smith testily, darkly suspicious of something which stood between him and his Talisker.

'Reason,' said Brown, 'reason – science – intelligence – all the things that used to be at a discount in politics, and are now the only things that matter. We have got rid of feudalism and clericalism and prejudice on the one hand, and doctrinairedom on the other.'

'And has all the world got *geist* like you?'

Brown laughed. 'Oh no! We have it in the Empire at least the rudiments of it. The other peoples, except Japan, refused it, and have suffered accordingly. To-day we divide the world between us. Japan has China and the American continent. Europe is a collection of small republics under our suzerainty, all except France, which we have neutral-ised, and keep as an independent centre of art and culture.'

'Give me some dates,' said Smith plaintively; 'my memory is so bad nowadays.'

'You seem to have become very stupid, old man,' said Brown. 'It's all due to that infamous tobacco of yours. I oughtn't to have to instruct you in these rudiments. The beginning was in 1911, the date of the first Haldane Ministry. In 1915 we fought the Triple Alliance. In 1916 Japan conquered and annexed the United States, and in 1920 there was the famous Conference of Ecclefechan between the Mikado and our Emperor. In 1921 the last Liberal died, and was preserved in the British Museum. In 1923—'

But at this moment Smith unfortunately chose to knock the ashes out of his pipe. As a Gladstonian of the old school, Brown's last remark had annoyed him greatly, and he was about to declare that the new régime, for all its mountaineering pride, was one from which beer and skittles, not to mention tobacco and Talisker, were deplor-ably absent. But the sound of his pipe-bowl, hammered against the mantelpiece, seemed to echo and reverberate with uncanny persistence . . .

And then he suddenly awoke to the fact that he was not in the Sligachan smoking-room, but in his bedroom at Cha-monix, and that the boots was beating at his door and striving in broken English to tell him that it was two o'clock in the morning.

Smith got up in a daze and struggled into his clothes. As a sign of his preoccupation he told me that he was half-way to the Blaitière chalet before it occurred to him to notice the state of the weather.

The Green Glen

'The Green Glen', one of the stories in *The Moon Endureth* (1912), was published in *Blackwood's Magazine* in January 1912 and is another story about the power of place. It was one of only two of his stories – the other was 'The Far Islands' – which Buchan included in an anthology, *Modern Short Stories* (1926).

I

I first saw the Glen when I was eleven years old, a small boy consumed with a passion for trout. Adventuring on a rusty bicycle I had penetrated to remote dales, and made baskets in streams which no *Anglers' Guide* ever heard of. One day I had fished the sources of the Cauldshaw, and, the sun being yet high, bethought me of the Fawn, which flowed on the other side of the narrow watershed. I shouldered my rod and tramped up the mossy spaces of the burn-head, till I waded deep in the bracken of the ridge. There on the summit the heather ended as if ruled by a gardener's line. I was looking into a narrow glen which ran from a round hope till a broad green hill baulked the view. From beginning to end there was no house, not even a sheepfold or a dyke. I remember my amazement at its indescribable greenness. There was the yellow-green of moss, the old velvet of mountain turf, the grey-green of bent on the hill-brow; but all was green, without tree or crag or heather bush to distract the eye. Through the middle of it ran the Fawn, a very fishable stream to my notion, and I ran down the brae with hope high in my heart.

But I never cast a fly in those waters. Long before I was down the hill the eeriness and the solitariness of the place weighed on my mind. There was no man here, and no sign of man. There were no whaups crying, or grouse to upbraid my presence. It was still as the grave, but for the lilt of the stream; and it was terribly green. I remembered a line of a song that ploughmen used to whistle – '*The wild glen sae green*' – and I thought how much deeper this green wildness was than any rock and heather. The still slopes and folds of hill seemed to my unquiet eye to stretch to eternity.

At the edge of the burn was a rude mound, embanked like some Roman fort. With a fluttering heart I began to put my rod together. The Fawn dashed and swirled in noble pools, but I could not keep my eyes on it. The green hills shut me in, and the awe of them brooded over me. I was mortally afraid, and not ashamed of my fear. I could not give a name to it, but something uncanny was in the air: not terrible exactly, or threatening, but inhumanly strange. I clutched my rod – the butt and middle piece were put together – and fled the way I had come. I do not think I stopped running till I fell panting by the side of the Cauldshaw among the friendly heather.

II

Twenty years later, when the doings of eleven are a faint memory, chance set me fishing the lower streams of the Fawn. It was a clear June day, but the waters were too low and my basket was light. I fished like an epicure, a cast in each pool sufficing for me; and presently I had rounded the shoulder of the green hill which cuts the valley in two. They call it the Green Dod, and there is no greener hill in that green country. I found myself in an upland glen, where the Fawn had sunk to a mountain burn. The place was very soothing and quiet, and idly I wandered on, drinking in the peace of the hills. Then something in the contours awakened a memory, and I recalled my boyish escapade. The years have their consolations, for what had once terrified now charmed. I laughed at the scared little sinner, whose trembling legs had once twinkled up those braes. I put by my rod and abandoned myself to the delights of the greenness. Far up on the hill shoulders white sheep were dotted, but the water-side was empty. Not even a water-crow was visible, and in the patches of bog there was no sign of snipe. The place was full of a delicious desolation. There were the strait green sides, the Green Dod at the foot, a green hope at the head, and only the clear singing water stirred in the sunny afternoon.

I found a seat on a mound, and basked in deep content. It was the height of pastoral, yet without sheep or shepherd. The Fawn was a true Border stream, jewelled in sunlight, but wan as death under grey skies. I wondered how I had hitherto missed this happy valley. Nature had wrought it in a kindly mood, and hidden it very far from men. It must, I thought, have had a gracious history. There was no terror in its solitude. I could not imagine the cry of death from the burn, or harsh deeds done on those green lawns. Who had owned it in old days? Perhaps some Roman, pushing north with his bronze soldiers against the Picts, had been caught by its grace, and christened it by the name of his woodland god. True Thomas may have walked by its streams. But its story must have been chiefly of elves and fairy folk, for it wore the fairy livery.

I looked at the mound on which I sat, and saw that it had once been the site of a dwelling. It was all crisp moorland turf, gemmed with eye-bright and milkwort, but the rampart had been made by man. Scraping with the butt-end of my rod, I laid bare a chiselled block. This had been no sheepfold or shepherd's cot, but a tower.

The discovery stirred a fresh strain of fancy. Some old raider had had his keep here, and filled the glen with ill-gotten cattle. I pictured the forays returning over the green hills in some autumn twilight. I saw beacons fired on the tops, and the winter snows reddened with blood. Just then a cloud came over the sun, and the grace of the valley vanished. Now the stream ran wan, and I saw that the glen was wild and very lonely. Terror had dwelt here as well as peace. I remembered the boy of eleven, who on this very mound had picked up his rod and run.

That evening at Hardriding I hunted the library for local histories. They could not tell me much, being mostly the casual compilations of local ministers. But I found one thing of interest. I had been right about True Thomas. It seemed that the Rhymer had honoured the Fawn with a couplet of doubtful Latin: –

> 'Ubi Faunus fluit
> Spes mortalis ruit.'

I had no notion what he meant, and suspected the hand of the Reverend Mr Gilfillan *circa* 1780.

III

A broken leg gave me some leisure that winter, and I spent it in searching for the history of what I had come to call the Green Glen. For two hundred years back it was plain going. Along with a dozen other valleys it had been swept into the net of the noble house which had built its fortunes on the fall of the turbulent little Border septs. Earlier it had been by turns in the hands of two families, both long perished – Home of Hardriding and Douglas of Cauldshaw. That took me back to the fourteenth century or thereabouts, where the history stopped short. But I found a charter of Melrose a century before, from which it appeared that the lands of Fawn, 'the nether and hither glens thereof', had been in the hands of the monks, who had profited by the good grazing. A chapel of Our Lady had stood by the burnside, endowed with a hundred merks a year by a certain Simon de Fries in penance for the slaying of an erring wife. There my tale ended, but I hazarded a guess. Fifty years ago a slab was found near Hadrian's Wall with a list of stations on the great road which ran north to the land of the Picts. You will find it copied in the Berlin *Corpus*, and there is much dispute about the identification of the names. One of them is a certain *Fauni Castellum*, which scholars have fastened on a dozen places between Ardoch and Melrose. I was myself convinced that the castellum was the mound in the Green Glen, the more so as Mr Gilfillan reported a find there of gold coins of the Antonines in 1758. It is true that the place was some miles from the main line of transit, but it would command the hill-roads from the West. Besides, might it not have been a sacred place, half fort, half shrine, an outpost of the dying faith? Why, otherwise, the strange name of the woodland god?

These were all my facts – too few on which to spin the delicate web of history. But my imagination was kindled, and I set to work. If I were right, this glen had a virtue which had drawn to it many races. Little as the recorded history was, it was far more than the due of an inconsiderable howe of the hills. Rome had made it a halting-place and consecrated it to her gods; the Church had built a shrine in it; two famous clans had fought furiously for its sake. My first impression was justified, for it had been no common place. Some ancient *aura* had brooded over its greenness and compelled men's souls.

Bit by bit from monkish Latin, from fragments of ballads, from cumbrous family histories, and from musty chronicles, I built up the shadow of a tale. Rome gave me nothing – the fog of years lay too thick over that greatest of mortal pages; but I hazarded a guess that the broken satyr's head, found in some unknown Border earthwork and now in the Grange collection, had come from my glen. Perhaps the Melrose monks had found it and copied it in their gargoyles. But of the Christian shrine I had something to tell. The chapel seems to have had an ill reputation for a holy place. The chapter of Melrose in or about 1250 held an inquisition into the doings of a certain John of Fawn, who tended the shrine with unhallowed service. There were complaints of his successor, a monk who bore the name of Lapidarius; and the grand climax was reached in the fate of one Andrew de Faun, a priest, says the record, who had the unpleasing gift 'diabolos convocandi'. He was hand in glove with Lord Soulis, whose castle of Hermitage lay some twenty miles over the hills. Of his iniquities it is recorded that the country folk grew weary, and one October night surprised him at the business. He confessed his sins under the pressure of boiling lead, was duly burned, and his ashes cast into Tweed to be borne to the cleansing sea.

To the monks succeeded the Barons, the first being the tragically fated house of Home. But side by side with the record of their moorland wars I found a ballad history.

Fawn had caught the fancy of the wandering minstrel. The heroine of the ghastly 'Riding of Etterick' had eyes 'grey as Fawn'. (The other reading 'grey as a fawn' is obvious nonsense.) The tryst for true love on Beltane's E'en was the Fawn side, and it was in the Green Glen that young Brokyn found himself asleep on his return from Fairyland.

'And when ye come to Fawn water,'

says the wise wife in 'May Margaret',

'I bid ye lout fu' low,
And say three prayers to Christes grace
Afore ye ride the flow.'

In the lovely fragment, 'The Thorn of Life', there is a variant, not given by Child, which tells how on Midsummer morning the lady washed herself with dew 'clear as dawn' – an absurd literary phrase which spoils the poem. My emendation 'Fawn' is, I take it, certain. In the later riding ballads the name is still more frequent. The doomed raider in 'Carlisle Town' swears that Fawn will run red as blood ere his wrongs are forgotten. In 'Castle Gay' the dying Home craves, like King David, for a draught of Fawn water; and in 'Lord Archibald's Goodnight' there is a strange line about 'the holy wells of Fawn'. No doubt the line is corrupt, but the form of the corruption testifies to the spell of the Green Glen.

The Homes of Hardriding marched through disorder and violence to catastrophe. Never more than a hill clan, and kin to no powerful house, they persisted for three centuries by sheer audacity and pride. They held the Fawn glen and built a tower in it, but their real seat was Hardriding in the lower valley. The wave of Douglas aggression flowed round them, but they stoutly resisted, and it was only the power of the great Warden of the Marches that seized Fawnside for the Cauldshaw branch of his house. The battle in which Piers Home died by the hand of young Cauldshaw was fought in the Green Glen. Presently the Douglases were in trouble with the King, and a younger

Piers, under a King's commission, won back his lands and chased Cauldshaw into Northumberland. The Douglas clan was as often as not in treaty with the English Warden, while the Hardriding folk were vehemently Scottish, and, alone of their name, gave a good account of themselves at Flodden. The fortunes of the two houses seesawed so long as lands were won and kept by the strong arm alone. By and by came the day of smooth things, when a parchment was more potent than the sword, and both Home and Douglas withered, like hill plants brought into a lowland garden.

It was all an unedifying tale of blood and treason, but in reading it I was struck by one curious fact. Every critical event in the fortunes of the two clans befell in the Green Glen. There the leaders died in battle or in duel, and there a shameless victor celebrated his mastery. It was, so to speak, the citadel, of which the possession was the proof of triumph. It can have had but little value in itself, for the tower by the burn was scarcely a fortalice, and was never seriously dwelled in. Indeed, it is referred to not as a castle but as a 'bower'. When a Douglas defied a Home he summoned him to meet him by the 'Bower o' Fawn'. This same Bower was the centre of a pretty tale, when for once the blood-stained record emerges into the clear air of pastoral. The Fawn glen did not always pass by war; once it fell to the Douglases by marriage. Marjory of Hardriding, walking one evening by the stream, fell in with the young Douglas, sore wounded in a forest hunt. In the Bower she tended his wounds, and hid him from her fierce clan. Love ripened, and one July morn came the heir of Cauldshaw to Hardriding gates on an errand of peace. But the Home was surly, and the Douglas retired with a bitter denial and an arrow in his corselet. Thereupon Maid Marjory took the matter into her own hands, and rode over the hills to her lover. A gallant lady this, for, after a hurried wedding at the Kirk o' Shaws, she returned with her man to the Fawn Bower to confront an angry father and six angrier brothers. She offered peace or war, but declared that, if war it should be, she herself would fight in the first rank of the Douglases. Whereupon, it is said, old Piers, struck with wonder and delight at the courage he had begotten, declared for peace, and the Green Glen was her dowry.

IV

The thing became an obsession with me, and I could not let this nook of history alone. Weary hours were spent in the search for Homes and Douglases. Why I wasted my time thus I cannot tell. I told myself it was part of the spell of the Green Glen. 'The place was silent and *aware*,' as Browning says. I could not think that the virtue had departed and that the romance of Fawn was a past tale. Now it had no visitants save a shepherd taking a short cut or a fisherman with a taste for moorland trout. But some day a horseman on a fateful errand would stir its waters, or the Bower witness a new pastoral. I told myself that the wise years might ordain a long interval, but sooner or later they would ring up the curtain on the play.

A needle in a haystack was a simple quest compared to mine. History, which loves to leave fringes and loose threads, had cut the record of Home and Douglas with her sharpest shears. The two families disappeared within the same decade. Cauldshaw had chosen the king's side in the Covenant wars, and the head of the house, Sir Adam, had been a noted persecutor of the godly. He came to his end by a bullet of the Black Macmichael's somewhere in the hills of Galloway. His son had fought in the Scots Brigade for the French king, and returned about 1710 to find an estate broken by fines and penalties. We see him last riding south with Mackintosh in the 'Fifteen, but history does not tell us of his fate. He may have died with Derwentwater, or, more likely, he may have escaped and lain low till the hunt passed. Cauldshaw was forfeited and sold, and there was an end of it. Thirty years later I find a Douglas, a locksmith in the High Street of Edinburgh, who may have been his son, since he was gently born and yet clearly of no other known Douglas sept. After that the shears are at work. My note at the end of my researches was, 'merged in the burgesses of Edinburgh'.

Hardriding showed a similar tale, save that the Homes stood for the Covenant. One of them, Piers or Patrick, swung in the Grassmarket, and was the subject of the eulogies of Wodrow and Patrick Walker. An odd type of saint, his godliness was proved chiefly by his ferocity against the King's officers, for whom he would lie in wait behind a dyke with a musket. He died gallantly, declaiming the 23rd Psalm. The Jacobite rising brought Hardriding round to the side of Cauldshaw. Home and Douglas rode south together, and the fate of the first at any rate is clear. He fell in the rout of Preston, charging with a mouthful of oaths and texts. He left landless sons who disappear into the mist, and the ancient name of Home of Hardriding died in the land. David Hume, the philosopher, in his cups used to claim kin with the house, but it is recorded that David's friends did not take him seriously.

v

About that time I used to try to analyse the impression the Green Glen made upon me. I went to it often and in all weathers, but especially in the soft June days and the flaming twilights of October. At first I thought that the attraction was the peace of it, Wordsworth's 'sleep that is among the lonely hills'. Certainly it was very quiet and hallowed, with that brooding stillness which is a positive thing and not a mere absence of unrest. I have gone there, worried and distraught, and returned at ease with the world. Once, I remember, I came to it after fighting a forlorn bye-election in an English slum, with my brain fagged and dull and my nerves a torment. The Glen healed me, plunging me into the deeps of cool old-world shadows. But I soon discovered that the charm was not an opiate, but a stimulant. Its spell was the spell of life. It stirred the blood, comforting failure and nursing hope, but it did not lull to sleep. Once after a bad illness I went to Hardriding to rest, but I could not face the Glen. It only fevered a sick man. Its call was to action, and its ancient genius had no love for weaklings.

Often I tried to test it, to see if others could feel as I did. I was ridiculously unsuccessful. The sportsmen who frequented Hardriding, finding no grouse in the Glen, fought shy of it, and, if chance took them there, lamented the absence of heather. 'Pretty place,' one young man observed to me, 'but no more Scotch than my hat. It might be Sussex. Where's the brown heath and shaggy wood? What! There isn't cover for a tomtit. It's a nasty big slice out of Harry's shooting to have that long bare place taking up room.' It was too remote for ladies to picnic in, but one who penetrated as far called it 'sweet', and said it reminded her of Dartmoor. The people of the neighbourhood were no better. Keepers took the same view as the Hardriding sportsmen, and the farmer whose lease covered it spoke of it darkly as 'Poverty Neuk'. 'Food for neither man nor beast,' he said. 'Something might be done with phosphates, but I've no money to spend. It would make a grand dam if any town wanted a water-supply.' Good businesslike views, but no hint anywhere of the strangeness which to me had made it a kind of sanctuary.

There was one exception, the shepherd of the Nine Stane Rig. He was a young man, with a fiery red head and a taste for poetry. He would declaim Burns and Hogg with gusto, and was noted at 'kirns' and weddings for his robust rendering of songs like 'When the Kye come Hame', and 'Robin Tamson's Smiddy'. I used to accompany him sometimes on his rounds, and he spoke to me of the Green Glen.

'It's a bonny bit,' he once said, waving his arm towards the Green Dod. 'And there's ae queer thing about it. Sheep'll no bide in it. Ye may pit a hirsel in it at nicht, and every beast'll be on the tap o' the rig by the mornin'. How d'ye account for that? Mr Yellowlees says the feedin's no guid, and that it wants phosphates. I dinna agree wi' him. I've herdit a' my days, and I never saw better feedin' than by yon burnside. I've no just fawthomed it yet, but I've an idea o' my ain. I think the glen is an auld kirkyaird. I mind when I herdit in Eskdalemuir there was a bit on the hill whaur Covenanters had been buried, and the sheep were aye sweir to gang near

it. Some day I'm thinkin' o' gettin' a spade and howkin'. I
micht find something queer . . .'

VI

I came to regard the Green Glen as my own exclusive
property, which shared with me a secret. It was a pleasant
intimacy, and I had resigned myself to its limits, conscious
that the curtain of the past was drawn too close to allow
more than one little chink to be seen. Then one day Fate
brought Linford across my path.

I had known him slightly for several years. I can see him
now as I first knew him, a big solemn young man, too heavy
for elegance, and an awkward weight for a horse. We first
met one spring at Valescure, and a lonely fortnight established a kind of friendship between us. He was a modest
being, full of halting sympathies and interests, for which he
rarely found words. His family had been settled for two
generations in Australia, sheep-farming in the good days
when the big profits were made. His father had made a
second fortune in a gold mine, and, disliking the land
legislation of the country, had sold his farms and brought
his boy to England. An undistinguished progress through a
public school and Oxford had left him without a profession,
and, his father having died, with no near relations, and a
ridiculous amount of money. He should have been a
soldier, but somehow had missed his chance. The man
was in no way slack, but he gave me the impression of
having no niche to fit into. He was very English in speech
and manners, but he seemed to stand outside all the
ordinary English occupations and look on. Not that he
didn't do most things well. He was a magnificent shot, a
first-rate horseman, and the best man to sail a boat I have
ever met. He read much, had travelled considerably, and
had a keen interest in scientific geography. I thought he had
found a job when he took a notion of exploring the
Brahmaputra gorges, but the expedition fell through and
his interest flagged. He belonged to many clubs, and had a
few hundred acquaintances; but beyond myself I don't
think he had a friend.

He used to come to see me, and I tried to understand what puzzled him. For puzzled he was – not unhappy or disillusioned, but simply puzzled with life. Somehow he did not fit in with the world around him. I used to think it would have been better if he had never left Australia. There he had a ready-made environment; here in England he had to make his own, and he did not seem to have the knack of it. People liked him, and thought him, for all his stiffness, a good fellow. But he never accepted anybody or anything as his own; he was always the observant and sympathetic stranger. I began to realise that my friend, with all his advantages, was desperately homeless.

To myself, as I thought about him, I prescribed marriage. *Vix ea nostra voco* might have been his motto about most things, but in a wife he would find something his very own. The thing was obvious, but I saw also that he would be a hard fellow to marry. He was hopelessly shy and curiously unimpressionable. I do not remember that he ever spoke to me of any woman, and he avoided every chance of meeting them. I only once saw his tall figure at a dance, when he looked like nothing so much as Marius among the ruins of Carthage.

Hunting was his main hobby, and one January I found myself staying under the same roof with him in the Cottesmore country. He was, as I have said, a bold and fine rider, but he had to know his horse, and on this occasion our host mounted both of us. There was an ugly banked fence where he misjudged his animal's powers, and came down in a heap on a hardish bit of ground. I thought his neck was broken, and prepared for the worst, as I helped three other white-faced men to get him clear. But it was only a slight concussion, a broken finger, and a dislocated shoulder. He had a bad night, but next day was little the worse for his fall, and, frost having set in, I spent most of the afternoon in his bedroom.

He wore a ring which I had often noticed, a little engraved carnelian in a heavy setting of Australian gold. In doctoring his hand it had been removed, and now lay on the dressing-table. We were talking idly of runs and spills, and, as we talked, I picked it up and examined it.

The stone was old and curious. There was no motto, and the carving seemed to be a heart transfixed by an arrow. I thought it the ordinary trumpery love token – Cupid and his darts – when I noticed something more. The heart was crowned, and the barb transfixing it was not an arrow but a spear.

The sight roused me to the liveliest interest. For the cognisance belonged to one house and one house alone. It was Douglas of Cauldshaw who had carried the family badge with this strange difference. Mary of Scots, it was said, had given him the spear, for to the last they had stood by that melancholy lady.

'Where did you get this?' I asked.

'What? The ring? It was my father's. An ugly thing.'

I looked at it again. 'It has an odd crest. Did you ever inquire about it?'

He said No. He knew little heraldry, and didn't want to pretend to what didn't belong to him. Then he corrected himself. He thought that the thing was a family relic, right enough. His father had got the stone in turn from his mother, and had had it reset. He thought, but he wasn't sure, that it had been a long time in his grandmother's family.

'What was her name?' I asked eagerly.

The answer was disappointing. 'Brown,' he said. 'They had the Wooramanga place.'

I asked if they came from Scotland. 'No,' he said. 'They were Yorkshire, I think. But wait a bit. I think – yes – I have heard my father say something about the Browns being Scotch – Brouns, you know.'

This was a false scent and I tried again. But Linford had nothing to tell me. He had no family papers or jewels or pictures, nothing but the one ring. I could see that he was puzzled at my interest, and to my horror offered to pay the Heralds' College to investigate matters. I made him promise to let the Heralds alone, and tried to get more about his grandmother. She had been a tall, thin old lady, as he remembered her, with a north-country accent. She had disliked Melbourne intensely. That was all he could tell; not a saying or a rhyme or a memory to link her with those who had borne the ring's cognisance.

I heard, however, another startling thing that afternoon. Linford, blushing delightfully, confessed that he was in love. He had no chance, of course, wasn't good enough, and all the rest of it. When I heard that the lady was Virginia Dasent I was inclined to agree with him. Miss Dasent was very high game for Linford to fly at – or for anybody.

VII

Language is too coarse a medium in which to give a true portrait of Miss Virginia. Airy diaphanous colours and the sharp fineness of marble are needed; and something more, something to recapture that grace, wild and birdlike and only half mortal, which for three seasons turned all our heads. She was an astounding success. Coming from nowhere, and as innocent as a child of ambition, she made every man her most hopeless and humble servant. I think her charm was her pure girlishness – neither childish nor womanly, you understand. She had the air of one who faces the world frankly but does not accept it. She was a changeling, a wanderer, a dainty solitary figure on the weary old roads of life. I remember thinking, when I first saw her, that she might have stood for a statue of incarnate Wonder.

I knew her a little, well enough to see the hopelessness of my friend's case. She was an American – from one of the Carolinas, I believe; and Lady Amysfort took her about in London. I do not think that they were related. I hope my friends beyond the Atlantic will forgive me for saying that Miss Virginia was like no American I have ever met. Not that she had any of the sad homeless vulgarity of the denationalised. She was a fervent patriot, and had a delicious variety of the national humour. But I could not fit her in with her great continent. Indeed, I could not place her anywhere in any society. She belonged to some fanciful world of her own; but all the time she seemed to me to be looking for something – perhaps for her lost material heritage.

I was more interested, however, in Linford than in Miss Dasent. I could find out no more from him about his forbears, but I wondered if the Glen could tell me anything. Supposing I took him there, unprepared, of course, by any warning of mine, might not he feel the spell of it? If he did, I would be convinced of the Douglas blood; for I was certain that not otherwise would so prosaic a being feel so subtle a charm.

I persuaded him to take the Hardriding shootings; with an option to purchase, too, for Harry's finances were now past praying for. The chance came two days before the Twelfth, when he and I were alone in the house. It was a mild, blue August day, with clear distances and a cool breeze, and as we rounded the Green Dod I thought that my Glen was nobly dressed for us. I had hoped for some cry of delight, but none came. Linford stalked through the bent, muttering something about black-game.

We came to the mound by the waterside, Maid Marjory's Bower, and stretched ourselves on the scented turf. Then a curious thing happened to me. A light wind came up the stream, rippling the pools and sending a grey shiver over the grasses. Suddenly I became oppressed with a mortal fear. I must have lain limp and white, looking dumbly at the opposite hill. I had no notion what I feared, but it was worse than my old boyish adventure, for, though I longed madly to flee, I knew I could not. The Green Glen was trying me, and if I failed I had lost its secret for ever. I shut my teeth, and for a second or two hung at the limit of my endurance. Then it all passed. I found myself lying back on the mound, desperately sleepy and dripping with sweat, as if I had run twenty miles.

I mopped my brow and looked at Linford. He was quite unperturbed, and had got out his pouch and was filling his pipe. He glanced at me curiously.

'You're in pretty bad condition, old chap,' he observed. 'You'll founder on the Twelfth if you drip like this in an afternoon saunter.'

He got up and stretched himself. 'Let's go back,' he said. 'There isn't a beast or bird in the place. I am glad I came here, for it will keep us from wasting time over it.'

I followed him, still shaky and acutely disappointed. The Glen had nothing to say to him. The ring was an accident, and the Cauldshaw stock was still to find. And yet, as we walked home, I began to doubt. The Glen had been not for Douglas or Home alone, but for both. What if a Home were needed to complete the circuit?

It was a possible explanation. Besides, the extraordinary seizure which had befallen me that afternoon seemed to argue that the visit had not been meaningless. I was perfectly well and normal, and I had sat on the mound a hundred times before. Might it not be that the Glen had been stirred, and was striving to tell us its secret? Then I began to laugh, and told myself that I was a fool to treat my fancies as solid facts.

VIII

That winter was made memorable to me, and a good many others, by Virginia Dasent. The Amysforts went to Egypt, leaving her very much to her own devices. She hunted a little and spent some time in country houses; but mostly she was to be found in London, a city for which she had an inordinate love. This was bad for Linford, who stayed devotedly in town, and being deprived of healthful exercise put on flesh and lost spirits. I found him in the club one afternoon in a very bad temper. I alone knew of his hopeless plight, and with me he did not trouble to keep up appearances.

'I get no forrarder,' he groaned. 'She tolerates me as she tolerates everybody else. Lord, how I hate that kind smile of hers! She isn't a woman, Jack. She's an adorable sort of bird that flits about and never settles. You know the way she holds her head forward and peers away beyond you. She's always preening for another flight.'

Love was making him a psychologist, for Miss Virginia's maddening charm lay in just that bird-like detachment. We had become very good friends, she and I; and often of a late afternoon we talked in the Amysforts' big ugly drawing-room. She liked me because I was interested in old things and odd bypaths, for I found that the child bubbled over with romance. A lonely girlhood in some Carolinian manor had given her fancy rich feeding. Half in a world of books, half in a world of pure dreaming, she took her airy way. She had about as much worldliness as St Theresa, and much less worldly knowledge. Frankly, I was a little afraid for her; some day disillusion would come, and come cruelly. There was a loneliness about her, as about Linford, but it was the loneliness of a happy preoccupation. Some day those wondering eyes would find the world less marvellous, and then her heart would break. Or would she carry her fresh childlike interest undimmed to the end? I could not tell, but I argued badly for Linford's chances. He was far too eligible – young, good-looking, preposterously rich. The man who was to win Miss Virginia's heart, I thought, must come riding in the fearless old fashion. Linford was as romantic in the ordinary sense of the word as a Republican senator of Virginia's native land.

That was my first impression, but I found cause to alter it slightly. As I came to know her better, new avenues opened up in her soul. She had an excellent brain, very clear, shrewd and subtle, and behind all her fancies I was aware of a solid rock of common-sense. She was not a ready talker, and never rhapsodised. Little odd phrases, a shrug and a laugh, gave the key to her whimsical world. But on a matter of prosaic fact I found her amazingly practical. More than once she offered me advice, with a little wise air which spoke of youth, but with a penetration, too, which took my breath away. I put my surprise into words. 'Of course I'm practical,' she said. 'I'm more than half Scotch, you know.'

I thought nothing of it at the time, for American girls have a habit of being either Scotch or early Norman. I remember asking her if she had ever been to Scotland, and she said – No; not yet. She had not had time. But some day . . .

I was inclined to be a little angry with both her and Linford. He went about like a sheep, a ridiculous figure of purposeless melancholy, and the deeper he sank in this mood the worse it was for his chances. As for the lady, I began to think her almost inhuman. I wondered if she were not perfectly heartless, hollow within like an Ell-woman. She seemed unconscious of the havoc she was causing everywhere. I think I would have preferred a common flirt to that unearthly aloofness. But her eyes used always to make me revise my judgments: they were so innocent and young. Some day she would awaken, I told myself. Some day the sleeping princess would be kissed into life. But I was pretty certain that, unless a miracle happened, it would be none of Linford's doing.

It was one morning in the Park in early May that she exploded the mine under my feet. She had been riding with Linford, and turned, as I came up, to accompany me. I don't know what they had been talking about, but her eyes were shining, her colour high, and her lips very tight.

'We have been discussing Scotch places,' she volunteered. 'It is very tiresome. I wanted a place, and Mr Linford seems to have got a long lease of it. He offered to make it over to me, but of course that was impossible. It's a great nuisance, for I had set my heart on it.'

I asked the name, and even as I asked I think I guessed the answer.

'Hardriding,' she said. 'A little old place in the Borders. My family lived there long ago, and I have always meant to make a pilgrimage to it. Caroline Amysfort is going to Bayreuth, so I shall set up as hostess on my own account. If I can't get Hardriding I must have Cauldshaw. Will you come and stay with me?'

I listened to her, I hope, with an impassive face, but inwardly I was a volcano of excitement. Hardriding and Cauldshaw! Home and Douglas! Was the circuit by some amazing chance to be completed? I wondered how soon I could decently make an appointment with Miss Virginia and get the whole story. She was going away for the week end, but would be free on Tuesday, rather late. I hugged my impatience for three beastly days.

I had expected a fragment, and found instead a complete and well-authenticated tale. I blessed that lovable American seriousness about genealogies. There was the pedigree neatly inscribed, with excerpts from registers and letters, as business-like, as irrefutable, as a share certificate. After old Sir Piers fell at Preston his eldest son, Gideon, fled to France, and thence to the Canadas. He fought under the French flag, and rose to a colonelcy before he fell at

Quebec. He had married a Frenchwoman, and their son – Lewis, I think – took to the sea and did good trade in the smuggling and privateering line along the New England coast. He settled in North Carolina, and, being rich from his ventures, bought a handsome property, and built a manor-house in the colonial style. With his grand-daughter the male line of Home – Miss Virginia pronounced it to rhyme with 'loam' – ended. She married a Dasent, son of a neighbouring squire, and was Miss Virginia's grandmother. There it was, all set down in black and white, and very prettily she expounded it to me. I had found the Hardriding stock at last. It had come back to me out of the mist with ample credentials.

Miss Virginia at Cauldshaw, Linford at Hardriding, and between them the Green Glen! Surely the stage was being set at last for the play. My first impulse was to tell her the whole romance. I pictured her delight; I saw the prosaic Linford take on the colour of poetry. But a scruple deterred me. It would be breaking faith with the Green Glen. If the spell were there it needed no preparation of mine for its working. Those starry influences called for respectful treatment. I would go to Hardriding, and some day – some mellow autumn day – Miss Virginia would cross the hills, and Linford would be there by the Bower to meet her!

Meanwhile all that summer the course of true love ran badly. The two were friends after a fashion, but Linford was such a clumsy and uneasy being, and Miss Virginia so swift and evasive, that it seemed impossible that that friendship could ripen. I got very sick of the whole business, angry with Linford, and puzzled about the lady. At one moment I called her inhuman, at another angelic; but, whatever view one took (and after all they came to the same conclusion), she was the most heartbreaking beauty. Her wild childlike eyes looked through one as if to a pleasant country beyond. There is a Greek fable, isn't there? about some hero who needed the touch of his mother the Earth to give him strength. I wondered if she would ever find that earth-kinship, which means common humanity.

IX

In early August the Lammas floods were high, so that sultriness was purged from the air and the world left clean and rain-washed and sweet-scented. I was staying at Cauldshaw, in a small party which tried in vain to induce its dancing hostess to be still. She was in wild spirits, out at all hours, a crony of shepherds, already learned in the ways of the moors. She had come back, she said, to her own country, and lived every hour in a whirl of delight and wonder. The long round-shouldered hills, the clear burns, the homely simplicity of the old land ravished her heart. I counted the days till I could take her to the Green Glen.

Then the party melted away, and it was arranged that she should pay a visit of state to Hardriding. I also was bidden, and Linford spent his days in a fever of expectation. Miss Virginia was scrupulous about the details. She would walk across the hills by the old raiding road from Cauldshaw. I showed her the way, which traversed the Green Glen, and on the map I pointed out the Bower. She clapped her hands with delight at my tale – the barest sketch – of the Home doings. 'What an adventure!' she cried. 'I shall tell you all about it at dinner. I feel like a princess coming home to her kingdom.'

I sincerely hoped that she was. If the Fates were kind this airy spirit should feel the antique spell of earth, and I dared to think that two wanderers might find a home.

To this hour I remember every incident of that autumn day. It was the 3rd of September. The morning broke cold and misty, but by ten o'clock the sun had burned up the rime, and the hills slept in a bright windless calm. I was shooting with Linford, and set out from Cauldshaw at eleven o'clock. Miss Virginia was to leave after luncheon, and, if she followed my directions, would be at Hardriding by six. She would reach the Green Glen about four o'clock, and I laid my plans accordingly.

I shot vilely, for I was full of a curious sense of anticipation. So was Linford, but nothing could impair his skill. We talked very little, I remember; but it took some manœuvring on my part to have the afternoon beat where I wanted it.

Linford would have had us try the moors near the house, for his mind was always turning to Hardriding; but after some persuasion I got him to keep to the hills by the Nine Stane Rig, where we looked down on the Green Glen. Had I told him that Miss Virginia was walking, he would have set off then and there to meet her, and spoiled everything. He kept asking me when she would start. 'She'll have to go round by the Red Ford,' he repeated, 'and that means Hardriding at tea-time. We needn't stay too long up here. Hardriding is her family place, so to speak, and I want to be there to welcome her.'

Shortly after three we stood on the summit of the Dun Rig, and as I watched the green shoulders of the Fawn Hope I saw a figure cross the sky-line. Then I told Linford the truth. I bade him go up the Glen to meet her and wait for her at the Bower. He looked at me shyly. 'You arranged all this?' he asked. 'Thanks very much, old man. You've been a pretty good friend to me.'

I set off for Hardriding without a glance behind. The Glen was now no place for me. Looking back at my frame of mind, I can see nothing but exhilaration. Some great thing was about to befall two people whom I loved. I had no doubt of the virtue of the place. By devious paths I had brought back to it its old masters. It had whispered its secret to me, and I had repaid it. For the moment I felt that time was not, that death was little, and change a mockery. The wise years let nothing die, and always the circle came full again, bringing back lost hopes and dreams. The still and golden afternoon spoke the same message to my heart. I felt the serene continuance of all things, the sense of something eternal behind the trivial ways of man.

I reached Hardriding a little after four, and according to my plan sat down to read and smoke. But I soon found that idleness was impossible. I was strung too high with expectation. I wandered into the library, and then into the garden, but my eyes were always turning to the shoulder of hill which marked the opening of the Fawn Glen. Then I resolved to go to meet Linford. Whatever had happened, it would be right for me to welcome Miss Virginia to Hardriding.

Before I had crossed the lawns my mood changed utterly. I suddenly became a prey to black forebodings. The doggerel Latin of True Thomas rang in my head like the croak of a raven:–

> 'Ubi Faunus fluit
> Spes mortalis ruit.'

I tried to laugh at it. I told myself that the verses were no doubt the work of a foolish eighteenth-century parson. What harm could follow the meeting of two friends in a hill glen where their forbears had fought and loved? But I reasoned in vain. A deadly depression overmastered me. The light had gone out of the sky, and the bent, all yellow in the westering sun, seemed wan as death.

> 'Where Fawn flows
> Man's hope goes.'

The dolorous refrain would not leave me.

I emerged from the park into the water-meadows where Fawn runs deep among flags and meadow-sweet. Beyond them I came to the lower glen, where the fir-clad slopes leave a thin strip of pasture by the stream. Here I should have met the two, but there was no sign of them. I looked at my watch and found it after five.

Then I began to quicken my pace. My depression had turned to acute anxiety. Before me was half a mile of open strath, and then the Green Dod, where the Glen turned sharply to the right. I ran that half-mile with dread in my heart of what I might see beyond it. But when I came to the Green Dod there was still no sign of a human being. The Fawn flows round the shoulder of hill in a narrow defile, at the upper end of which begins the Green Glen. I resolved to wait there, for I realised that I could not enter the Glen. I can give no reason for this, but I knew the truth of it. My feet could not have carried me round the shoulder of hill.

I did not wait long. Suddenly down the defile came a single figure. It was Linford, but even to my distraught sight a different Linford from him I had known. As I have said he was a big fellow, a little ungainly, a little afraid of his size. But now he was a noble figure of a man, and as he strode along there was a strange mastery and dignity in him. But why was he alone? I blinked my eyes, for I saw that he was not alone. He carried in his arms something slim and white and very quiet. I crouched behind a boulder as he came near, but he had no eyes for anything but his burden. His head was bent over it, and his face was wild and drawn with grief. Then I saw that a fair head lay limply in the crook of his arm, and that the face was very pale . . .

The doctors called it heart failure. Miss Virginia, said one of them in a moment of poetry, had for years had a frail chariot for her body and the horses of her spirit had driven too fiercely. She must have had heart trouble, though no one had diagnosed it. The hill walk from Cauldshaw had been too much for her. The same man spoke wisely about the evils of our modern life. 'Most people to-day,' he said, 'have temperaments that prey on their bodies. They must live at white heat and the shell cracks . . .'

Years afterwards, when time had taken the edge off his grief, Linford told me something of what happened. 'She met me, looking very well and jolly, and we walked to the place you call the Bower. You may laugh at me, but I tell you I had a presentiment that something was going to happen, but I couldn't be sure whether it was good or bad . . . She looked all round the Glen and sighed happily, as if she had found what she liked very much. Then suddenly she gave a little cry and went very white. I caught her, and saw that she was all in a shiver. She was staring at the burn, and her eyes were round and frightened like a deer's. Then she smiled again, and turned to me with a look – Oh, my God, I can never forget it! It was so kind and happy and . . . She must have cared for me all the time, and like a blind fool I didn't know it. She put her arms round my neck and said, "My ain true love" – I suppose she was quoting from a Scotch song. And just as I was bursting with joy I felt her cheek grow cold . . .'

Now it is a curious thing, but in the *Scotichronicon* of Hume of Calzeat – it is in manuscript, and I do not think any one living has read it besides myself – there is a version of the story of Maid Marjory. And according to that version, when the lady confronted her father in the Green Glen, she put her arm around the Douglas's neck, and said, 'My ain true love'.

The Riding of Ninemileburn

An historical story about a Border raid, this was first published in *Blackwood's Magazine* in April 1912 and included in *The Moon Endureth* (1912).

Sim bent over the meal ark and plumbed its contents with his fist. Two feet and more remained: provender – with care – for a month, till he harvested the waterside corn and ground it at Ashkirk mill. He straightened his back, better pleased; and, as he moved, the fine dust flew into his throat and set him coughing. He choked back the sound till his face crimsoned.

But the mischief was done. A woman's voice, thin and weary, came from the ben-end.

The long man tiptoed awkwardly to her side. 'Canny, lass,' he crooned. 'It's me back frae the hill. There's a mune and a clear sky, and I'll hae the lave under thack and rape the morn. Syne I'm for Ninemileburn, and the coo 'ill be i' the byre by Setterday. Things micht be waur, and we'll warstle through yet. There was mair tint at Flodden.'

The last rays of October daylight that filtered through the straw lattice showed a woman's head on the pillow. The face was white and drawn, and the great black eyes – she had been an Oliver out of Megget – were fixed in the long stare of pain. Her voice had the high lilt and the deep undertones of the Forest.

'The bairn 'ill be gone ere ye ken, Sim,' she said wearily. 'He canna live without milk, and I've nane to gie him. Get the coo back or lose the son I bore ye. If I were my ordinar' I wad hae't in the byre, though I had to kindle Ninemileburn ower Wat's heid.'

She turned miserably on her pillow and the babe beside her set up a feeble crying. Sim busied himself with stirring up the peat fire. He knew too well that he would never see the milk-cow till he took with him the price of his debt or gave a bond on harvested crops. He had had a bad lambing, and the wet summer had soured his shallow lands. The cess to Branksome was due, and he had no means to pay it. His father's cousin of the Ninemileburn was a brawling fellow, who never lacked beast in byre or corn in bin, and to him he had gone for the loan. But Wat was a hard man, and demanded surety; so the one cow had travelled the six moorland miles and would not return till the bond was cancelled. As well might he try to get water from stone as move Wat by any tale of a sick wife and dying child.

The peat smoke got into his throat and brought on a fresh fit of coughing. The wet year had played havoc with his chest, and his lean shoulders shook with the paroxysms. An anxious look at the bed told him that Marion was drowsing, so he slipped to the door.

Outside, as he had said, the sky was clear. From the plashy hillside came the rumour of swollen burns. Then he was aware of a man's voice shouting.

'Sim,' it cried, 'Sim o' the Cleuch . . . Sim.' A sturdy figure came down through the scrog of hazel and revealed itself as his neighbour of the Dodhead. Jamie Telfer lived five miles off in Ettrick, but his was the next house to the Cleuch shieling.

Telfer was running, and his round red face shone with sweat. 'Dod, man, Sim, ye're hard o' hearing. I was routin' like to wake the deid, and ye never turned your neck. It's the fray I bring ye. Mount and ride to the Carewoodrig. The word's frae Branksome. I've but Ranklehope to raise, and then me and William's Tam will be on the road to join ye.'

'Whatna fray?' Sim asked blankly.

'Ninemileburn. Bewcastle's marching. They riped the place at cockcrow, and took twenty-six kye, five horse, and a walth o' plenishing. They were seen fordin' Teviot at ten afore noon, but they're gaun round by Ewes Water, for they durstna try the Hermitage Slack. Forbye they move slow, for the bestial's heavy wark to drive. They shut up Wat in the auld peel, and he didna win free till bye midday. Syne he was off to Branksome, and the word frae Branksome is to raise a' Ettrick, Teviotdale, Ale Water, and the Muirs o' Esk. We look to win up wi' the lads long ere they cross Liddel, and that at the speed they gang will be gey an' near sunrise. It's a braw mune for the job.'

Jamie Telfer lay on his face by the burn and lapped up water like a dog. Then without another word he trotted off across the hillside beyond which lay the Ranklehope.

Sim had a fit of coughing and looked stupidly at the sky. Here was the last straw. He was dog-tired, for he had had little sleep the past week. There was no one to leave with Marion, and Marion was too weak to tend herself. The word was from Branksome, and at another time Branksome was to be obeyed. But now the thing was past reason. What use was there for a miserable careworn man to ride among the swank well-fed lads in the Bewcastle chase?

And then he remembered his cow. She would be hirpling with the rest of the Ninemileburn beasts on the road to the Border. The case was more desperate than he had thought. She was gone for ever unless he helped Wat to win her back. And if she went, where was the milk for the child?

He stared hopelessly up at a darkening sky. Then he went to the lean-to where his horse was stalled. The beast was fresh, for it had not been out for two days – a rough Forest shelty with shaggy heels and a mane like a thicket. Sim set his old saddle on it, and went back to the house.

His wife was still asleep, breathing painfully. He put water on the fire to boil, and fetched a handful of meal from the ark. With this he made a dish of gruel, and set it by the bedside. He drew a pitcher of water from the well, for she might be thirsty. Then he banked up the fire and steeked the window. When she woke she would find food and drink, and he would be back before the next darkening. He dared not look at the child.

The shelty shied at a line of firelight from the window, as Sim flung himself wearily on its back. He had got his long ash spear from its place among the rafters, and donned his leather jacket with the iron studs on breast and shoulder. One of the seams gaped. His wife had been mending it when her pains took her.

He had ridden by Commonside and was high on the Caerlanrig before he saw signs of men. The moon swam in a dim dark sky, and the hills were as yellow as corn. The round top of the Wisp made a clear mark to ride by. Sim was a nervous man, and at another time would never have dared to ride alone by the ruined shieling of Chasehope, where folk said a witch had dwelt long ago and the Devil still came in the small hours. But now he was too full of his cares to have room for dread. With his head on his breast he let the shelty take its own road through the mosses.

But on the Caerlanrig he came on a troop of horse. They were a lusty crowd, well-mounted and armed, with iron basnets and corselets that jingled as they rode. Harden's men, he guessed, with young Harden at the head of them. They cried him greeting as he fell in at the tail. 'It's Long Sim o' the Cleuch,' one said; 'he's sib to Wat or he wadna be here. Sim likes his ain fireside better than the 'Bateable Land.'

The companionship of others cheered him. There had been a time, before he brought Marion from Megget, when he was a well-kenned figure on the Borders, a good man at weaponshows and a fierce fighter when his blood was up. Those days were long gone; but the gusto of them returned. No man had ever lightlied him without paying scot. He held up his head and forgot his cares and his gaping jacket. In a little they had topped the hill, and were looking down on the young waters of Ewes.

The company grew, as men dropped in from left and right. Sim recognised the wild hair of Charlie of Geddinscleuch, and the square shoulders of Adam of Frodslaw. They passed Mosspaul, a twinkle far down in the glen, and presently came to the long green slope which is called the Carewoodrig, and which makes a pass from Ewes to Hermitage. To Sim it seemed that an army had encamped on it. Fires had been lit in a howe, and wearied men slept by them. These were the runners, who all day had been warning the dales. By one fire stood the great figure of Wat o' the Ninemileburn, blaspheming to the skies and counting his losses. He had girded on a long sword, and for better precaution had slung an axe on his back. At the sight of young Harden he held his peace. The foray was Branksome's and a Scott must lead.

Dimly and stupidly, for he was very weary, Sim heard word of the enemy. The beasts had travelled slow, and would not cross Liddel till sunrise. Now they were high up on Tarras water, making for Liddel at a ford below the Castletown. There had been no time to warn the Elliots, but the odds were that Lariston and Mangerton would be out by morning.

'Never heed the Elliots,' cried young Harden. 'We can redd our ain frays, lads. Haste and ride, and we'll hae Geordie Musgrave long ere he wins to the Ritterford. Borrowstonemoss is the bit for us.' And with the light Scott laugh he was in the saddle.

They were now in a land of low marshy hills, which made ill-going. A companion gave Sim the news. Bewcastle had five-score men and the Scots four-score and three. 'It's waur to haud than to win,' said the man. 'Ae man can tak' ten beasts when three 'ill no keep them. There'll be bluidy war on Tarras side ere the nicht's dune.'

Sim was feeling his weariness too sore for speech. He remembered that he had tasted no food for fifteen hours. He found his meal-poke and filled his mouth, but the stuff choked him. It only made him cough fiercely, so that Wat o' the Ninemileburn, riding before him, cursed him for a broken-winded fool. Also he was remembering about Marion, lying sick in the darkness twenty miles over the hills.

The moon was clouded, for an east wind was springing up. It was ill riding on the braeface, and Sim and his shelty floundered among the screes. He was wondering how long it would all last. Soon he must fall down and be the scorn of the Border men. The thought put Marion out of his head again. He set his mind on tending his horse and keeping up with his fellows.

Suddenly a whistle from Harden halted the company. A man came running back from the crown of the rig. A whisper went about that Bewcastle was on the far side, in the little glen called the Brunt Burn. The men held their breath, and in the stillness they heard far off the sound of hooves on stones and the heavy breathing of cattle.

It was a noble spot for an ambuscade. The Borderers scattered over the hillside, some riding south to hold the

convoy as it came down the glen. Sim's weariness lightened. His blood ran quicker; he remembered that the cow,
his child's one hope, was there before him. He found
himself next his cousin Wat, who chewed curses in his
great beard. When they topped the rig they saw a quarter of
a mile below them the men they sought. The cattle were
driven in the centre, with horsemen in front and rear and
flankers on the braeside.

'Hae at them, lads,' cried Wat o' the Ninemileburn, as he
dug spurs into his grey horse. From farther down the glen
he was answered with a great shout of 'Branksome'.

Somehow or other Sim and his shelty got down the steep
braeface. The next he knew was that the raiders had turned to
meet him – to meet him alone, it seemed; the moon had come
out again, and their faces showed white in it. The cattle, as the
driving ceased, sank down wearily in the moss. A man with an
iron ged turned, cursing, to receive Wat's sword on his
shoulderbone. A light began to blaze from down the burn
– Sim saw the glitter of it out of the corner of an eye – but the
men in front were dark figures with white faces.

The Bewcastle lads were stout fellows, well used to hold
as well as take. They closed up in line around the beasts,
and the moon lit the tops of their spears. Sim brandished
his ash-shaft, which had weighed heavily these last hours,
and to his surprise found it light. He found his voice, too,
and fell a-roaring like Wat.

Before he knew he was among the cattle. Wat had broken
the ring, and men were hacking and slipping among the
slab sides of the wearied beasts. The shelty came down over
the rump of a red bullock, and Sim was sprawling on his
face in the trampled grass. He struggled to rise, but some
one had him by the throat.

Anger fired his slow brain. He reached out his long arms
and grappled a leather jerkin. His nails found a seam and
rent it, for he had mighty fingers. Then he was gripping
warm flesh, tearing it like a wild beast, and his assailant with
a cry slackened his hold.

'Whatna wull-cat . . .' he began, but he got no further.
The hoof of Wat's horse came down on his head and
brained him. A spatter of blood fell on Sim's face.

The man was half wild. His shelty had broken back for the hill, but his spear lay a yard off. He seized it and got to his feet, to find that Wat had driven the English over the burn. The cattle were losing their weariness in panic, and tossing wild manes among the Scots. It was like a fight in a winter's byre. The glare on the right grew fiercer, and young Harden's voice rose, clear as a bell, above the tumult. He was swearing by the cross of his sword.

On foot, in the old Border way, Sim followed in Wat's wake, into the bog and beyond the burn. He laired to his knees, but he scarcely heeded it. There was a big man before him, a foolish, red-haired fellow, who was making great play with a cudgel. He had shivered two spears and was singing low to himself. Farther off Wat had his axe in hand and was driving the enemy to the brae. There were dead men in the moss. Sim stumbled over a soft body, and a hand caught feebly at his heel. 'To me, lads,' cried Wat. 'Anither birse and we hae them broken.'

But something happened. Harden was pushing the van of the raiders up the stream, and a press of them surged in from the right. Wat found himself assailed on his flank, and gave ground. The big man with the cudgel laughed loud and ran down the hill, and the Scots fell back on Sim. Men tripped over him, and as he rose he found the giant above him with his stick in the air.

The blow fell, glancing from the ash-shaft to Sim's side. Something cracked and his left arm hung limp. But the furies of hell had hold of him now. He rolled over, gripped his spear short, and with a swift turn struck upwards. The big man gave a sob and toppled down into a pool of the burn.

Sim struggled to his feet, and saw that the raiders were beginning to hough the cattle. One man was driving a red spear into a helpless beast. It might have been the Cleuch cow. The sight maddened him, and like a destroying angel he was among them. One man he caught full in the throat, and had to set a foot on his breast before he could tug the spear out. Then the head shivered on a steel corselet, and Sim played quarterstaff with the shaft. The violence of his onslaught turned the tide. Those whom Harden drove up were caught in a vice, and squeezed out, wounded and dying and mad with fear, on to the hill above the burn. Both sides were weary men, or there would have been a grim slaughter. As it was, none followed the runners, and every now and again a Scot would drop like a log, not from wounds but from dead weariness.

Harden's flare was dying down. Dawn was breaking, and Sim's wild eyes cleared. He saw the press of cattle, dazed with fright, and the red and miry heather. Queer black things were curled and stretched athwart it. He noticed a dead man beside him, perhaps of his own slaying. It was a shabby fellow, in a jacket that gaped like Sim's. The face was thin and patient, and the eyes, even in death, looked puzzled and reproachful. It would be one of the plain folk who had to ride, willy-nilly, on bigger men's quarrels. Sim found himself wondering if he, also, had a famished wife and child at home. The fury of the night had gone, and Sim began to sob from utter tiredness.

He slept in what was half a swoon. When he woke the sun was well up in the sky and the Scots were cooking food. His arm irked him, and his head burned like fire. He felt his body and found nothing worse than bruises, and one long shallow scar where his jacket was torn.

A Teviotdale man brought him a cog of brose. Sim stared at it and sickened: he was too far gone for food. Young Harden passed, and looked curiously at him. 'Here's a man that hasna spared himsel',' he said. 'A drop o' French cordial is the thing for you, Sim.' And out of a leathern flask he poured a little draught which he bade Sim swallow.

The liquor ran through his veins and lightened the ache of his head. He found strength to rise and look round. Surely they were short of men. If these were all that were left Bewcastle had been well avenged.

Jamie Telfer enlightened him. 'When we had gotten the victory, there were some o' the lads thocht that Bewcastle sud pay scot in beasts as weel as men. Sae Wat and a score mair rade off to lowse Geordie Musgrave's kye. The road's clear, and they'll be back ower Liddel by this time. Dod, there'll be walth o' plenishin' at the Ninemileburn.'

Sim was cheered by the news. If Wat got back more than his own he might be generous. They were cooking meat round the fire, the flesh of the cattle killed in the fight. He went down to the nearest blaze, and was given a strip of roast which he found he could swallow.

'How mony beasts were killed?' he asked incuriously, and was told three. Saugh poles had been set up to hang the skins on. A notion made Sim stagger to his feet and go to inspect them. There could be no mistake. There hung the brindled hide of Marion's cow.

Wat returned in a cloud of glory, driving three-and-twenty English beasts before him – great white fellows that none could match on the Scottish side. He and his lads clamoured for food, so more flesh was roasted, till the burnside smelt like a kitchen. The Scots had found better than cattle, for five big skins of ale bobbed on their saddles. Wat summoned all to come and drink, and Harden, having no fear of reprisals, did not forbid it.

Sim was becoming a man again. He had bathed his bruises and scratches in the burn, and Will o' Phawhope, who had skill as a leech, had set his arm and bound it to his side in splints of ash and raw hide. He had eaten grossly of flesh – the first time since the spring, and then it had only been braxy lamb. The ale had warmed his blood and quickened his wits. He began to feel pleased with himself. He had done well in the fray – had not young Harden praised him? – and surly Wat had owned that the salvage of so many beasts was Sim's doing. 'Man, Sim, ye wrocht michtily at the burnside,' he had said. 'The heids crackit like nits when ye garred your staff sing. Better you wi' a stick than anither man wi' a sword.' It was fine praise, and warmed Sim's chilly soul. For a year he had fought bitterly for bread, and now glory had come to him without asking.

Men were drawn by lot to drive the cattle, and others to form a rearguard. The rest set off for their homes by the nearest road. The shelty had been recovered, and Sim to his pride found himself riding in the front with Wat and young Harden and others of the Scott and Elliot gentry.

The company rode fast over the green hills in the clear autumn noon. Harden's blue eyes danced, and he sang snatches in his gay voice. Wat rumbled his own praises and told of the raid over Liddel. Sim felt a new being from the broken man who the night before had wearily jogged on the same road. He told himself he took life too gravely and let care ride him too hard. He was too much thirled to the Cleuch and tied to his wife's apron. In the future he would see his friends, and bend the bicker with the rest of them.

By the darkening they had come to Ninemileburn, where Harden's road left theirs. Wat had them all into the bare dwelling, and another skin of ale was broached. A fire was lit and the men sprawled around it, singing songs. Then tales began, and they would have sat till morning, had not Harden called them to the road. Sim, too, got to his feet. He was thinking of the six miles yet before him, and as home grew nearer his spirits sank. Dimly he remembered the sad things that waited his home-coming.

Wat made him a parting speech. 'Gude e'en to ye, cousin Sim. Ye've been a kind man to me the day. May I do as weel by you if ever the fray gangs by the Cleuch. I had a coo o' yours in pledge, and it was ane o' the beasts the Musgraves speared. By the auld law your debt still stands, and if I likit I could seek anither pledge. But there'll be something awin' for rescue-shot, and wi' that and the gude wark ye've dune the day, I'm content to ca' the debt paid.'

Wat's words sounded kind, and no doubt Wat thought himself generous. Sim had it on his tongue to ask for a cow – even on a month's loan. But pride choked his speech. It meant telling of the pitiful straits at the Cleuch. After what had passed he must hold his head high amongst those full-fed Branksome lads. He thanked Wat, cried farewell to the rest, and mounted his shelty.

The moon was rising and the hills were yellow as corn. The shelty had had a feed of oats, and capered at the shadows. What with excitement, meat, and ale, and the dregs of a great fatigue, Sim's mind was hazy, and his cheerfulness returned. He thought only on his exploits. He had done great things – he, Sim o' the Cleuch – and every man in the Forest would hear of them and praise his courage. There would be ballads made about him; he could hear the blind violer at the Ashkirk change-house singing songs which told how Sim o' the Cleuch smote Bewcastle in the howe of the Brunt Burn – ash against steel, one against ten. The fancy intoxicated him; he felt as if he, too, could make a ballad. It would speak of the soft shiny night with the moon high in the heavens. It would tell of the press of men and beasts by the burnside, and the red glare of Harden's fires, and Wat with his axe, and above all of Sim with his ash shaft and his long arms, and how Harden drove the raiders up the burn and Sim smote them silently among the cattle. Wat's exploits would come in, but the true glory was Sim's. But for him Scots saddles might have been empty and every beast safe over Liddel.

The picture fairly ravished him. It carried him over the six miles of bent and down by the wood of hazel to where the Cleuch lay huddled in its nook of hill. It brought him to the door of his own silent dwelling. As he pushed into the darkness his heart suddenly sank . . .

With fumbling hands he kindled a rushlight. The peat fire had long sunk and left only a heap of white ashes. The gruel by the bed had been spilled and was lying on the floor. Only the jug of water was drained to the foot.

His wife lay so still that he wondered. A red spot burned in each cheek, and, as he bent down, he could hear her fast breathing. He flashed the light on her eyes and she slowly opened them.

'The coo, Sim,' she said faintly. 'Hae ye brocht the coo?'

The rushlight dropped on the floor. Now he knew the price of his riding. He fell into a fit of coughing.

Watches of the Night

A slight story published in *The Scottish Mountaineering Club Journal* 1921–3, it contrasts the pleasant dreams of a climber and the reality of a night climb.

Nine-thirty p.m. – The 'Gardien' has just put out the light and bumped noisily into his cubby-hole. The hut is as dark as the pit; an uneasy quiet reigns, and I compose myself to sleep.

This (my reason tells me) is the precious hour of rest; the storehouse of the body's strength against the toil and tribulation of the morning; not a moment must be lost! Come, now, let me concentrate upon oblivion: I will speak softly – perhaps I shall catch it unawares – Sleep . . . Sleep . . . (It would be easier, all the same, if there were fewer lumps in this mattress, and if the straw were less prickly within the pillow.)

Sleep . . .

It is a grim business. Half an hour has gone already. I have tried all manner of ways; on the right side, and on the left; I have passed in hot pursuit down all the byways of my mind; I have lain in wait among the shadows of idle thought – and sleep eludes me still! It has been deaf to my prayers; it has scorned my little scientific ruses; it has treated my mathematical contrivances with contempt. As usual, it has played the woman with my over-anxious wooing, and taken a delight in denying the too assiduous lover. Fool that I am! To conquer, my wooing should, of course, be the wooing of the Apache: I must be careless and brutal, seemingly indifferent, lazily sure of my success. Men of genius have always done this. Napoleon, for instance, found sleep the moment he desired it, even on the eve of a critical battle. Wonderful!

I fear in this respect I do not resemble Napoleon. It is unfortunate.

Raymond does though; he is off already – the lucky devil. So does the Gardien. *Nom d'un nom!* How the man snores! It is like a double-bass played by clockwork: in spasms it is like the thunder of the Atlantic on a rock-bound shore.

Why don't they make men wear silencers? They have to have them on motor bicycles and things. Compulsory silencers – for use in all S.A.C. huts – a brilliant idea! (I am often exceptionally brilliant on these occasions.) It will be defended not to use them when requested to do so by other Clubists – another excellent precept for voyagers! And why not? After all, they climb Everest in gas-masks; at least, they do on the posters. Why not have some similar sort of apparatus, instruments of silence for the cabane? Surely Mr Unna could invent an ingenious device?

I wonder if it would matter very much if I murdered the Gardien quite quietly? He is probably insured. Not that it would be of much use, for another in all respects like unto him would take his place in the morning.

Hang it all! I MUST get to sleep! It is getting on for eleven o'clock by now: only two hours more, and then – breakfast and that infernal moraine. Perhaps if I try the counting game again . . .

One . . . Two . . . Three . . . Yes; we shall take quite three hours to reach the ridge. And then – how many hours? I wonder! Old Dübi is nearly lyrical about it: the stern decorum of topographical science is quite overcome; it has even compassed the majestic word 'anfractuosities' in its service; these are, apparently, numerous, and many of them are difficult (*varappe scabreuse*). Finally there will be an *arête de neige tranchante*, not seldom *garnie d'une corniche* – however, that part looked all right, as far as we could see. But, in any case, we shall have our work cut out; there will be more than one tense moment before we find the summit under foot and are at liberty to descend that glorious sweep of ridge which leads to the broad slopes beyond.

We shall . . . we shall . . .

What did you say, Raymond?

This valley, into which we are so unaccountably descending, seems strange to you? My good sir! Why – of
course – it's the . . . it's the . . . Well – funny thing – now
you come to mention it, it DOES seem a bit unfamiliar, even
to me . . . It must be . . . But – never mind – we shall soon
come upon things we recognise – when we get a little lower.

The curious part about it is that the Swiss map seems
wrong somehow. I've never known it happen before. It's
really quite extraordinary! We shall have to put a pithy little
note about it in the next *A.J.*: 'Alpine topography still
incomplete – lingering defects in Swiss maps – theory of
"wet" drinks among (dry) Federal surveyors.' It'll cause a
minor sensation! Theory questioned by Prof. X., angrily
pooh-poohed by the Rev. Y., supported by General Z., and
so on, to another merry controversy!

It is a very beautiful valley, Raymond! Those pastures –
what an exquisite shade of green! How deliciously cool will
be those woods after this furnace of a moraine . . .

We are going down – down – down the pathway under
the pines. The sunlight creeps stealthily in through the
leaves and spreads a quivering trellis-work of light at our
feet. Here and there little streams play hide-and-seek with
great moss-clad boulders, and gurgle happily under bushes
of alpen rose: we drink as we pass downward and are well
content. Anything may happen in these woods. We may
wander on for ever . . .

Hullo – what is this?

We have come to a clearing in the forest, a grassy glade
among the pines, and in the middle of it stands a large chalet,
many windowed, generously roofed, and richly carved about
the corners and under the eaves. The very sight of the place is
an invitation. The perfect valley must possess a perfect inn.
We approach and enter as a matter of course. We have
scarcely crossed the threshold before a stately old man, clad
in flowing robes of purple edged with gold, comes forward to
meet us with a smile of welcome. Strange . . . but it is almost
certainly the concierge. We murmur the usual phrases about
food and beds. 'But yes, Messieurs, everything is prepared!
The Messieurs will surely bathe before they sit down to eat?
All is in readiness. Excusez.' With the utmost deference he

relieves us of our axes and sacks. If we will be so good as to follow him. He leads the way down several passages, and then, opening a door suddenly, ushers us into a darkened chamber. As soon as our eyes grow accustomed to the gloom, we see that it is a beautifully appointed *chambre de bain*, floored with black marble, and in the centre is a circular pool of clear water from which the steam is rising softly to fill the chamber with a delicious perfume, as of a garden of roses on summer's morning. 'Messieurs will take an *apéritif* while they prepare for the bath . . . and a cigarette, perhaps?' 'Certainly we will, mon ami!' Silent-footed attendants appear from out the shadows, bearing stimulating drinks. Hastily we shed our clothing and leap into the pool. The temperature is perfect; we abandon ourselves to an ecstasy of physical well-being and delight.

Dimly I am aware of Raymond's sun-burnt visage, like a great blood-orange, floating in a cloud of steam.

'Ah!' says he, in a deep languorous voice, 'this is wonderful! Amazingly . . . incredibly . . . wonderful.'

The bath is over. The attendants bring us clean raiment, soft and very pleasant to the touch. I dress myself at leisure. Then I wander out into a spacious hall. Through a curtained doorway I get a peep into an inner room which is full of light. A magnificent banquet is being prepared within! The table groans under great bowls of silver filled with flowers and luscious fruits: melons, grapes, figs, peaches, and pomegranates. Numberless little dishes are there also, laden with the trifles which toy with the palate at unimportant intervals. From somewhere underground there comes the inviting aroma of savoury meat well cooked. Comely maidens pass with beakers of sparkling wine.

'This,' I find myself murmuring, 'is a fit reward of toil. This must be the climber's Valhalla.'

Hark!

That will be the dinner gong! The feast is about to begin. I feel I possess a hunger worthy of the occasion. We will go in. The sound of the gong is faint at first; it has a deep note, soft and seemingly distant. How sweetly it rouses the echoes of that sombre hall! Then it grows louder and more shrill; louder yet – until now it is drumming in my ears.

Ding-dong – ding-dong – ding-dong – ding-ding-ding-ding-ding . . .

DAMN!!

Where are my matches? Stop that infernal din, will you? I'm awake. One o'clock.

Through the window of the hut I can see a cold, triangular wedge of stars. It is a perfect night.

I tumble out of bed and start to light the fire. There is a stir among Raymond's blankets; he sits up and rubs his eyes. Has he, too, I wonder, been piped out of Elysium on the note of the alarm?

The Frying-pan and the Fire

The Duke of Burminster's story in *The Runagates Club* (1928), first appeared as 'Human Quarry' in *Pall Mall Magazine* in April 1928, and with its theme of degenerate middle age and a sporting bet there are certain parallels with *John Macnab* (1925), though closer analogies might be made with the Dickson McCunn trilogy. In it Burminster explains just how he came to appear on the station at Langshiels with a muddy face, a scratched nose, dressed in a strange assortment of torn clothes and was then escorted by a band to a political meeting in the Town Hall.

From the Bath, in its most exotic form, degenerate patrician youth passed to the coarse delights of the Circus, and thence to that parody of public duties which it was still the fashion of their class to patronise.

VON LETTERBECK: Imperial Rome

I THE FRYING-PAN

Lamancha had been staying for the week-end at some country house, and had returned full of wrath at the way he had been made to spend his evenings. 'I thought I hated bridge,' he said, 'but I almost longed for it as a change from cracking my brain and my memory to find lines from poets I had forgotten to describe people I didn't know. I don't like games that make me feel a congenital idiot. But there was one that rather amused me. You invented a preposterous situation and the point was to explain naturally how it came about. Drink, lunacy and practical joking were barred as explanations. One problem given was the Bishop of London on a camel, with a string of sea-trout round his neck, playing on a penny whistle on the Hoe at Plymouth. There was a fellow there, a Chancery K.C., who provided a perfectly sensible explanation.'

'I have heard of stranger things,' said Sandy Arbuthnot, and he winked at Burminster, who flushed and looked uncomfortable. As the rest of our eyes took the same direction the flush deepened on that round cheerful face.

'It's no good, Mike,' said Arbuthnot. 'We've been waiting months for that story of yours, and this is the place and the hour for it. We'll take no denial.'

'Confound you, Sandy, I can't tell it. It's too dashed silly.'

'Not a bit of it. It's full of profound philosophical lessons, and it's sheer romance, as somebody has defined the thing – strangeness flowering from the commonplace. So pull up your socks and get going.'

'I don't know how to begin,' said Burminster.

'Well, I'll start it for you . . . The scene is the railway station of Langshiels on the Scottish Borders on a certain day last summer. On the platform are various gentlemen in their best clothes with rosettes in their buttonholes – all strictly sober, it being but the third hour of the afternoon. There are also the rudiments of a brass band. Clearly a distinguished visitor is expected. The train enters the station, and from a third-class carriage descends our only Mike with a muddy face and a scratched nose. He is habited in dirty white cord breeches, shocking old butcher boots, a purple knitted waistcoat, and what I believe is called a morning coat; over all this splendour a ticky ulster – clearly not his own since it does not meet – and on his head an unspeakable bowler hat. He is welcomed by the deputation and departs, attended by the band, to a political meeting in the Town Hall. But first – I quote from the local paper – "The Duke, who had arrived in sporting costume, proceeded to the Station Hotel, where he rapidly changed." We want to know the reason of these cantrips.'

Burminster took a long pull at his tankard, and looked round the company with more composure.

'It isn't much of a story, but it's true, and, like nearly every scrape I ever got into, Archie Roylance was at the bottom of it. It all started from a discussion I had with Archie. He was staying with me at Larristane, and we got talking about the old Border raiders and the way the face of the countryside had changed and that sort of thing. Archie said that, now the land was as bare as a marble-topped table and there was no cover on the hills to hide a tomtit, a man couldn't ride five miles anywhere between the Cheviots and the Clyde without being seen by a dozen people. I said that there was still plenty of cover if you knew how to use it – that you could hide yourself as well on bent and heather as in a thick wood if you studied the shadows and the lie of the land, same as an aeroplane can hide itself in an empty sky. Well, we argued and argued, and the upshot was that I backed myself to ride an agreed course, without Archie spotting me. There wasn't much money on it – only an even sovereign – but we both worked ourselves up into considerable keenness. That was where I fell down. I might have known that anything Archie was keen about would end in the soup.

'The course we fixed was about fifteen miles long, from Gledfoot bridge over the hills between Gled and Aller and the Blae Moor to the Mains of Blae. That was close to Kirk Aller, and we agreed, if we didn't meet before, to foregather at the Cross Keys and have tea and motor home. Archie was to start from a point about four miles north-east of Gledfoot and cut in on my road at a tangent. I could shape any course I liked, but I couldn't win unless I got to the Mains of Blae before five o'clock without being spotted. The rule about that was that he must get within speaking distance of me – say three hundred yards – before he held me up. All the Larristane horses were at grass, so we couldn't look for pace. I chose an old hunter of mine that was very leery about bogs; Archie picked a young mare that I had hunted the season before and that he had wanted to buy from me. He said that by rights he ought to have the speedier steed, since, if he spotted me, he had more or less to ride me down.

'We thought it was only a pleasant summer day's diversion. I didn't want to give more than a day to it, for I had guests arriving that evening, and on the Wednesday – this was a Monday – I had to take the chair for Deloraine at a big Conservative meeting at Langshiels, and I meant to give a lot of time to preparing a speech. I ought to say that neither of us knew the bit of country beyond its general lines, and we were forbidden to carry maps. The horses were sent on, and at 9.30 a.m. I was at Gledfoot bridge ready to start. I was wearing khaki riding breeches, polo boots, an old shooting coat and a pretty old felt hat. I mention my costume, for later it became important.

'I may as well finish with Archie, for he doesn't come any more into this tale. He hadn't been half an hour in the saddle when he wandered into a bog, and it took him till three in the afternoon to get his horse out. Consequently he chucked in his hand, and went back to Larristane. So all the time I was riding cunning and watching out of my right eye to see him on the skyline he was sweating and blaspheming in a peat moss.

'I started from Gledfoot up the Rinks burn in very good spirits, for I had been studying the big Ordnance map and I believed I had a soft thing. Beyond the Rinks Hope I would cross the ridge to the top of the Skyre burn, which at its head is all split up into deep grassy gullies. I had guessed this from the map, and the people at Gledfoot had confirmed it. By one or other of these gullies I could ride in good cover till I reached a big wood of firs that stretched for a mile down the left bank of the burn. Archie, to cut in on me, had a pretty steep hill to cross, and I calculated that by the time he got on the skyline I would be in the shelter of one of the gullies or even behind the wood. Not seeing me on the upper Skyre, he would think that I had bustled a bit and would look for me lower down the glen. I would lie doggo and watch for him, and when I saw him properly started I meant to slip up a side burn and get into the parallel glen of the Hollin. Once there I would ride like blazes, and either get to the Blae Moor before him – in which case I would simply canter at ease up to the Mains of Blae – or, if I saw him ahead of me, fetch a circuit among the plantings and come in on the farm from the other side. That was the general layout, but I had other dodges in hand in case Archie tried to be clever.

'So I tittuped along the hill turf beside the Rinks burn, feeling happy and pretty certain I would win. My horse, considering he was fresh from the grass, behaved very well, and we travelled in good style. My head was full of what I was going to say at Langshiels, and I thought of some rather fine things – "Our opponents would wreck the old world in order to build a new, but you cannot found any system on chaos, not even Communism" – I rather fancied that. Well, to make a long story short, I got to the Rinks Hope in thirty minutes, and there I found the herd gathering his black-faced lambs.

'Curiously enough I knew the man – Prentice they called him – for he had been one of the young shepherds at Larristane. So I stopped to have a word with him, and watched him at work. He was short-handed for the job, and he had a young collie only half-trained, so I offered to give him a hand and show my form as a mounted stockman. The top of that glen was splendid going, and I volunteered to round up the west hirsel. I considered that I had plenty of time and could spare ten minutes to help a pal.

'It was a dashed difficult job, and it took me a good half-hour, and it was a mercy my horse didn't get an over-reach among the mossy well-heads. However, I did it, and when I started off again both I and my beast were in a lather of sweat. That must have confused me, and the way I had been making circles round the sheep, for I struck the wrong feeder, and instead of following the one that led to the top of the Skyre burn I kept too much to my left. When I got to the watershed I looked down on a country utterly different from what I had expected. There was no delta of deep gullies, but a broad green cup seamed with stone walls, and below it a short glen which presently ran out into the broader vale of the Aller.

'The visibility was none too good, so I could not make out the further prospect. I ought to have realised that this was not the Skyre burn. But I only concluded that I had misread the map, and besides, there was a big wood lower down which I thought was the one I had remarked. There was no sign of Archie as yet on the high hills to my right, so I decided I had better get off the skyline and make my best speed across that bare green cup.

'It took me a long time, for I had a lot of trouble with the stone dykes. The few gates were all fastened up with wire, and I couldn't manage to undo them. So I had to scramble over the first dyke, and half pull down the next, and what with one thing and another I wasted a shocking amount of time. When I got to the bottom I found that the burn was the merest trickle, not the strong stream of the Skyre, which is a famous water for trout. But there, just ahead of me, was the big wood, so I decided I must be right after all.

'I had kept my eye lifting to the ridge on the right, and suddenly I saw Archie. I know now that it wasn't he, but it was a man on a horse and it looked his living image. He was well down the hillside and he was moving fast. He didn't appear to have seen me, but I realised that he would in a minute, unless I found cover.

'I jogged my beast with the spur, and in three seconds was under cover of the fir-wood. But here I found a track, and it struck me that it was this track which Archie was following, and that he would soon be up with me. The only thing to do seemed to be to get inside the wood. But this was easier said than done, for a great wall with broken bottles on the top ran round that blessed place. I had to do something pretty quick, for I could hear the sound of hoofs behind me, and on the left there was nothing but the benty side of a hill

'Just then I saw a gate, a massive thing of close-set oak splints, and for a mercy it was open. I pushed through it and slammed it behind me. It shut with a sharp click as if it was a patent self-locking arrangement. A second later I heard the noise of a horse outside and hands trying the gate. Plainly they couldn't open it. The man I thought was Archie said "Damn" and moved away.

'I had found sanctuary, but the question now was how to get out of it. I dismounted and wrestled with the gate, but it was as firm as a rock. About this time I began to realise that something was wrong, for I couldn't think why Archie should have wanted to get through the gate if he hadn't seen me, and, if he had seen me, why he hadn't shouted, according to our rules. Besides, this wasn't a wood, it was the grounds of some house, and the map had shown no house in the Skyre glen . . . The only thing to do was to find someone to let me out. I didn't like the notion of riding about in a stranger's policies, so I knotted my bridle and let my beast graze, while I proceeded on foot to prospect.

'The ground shelved steeply, and almost at once my feet went from under me and I slithered down a bank of raw earth. You see there was no grip in the smooth soles of my polo boots. The next I knew I had banged hard into the back of a little wooden shelter which stood on a sunny mantelpiece of turf above the stream. I picked myself up and limped round the erection, rubbing the dirt from my eyes, and came face to face with a group of people.

'They were all women, except one man, who was reading aloud to them, and they were all lying in long chairs. Pretty girls they seemed to be from the glimpse I had of them, but rather pale, and they all wore bright-coloured cloaks.

'I daresay I looked a bit of a ruffian, for I was very warm and had got rather dirty in slithering down, and had a rent in my breeches. At the sight of me the women gave one collective bleat like a snipe, and gathered up their skirts and ran. I could see their cloaks glimmering as they dodged like woodcock among the rhododendrons.

'The man dropped his book and got up and faced me. He was a young fellow with a cadaverous face and side-whiskers, and he seemed to be in a funk of something, for his lips twitched and his hands shook as if he had fever. I could see that he was struggling to keep calm.

'"So you've come back, Mr Brumby," he said. "I hope you had a g-good time?"

'For a moment I had a horrid suspicion that he knew me, for they used to call me "Brummy" at school. A second look convinced me that we had never met, and I realised that the word he had used was Brumby. I hadn't a notion what he meant, but the only thing seemed to be to brazen it out. That was where I played the fool. I ought to have explained my mistake there and then, but I still had the notion that Archie was hanging about, and I wanted to dodge him. I dropped into a long chair, and said that I had come back and that it was a pleasant day. Then I got out my pipe.

'"Here, you mustn't do that," he said, "It isn't allowed."

'I put my pipe away, and wondered what lunatic asylum I had wandered into. I wasn't permitted to wonder long, for up the path from the rhododendrons came two people in a mighty hurry. One was an anxious-faced oldish man dressed like a valet, and the other a middle-aged woman in nurse's uniform. Both seemed to be excited, and both to be trying to preserve an air of coolness.

'"Ah, Schwester," said the fellow with the whiskers. "Here is Mr Brumby back again and none the worse."

'The woman, who had kind eyes and a nice gurgling voice, looked at me reproachfully.

'"I hope you haven't taken any harm, sir," she said. "We had better go back to the house, and Mr Grimpus will give you a nice bath and a change, and you'll lie down a bit before luncheon. You must be very tired, sir. You'd better take Mr Grimpus's arm."

'My head seemed to be spinning, but I thought it best to lie low and do what I was told till I got some light. Silly ass that I was, I was still on the tack of dodging Archie. I could easily have floored Grimpus, and the man with the whiskers wouldn't have troubled me much, but there was still the glass-topped wall to get over, and there might be heftier people about, grooms and gardeners and the like. Above all, I didn't want to make any more scenes, for I had already scared a lot of sick ladies into the rhododendrons.

'So I went off quite peaceably with Grimpus and the sister, and presently we came to a house like a small hydropathic, hideously ugly but beautifully placed, with a view south to the Aller Valley. There were more nurses in the hall and a porter with a jaw like a prize-fighter. Well, I went up in a lift to the second floor, and there was a bedroom and a balcony, and several trunks, and brushes on the dressing-table lettered H. B. They made me strip and get into a dressing-gown, and then a doctor arrived, a grim fellow with gold spectacles and a soft, bedside manner. He spoke to me soothingly about the beauty of the weather and how the heather would soon be in bloom on the hill; he also felt my pulse and took my blood pressure, and talked for a long time in a corner with the sister. If he said there was anything wrong with me he lied, for I had never felt fitter in my life except for the bewilderment of my brain.

'Then I was taken down in a lift to the basement, and Grimpus started out to give me a bath. My hat! That was a bath! I lay in six inches of scalding water, while a boiling cataract beat on my stomach; then it changed to hot hail and then to gouts that hit like a pickaxe; and then it all turned to ice. But it made me feel uncommonly frisky. After that they took me back to my bedroom and I had a gruelling massage, and what I believe they call violet rays. By this time I was fairly bursting with vim, but I thought it best to be quite passive, and when they told me I must try to sleep before luncheon, I only grinned and put my head on the pillow like a child. When they left me I badly wanted to smoke, but my pipe had gone with my clothes, and I found laid out for me a complete suit of the man Brumby's flannels.

'As I lay and reflected I began to get my bearings. I knew where I was. It was a place called Craigiedean, about six miles from Kirk Aller, which had been used as a shell-shock hospital during the War and had been kept on as a home for nervous cases. It wasn't a private asylum, as I had thought at first; it called itself a Kurhaus, and was supposed to be the last thing in science outside Germany. Now and then, however, it got some baddish cases, people who were almost off their rocker, and I fancied that Brumby was one. He was apparently my double, but I didn't believe in exact doubles, so I guessed that he had just arrived, and hadn't given the staff time to know him well before he went off on the bend. The horseman whom I had taken for Archie must have been out scouring the hills for him.

'Well, I had dished Archie all right, but I had also dished myself. At any moment the real Brumby might wander back, and then there would be a nice show up. The one thing that terrified me was that my identity should be discovered, for this was more or less my own country-side, and I should look a proper ass if it got about that I had been breaking into a nerve-cure place, frightening women, and getting myself treated like a gentle loony. Then I remembered that my horse was in the wood and might be trusted to keep on grazing along the inside of the wall where nobody went. My best plan seemed to be to wait my chance, slip out of the house, recover my beast and find some way out of the infernal park. The wall couldn't be everywhere, for after all the place wasn't an asylum.

'A gong sounded for luncheon, so I nipped up, and got into Brumby's flannels. They were all right for length, but a bit roomy. My money and the odds and ends from my own pockets were laid out on the dressing-table, but not my pipe and pouch, which I judged had been confiscated.

'I wandered downstairs to a big dining-room, full of little tables, with the most melancholy outfit seated at them that you ever saw in all your days. The usual thing was to have a table to oneself, but sometimes two people shared one – husband and wife, no doubt, or mother and daughter. There were eight males including me, and the rest were females of every age from flappers to grand-mothers. Some looked pretty sick, some quite blooming, but all had a watchful air, as if they were holding themselves in and pursuing some strict regime. There was no conversation, and everybody had brought a book or a magazine which they diligently studied. In the centre of each table, beside the salt and pepper, stood a little fleet of medicine bottles. The sister who led me to my place planted down two beside me.

'I soon saw the reason of the literary absorption. The food was simply bestial. I was hungry and thirsty enough to have eaten two beefsteaks and drunk a quart of beer, and all I got was three rusks, a plate of thin soup, a purée of vegetables and a milk pudding in a teacup. I envied the real Brumby, who at that moment, if he had any sense, was doing himself well in a public-house. I didn't dare to ask for more in case of inviting awkward questions, so I had plenty of leisure to observe the company. Nobody looked at anybody else, for it seemed to be the fashion to pretend you were alone in a wilderness, and even the couples did not talk to each other. I made a cautious preliminary survey to see if there was anyone I knew, but they were all strangers. After a time I felt so lonely that I wanted to howl.

'At last the company began to get up and straggle out. The sister whom I had seen first – the others called her Schwester and she seemed to be rather a boss – appeared with a bright smile and gave me my medicine. I had to take

two pills and some horrid drops out of a brown bottle. I
pretended to be very docile, and I thought that I'd take the
chance to pave the way to getting to my horse. So I said that
I felt completely rested, and would like a walk that afternoon. She shook her head.

'"No, Mr Brumby. Dr Miggle's orders are positive that
you rest today."

'"But I'm feeling really very fit," I protested. "I'm the
kind of man who needs a lot of exercise."

'"Not yet," she said with a patient smile. "At present
your energy is morbid. It comes from an irregular nervous
complex, and we must first cure that before you can lead a
normal life. Soon you'll be having nice long walks. You
promised your wife, you know, to do everything that you
were told, and it was very wrong of you to slip out last night
and make us all so anxious. Dr Miggle says that must *never*
happen again." And she wagged a reproving finger.

'So I had a wife to add to my troubles. I began now to be really
worried, for not only might Brumby turn up any moment, but
his precious spouse, and I didn't see how I was to explain to her
what I was doing in her husband's trousers. Also the last
sentence disquieted me. Dr Miggle was determined that I
should not bolt again, and he looked a resolute lad. That
meant that I would be always under observation, and that at
night my bedroom door would be locked.

'I made an errand to go up to my room, while Grimpus
waited for me in the hall, and had a look at the window.
There was a fine thick Virginia creeper which would make it
easy to get to the floor beneath, but it was perfectly
impossible to reach the ground, for below was a great
chasm of a basement. There was nothing doing that
way, unless I went through the room beneath, and that
meant another outrage and probably an appalling row.

'I felt very dispirited as I descended the stairs, till I saw a
woman coming out of that identical room . . . Blessed if it
wasn't my Aunt Letitia!

'I needn't have been surprised, for she gave herself out as
a martyr to nerves, and was always racing about the world
looking for a cure. She saw me, took me for Brumby, and
hurried away. Evidently Brumby's doings had got about,

and there were suspicions of his sanity. The moment was not propitious for following her, since Grimpus was looking at me.

'I was escorted to the terrace by Grimpus, tucked up in a long chair, and told to stay there and bask in the sun. I must not read, but I could sleep if I liked. I never felt less like slumber, for I was getting to be a very good imitation of a mental case. I must get hold of Aunt Letitia. I could see her in her chair at the other end of the terrace, but if I got up and went to her she would take me for that loony Brumby and have a fit.

'I lay cogitating and baking in the sun for about two hours. Then I observed that sisters were bringing out tea or medicines to some of the patients and I thought I saw a chance of a move. I called one of them to me, and in a nice invalidish voice complained that the sun was too hot for me and that I wanted to be moved to the other end where there was more shade. The sister went off to find Grimpus and presently that sportsman appeared.

' "I've had enough to this sun-bath," I told him, "and I feel a headache coming. I want you to shift me to the shade of the beeches over there."

' "Very good, sir," he said, and helped me to rise, while he picked up chair and rugs. I tottered delicately after him, and indicated a vacant space next to Aunt Letitia. She was dozing, and mercifully did not see me. The chair on my other side was occupied by an old gentleman who was sound asleep.

'I waited for a few minutes and began to wriggle my chair a bit nearer. Then I made a pellet of earth from a crack in the paving stones and jerked it neatly on to her face.

' "Hist!" I whispered. "Wake up, Aunt Letty."

'She opened one indignant eye, and turned it on me, and I thought she was going to swoon.

' "Aunt Letty," I said in an agonised voice. "For Heaven's sake don't shout. I'm not Brumby. I'm your nephew Michael."

'Her nerves were better than I thought, for she managed to take a pull on herself and listen to me while I muttered my tale. I could see that she hated the whole affair, and had some kind of grievance against me for outraging the sanctity of her pet cure. However, after a bit of parleying, she behaved like a brick.

' "You are the head of our family, Michael," she said, "and I am bound to help you out of the position in which your own rashness has placed you. I agree with you that it is essential to have no disclosure of identity. It is the custom here for patients to retire to their rooms at eight-thirty. At nine o'clock I shall have my window open, and if you enter by it you can leave by the door. That is the most I can do for you. Now please be silent, for I am ordered to be very still for an hour before tea."

'You can imagine that after that the time went slowly. Grimpus brought me a cup of tea and a rusk, and I fell asleep and only woke when he came at half-past six to escort me indoors. I would have given pounds for a pipe. Dinner was at seven, and I said that I would not trouble to change, though Brumby's dress-clothes were laid out on the bed. I had the needle badly, for I had a horrid fear that Brumby might turn up before I got away.

'Presently the doctor arrived, and after cooing over me a bit and feeling my pulse, he started out to cross-examine me about my past life. I suppose that was to find out the subconscious complexes which were upsetting my wits. I decided to go jolly carefully, for I suspected that he had either given Brumby the once-over or had got some sort of report about his case. I was right, for the first thing he asked me was about striking my sister at the age of five. Well, I haven't got a sister, but I had to admit to beating Brumby's, and I said the horrible affair still came between me and my sleep. That seemed to puzzle him, for apparently I oughtn't to have been thinking about it; it should have been buried deep in my unconscious self, and worrying me like a thorn in your finger which you can't find. He asked me a lot about my nurse, and I said that she had a brother who went to gaol for sheep stealing. He liked that, and said it was a fruitful line of inquiry. Also he wanted to know about my dreams, and said I should write them down. I said I had dreamed that a mare called Nursemaid won the Oaks, but found there was no such animal running. That cheered him up a bit, and he said that he thought my nurse might be the clue. At that I very nearly gave the show away by laughing, for my nurse was old Alison Hyslop, who is now the housekeeper at Larristane, and if anybody called her a clue she'd have their blood.

'Dinner was no better than luncheon – the same soup and rusks and vegetables, with a bit of ill-nourished chicken added. This time I had to take three kinds of medicine instead of two. I told the sister that I was very tired, and Grimpus took me upstairs at eight o'clock. He said that Dr Miggle proposed to give me another go of violet rays, but I protested so strongly that I was too sleepy for his ministrations that Grimpus, after going off to consult him, announced that for that evening the rays would be omitted. You see I was afraid that they would put me to bed and remove my clothes, and I didn't see myself trapesing about the country in Brumby's pyjamas.

'As Grimpus left me I heard the key turn in the lock. It was as well that I had made a plan with Aunt Letitia.

'At nine o'clock I got out of my window. It was a fine night, with the sun just setting and a young moon. The Virginia creeper was sound, and in less than a minute I was outside Aunt Letitia's window. She was waiting in a dressing-gown to let me in, and I believe the old soul really enjoyed the escapade. She wanted to give me money for my travels, but I told her that I had plenty. I poked my nose out, saw that the staircase and hall were empty, and quietly closed the door behind me.

'The big hall door was shut, and I could hear the prize-fighting porter moving in his adjacent cubby hole. There was no road that way, so I turned to the drawing-room, which opened on the terrace. But that was all in darkness, and I guessed that the windows were shuttered. There was nothing for it but to try downstairs. I judged that the servants would be at supper, so I went through a green-baize swing-door and down a long flight of stone steps.

'Suddenly I blundered into a brightly lit kitchen. There was no one in it, and beyond was a door which looked as if it might lead to the open air. It actually led to a scullery, where a maid was busy at a tap. She was singing to herself a song called "When the kye come hame", so I knew she belonged to the countryside. So did I, and I resolved to play the bold game.

' "Hey, lassie," I said. "Whaur's the road out o' this hoose? I maun be back in Kirk Aller afore ten."

'The girl stopped her singing and stared at me. Then in response to my grin she laughed.

' "Are ye frae Kirk Aller?" she asked.

' "I've gotten a job there," I said. "I'm in the Cally station, and I cam' up about a parcel for ane o' the leddies here. But I come frae further up the water, Larristane way."

' "D'ye say sae? I'm frae Gledside mysel'. What gars ye be in sic a hurry? It's a fine nicht and there's a mune."

'She was a flirtatious damsel, but I had no time for dalliance.

' "There's a lassie in Kirk Aller will take the heid off me if I keep her waitin'."

'She tossed her head and laughed, "Haste ye then, my mannie. Is it Shanks' powny?"

' "Na, na, I've a bicycle ootbye."

' "Well, through the wash-hoose and up the steps and roond by the roddydendrums and ye're in the yaird. Guid nicht to ye."

'I went up the steps like a lamplighter and dived into the rhododendrons, coming out on the main avenue. It ran long and straight to the lodge gates, and I didn't like the look of it. My first business was to find my horse, and I had thought out more or less the direction. The house stood on the right bank of the burn, and if I kept to my left I would cross the said burn lower down and could then walk up the other side. I did this without trouble. I forded the burn in the meadow, and was soon climbing the pinewood which clothed the gorge. In less than twenty minutes I had reached the gate in the wall by which I had entered.

'There was no sign of my horse anywhere. I followed the wall on my left till it curved round and crossed the burn, but the beast was not there, and it was too dark to look for hoof-marks. I tried to my right and got back to the level of the park, but had no better luck. If I had had any sense I would have given up the quest, and trusted to getting as far as Gledsfoot on my own feet. The horse might be trusted to turn up in his own time. Instead I went blundering on in the half-light of the park, and presently blundered into trouble.

'Grimpus must have paid another visit to my room, found me gone, seen the open window, and started a hue-and-cry. They would not suspect my Aunt Letitia, and must have thought that I had dropped like a cat into the basement. The pursuit was coming down the avenue, thinking I had made for the lodge gates, and as ill-luck would have it, I had selected that moment to cross the drive, and they spotted me. I remember that out of a corner of one eye I saw the lights of a fly coming up the drive, and I wondered if Brumby had selected this inauspicious moment to return.

'I fled into the park with three fellows after me. Providence never meant me for a long-distance runner, and, besides, I was feeling weak from lack of nourishment. But I was so scared of what would happen if I was caught that I legged it like a miler, and the blighters certainly didn't gain on me.

'But what I came to was the same weary old wall with the bottle glass on the top of it. I was pretty desperate, and I thought I saw a way. A young horse-chestnut tree grew near the wall and one bough overhung it. I made a jump at the first branch, caught it, and with a bit of trouble swung myself up into the crutch. This took time, and one of the fellows came up and made a grab at my leg, but I let him have Brumby's rubber-soled heel in the jaw.

'I caught the bigger branch and wriggled along it till I was above and beyond the wall. Then the dashed thing broke with my twelve stone, and I descended on what looked like a highroad.

'There was no time to spare, though I was a bit shaken, for the pursuit would not take long to follow me. I started off down that road looking for shelter, and I found it almost at once. There was a big covered horse-van moving ahead of me, with a light showing from the interior. I sprinted after it, mounted the step and stuck my head inside.

'"Can I come in?" I panted. "Hide me for ten minutes and I'll explain."

'I saw an old, spectacled, whiskered face. It was portentously solemn, but I thought I saw a twinkle in the eye.

' "Ay," said a toothless mouth, "ye can come in." A hand grabbed my collar, and I was hauled inside. That must have been just when the first of my pursuers dropped over the wall.'

II THE FIRE

'I had got into a caravan which was a sort of bedroom, and behind the driver's seat was a double curtain. There I made myself inconspicuous while the old man parleyed with the pursuit.

' "Hae ye seen a gentleman?" I could hear a panting voice. "Him that drappit ower the wa'? He was rinnin' hard."

' "What kind of a gentleman?"

' "He had on grey claithes – aboot the same height as mysel'." The speaker was not Grimpus.

' "Naebody passed me," was the strictly truthful answer. "Ye'd better seek the ither side o' the road among the bracken. There's plenty hidy-holes there. Wha's the man?"

' "Ane o' the doctor's folk." I knew, though I could not see, that the man had tapped his forehead significantly. "Aweel, I'll try back. Guid nicht to ye."

'I crept out of my refuge and found the old man regarding me solemnly under the swinging lamp.

' "I'm one of the auld-fashioned Radicals," he announced, "and I'm for the liberty o' the individual. I dinna hold wi' lockin' folks up because a pernicketty doctor says they're no wise. But I'd be glad to be assured, sir, that ye're not a dangerous lunattic. If ye are, Miggle has nae business to be workin' wi' lunattics. His hoose is no an asylum."

' "I'm as sane as you are," I said, and as shortly as I could I told him my story. I said I was a laird on Gledwater-side – which was true, and that my name was Brown – which wasn't. I told him about my bet with Archie and my ride and its disastrous ending. His face never moved a muscle; probably he didn't believe me, but because of his political principles he wasn't going to give me away.

' "Ye can bide the night with me," he said. "The morn we'll be busy and ye can gang wherever ye like. It's a free country in spite o' our God-forsaken Government."

'I blessed him, and asked to whom I was indebted for this hospitality.

' "I'm the Great McGowan," he said. "The feck o' the pawraphernalia is on ahead. We open the morn in Kirk Aller."

'He had spoken his name as if it were Mussolini or Dempsey, one which all the world should know. I knew it too, for it had been familiar to me from childhood. You could have seen it any time in the last twenty years flaming upon hoardings up and down the Lowlands – The Great McGowan's Marvellous Multitudinous Menagerie – McGowan's Colossal Circassian Circus – The Only Original McGowan.

'We rumbled on for another half-mile, and then turned from the road into a field. As we bumped over the grass I looked out of the door and saw about twenty big caravans and wagons at anchor. There was a strong smell of horses and of cooking food, and above it I seemed to detect the odour of unclean beasts. We took up our station apart from the rest, and after the proprietor had satisfied himself by a brief inspection that the whole outfit was there, he announced that it was time to retire. Mr McGowan had apparently dined, and he did not offer me food, which I would have welcomed, but he mixed me a rummer of hot toddy. I wondered if it would disagree with the various medicines I had been compelled to take, and make me very sick in the night. Then he pointed out my bunk, undressed himself as far as his shirt, pulled a nightcap over his venerable head, and in five minutes was asleep. I had had a wearing day, and in spite of the stuffiness of the place it wasn't long before I dropped off also.

'I awoke next morning to find myself alone in the caravan. I opened the window and saw that a fine old racket was going on. The show had started to move, and as the caravan bumped over the turf various specimens inside were beginning to give tongue. It was going to be a gorgeous day and very hot. I was a little bit anxious about my next move, for Kirk Aller was unpleasantly near Craigiedean and Dr Miggle. In the end I decided that my best plan would be to take the train to Langshiels and there hire a car to Larristane, after sending a telegram to say I was all right, in case my riderless steed should turn up before me. I hadn't any headgear, but I thought I could buy something in Kirk Aller, and trust to luck that nobody from the Kurhaus spotted me in the street. I wanted a bath and a shave and breakfast, but I concluded I had better postpone them till I reached the hotel at Langshiels.

'Presently Mr McGowan appeared, and I could see by his face that something had upset him. He was wearing an old check dressing-gown, and he had been padding about in his bare feet on the dewy grass.

' "Ye told me a story last night, Mr Brown," he began solemnly, "which I didna altogether believe. I apologise for being a doubting Thomas. I believe every word o't, for I've just had confirmation."

'I mumbled something about being obliged to him, and he went on.

' "Ay, for the pollis were here this morning – seeking you. Yon man at Craigiedean is terrible ill-set against ye, Mr Brown. The pollisman – his name's Tam Doig, I ken him fine – says they're looking for a man that personated an inmate, and went off wi' some o' the inmate's belongings. I'm quotin' Tam Doig. I gave Tam an evasive answer, and he's off on his bicycle the other road, but – I ask ye as a freend, Mr Brown – what is precisely the facts o' the case?"

' "Good God!" I said. "It's perfectly true. These clothes I'm wearing belong to the man Brumby, though they've got my own duds in exchange. He must have come back after I left. What an absolutely infernal mess! I suppose they could have me up for theft."

' "Mair like obtaining goods on false pretences, though I think ye have a sound answer. But that's no the point, Mr Brown. The doctor is set on payin' off scores. Ye've entered his sawnatorium and gone through a' the cantrips he provides, and ye've made a gowk o' him. He wants to make an example o' *you*. Tam Doig was sayin' that he's been bleezin' half the night on the telephone, an' he'll no rest till ye're grippit. Now ye tell me that ye're a laird and a man o' some poseetion, and I believe ye. It wad be an ill job for you and your freends if ye was to appear before the Shirra."

'I did some rapid thinking. So far I was safe, for there was nothing about the clothes I had left behind to identify me. I was pretty certain that my horse had long ago made a bee-line for the Larristane stables. If I could only get home without being detected, I might regard the episode as closed.

' "Supposing I slip off now," I said. "I have a general notion of the land, and I might get over the hills without anybody seeing me."

'He shook his head. "Ye wouldn't travel a mile. Your description has been circulated and a' body's lookin' for ye – a man in a grey flannel suit and soft shoes wi' a red face and nae hat. Guid kens what the doctor has said about ye, but the countryside is on the look-out for a dangerous, and maybe lunattic, criminal. There's a reward offered of nae less than twenty pound."

' "Can you not take me with you to Kirk Aller?" I asked despairingly.

' "Aye, ye can stop wi' me. But what better wad ye be in Kirk Aller? That's where the Procurator Fiscal bides."

'Then he put on his spectacles and looked at me solemnly.

' "I've taken a fancy to ye, Mr Brown, and ye can tell the world that. I ask you, are ye acquaint wi' horses?"

'I answered that I had lived among them all my life, and had been in the cavalry before I went into the Air Force.

' "I guessed it by your face. Horses have a queer trick o' leavin' their mark on a body. Now, because I like ye, I'll make a proposeetion to ye that I would make to no other man . . . I'm without a ring-master. Joseph Japp, who for ten years has had the job with me, is lyin' wi' the influenzy at Berwick. I could make shift with Dublin Davie, but Davie has no more presence than a messan dog, and forbye Joseph's clothes wouldna fit him. When I cast my eyes on ye this mornin' after hearin' Tam Doig's news, I says to mysel', 'Thou art the man.' "

'Of course I jumped at the offer. I was as safe in Kirk Aller, as Joseph Japp's understudy, as I was in my own house. Besides, I liked the notion; it would be a good story to tell Archie. But I said it could only be for one night, and that I must leave tomorrow, and he agreed. "I want to make a good show for a start in Kirk Aller – forbye, Joseph will be ready to join me at Langshiels."

'I borrowed the old boy's razor and had a shave and a wash, while he was cooking breakfast. After we had fed he fetched my predecessor's kit. It fitted me well enough, but Lord! I looked a proper blackguard. The cord breeches had been recently cleaned, but the boots were like a pair of dilapidated buckets, and the coat would have made my tailor weep. Mr McGowan himself put on a frock-coat and a high collar and spruced himself up till he looked exactly like one of those high-up Irish dealers you see at the Horse Show – a cross between a Cabinet Minister and a Methodist parson. He said the ring-master should ride beside the chief exhibit, so we bustled out and I climbed up in front of a wagon which bore a cage containing two very low-spirited lions. I was given a long whip, and told to make myself conspicuous.

'I didn't know Kirk Aller well, so I had no fear of being recognised either as myself or as the pseudo-Brumby. The last time I had been there was when I had motored over from Larristane to dine with the Aller Shooting Club. My present entry was of a more sensational kind. I decided to enjoy myself and to attract all the notice I could, and I certainly succeeded. Indeed, you might say I received an ovation. As it happened it was a public holiday, and the streets were pretty full. We rumbled up the cobbled Westgate, and down the long High Street, with the pavements on both sides lined with people and an attendant mob of several hundred children. The driver was a wizened little fellow in a jockey cap, but I was the principal figure on the box. I gave a fine exhibition with my whip, and when we slowed down I picked out conspicuous figures in the crowd and chaffed them. I thought I had better use Cockney patter, as being more in keeping with my job, and I made a happy blend of the table-talk of my stud-groom and my old batman in the regiment. It was rather a high-class performance and you'd be surprised how it went down. There was one young chap with a tremendous head of hair that I invited to join his friends in the cage, and just then one of the dejected lions let out a growl, and I said that Mamma was calling to her little Percy. And there was an old herd from the hills, who had been looking upon the wine-cup, and who, in a voice like a fog-horn, wanted to know what we fed the beasts on. Him I could not refrain from answering in his own tongue. "Braxy, my man," I cried, "The yowes ye lost when we were fou last Boswell's Fair." I must have got home somehow, for the crowd roared, and his friends thumped the old chap on the back and shouted: "That's a guid ane! He had you there, Tam."

'My triumphant procession came to an end on the Aller Green, where the show was to be held. A canvas palisade had been set up round a big stretch of ground, and the mob of children tailed off at the gate. Inside most of our truck had already arrived. The stadium for the circus had been marked off, and tiers of wooden seats were being hammered together. A big tent had been set up, which was to house the menagerie, and several smaller tents were in process of erection. I noticed that the members of the troupe looked at me curiously till Mr McGowan arrived and introduced me. "This is Mr Brown, a friend of mine," he said, "who will take on Joe Japp's job for the night." And, aside to me, "Man, I heard ye comin' down the High Street. Ye did fine. Ye're a great natural talent for the profession." After that we were all very friendly, and the whole company had a snack together in one of the tents – bread and cheese and bottled beer.

'The first thing I did was to make a bundle of Brumby's clothes, which Mr McGowan promised to send back to Craigiedean when the coast was clear. Then I bribed a small boy to take a telegram to the Post Office – to Archie at Larristane, saying I had been detained and hoped to return next day. After that I took off my coat and worked like a beaver. It was nearly six o'clock before we had everything straight, and the show opened at seven, so we were all a bit the worse for wear when we sat down to high tea. It's a hard job an artiste's, as old McGowan observed.

'I never met a queerer, friendlier, more innocent company, for the proprietor seemed to have set out to collect originals, and most of them had been with him for years. The boss of the menagerie was an ex-sailor, who had a remarkable way with beasts; he rarely spoke a word, but just grinned and whistled through broken teeth. The clown, who said his name was Sammle Dreep, came from Paisley, and was fat enough not to need the conventional bolster. Dublin Davie, my second in command, was a small Irishman who had been an ostler, and limped owing to having been with the Dublin Fusiliers at Gallipoli. The clown had a wife who ran the commissariat, when she wasn't appearing in the ring as Zenobia, the Pride of the Sahara. Then there were the Sisters Wido – a young married couple with two children; and the wife of a man who played the clarionet – figured in the bill as Elise the Equestrienne. I had a look at the horses, which were the ordinary skinny, broad-backed, circus ponies. I found out later that they were so well trained that I daresay they could have done their turns in the dark.

'At a quarter to seven we lit the naphtha flares and our orchestra started in. McGowan told me to get inside Japp's dress clothes, and rather unwillingly I obeyed him, for I had got rather to fancy my morning's kit. I found there was only a coat and waistcoat, for I was allowed to retain the top-boots and cords. Happily the shirt was clean, but I had a solitaire with a sham diamond as big as a shilling, and the cut of the coat would have been considered out-of-date by a self-respecting waiter in Soho. I had also a scarlet silk handkerchief to stuff in my bosom, a pair of dirty white kid gloves, and an immense coach whip.

'The menagerie was open, but that night the chief attraction was the circus, and I don't mind saying that about the best bit of the circus was myself. In one of the intervals McGowan insisted on shaking hands and telling me that I was wasted in any other profession than a showman's. The fact is I was rather above myself, and entered into what you might call the spirit of the thing. We had the usual Dick Turpin's ride to York, and an escape of Dakota Dan (one of the Sisters Wido) from Red Indians (the other Wido, Zenobia and Elise, with about a ton of feathers on their heads). The Equestrienne equestered, and the Widos hopped through hoops, and all the while I kept up my patter and spouted all the rot I could remember.

'The clown was magnificent. He had a Paisley accent you could have cut like a knife, but he prided himself on talking aristocratic English. He had a lot of badinage with Zenobia about her life in the desert. One bit I remember. She kept on referring to bulbuls, and asked him if he had ever seen a bull-bull. He said he had, for he supposed it was a male coo-coo. But he was happiest at my expense. I never heard a chap with such a flow of back-chat. A funny thing – but when he wasn't calling me "Little Pansy-face", he ad-dressed me as "Your Grace" and "Me Lord Dook", and hoped that the audience would forgive my négligé attire, seeing my coronet hadn't come back from the wash.

'Altogether the thing went down with a snap from beginning to end, and when old McGowan, all dressed up with a white waistcoat, made a speech at the end and explained about the next performances he got a perfect hurricane of applause. After that we had to tidy up. There was the usual trouble with several procrastinating drunks, who wanted to make a night of it. One of them got into the ring and tried to have a row with me. He was a big loutish fellow with small eyes and red hair, and had the look of a betting tout. He stuck his face close to mine and bellowed at me:

' "I ken ye fine, ye—! I seen ye at Lanerick last back-end . . . Ye ca'd yoursel' Gentleman Geordie, and ye went off wi' my siller. By God, I'll get it out o' ye, ye— welsher."

'I told him that he was barking up the wrong tree, and that I was not a bookie and had never been near Lanerick, but he refused to be convinced. The upshot was that Davie and I had to chuck him out, blaspheming like a navy and swearing that he was coming back with his pals to do me in.

'We were a very contented lot of mountebanks at supper that night. The takings were good and the menagerie also

had been popular, and we all felt that we had been rather
above our form. McGowan, for whom I was acquiring a
profound affection, beamed on us, and produced a couple
of bottles of blackstrap to drink the health of the Colossal
Circassian Circus. That old fellow was a nonesuch. He kept
me up late – for I stopped with him in his caravan –
expounding his philosophy of life. It seemed he had been
intended for the kirk, but had had too much *joie de vivre* for
the pulpit. He was a born tramp, and liked waking up most
days in a new place, and he loved his queer outfit and saw
the comedy of it. "For three and thirty years I've travelled
the country," he said, "and I've been a public benefactor,
Mr Brown. I've put colour into many a dowie life, and I've
been a godsend to the bairns. There's no vulgarity in my
performances – they're a' as halesome as spring water." He
quoted Burns a bit, and then he got on to politics, for he
was a great Radical, and maintained that Scotland was
about the only true democracy, because a man was valued
precisely for what he was and no more. "Ye're a laird,
Mr Brown, but ye're a guid fellow, and this night ye've
shown yourself to be a man and a brither. What do you and
me care for mawgnates? We take no stock in your Andra
Carnegies and your Dukes o' Burminster." And as I
dropped off to sleep he was obliging with a verse of "A
man's a man for a' that."

'I woke in excellent spirits, thinking what a good story I
should have to tell when I returned to Larristane. My plan
was to get off as soon as possible, take the train to
Langshiels, and then hire. I could see that McGowan
was sorry to part with me, but he agreed that it was too
unhealthy a countryside for me to dally in. There was to be
an afternoon performance, so everybody had to hustle, and
there was no reason for me to linger. After breakfast I
borrowed an old ulster from him, for I had to cover up my
finery, and a still older brown bowler to replace the topper I
had worn on the preceding day.

'Suddenly we heard a fracas, and the drunk appeared
who had worried me the night before. He had forced his
way in and was pushing on through an expostulating
crowd. When he saw me he made for me with a trail of

blasphemy. He was perfectly sober now and looked very ugly.

' "Gie me back my siller," he roared. "Gie me back the five-pund note I won at Lanerick when I backed Kettle o' Fish." If I hadn't warded him off he would have taken me by the throat.

'I protested again that he was mistaken, but I might as well have appealed to a post. He swore with every variety of oath that I was Gentleman Geordie, and that I had levanted with his winnings. As he raved I began to see a possible explanation of his madness. Some bookmaker, sporting my sort of kit, had swindled him. I had ridden several times in steeplechases at Lanerick and he had seen me and got my face in his head, and mixed me up with the fraudulent bookie.

'It was a confounded nuisance, and but for the principle of the thing I would have been inclined to pay up. As it was we had to fling him out, and he went unwillingly, doing all the damage he could. His parting words were that he and his pals weren't done with me, and that though he had to wait fifty years he would wring my neck.

'After that I thought I had better waste no time, so I said good-bye to McGowan and left the show-ground by the back entrance close to the Aller. I had a general notion of the place, and knew that if I kept down the river I could turn up a lane called the Water Wynd, and get to the station without traversing any of the main streets. I had ascertained that there was a train at 10.30 which would get me to Langshiels at 11.15, so that I could be at Larristane for luncheon.

'I had underrated the persistence of my enemy. He and his pals had picketed all the approaches to the show, and when I turned into the Water Wynd I found a fellow there, who at the sight of me blew a whistle. In a second or two he was joined by three others, among them my persecutor.

' "We've gotten ye noo," he shouted, and made to collar me.

' "If you touch me," I said, "it's assault, and a case for the police."

' "That's your game, is it?" he cried. "Na, na, we'll no trouble the pollis. They tell me the Law winna help me to

recover a bet, so I'll just trust to my nieves. Will ye pay up,
ye—, or take the bloodiest bashin' ye ever seen?"

'I was in an uncommon nasty predicament. There was
nobody in the Wynd but some children playing, and the
odds were four to one. If I fought I'd get licked. The
obvious course of safety was to run up the Wynd towards
the High Street, where I might find help. But that would
mean a street row and the intervention of the police, a case
in court, and the disclosure of who I was. If I broke through
and ran back to McGowan I would be no farther forward.
What was perfectly clear was that I couldn't make the
railway station without landing myself in the worst kind
of mess.

'There wasn't much time to think, for the four men were
upon me. I hit out at the nearest, saw him go down, and
then doubled up the Wynd and into a side alley on the
right.

'By the mercy of Providence this wasn't a cul-de-sac, but
twisted below the old walls of the burgh, and then became a
lane between gardens. The pursuit was fairly hot, and my
accursed boots kept slipping on the cobbles and cramped
my form. They were almost upon me before I reached the
lane, but then I put on a spurt, and was twenty yards ahead
when it ended in a wall with a gate. The gate was locked,
but the wall was low, and I scrambled over it, and dropped
into the rubbish heap of a garden.

'There was no going back, so I barged through some
gooseberry bushes, skirted a lawn, squattered over a big
square of gravel, and charged through the entrance gates of
a suburban villa. My enemies plainly knew a better road, for
when I passed the entrance they were only a dozen yards off
on my left. That compelled me to turn to the right, the
direction away from Kirk Aller. I was now on a highway
where I could stretch myself, and it was not long before I
shook off the pursuit. They were whiskyfied ruffians and
not much good in a hunt. It was a warm morning, but I did
not slacken till I had put a good quarter of a mile between
us. I saw them come round a turn, lumbering along,
cooked to the world, so I judged I could slow down to
an easy trot.

'I was cut off from my lines of communication, and the only thing to do was to rejoin them by a detour. The Aller valley, which the railway to Langshiels followed, gave me a general direction. I remembered that about six miles off there was a station called Rubersdean, and that there was an afternoon train which got to Langshiels about three o'clock. I preferred to pick it up there, for I didn't mean to risk showing my face inside Kirk Aller again.

'By this time I had got heartily sick of my adventures. Being chased like a fox is amusing enough for an hour or two, but it soon palls. I was becoming a regular outlaw – wanted by the police for breaking into a nursing-home and stealing a suit, and very much wanted by various private gentlemen on the charge of bilking. Everybody's hand seemed to be against me, except old McGowan's, and I had had quite enough of it. I wanted nothing so much as to be back at Larristane, and I didn't believe I would tell Archie the story, for I was fed up with the whole business.

'I didn't dare go near a public-house, and the best I could do for luncheon was a bottle of ginger-beer and some biscuits which I bought at a sweetie-shop. To make a long story short, I reached Rubersdean in time, and as there were several people on the platform I waited till the train arrived before showing myself. I got into a third-class carriage at the very end of it.

'The only occupants were a woman and a child, and my appearance must have been pretty bad, for the woman looked as if she wanted to get out when she saw me. But I said it was a fine day and 'guid for the crops', and I suppose she was reassured by my Scotch tongue, for she quieted down. The child was very inquisitive, and they discussed me in whispers. "What's that man, Mamaw?" it asked. "Never mind, Jimmie." "But I want to ken, Mamaw." "Wheesht, dearie. He's a crool man. He kills the wee mawpies." At that the child set up a howl, but I felt rather flattered, for a rabbit-trapper was a respectable profession compared to those with which I had recently been credited.

'At the station before Langshiels they collect the tickets. I had none, so when the man came round I could only offer a Bank of England five-pound note. He looked at it very suspiciously, asked me rudely if I had nothing smaller, consulted the station-master, and finally with a very ill grace got me change out of the latter's office. This hung up the train for a good five minutes, and you could see by their looks that they thought I was a thief. The thing had got so badly on my nerves that I could have wept. I counted the minutes till we reached Langshiels, and I was not cheered by the behaviour of my travelling companion. She was clearly convinced of the worst, and when we came out of a tunnel she was jammed into the farthest corner, clutching her child and her bag, and looking as if she had escaped from death. I can tell you it was a thankful man that shot out on to the platform at Langshiels . . .

'I found myself looking into the absolutely bewildered eyes of Tommy Deloraine . . . I saw a lot of fellows behind him with rosettes and scared faces, and I saw what looked like a band . . .

'It took me about a hundredth part of a second to realise that I had dropped out of the frying-pan into the fire. You will scarcely believe it, but since I had rehearsed my speech going up the Rinks burn, the political meeting at Langshiels had gone clean out of my head. I suppose I had tumbled into such an utterly new world that no link remained with the old one. And as my foul luck would have it, I had hit on the very train by which I had told Deloraine I would travel.

' "For heaven's sake, Tommy, tell me where I can change," I hissed. "Lend me some clothes or I'll murder you."

'Well, that was the end of it. I got into a suit of Tommy's at the Station Hotel – luckily he was about my size – and we proceeded with the brass band and the rosetted committee to the Town Hall. I made a dashed good speech, though I say it who shouldn't, simply because I was past caring what I did. Life had been rather too much for me the last two days.'

Burminster finished his tankard, and a light of reminiscence came into his eye.

'Last week,' he said. 'I was passing Buckingham Palace. One of the mallards from St James's Park had laid away, and had hatched out a brood somewhere up Constitution Hill. The time had come when she wanted to get the ducklings back to the water. There was a big crowd, and through the midst of it marched two bobbies with the mother-duck between them, while the young ones waddled behind. I caught the look in her eye, and, if you believe me, it was the comicalest mixture of relief and embarrassment, shyness, self-consciousness and desperation.

'I would like to have shaken hands with that bird. I knew exactly how she felt.'

Skule Skerry

Anthony Hurrell, a distinguished ornithologist, recounts
in *The Runagates Club* (1928) his visit to a strange island,
Skule Skerry, which is solely inhabited by birds. There
he feels he has 'fallen into a world that killed life, a sort of
Valley of the Shadow of Death' and is told his hallucinations are the result of 'a physical affliction produced by
natural causes, explicable, though as yet not fully explained'. Buchan was prone to similar hallucinations.

Who's there, besides foul weather?
King Lear.

Mr Anthony Hurrell was a small man, thin to the point of
emaciation, but erect as a ramrod and wiry as a cairn
terrier. There was no grey in his hair, and his pale far-
sighted eyes had the alertness of youth, but his lean face was
so wrinkled by weather that in certain lights it looked
almost venerable, and young men, who at first sight had
imagined him their contemporary, presently dropped into
the 'sir' reserved for indisputable seniors. His actual age
was, I believe, somewhere in the forties. He had inherited a
small property in Northumberland, where he had accumu-
lated a collection of the rarer wildfowl; but much of his life
had been spent in places so remote that his friends could
with difficulty find them on the map. He had written a
dozen ornithological monographs, was joint editor of the
chief modern treatise on British birds, and had been the
first man to visit the *tundras* of the Yenisei. He spoke little
and that with an agreeable hesitation, but his ready smile,
his quick interest, and the impression he gave of having a
fathomless knowledge of strange modes of life, made him a
popular and intriguing figure among his friends. Of his

doings in the War he told us nothing; what we knew of them – and they were sensational enough in all conscience – we learned elsewhere. It was Nightingale's story which drew him from his customary silence. At the dinner following that event he made certain comments on current explanations of the super-normal. 'I remember once,' he began, and before we knew he had surprised us by embarking on a tale.

He had scarcely begun before he stopped. 'I'm boring you,' he said deprecatingly. 'There's nothing much in the story . . . You see, it all happened, so to speak, inside my head . . . I don't want to seem an egotist . . .'

'Don't be an ass, Tony,' said Lamancha. 'Every adventure takes place chiefly inside the head of somebody. Go on. We're all attention.'

'It happened a good many years ago,' Hurrell continued, 'when I was quite a young man. I wasn't the cold scientist then that I fancy I am to-day. I took up birds in the first instance chiefly because they fired what imagination I possess. They fascinated me, for they seemed of all created things the nearest to pure spirit – those little beings with a normal temperature of 125°. Think of it. The goldcrest, with a stomach no bigger than a bean, flies across the North Sea! The curlew sandpiper, which breeds so far north that only about three people have ever seen its nest, goes to Tasmania for its holidays! So I always went bird-hunting with a queer sense of expectation and a bit of a tremor, as if I were walking very near the boundaries of the things we are not allowed to know. I felt this especially in the migration season. The small atoms, coming God knows whence and going God knows whither, were sheer mystery – they belonged to a world built in different dimensions from ours. I don't know what I expected, but I was always waiting for something, as much in a flutter as a girl at her first ball. You must realise that mood of mine to understand what follows.

'One year I went to the Norland Islands for the spring migration. Plenty of people do the same, but I had the notion to do something a little different. I had a theory that migrants go north and south on a fairly narrow road. They have their corridors in the air as clearly defined as a highway, and keep an inherited memory of these corridors, like the stout conservatives they are. So I didn't go to the Blue Banks or to Noop or to Hermaness or any of the obvious places, where birds might be expected to make their first landfall.

'At that time I was pretty well read in the sagas, and had taught myself Icelandic for the purpose. Now it is written in the Saga of Earl Skuli, which is part of the Jarla Saga or Saga of the Earls, that Skuli, when he was carving out his earldom in the Scots islands, had much to do with a place called the Isle of the Birds. It is mentioned repeatedly, and the saga-man has a lot to say about the amazing multitude of birds there. It couldn't have been an ordinary gullery, for the Northmen saw too many of these to think them worth mentioning. I got it into my head that it must have been one of the alighting places of the migrants, and was probably as busy a spot to-day as in the eleventh century. The saga said it was near Halmarsness, and that is on the west side of the island of Una, so to Una I decided to go. I fairly got that Isle of Birds on the brain. From the map it might be any one of a dozen skerries under the shadow of Halmarsness.

'I remember that I spent a good many hours in the British Museum before I started, hunting up the scanty records of those parts. I found – I think it was in Adam of Bremen – that a succession of holy men had lived on the isle, and that a chapel had been built there and endowed by Earl Rognvald, which came to an end in the time of Malise of Strathearn. There was a bare mention of the place, but the chronicler had one curious note. "*Insula Avium,*" ran the text, "*quæ est ultima insula et proxima Abysso.*" I wondered what on earth he meant. The place was not ultimate in any geographical sense, neither the farthest north nor the farthest west of the Norlands. And what was the "abyss"? In monkish Latin the word generally means Hell – Bunyan's Bottomless Pit – and sometimes the grave; but neither meaning seemed to have much to do with an ordinary sea skerry.

'I arrived at Una about eight o'clock in a May evening, having been put across from Voss in a flit-boat. It was a quiet evening, the sky without clouds but so pale as to be almost grey, the sea grey also but with a certain iridescence in it, and the low lines of the land a combination of hard greys and umbers, cut into by the harder white of the lighthouse. I can never find words to describe that curious quality of light that you get up in the North. Sometimes it is like looking at the world out of deep water – Farquharson used to call it "milky", and one saw what he meant. Generally it is a sort of essence of light, cold and pure and distilled, as if it were reflected from snow. There is no colour in it, and it makes thin shadows. Some people find it horribly depressing – Farquharson said it reminded him of a churchyard in the early morning where all his friends were buried – but personally I found it tonic and comforting. But it made me feel very near the edge of the world.

'There was no inn, so I put up at the post office, which was on a causeway between a fresh-water loch and a sea voe, so that from the doorstep you could catch brown trout on one side and sea-trout on the other. Next morning I set off for Halmarsness, which lay five miles to the west over a flat moorland all puddled with tiny lochans. There seemed to be nearly as much water as land. Presently I came to a bigger loch under the lift of ground which was Halmarsness. There was a gap in the ridge through which I looked straight out to the Atlantic, and there in the middle distance was what I knew instinctively to be my island.

'It was perhaps a quarter of a mile long, low for the most part, but rising in the north to a grassy knoll beyond the reach of any tides. In parts it narrowed to a few yards' width, and the lower levels must often have been awash. But it was an island, not a reef, and I thought I could make out the remains of the monkish cell. I climbed Halmarsness, and there, with nesting skuas swooping angrily about my head, I got a better view. It was certainly my island, for the rest of the archipelago were inconsiderable skerries, and I realised that it might well be a resting-place for migrants, for the mainland cliffs were too thronged with piratical skuas and other jealous fowl to be comfortable for weary travellers.

'I sat for a long time on the headland looking down from the three hundred feet of basalt to the island half a mile off – the last bid of solid earth between me and Greenland. The sea was calm for Norland waters, but there was a snowy edging of surf to the skerries which told of a tide rip. Two miles farther south I could see the entrance to the famous Roost of Una, where, when tide and wind collide, there is a wall like a house, so that a small steamer cannot pass it. The only sign of human habitation was a little grey farm in the lowlands toward the Roost, but the place was full of the evidence of man – a herd of Norland ponies, each tagged with its owner's name – grazing sheep of the piebald Norland breed – a broken barbed-wire fence that drooped over the edge of the cliff. I was only an hour's walk from a telegraph office, and a village which got its newspapers not more than three days late. It was a fine spring noon, and in the empty bright land there was scarcely a shadow . . . All the same, as I looked down at the island I did not wonder that it had been selected for attention by the saga-man and had been reputed holy. For it had an air of concealing something, though it was as bare as a billiard-table. It was an intruder, an irrelevance in the picture, planted there by some celestial caprice. I decided forthwith to make my camp on it, and the decision, inconsequently enough, seemed to me to be something of a venture.

'That was the view taken by John Ronaldson, when I talked to him after dinner. John was the post-mistress's son, more fisherman than crofter, like all Norlanders, a skilful sailor and an adept at the dipping lug, and noted for his knowledge of the western coast. He had difficulty in understanding my plan, and when he identified my island he protested.

'"Not Skule Skerry!" he cried. "What would take ye there, man? Ye'll get a' the birds ye want on Halmarsness and a far better bield. Ye'll be blawn away on the skerry, if the wund rises."

'I explained to him my reasons as well as I could, and I answered his fears about a gale by pointing out that the island was sheltered by the cliffs from the prevailing winds, and could be scourged only from the south, south-west, or west, quarters from which the wind rarely blew in May. "It'll be cauld," he said, "and wat." I pointed out that I had a tent and was accustomed to camping. "Ye'll starve" – I expounded my proposed methods of commissariat. "It'll be an ill job getting ye on and off" – but after cross-examination he admitted that ordinarily the tides were not difficult, and that I could get a rowboat to a beach below the farm I had seen – its name was Sgurravoe. Yet when I had said all this he still raised objections, till I asked him flatly what was the matter with Skule Skerry.

'"Naebody gangs there," he said gruffly.

'"Why should they?" I asked. "I'm only going to watch the birds."

'But the fact that it was never visited seemed to stick in his throat, and he grumbled out something that surprised me. "It has an ill name," he said. But when I pressed him he admitted that there was no record of shipwreck or disaster to account for the ill name. He repeated the words "Skule Skerry" as if they displeased him. "Folk dinna gang near it. It has aye had an ill name. My grandfather used to say that the place wasna canny."

'Now your Norlander has nothing of the Celt in him, and is as different from the Hebridean as a Northumbrian from a Cornishman. They are a fine, upstanding, hard-headed race, almost pure Scandinavian in blood, but they have as little poetry in them as a Manchester Radical. I should have put them down as utterly free from superstition, and, in all my many visits to the islands, I have never yet come across a folk-tale – hardly even a historical legend. Yet here was John Ronaldson, with his weather-beaten face and stiff chin and shrewd blue eyes, declaring that an innocent-looking island "wasna canny", and showing the most remarkable disinclination to go near it.

'Of course all this only made me keener. Besides, it was called Skule Skerry, and the name could only come from Earl Skuli; so it was linked up authentically with the oddments of information I had collected in the British Museum – the Jarla Saga and Adam of Bremen and all the rest of it. John finally agreed to take me over next morning in his boat, and I spent the rest of the day in collecting my kit. I had a small tent, and a Wolseley valise and half a dozen rugs, and, since I had brought a big box of tinned stuffs from the Stores, all I needed was flour and meal and some simple groceries. I learned that there was a well on the island, and that I could count on sufficient driftwood for my fire, but to make certain I took a sack of coals and another of peats. So I set off next day in John's boat, ran with the wind through the Roost of Una when the tide was right, tacked up the coast, and came to the skerry early in the afternoon.

'You could see that John hated the place. We ran into a cove on the east side, and he splashed ashore as if he expected to have his landing opposed, looking all the time sharply about him. When he carried my stuff to a hollow under the knoll, which gave a certain amount of shelter, his head was always twisting round. To me the place seemed to be the last word in forgotten peace. The swell lipped gently on the reefs and the little pebbled beaches, and only the babble of gulls from Halmarsness broke the stillness.

'John was clearly anxious to get away, but he did his duty by me. He helped me to get the tent up, found a convenient place for my boxes, pointed out the well and filled my water bucket, and made a zareba of stones to protect my camp on the Atlantic side. We had brought a small dinghy along with us, and this was to be left with me, so that when I wanted I could row across to the beach at Sgurravoe. As his last service he fixed an old pail between two boulders on the summit of the knoll, and filled it with oily waste, so that it could be turned into a beacon.

' "Ye'll maybe want to come off," he said, "and the boat will maybe no be there. Kindle your flare, and they'll see it at Sgurravoe and get the word to me, and I'll come for ye though the Muckle Black Silkie himsel' was hunkerin' on the skerry."

'Then he looked up and sniffed the air. "I dinna like the set of the sky," he declared. "It's a bad weatherhead. There'll be mair wund than I like in the next four-and-twenty hours."

'So saying, he hoisted his sail, and presently was a speck on the waters towards the Roost. There was no need for him to hurry, for the tide was now wrong, and before he could pass the Roost he would have three hours to wait on this side of the Mull. But the man, usually so deliberate and imperturbable, had been in a fever to be gone.

'His departure left me in a curious mood of happy loneliness and pleasurable expectation. I was left solitary with the seas and the birds. I laughed to think that I had found a streak of superstition in the granite John. He and his Muckle Black Silkie! I knew the old legend of the North which tells how the Finns, the ghouls that live in the deeps of the ocean, can on occasion don a seal's skin and come to land to play havoc with mortals. But *diablerie* and this isle of mine were worlds apart. I looked at it as the sun dropped, drowsing in the opal-coloured tides, under a sky in which pale clouds made streamers like a spectral *aurora borealis*, and I thought that I had stumbled upon one of those places where Nature seems to invite one to her secrets. As the light died the sky was flecked as with the roots and branches of some great nebular tree. That would be the "weatherhead" of which John Ronaldson had spoken.

'I set my fire going, cooked my supper, and made everything snug for the night. I had been right in my guess about the migrants. It must have been about ten o'clock when they began to arrive – after my fire had died out and I was smoking my last pipe before getting into my sleeping-bag. A host of fieldfares settled gently on the south part of the skerry. A faint light lingered till after midnight, but it was not easy to distinguish the little creatures, for they were aware of my presence and did not alight within a dozen yards of me. But I made out bramblings and buntings and what I thought was the Greenland wheatear; also jack snipe and sanderling; and I believed from their cries that the curlew sandpiper and the whimbrel were there. I went to sleep in a state of high excitement, promising myself a fruitful time on the morrow.

'I slept badly, as one often does one's first night in the open. Several times I woke with a start, under the impression that I was in a boat rowing swiftly with the tide. And every time I woke I heard the flutter of myriad birds, as if a velvet curtain were being slowly switched along an oak floor. At last I fell into deeper sleep, and when I opened my eyes it was full day.

'The first thing that struck me was that it had got suddenly colder. The sky was stormily red in the east, and masses of woolly clouds were banking in the north. I lit my fire with numbed fingers and hastily made tea. I could see the nimbus of seafowl over Halmarsness, but there was only one bird left on my skerry. I was certain from its forked tail that it was a Sabine's gull, but before I got my glass out it was disappearing into the haze towards the north. The sight cheered and excited me, and I cooked my breakfast in pretty good spirits.

'That was literally the last bird that came near me, barring the ordinary shearwaters and gulls and cormorants that nested round about Halmarsness. (There was not one single nest of any sort on the island. I had heard of that happening before in places which were regular halting-grounds for migrants.) The travellers must have had an inkling of the coming weather and were waiting somewhere well to the south. For about nine o'clock it began to blow. Great God, how it blew! You must go to the Norlands if you want to know what wind can be. It is like being on a mountain-top, for there is no high ground to act as a wind-break. There was no rain, but the surf broke in showers and every foot of the skerry was drenched with it. In a trice Halmarsness was hidden, and I seemed to be in the centre of a maelstrom, choked with scud and buffeted on every side by swirling waters.

'Down came my tent at once. I wrestled with the crazy canvas and got a black eye from the pole, but I managed to drag the ruins into the shelter of the zareba which John had built, and tumble some of the bigger boulders on it. There it lay, flapping like a sick albatross. The water got into my food boxes, and soaked my fuel, as well as every inch of my clothing . . . I had looked forward to a peaceful day of watching and meditation, when I could write up my notes; and instead I spent a morning like a Rugger scrum. I might have enjoyed it, if I hadn't been so wet and cold, and could have got a better lunch than some clammy mouthfuls out of a tin. One talks glibly about being "blown off" a place, generally an idle exaggeration – but that day I came very near the reality. There were times when I had to hang on for dear life to one of the bigger stones to avoid being trundled into the yeasty seas.

'About two o'clock the volume of the storm began to decline, and then for the first time I thought about the boat. With a horrid sinking of the heart I scrambled to the cove where we had beached it. It had been drawn up high and dry, and its painter secured to a substantial boulder. But now there was not a sign of it except a ragged rope-end round the stone. The tide had mounted to its level, and tide and wind had smashed the rotten painter. By this time what was left of it would be tossing in the Roost.

'This was a pretty state of affairs. John was due to visit me next day, but I had a cold twenty-four hours ahead of me. There was of course the flare he had left me, but I was not inclined to use this. It looked like throwing up the sponge and confessing that my expedition had been a farce. I felt miserable, but obstinate, and, since the weather was clearly mending, I determined to put the best face on the business, so I went back to the wreckage of my camp, and tried to tidy up. There was still far too much wind to do anything with the tent, but the worst of the spindrift had ceased, and I was able to put out my bedding and some of my provender to dry. I got a dry jersey out of my pack, and, as I was wearing fisherman's boots and oilskins, I managed to get some slight return of comfort. Also at last I succeeded in lighting a pipe. I found a corner under the knoll which gave me a modicum of shelter, and I settled myself to pass the time with tobacco and my own thoughts.

'About three o'clock the wind died away completely. That I did not like, for a dead lull in the Norlands is often the precursor of a new gale. Indeed, I never remembered a time when some wind did not blow, and I had heard that when such a thing happened people came out of their houses to ask what the matter was. But now we had the deadest sort of calm. The sea was still wild and broken, the tides raced by like a mill-stream, and a brume was gathering which shut out Halmarsness – shut out every prospect except a narrow circuit of grey water. The cessation of the racket of the gale made the place seem uncannily quiet. The present tumult of the sea, in comparison with the noise of the morning, seemed no more than a mutter and an echo.

'As I sat there I became conscious of an odd sensation. I seemed to be more alone, more cut off, not only from my fellows but from the habitable earth, than I had ever been before. It was like being in a small boat in mid-Atlantic – but worse, if you understand me, for that would have been loneliness in the midst of a waste which was nevertheless surrounded and traversed by the works of man, whereas now I felt that I was clean outside man's ken. I had come somehow to the edge of that world where life is, and was very close to the world which has only death in it.

'At first I do not think there was much fear in the sensation – chiefly strangeness, but the kind of strangeness which awes without exciting. I tried to shake off the mood, and got up to stretch myself. There was not much room for exercise, and as I moved with stiff legs along the reefs I slipped into the water, so that I got my arms wet. It was cold beyond belief – the very quintessence of deathly Arctic ice, so cold that it seemed to sear and bleach the skin.

'From that moment I date the most unpleasant experience of my life. I became suddenly the prey of a black depression, shot with the red lights of terror. But it was not a numb terror, for my brain was acutely alive . . . I had the sense to try to make tea, but my fuel was still too damp, and the best I could do was to pour half the contents of my brandy flask into a cup and swallow the stuff. That did not properly warm my chilled body, but – since I am a very temperate man – it speeded up my thoughts instead of calming them. I felt myself on the brink of a childish panic.

'One thing I thought I saw clearly – the meaning of Skule Skerry. By some alchemy of nature, at which I could only guess, it was on the track by which the North exercised its spell, a cableway for the magnetism of that cruel frozen Uttermost, which man might penetrate but could never subdue or understand. Though the latitude was only 61°, there were folds and tucks in space, and this isle was the edge of the world. Birds knew it, and the old Northmen, who were primitive beings like the birds, knew it. That was why an inconsiderable skerry had been given the name of a conquering Jarl. The old Church knew it, and had planted a chapel to exorcise the demons of darkness. I wondered what sights the hermit, whose cell had been on the very spot where I was cowering, had seen in the winter dusks.

'It may have been partly the brandy acting on an empty stomach, and partly the extreme cold, but my brain, in spite of my efforts to think rationally, began to run like a dynamo. It is difficult to explain my mood, but I seemed to be two persons – one a reasonable modern man trying to keep sane and scornfully rejecting the fancies which the other, a cast-back to something elemental, was furiously spinning. But it was the second that had the upper hand . . . I felt myself loosed from my moorings, a mere waif on uncharted seas. What is the German phrase? *Urdummheit* – Primal Idiocy? That was what was the matter with me. I had fallen out of civilisation into the Outlands and was feeling their spell . . . I could not think, but I could remember, and what I had read of the Norse voyagers came back to me with horrid persistence. They had known the outland terrors – the Sea Walls at the world's end, the Curdled Ocean with its strange beasts. Those men did not sail north as we did, in steamers, with modern food and modern instruments, huddled into crews and expeditions. They had gone out almost alone, in brittle galleys, and they had known what we could never know.

'And then, I had a shattering revelation. I had been groping for a word and I suddenly got it. It was Adam of Bremen's "*proxima Abysso*". This island was next door to the Abyss, and the Abyss was that blanched world of the North which was the negation of life.

'That unfortunate recollection was the last straw. I remember that I forced myself to get up and try again to kindle a fire. But the wood was still too damp, and I realised with consternation that I had very few matches left, several boxes having been ruined that morning. As I staggered about I saw the flare which John had left for me, and had almost lit it. But some dregs of manhood prevented me – I could not own defeat in that babyish way – I must wait till John Ronaldson came for me next morning. Instead I had another mouthful of brandy, and tried to eat some of my sodden biscuits. But I could scarcely swallow; the infernal cold, instead of rousing hunger, had given me only a raging thirst.

'I forced myself to sit down again with my face to the land. You see, every moment I was becoming more childish. I had the notion – I cannot call it a thought – that down the avenue from the North something terrible and strange might come. My nervous state must have been pretty bad, for though I was cold and empty and weary I was scarcely conscious of physical discomfort. My heart was fluttering like a scared boy's; and all the time the other part of me was standing aside and telling me not to be a damned fool . . . I think that if I had heard the rustle of a flock of migrants I might have pulled myself together, but not a blessed bird had come near me all day. I had fallen into a world that killed life, a sort of Valley of the Shadow of Death.

'The brume spoiled the long northern twilight, and presently it was almost dark. At first I thought that this was going to help me, and I got hold of several of my half-dry rugs, and made a sleeping-place. But I could not sleep, even if my teeth had stopped chattering, for a new and perfectly idiotic idea possessed me. It came from a recollection of John Ronaldson's parting words. What had he said about the Black Silkie – the Finn who came out of the deep and hunkered on this skerry? Raving mania! But on this lost island in the darkening night, with icy tides lapping about me, was any horror beyond belief?

'Still, the sheer idiocy of the idea compelled a reaction. I took hold of my wits with both hands and cursed myself for a fool. I could even reason about my folly. I knew what was wrong with me. I was suffering from *panic* – a physical affection produced by natural causes, explicable, though as yet not fully explained. Two friends of mine had once been afflicted with it: one in a lonely glen in the Jotunheim, so that he ran for ten miles over stony hills till he found a saeter and human companionship; the other in a Bavarian forest, where both he and his guide tore for hours through the thicket till they dropped like logs beside a highroad. This reflection enabled me to take a pull on myself and to think a little ahead. If my troubles were physical then there would be no shame in looking for the speediest cure. Without further delay I must leave this God-forgotten place.

'The flare was all right, for it had been set on the highest point of the island, and John had covered it with a peat. With one of my few remaining matches I lit the oily waste, and a great smoky flame leapt to heaven.

'If the half-dark had been eerie, this sudden brightness was eerier. For a moment the glare gave me confidence, but as I looked at the circle of moving waters evilly lit up all my terrors returned . . . How long would it take John to reach me? They would see it at once at Sgurravoe – they would be on the look-out for it – John would not waste time, for he had tried to dissuade me from coming – an hour – two hours at the most . . .

'I found I could not take my eyes from the waters. They seemed to flow from the north in a strong stream, black as the heart of the elder ice, irresistible as fate, cruel as hell. There seemed to be uncouth shapes swimming in them, which were more than the flickering shadows from the flare . . . Something portentous might at any moment come down that river of death . . . Someone . . .

'And then my knees gave under me and my heart shrank like a pea, for I saw that the someone had come.

'He drew himself heavily out of the sea, wallowed for a second, and then raised his head and, from a distance of five yards, looked me blindly in the face. The flare was fast dying down, but even so at that short range it cast a strong light, and the eyes of the awful being seemed to be dazed by it. I saw a great dark head like a bull's – an old face wrinkled as if in pain – a gleam of enormous broken teeth – a dripping beard – all formed on other lines than God has made mortal creatures. And on the right of the throat was a huge scarlet gash. The thing seemed to be moaning, and then from it came a sound – whether of anguish or wrath I cannot tell – but it seemed to be the cry of a tortured fiend.

'That was enough for me. I pitched forward in a swoon, hitting my head on a stone, and in that condition three hours later John Ronaldson found me.

'They put me to bed at Sgurravoe with hot earthenware

bottles, and the doctor from Voss next day patched up my head and gave me a sleeping draught. He declared that there was little the matter with me except shock from exposure, and promised to set me on my feet in a week.

'For three days I was as miserable as a man could be, and did my best to work myself into a fever. I had said not a word about my experience, and left my rescuers to believe that my only troubles were cold and hunger, and that I had lit the flare because I had lost the boat. But during these days I was in a critical state. I knew that there was nothing wrong with my body, but I was gravely concerned about my mind.

'For this was my difficulty. If that awful thing was a mere figment of my brain, then I had better be certified at once as a lunatic. No sane man could get into such a state as to see such portents with the certainty with which I had seen that creature come out of the night. If, on the other hand, the thing was a real presence, then I had looked on something outside natural law, and my intellectual world was broken in pieces. I was a scientist, and a scientist cannot admit the supernatural. If with my eyes I had beheld the monster in which Adam of Bremen believed, which holy men had exorcised, which even the shrewd Norlanders shuddered at as the Black Silkie, then I must burn my books and revise my creed. I might take to poetry or theosophy, but I would never be much good again at science.

'On the third afternoon I was trying to doze, and with shut eyes fighting off the pictures which tormented my brain. John Ronaldson and the farmer of Sgurravoe were talking at the kitchen door. The latter asked some question, and John replied:

' "Aye, it was a wall-ross and nae mistake. It cam ashore at Gloop Ness and Sandy Fraser has gotten the skin of it. It was deid when he found it, but no long deid. The puir beast would drift south on some floe, and it was sair hurt, for Sandy said it had a hole in its throat ye could put your nieve in. There hasna been a wall-ross come to Una since my grandfather's day."

'I turned my face to the wall and composed myself to sleep. For now I knew that I was sane, and need not forswear science.'

Glossary

aboon/abune, above/over
ae, one
ahint, behind
aiblins, perhaps
ain, own
aince, once
aiten, oaten
alang, along
amang, among
ane, one
atween, between
aucht, anything
auchteen, eighteen
auld, old
auldfarrant, old-fashioned
awa, away
bade, bid
bannocks, pancakes
bairn, child
bairnliest, babiest
baith, both
bauchled, distorted
bauks, untilled land
bauld, bold
bawbee, halfpenny
bawl, shout
bawsened, white-faced
begood, begun
belchin', preaching
ben, through
beuk, book
bicker, drinking cup
bickerin', arguing
biddins, orders
bield, shelter
birk, birch
blae, blue

blate, shy
blaw, blow
bleeze, blaze
bluid, blood
brae, hill
braid, broad
braw, fine
braxy, diseased
breeks, trousers
broo, brow
bucht, sheep pen
buid, bid
buits, boots
bund, bond/bound
burnie, brook
buskit, dressed
busses, bushes
bye, beside/near
byliff, bailiff
ca', call
ca'ed, called
canna, cannot
canty, lively
carle, old man
cauld, cold
chappin, knocking
chaumer, chamber
chield, boy
chuckies, chickens
claes, clothes
clamjamfried, worthless
clart/y, dirt/y
claught, clutched
clinkit, struck
cockit, heaped
coorts, courts
coup, upset

couthy, kindly

crackin', chatting

crow, crow/boast

creashy, greasy

crood, crowd

croun, crown

crously, briskly

cuif, fool

cuisten, cast

cundies, conduits

dacent, decent

dae, do

dander, stroll

daunder, saunter

daured, dared

dawf, remove

delve, dig

denty, dainty

ding, knock

dochter, daughter

Dod, George

doo, dove/pigeon

doots, doubts

doucely, quiet

doun, down

dowie, sad

drée, endure

dreich/est, dull/est

drooned, drowned

dwaibly, feeble

een, eyes

eneuch, enough

errin', errant

ettle, attempt

faes, foes

farles, oatcakes

fauld, fold

faun, fallen

fauts, faults

ferlie, strange

feucht, fight

fleechin', flattering

fleein', flying

floo'rs, flowers

flytit, scolded

frae, from

freend, friend

frem't, foreign

fricht, fright

fan, when

furthy, frank

gaed, went

gait, stride

gangs, goes

garred, made

gaucy, plump

ghaist, ghost

gie/n, give/n

glaikit, stupid

glaury, muddy

gleg, horsefly

gleg's, bright

gloomin', frowning

glower, glare

glumchin, looking sad

goud, gold

gowans, daisies

gowk, fool

greetin', crying

grue, ice

grumlin', grumbling

grund, ground

guddlin', tickling trout

guid, good

hae, have

hain/in's, enclose/ures

hairst, harvest

hale, whole

halms, stalks/shaws

happit, wrapped

haughlands, highlands

heinchin, chicken

heuchs, exclamations

hirsel, collection

hoddit, held

hoodie craws, black-head
 crows

howkin', digging

hunkerin', squatting

ilka, every

ither, other

jee, stir

jimped, leaped
jouked, ducked
kent, known
kenned, knew
kep, cap
kets, carrion
kittle, tickle
kinle, light
kye, cattle
lauchin', laughing
lee, lie
lickit, defeated
licht, light
loon, boy
Losh, Lord
loup, leap
louse, free
lowe, flame
mair, more
mairrit, married
makkers, poets
maud, plaid
maukit, infested
maun, must
massy, massive
meuse, honour
micht, might
midden, dung heap
misdoot, misdoubt
mools, moles
mou, mouth
muckle, much/great
nae, no
nane, none
neebors, neighbours
niffer, barter/haggle
nieves, fists
nocht, nothing
nou, now
'oo, wool
ower, over
orra, odd
paiks, strikes/poles
parritch, porridge
piked, gathered
plock, third of a penny

ploom, plum
ploos, ploughs
plowtered, waded
poke, grope
pooches, pockets/pouches
poopits, pulpits
poether, powder
puir, poor
puirtith, poverty
quate, quiet
rade, afraid
rape, rope
raws, rows
rax, stretch
reddin', clearing
reid, read
richt, right
roopy, hoarsely
rauk, fag
roup, auction
rows, rolls
sae, so
sair, sore
saunts, saints
scabbit, scabbed
scaith, scathe
scaud, scald
schauchled, shackled
schauchlin', shaking
sel, self
shairn/y, cows dung/daubed in
shouther, shoulder
shilpit, pale
siccan, such
siller, silver
sin, since
skeely, skilled
skelped, smacked
skreich, break of day
snoddit, tidied
snoukin', to smell as a dog
snoutit, snouted
spainin', weaning
spak, spoke
speir, ask
speldered, split

spiore, explore

staig, stag

staucherin', staggering

stausome, disgusting

steeked, latched

stell, prop

stench, strong

stert/it, start/ed

stievest, stiffest

stirk, cow

stramash, uproar

straucht, straight

sudna, should not

swirds, swords

tackets, tacks

taen, taken

tak, take

tautit, matted

tawmont, two months

tentier, careful

teuch, tough

thack, thatch

thegither, together

thole, bear

thrall, worry

thrang, stubborn

thrapple, throat

threep/it, whistle/d

thristles, thistles

tine, lose

tippeny, two pence

toddy, whisky

toom, empty

toun, town

traivelled, travelled

trig/s, trim/tidy

tups, rams

twae, two

unco, extraordinarily

unction, auction

wae/fu', woe/ful

walie, feeble

wame, belly/womb

wanchancy, unlucky

warstled, wrestled

wauf, wave

wauks, wakens

wean, child

wecht, weight

weird, fate

whae, who

whaup, curlew

whaur, where

whase, whose

whilk, which

wight, creature

wrocht, worked

yaird, yard

yammerin', whining

ye, you

yestreen, yesterday

yett, gate

yill, ale

yin, one

yon, that/yonder

yowe, cattle

Selected John Buchan Reading List

In recent years John Buchan has undergone a distinct revival with five different publishers bringing out some of his best-known novels, often with new introductions and critical notes. The Scottish publisher, B&W, who have championed some of the lesser-known books, have a dozen titles in print, followed by Penguin with ten, OUP with nine in their World's Classic series, Alan Sutton with five and Canongate with one.

The Richard Hannay novels are available in omnibus editions from Penguin and B&W. *The Thirty-Nine Steps*, *Greenmantle*, *Mr Standfast* and *The Three Hostages* are all available from either OUP or Penguin, while B&W have *The Courts of the Morning* and Penguin *The Island of Sheep*.

The Edward Leithen novels are not currently available in an omnibus edition but *John Macnab* is in print with both Penguin and OUP and *Sick Heart River* with OUP and B&W. Other Leithen titles include *The Power-House* and *The Gap in the Curtain* with B&W and *The Dancing Floor* with Penguin. The Dickson McCunn trilogy, *Huntingtower*, *Castle Gay* and *The House of the Four Winds*, is available from Penguin or separately from Alan Sutton.

B&W have five of the historical novels in print – *A Lost Lady of Old Years*, *The Blanket of the Dark*, *John Burnet of Barns*, *The Free Fishers* and *Midwinter*. Buchan's favourite novel, *Witch Wood*, is available from OUP and Canongate. Two interesting recent reissues are Buchan's last collection of short stories, *The Runagates Club*, from Alan Sutton and his political novel, *A Prince of the Captivity* from B&W. His classic adventure story about Black Nationalism, *Prester John*, is available from both Penguin and OUP. For some reason Buchan's biographies of Sir Walter Scott and Cromwell remain out of print but Prion have reissued his biography of the Marquis of Montrose.

The most recent biography is Andrew Lownie's *John Buchan: The Presbyterian Cavalier*, published in paperback by Canongate. Lownie has also edited Buchan's complete short stories in three volumes for Thistle Publishing and Buchan's poems for Scottish Cultural Press.

CANONGATE CLASSICS

Books listed in alphabetical order by author.

The Gowk Storm Nancy Brysson Morrison
ISBN 0 86241 222 6   £3.95
An Autobiography Edwin Muir
ISBN 0 86241 423 7   £5.99
The Wilderness Journeys (The Story of My Boyhood and Youth,
A Thousand Mile Walk to the Gulf, My First Summer in the
Sierra, Travels in Alaska, Stickeen) John Muir
ISBN 0 86241 586 1   £8.99
Imagined Selves: (Imagined Corners, Mrs Ritchie, Mrs Grundy in
Scotland, Women: An Inquiry, Women in Scotland) Willa Muir
ISBN 0 86241 605 1   £8.99
Homeward Journey John MacNair Reid
ISBN 0 86241 178 5   £3.95
A Twelvemonth and a Day Christopher Rush
ISBN 0 86241 439 3   £4.99
End of an Old Song J. D. Scott
0 86241 311 7   £4.95
Grampian Quartet: (The Quarry Wood, The Weatherhouse, A Pass
in the Grampians, The Living Mountain) Nan Shepherd
ISBN 0 86241 589 6   £8.99
Consider the Lilies Iain Crichton Smith
ISBN 0 86241 415 6   £4.99
Diaries of a Dying Man William Soutar
ISBN 0 86241 347 8   £4.99
Listen to the Voice: Selected Stories Iain Crichton Smith
ISBN 0 86241 434 2   £5.99
Shorter Scottish Fiction Robert Louis Stevenson
ISBN 0 86241 555 1   £4.99
Tales of Adventure (Black Arrow, Treasure Island, 'The Sire de
Malétroit's Door' and other stories) Robert Louis Stevenson
ISBN 0 86241 687 6   £7.99
Tales of the South Seas (Island Landfalls, The Ebb-tide,
The Wrecker) Robert Louis Stevenson
ISBN 0 86241 643 4   £7.99
The Scottish Novels: (Kidnapped, Catriona, The Master of
Ballantrae, Weir of Hermiston) Robert Louis Stevenson
ISBN 0 86241 533 0   £5.99
The People of the Sea David Thomson
ISBN 0 86241 550 0   £4.99
City of Dreadful Night James Thomson
ISBN 0 86241 449 0   £4.99
Three Scottish Poets: MacCaig, Morgan, Lochead
ISBN 0 86241 400 8   £4.99
Black Lamb and Grey Falcon Rebecca West
ISBN 0 86241 428 8   £10.99

Most Canongate Classics are available at good bookshops. You can
also order direct from Canongate Books Ltd – by post: 14 High Street,
Edinburgh EH1 1TE, or by telephone: 0131 557 5111. There is no charge
for postage and packing to customers in the United Kingdom.